Acknowledgments

I want to give special thanks to: Linda Marrow, my editor, for sharing my vision; Donna Kitt, for endless hours of word processing; Esther Anthony, my big sister in Christ, for her prayers.

*For the first time in her life,
Lauren stared at a pair of lips
that she wanted desperately
to feel on hers. . . .*

Roget answered her silent plea. Their lips met. Softly at first—and then wildly, passionately, she kissed him until her head spun and her heart leapt into her throat and strangled her breath. Horses and riders thundered past them, but Lauren heard nothing except the raucous thumping in her breast. Roget's arms circled her waist and pulled her to him, and Lauren's body responded eagerly to the pressure of his touch. Everything in her cried out for him, as she fought to control the spontaneous inferno that licked its way up from her womb and sought to extinguish itself in the warm, sultry lips that covered hers. Her arms ached to hold him, to feel the broad, muscular expanse of his back beneath her fingers. But if she yielded to her desires at this moment, she would be destined to be his mistress. Shocked by the things she was feeling, Lauren's head spun in circles. There were things she wanted from him, but, improbable as it was, she wanted to be his wife and not his mistress, and she would risk everything to that end. . . .

MURMUR OF RAIN

PATRICIA VAUGHN

POCKET STAR BOOKS

New York London Toronto Sydney Tokyo Singapore

This book is a work of fiction. Names, characters, places and incidents are products of the author's imagination or are used fictitiously. Any resemblance to actual events or locales or persons, living or dead, is entirely coincidental.

An *Original* Publication of POCKET BOOKS

A Pocket Star Book published by
POCKET BOOKS, a division of Simon & Schuster Inc.
1230 Avenue of the Americas, New York, NY 10020

ISBN: 0-671-52004-0

First Pocket Books printing March 1996

10 9 8 7 6 5 4 3 2 1

POCKET STAR BOOKS and colophon are registered trademarks of Simon & Schuster Inc.

Cover art by Dominick Finelle

Printed in the U.S.A.

This book is dedicated to

God, my heavenly father,
who makes the impossible possible.

Norman and Marion Vaughn, my parents,
without whom I or this book would
not have been created.

Gayle, Carole, and John, my friends,
for their unwavering support.

George, who gave me the inspiration.

Vivian Stephens, my agent, editor, friend,
for holding fast the dream.

MURMUR OF RAIN

Prologue

Paris 1870

Amid clamoring wheels and pounding hooves, the horse-drawn omnibus barreled around the corner onto boulevard Saint-Martin and out of control. Frantic men and women scattered in every direction, their eyes frozen in sudden fear as the wayward vehicle plunged into them while they crossed the street. Shrill, spine-wrenching cries arose from female throats, piercing the air with their sound, while uttered moans of terror lodged deep in the larynxes of the men.

An ebony-skinned woman carrying a small child, caught by surprise and unable to move fast enough, opened her mouth and let out a primal scream. Shoving her child to safety, the young woman struggled frantically to free her skirts from the spoked wheels but to no avail. Within seconds, her body was crushed beneath the wheels of the vehicle.

Two *gendarmes* witnessed the frenzied commotion and rushed toward the activity. Reaching the street, they stared in horror at the scene before them. Motivated by his strong sense of duty, Gendarme Gereaux's stocky, well-seasoned legs propelled him forward to assist the hapless victim, while his novice partner stood there looking as if he would throw up his lunch any minute. The crowd of pedestrians that had scattered frantically in every direction now

1

wandered back to the scene. Out of nowhere, a high-pitched sound sliced through the air, and an offical carriage ground to a halt. A captain, his uniform decorated with medals and gold braid, climbed down and pushed his way through the crush of bodies. Striding toward the object of the pandemonium, he knelt on one knee next to Gendarme Gereaux. "Is she still alive?" he questioned the officer.

"Just barely."

Rising to his feet, the captain strode back to the carriage and returned with a blanket to protect the shivering body from the brisk October air. *"Monsieur le gendarme,* keep these people back," he barked at the other officer who stood there looking sickly pale. Then enlisting one of the street boys who lurked about to earn a coin, he sent him racing to the hospital to fetch a doctor.

"Is there a muff, a reticule, anything . . . to find out who she is?" The captain searched for a clue, but only blank faces stared back at him. As he turned away from them, a pompous male voice caught his ear.

"There is some Frenchman near the Latin Quarter who's married to one of those Africans. Almost dark as teakwood, she is. Beats me why a white man wants to marry something that dark when there are so many Frenchwomen with delicate white skin." The man gazed down at the bloody, mangled form lying on the cobblestone street. "Those people should stay in Africa . . . They don't know how to live in our—"

"Did you say you know where this white man lives, *monsieur?"* the captain broke in impatiently.

"No." The man hesitated, shifting his weight uncomfortably. The other faces glared at him as if to say, Why are you wasting our time? He stiffened and blood rushed into his face. "How should I know where a black woman lives?"

"I know where she lives." A tenor voice floated over the crowd. A boy made his way through the press of bodies, ducking between them until he popped into the opening.

"Could you go and get this man?" the captain asked.

"Oui, mon capitaine." His young chest swelled with pride that he could be in the service of the *gendarmes.* Saluting

2

the captain with a hand pressed against his cap, he took off and ran all the way to the Left Bank.

As his eyes followed the boy, Gendarme Gereaux noticed a colorful beaded ornament lying a few feet from the woman on the ground. He picked it up.

"What's that?" his partner asked.

"I don't know. Looks like one of those bracelets that those Africans wear . . . Must belong to her."

"It must have come off from the impact when the carriage struck her."

The seasoned *gendarme* pulled out his white handkerchief. Wrapping the bracelet in it, he put the bloodstained cloth back in his pocket.

Just then a young man in a soiled white coat appeared and attempted to fight his way through the crowd. "Please, let me through," he pleaded. "I'm the doctor." But the people moved barely an inch.

The captain moved toward them, his two arms stretched across the breadth of them and began forcing them back onto the sidewalk.

"Mesdames, messieurs, let us give the unfortunate victim some room." The other two *gendarmes* moved into line and formed a barrier against the gawking spectators, letting the doctor pass between them. With one hand holding his spectacles and the other clutching a black bag, he rushed toward the mangled body of the woman. And mangled she was, beyond anything he had ever seen. As he began to examine her, an expression of hopelessness slid over his face. Hearing her faint gasps for air, the young doctor leaned over her as she attempted to speak. He heard the thin, raspy sounds that came from her lips but could not understand the words.

"What's she saying?" the captain inquired anxiously.

"I don't know." The doctor knelt closer, putting his ear to her mouth.

Again, she muttered the faint, raspy words. *"Ma fille."* He looked up at the captain, confused. "She said, *'ma fille.'* She seems to be asking for her child."

"Child." The captain repeated the word in a tone that echoed his own confusion. Tugging at the strap under his chin, he turned to the crowd of onlookers. "Has anyone seen a child?" he asked curiously. "Did this woman have a child with her?"

Their blank white faces stared at him vacantly. But within moments, a woman pushed her way through the crowd. She was a Frenchwoman carrying a brown-skinned little girl with a head full of soft, bushy curls that covered her head like a halo. The captain's expression questioned the woman.

"I caught her, I did. It was the least a person could do. I was right there—the minute it happened," she said rapidly. Her animated face relived the moment. "Those wheels almost got me, too—he was goin' so fast—but I got out of the way. And then just before it got her, she hurled the little girl from her arms. But people were running in every which way, trying to escape the thing themselves and no one saw, or cared, for that matter. Yet something made me stop and reach out my arms to grab the child. I suppose it was the least I could do . . . considering that the Good Lord spared me the same fate."

Jean Dufort pushed his way frantically through the crowd. Breathless and wrenched with fear, he bounded toward the nucleus of activity centered in the street. Reluctantly, he dropped his eyes to look at the dark face. "Oh, my God," he murmured, burying a ghostlike face in his hands.

Dreading the fact that he had to intrude on the man's anguish, the doctor looked up at him. "There's not much we can do for her . . . just ease the pain . . . She's too broken . . . I'm sorry. You might as well take her home . . . Let her die in peace. Being in the hospital will do her no good." After giving her a heavy dose of morphine, the doctor instructed the *gendarmes* as they lifted the young woman and laid her in an ambulance wagon.

Still holding the child, the Frenchwoman pushed forward and noticing that the girl's eyes matched exactly the light hazel color of the man's, she shoved the child into his arms. Shivering, Jean Dufort climbed into the ambulance holding his daughter. The October air was chilly, and he had run out without a coat.

4

Gendarme Gereaux reached into his pocket and pulled out the handkerchief. "I found this lying near her in the street," he said, handing Dufort the bracelet. "I thought it must be hers."

"*Oui . . . oui . . .* it is hers. *Merci.*" Freeing a hand from the child, he reached out and took it. *Oh, God, how hard she must have been hit for it to be forced from her arm,* he thought.

A short distance away, the driver of the fatal vehicle still sat in his seat, a glassy stare echoing his catatonic state. "I couldn't control them . . . I couldn't control them . . . ," he said, repeating the words over and over again.

Jean Dufort stood over their bed and ached with remorse as he looked down at his wife's broken, twisted form. He could only pray that death would put her out of her misery. He should never have brought her to France.

The last five years had gone by so quickly that there were times when he imagined he was sleepwalking. As his thoughts fled back to Guiana, he remembered Ndate as he had seen her for the first time. A snake bite he had gotten some weeks before in the cane field was not healing properly; it seemed infected, and the native blacks said that Ndate Yala would know what to do—she had a gift for healing. He could still see Ndate, tall, proud, and dignified, as she strolled into his room at the refinery greathouse, bearing a carriage he had never seen in a woman just twenty-one years old. Even with pain gripping his leg, he was fascinated with the rhythmic sway in her hips and the soft, bushy hair that covered her head like the halo of an angel.

"You asked to see me, *monsieur,*" she inquired saucily.

"*Oui, mademoiselle.* As you can see, I'm having a problem." He nodded at the bare, swollen leg he had propped on a pillow.

She looked at his whiteness with wary eyes.

"Is there something wrong?" he questioned.

"No, *monsieur.*"

"You look at me with such disdain," he said, nervously twisting the edges of his seal-brown moustache.

"You're a white man . . . White men dragged my mother

from Africa." Her long graceful fingers touched the infected yellow-green spot on his leg, and he felt the pain radiate through his body. "A snake bite?" she asked flatly.

"Oui."

As she rolled up the sleeves of her simple cotton dress and dug into the sack that she had slung from her shoulder, he noticed the beaded bracelet on her arm.

After treating his leg, every day for a week she came and applied poultices made of herbs and barks and strange substances he knew nothing of. When the week ended, the swelling and discoloration had gone. During that week, he used each visit to draw her into conversation about herself, thinking it was curiosity that tugged at him. But the more he knew about her, the more the fascination grew. She told him that she had been born into slavery, but emancipation came in 1848 when she was four years old and she remembered only the stories her mother had recounted to her. She had learned healing from her mother, who had carried the secrets from Africa entrenched in her memory. How easily the barriers between him and Ndate had crumbled away when she told him how her mother was brought to French Guiana chained in the galley of a slave ship. He could still feel the sadness that welled inside him when Ndate said, "My mother survived with this bracelet and knowing that I was inside her belly." Suddenly, Jean had grown red with anger that men could be so inhuman to other men, not to mention women.

Ndate chuckled at his anger. "You certainly don't act like a white man," she said.

"Do you ever take that off?" he questioned, his eyes perusing the intricately beaded ornament and the slender dark arm it circled. "May I see it?" She pulled it from her arm with much effort and handed it to him.

"Does it mean something special?"

"It was a gift to my mother from her mother on her coming of age. The custom in their family was for a woman to wear it until she passed it on to her daughter. It was the only thing my mother could give me to link me to my heritage."

Once his leg had healed, they instinctively avoided each other. As an accountant for the sugar refinery, he had been forced before going there to sign a statement swearing that

6

he would not fraternize with the women. Marriages between French citizens and the black population were forbidden, and it was company policy to discourage their fraternization. Ironically though, French prisoners that were deported there were encouraged to marry with the blacks.

Yet, without intending to, Jean Dufort and Ndate Yala had fallen in love. After weeks of not seeing each other, he had by chance walked into her path as she gathered bark by the river. How easily they had made love that day beneath the shade of a rustling palm tree. But then they realized they had broken the law. Black and white had virtually melted away in their passion and murmured sighs. For months they met in secret rendevous until that fateful day when his work there was finished.

Jean Dufort had no intention of leaving Ndate behind, pregnant with his child. He loved her. It cost him literally every *centime* he had saved to get her out of Guiana—to bribe the ship steward to let her stow away in his cabin, and he knew there would be legal problems when she arrived in France with no papers. He would have to say that he brought her back as a servant. But she was with him, and to him, that was the only concern. As soon as he could find a way to skirt the legal problems, they would be married.

Gazing down at her now, as she faced death, those days were a lifetime ago.

"Ndate," he whispered, his lips murmuring her name.

At that moment, as if reading his thoughts, she struggled for his hand, her long, graceful fingers among the few bones in her body that were not mangled. With strength enough to grasp but one finger, she clasped it weakly and then went limp. She was gone. Deep in the pit of his stomach, he felt sick from the sense of loss.

With tears stinging his hazel eyes, he stared at the tribal bracelet that had always circled her arm. Picking up the intricately beaded ornament, the Frenchman turned it round in his hand. Ndate had worn it the day he met her and every day since. It was the only thing her mother had possessed from her homeland and the Borrero tribe from which she had come. Dragged from Senegal, newly married and with child, this bracelet had been her strength during the long, bitter journey from Africa to French Guiana. It was the one legacy she could leave her daughter that symbolized her heritage.

Jean Dufort placed the bracelet beside his wife on the bed, thinking that he would bury it with her, but more pressing matters usurped his thoughts. In the next room, his three-year-old daughter wailed at the top of her lungs for her mother.

Manon Allard watched through the curtains that covered her ground-floor window as Jean Dufort hurried along the sidewalk. A worried expression marred his otherwise handsome face. He was such a nice young man, left alone with his small child. Buttoning the little girl into her coat, Madame Allard pushed Lauren's brown hands into her mittens and led her to the door with the promise that she would soon see her *papan*. Perhaps tomorrow the girl would get used to their arrangement and be less fretful, she thought.

As the child's father knocked, Madame Allard pulled open the door.

"Bonjour, madame," he said, removing his gray stovepipe hat.

"Papan!" Lauren broke away from the strange woman who looked nothing like her mother and ran to her father, wrapping herself about his knees.

"Mon chou," he chuckled lightly. Scooping her up, he settled her in his free arm. "I hope she wasn't too much trouble." His tone bordered on an apology.

"She's a good girl," Madame Allard replied, "but of course she misses her mother."

As he replaced his hat, a dull ache surrounded his heart. *"Merci, madame,* for your kindness."

Madame Allard watched them disappear through her front door. Her offer to mind the child during the day was as much a selfish motive as it was a charitable one. He could only pay a little, but she did not care about the money. Since being widowed last year, she needed something to occupy her days besides lamenting over her gray hairs and matronly figure. She had never been blessed with children of her own, and being able to have a child in her life was payment enough.

But each morning that Jean Dufort brought his daughter to Madame Allard's flat, the girl cried and fretted when her father left. Manon Allard invented games, designed numerous toys, and acted out pantomimes, all the things she imagined she would have done to amuse her own child, but the girl would not be amused. How did you comfort a child who longed for her mother? She had no idea how to penetrate the confusion that lay buried deep in the soul of those young eyes. And what eyes—she had never seen eyes so lucid that anger made them glow yellow.

At the end of one of those exasperating days, Madame Allard went into the salon, opened the piano, and began to play. Not having played since her husband's death, she played now out of feverish frustration, venting her own feelings of disappointment. The sounds filled the room and as her spirits soared with the music, she did not notice Lauren as she wandered to the doorway. Suddenly quiet, the child stood there wide-eyed, fascination gleaming in her face as she absorbed the sounds. But soon the teakettle summoned Madame Allard to the kitchen, and she left hurriedly, leaving the piano lid wide open. When she returned, her feet stopped short as she approached the doorway, and she watched the child, propelled by curiosity, scamper onto the bench. With great, wondrous glee, Lauren plunked her small brown fingers on the keys and chuckled with delight at the sounds that were created. "That's it," the older woman thought aloud, "I'll teach her to play the piano."

Every morning after that memorable occurrence, Jean Dufort happily took his daughter next door to Madame Allard's flat and took her home again each evening when he returned. Lauren loved her lessons on the piano. She began to look forward to the days there, and with time, Lauren learned to love Madame Allard.

On his days off, Jean Dufort took his daughter walking through the streets and alleyways of Paris. They explored the monuments and the cathedrals, but most of all they wandered through the many parks that decorated the city.

He marveled at her small, graceful, honey-colored hand and the way it clutched his so trustingly. Constantly, he was amused when she stopped to put her nose into every flower and stretch her hand out to pet every dog. There was so much of Ndate in her, he thought. And year after year went by in that manner, until one day, Lauren was no longer a child, but a young woman facing adolescence.

Jean Dufort knew he had to think seriously about his daughter. Her life would not be an easy one. Madame Allard had moved to Orleans a year ago to care for her ailing sister, and he was at the end of his wits, not knowing how to prepare a girl of twelve to face her life. Monsieur de Villiers, the owner of one of the estates whose books he kept, had offered his influence to get Lauren enrolled in a private girls' school, but how could he possibly afford it? There were times when he wished their child had been a boy. A man of mixed blood could always get by—but a woman? Who would take care of her? Who would she marry? He loved this girl-child who had Ndate's alluring mouth and his hazel eyes, yet her eyes had an opalescent quality that his did not have. Hers were a mirror reflecting her soul, and her most poignant feelings shown in them.

Raising Lauren alone had not been easy for him, but she needed a mother now, more than ever, a mother to teach her all the things a man did not know about being a woman. He thanked God that his sister, Claude, had been there for her last month when she started her womanly cycle, but Claude had little time for being a mother. Needless to say, he had not waited until Lauren's coming of age to give her Ndate's bracelet, because he had sensed her need for something of her mother long before now.

A whispered sigh escaped his lips. "Ndate . . . Ndate why did you have to leave us? Our daughter needs you . . . I need you." Jean Dufort clamped his lips together and straightened his spine. No doubt his daughter would have to make her own way in the world. She would need the best possible education. He would work more hours, take a second job, bring work home. He would do what he had to do, he decided. And within six months, much against her wishes, Lauren Dufort found herself enrolled at Madame Poisson's École de Jeunes Filles.

Lauren lay in bed, staring at the ceiling through the darkness. "Lauren." She cringed, not wanting to acknowledge her roommate's voice.

"Lauren, I know you are awake," Marie Thérèse insisted. "Why will you not do it with me? It would be such fun. Haven't you ever wanted to ride with your legs gripping the horse, like men do, feeling all that power between them? I always envied my brothers," she continued mockingly, "not having to ride with one leg hooked over a prong . . . Lauren!"

"Oui." Lauren's voice hesitated. "I don't know . . . We could get into a lot of trouble. And I've—I've never ridden that way. All I know about riding is what I've learned here."

"I will show you. It is really easy, much easier than riding sidesaddle. But that is the way ladies ride," she said, imitating Madame Luce, their riding instructor, as she sat her horse. "I saw some English saddles in the stable. We could sneak down there and ride all night—no one need ever know."

"I—I don't know," Lauren replied.

"Oh, do not be such a Goody Two-shoes," the girl said, exasperated. "Why should boys have all the fun? Do you not want to even try it?"

"Oui, but . . ." It would be fun, Lauren thought, as long as no one knew.

"Then you will do it?" she prodded.

"All right."

"Magnifique!" Marie Thérèse clutched her hands together with delight. While her mind raced along plotting the illicit adventure, Lauren drifted into an uneasy sleep.

The next afternoon when they had their riding lesson, Marie Thérèse made note of where the saddles were stored. While their classmates were trying to imitate Madame Luce's sitting position, after mounting, Marie Thérèse encouraged Lauren to lag behind so that they could memorize the execution of her plan.

That night while the others were asleep, Lauren and her roommate got up, stuffed pillows beneath their blankets, pulled riding boots on beneath their skirts, and tiptoed through the dark halls, feeling their way, until they reached the first floor. There, they dared to light a candle. Whispering and stifling their giggles, they slipped out the kitchen door and tramped over the dirt to the stables. Moonlight lit a path through the velvet darkness as though it had been waiting for them to come. They stole into the stable, and Marie Thérèse held the flickering light before her as she perused the stalls. The animals opened their eyes and snorted, skittish at the intrusion.

"I've seen the grooms ride these two," she said, her finger pointing toward two sleek brown fillies. "They must be used to carrying men astride."

"Are you sure?" Lauren felt her heart thump raucously in her chest. She tried to swallow, but her throat felt like dry wood.

Resting the candle on the mounting step, Marie Thérèse twisted her long blond hair into a coil behind her back and prodded Lauren to help her with the saddles. Together they lifted each saddle from the rack and hoisted it on the animal's back, and then Marie Thérèse showed Lauren how to fasten the straps. With the two horses saddled, Lauren stood there bewildered, not knowing what to do next. When she rode the sidesaddle, a groom helped her onto the horse.

"You silly goose!" Marie Thérèse exclaimed, ripping the bottom ruffle from her skirt. "Just watch me." Putting her left foot into the stirrup, she swung the right one over the horse's back. Reluctantly, Lauren followed her demonstration, and they walked the horses quietly out of the stable until they reached the wooded trail. All of a sudden, Marie Thérèse dug her heels into her mount's sides. "Let's go, girl," she cried, and the horse plunged into the woods. Still getting accustomed to the strange new position, Lauren needed all the strength she could muster just to hang onto her horse. With their hooves guided only by the moonlight, the two horses raced over the dark road, forcing the wind to rush in their riders' faces and the low-hanging branches to tear at their clothing and hair. Marie Thérèse's blond hair flew behind her like streamers on a Maypole, and Lauren felt the gush of air lift her springy brown curls as if she were about to fly. The sensation was exhilarating, she thought, and she soon learned to handle her horse in this fashion as well as, if not better than, Marie Thérèse.

Every night after that, they stole into the stables and reenacted the same adventure. Lauren's heart still raced, but she accepted it as part of the excitement. Her curiosity was piqued, and she now understood Marie Thérèse's obsession. She had not realized that something forbidden could be so exciting. But what she also did not realize was that the grooms had become suspicious when they found the two fillies always overheated and lethargic in the morning.

One night, just before dawn broke, Lauren and her companion came racing toward the stables as it began to rain. Laughing wildly, their skirts hiked high enough to expose their young thighs, the two girls nearly collided with Madame Poisson as she waited in the shadows.

"Madame Poisson!" Lauren gasped. Abruptly halting her mount, Lauren slid from the saddle.

"So, it is you!" she said, her eyes gliding over Lauren with contempt. "I should have known."

Marie Thérèse slid from her saddle, smoothed her skirt, and became demurely innocent. She said nothing.

"Inside with you, child," the older woman ordered, taken in by the pale angelic expression. Marie Thérèse slipped past Lauren and tread lightly across the yard and into the house. "Mademoiselle Dufort, I want to see your father. This is an outrage," she said, staring down the bony plane of her nose.

"Madame, I—" But Lauren's pleas fell on deaf ears. Madame Poisson lifted her skirt and picked her way toward the main house.

Two days later, Jean Dufort was ushered into Madame Poisson's office. Lauren sat between her father and the head mistress, her honey brown hands folded in her lap while the rains of injustice beat down on her young head.

"Monsieur Dufort, we accepted your daughter on the recommendation of Monsieur de Villiers. We like to think that we are benevolent toward a few girls who are"—she paused, searching for the right word—"less fortunate. But we cannot have your daughter introducing her plebian ideas to young ladies."

Seeing her father flush red with shame, Lauren fumed. "Mademoiselle Poisson, I—Marie Thérèse—"

"Quiet, Mademoiselle Dufort! Young ladies are seen and not heard."

"But I—"

"Lauren, not now," her father scolded irascibly.

"Marie Thérèse is from one of the oldest, most prestigious families in France," Madame Poisson expounded further. "If her father hears of this outrage, there will be hell to pay."

Scorching tears threatened to burn through Lauren's eyelids as she sat there fuming at the injustice of her situation.

"I would suggest that you discipline your daughter severely. If this happens again, I will have no choice but to ask her to leave. I will not have her corrupting the morals of young ladies of breeding."

Dufort strongly resented the way this woman spoke to his daughter, but he said nothing. Once he had Lauren alone, he scolded her out of frustration and then tried to atone by patiently listening to her explanation.

"S'il vous plaît, Papan, do I have to stay here?" she pleaded.

"Just try to be a good girl, *mon chou,"* he said, smiling gently, "and don't cause trouble." Stubborn tears welled in her innocent eyes. Wrapping his arms around her, he held her to him, and Lauren clung to him. He knew that his child could not have instigated the incident. She had never ridden a horse before coming to the school, but he could not protest and risk having her expelled. So, at thirteen, Lauren was quite aware of her station in life.

After that mishap, Lauren and Marie Thérèse were separated as roommates, and Lauren roomed with a girl from a less prestigious background. It was a wise move, Lauren thought, because each time she saw Marie Thérèse, she felt the urge to strangle her scrawny neck. Having learned not to trust the other girls, Lauren kept to herself. Madame Debussy, the music teacher, had said many times that hers was an exceptional talent, and so Lauren concentrated on perfecting her skill at the piano. In this manner she survived the next three years of her life.

Not until she was sixteen did Lauren come face-to-face with her father's failing health. She noticed how quickly he tired when he walked with her in the park and how he struggled for breath after climbing the stairs to their flat.

"*Papan*, you need not work so hard," Lauren pleaded, clinging to his arm. Jean Dufort stood at the top of the stairs gasping for breath and prayed to God that it were possible. He did not have the strength to walk the few steps to his modest flat, but still he continued to work long hours and get little sleep. It took all he could earn to pay the bills that kept her in school.

"I could quit school," Lauren said as if reading his thoughts. "*Papan*, why do I have to go back there? I feel so out of place. They all have expensive gowns . . . and fancy carriages. *Papan*, please let me quit. I could come home and take care of you." Her eyes sparkled with the thought.

But he reacted the same as he always had when she mentioned quitting school. A wild glare rose in her father's eyes and the veins bulged against his temples until she thought they would burst. "You will finish school as I have planned!" he bellowed. His voice was so loud that it shook the walls.

Lauren shrunk away from him, feeling the anger and frustration well up inside her chest. "But I hate being there! I feel like the scullery maid walking next to them."

As he felt his daughter's unhappiness, Jean softened and drew her into his arms.

"Oh, *Papan*, you're sick," she sobbed.

"It will be all right," he said, wiping her tears with his hand. "And one day, I promise, you *will* understand."

But everything failed to be all right. In less than a year, Jean Dufort's heart stopped beating. Weakened by the years of working long hours in a cold, damp warehouse and never having recovered his joie de vivre after the loss of Ndate, he lacked the motivation to struggle through life any longer. His driving force had been his daughter Lauren and her education, and having accomplished that, his heart just gave up.

Only weeks after her seventeenth birthday, Lauren Dufort stood in the small church cemetery, on the outskirts of Paris, staring down at the raw, dark plot of earth that had swallowed her father's body. Hot tears streamed over her cheeks as she read the slab of stone:

Ndate Yala Dufort
1844–1870
Jean Benoit Dufort
1840–1884

Lauren ground her teeth into her bottom lip, trying to stifle the loneliness that crept through her soul. *"Papan, what will I do without you?"*

Chapter

1

1891

Blustery March winds seized the skirt of Lauren de Martier's traveling suit and tangled it hopelessly about her honey-colored legs. Unshielded from the whipping wind, she stood on the dock at Le Havre and watched as porters and crew loaded passengers and freight aboard the giant ocean liner. Not in her wildest dreams would she have imagined two months ago that she would be eagerly leaving Paris forever.

Paris, with its beautiful Gothic buildings, the mysteries of its tiny winding alleys, and the tales that lurked within them, was her home. She was born here. Her mother had died here—in that grisly accident. Lauren planted firmly in her mind's eye all the things in Paris that had delighted her as a child, les Tuilleries, Notre Dame, and Île Saint Louis, but they would not stay. They faded into the distance as though they belonged to something long past.

The ancient seaport town of Le Havre lay in the hills surrounding the pier, its oddly tiled houses basking in the early spring sunshine. The wind grew stronger, and to Lauren, it seemed the sun shone more brightly than ever. Waves crashing against the ship caused the steel vessel to heave to and fro even though it was securely anchored. It was a beautiful day, almost too beautiful to leave France, Lauren thought.

An officer approached, tipping his hat. *"Madame,* are you a passenger on this voyage?"

"Oui," she answered in her best drawing room French. "My husband went to see about our luggage."

"Very well, *madame,* but I hope he hurries. We'll be taking up anchor in about ten minutes." Lauren mused as he walked away. Being addressed as *madame* was still strange to her.

Even she, with all her adventurous spirit, was surprised that she was leaving France to start life with a man she had known scarcely two months in a country about which she knew decidedly less. But she had known from the moment she first stared into his eyes that she would have gone anywhere with Roget.

Elegant women dressed in the finest haute couture bustled past her, accompanied by gentlemen in wool broadcloth invernesses and narrow striped trousers. Was this illustrious assortment of people going to Haiti? Lauren felt illiterate, knowing so little about her mother's people, her husband's people, and the most dominant part of herself.

Emerald green faille swished and gave way to raucous rustling noises, as the wind twisted yards of voluminous skirt about Lauren's ankles. Glancing over her shoulder, Lauren was surprised to see her husband, Roget, her aunt Claude, and Pierre rushing along the walkway to where she stood.

"Claude—Pierre—why are you here in Le Havre?" Her tone was an odd coupling of overt delight and reticent curiosity. They had said their good-byes the previous day. What could have prompted her aunt to travel all the way to Le Havre from Paris? The older woman grabbed her niece and hugged her passionately, tears dampening two pairs of eyes. As they embraced, Claude stealthily freed a hand and slipped an envelope into Lauren's fur muff.

"Read this when you are alone," she whispered. *"Au revoir, chérie."* With a feigned gesture that appeared to be the waving of a hand, Claude brushed the tears from her dark eyes. Pierre exchanged a hurried handshake with Roget and bestowed Lauren with a fatherly peck on her flushed cheek as the officer hustled them on board.

"You will take good care of my birds," Lauren called anxiously to Claude.

"Oui, chérie," her aunt's reply rang through the air.

The gangplank lifted slowly off the ground. Lauren stared blindly into the distance until Le Havre faded from view. It was then that she uttered a silent farewell to France and prepared to meet the country that demanded her husband's intensely ambivalent loyalties.

Inside their stateroom, Roget flung his tailcoat, followed by the waistcoat, onto the small double berth and disappeared into the cramped dressing room. Lauren remembered the envelope stuffed carelessly in her muff. Seizing it from where it lay nestled in the gray fur, her eyes searched the minuscule room and fixed on the shiny surface of her workbox. Here was where she had placed her two most cherished possessions: a time-worn, barely visible daguerreotype of her mother and father and her mother's tribal bracelet. The exquisite ivory sewing box, inlaid with mother-of-pearl, had left her speechless when Bertrand presented it to her on her wedding day. Tears had flooded her eyes when she realized that Bertrand had chosen such a delicate thing to give her as a gift. Lauren was painfully aware that she would miss him. Claude, Pierre, and Bertrand had been her family for seven years. Now she would have to become acquainted with a new family—a family of strangers.

Nervously, Lauren fingered the crumpled envelope and then quickly shoved it into the obscure pocket, making certain that none of the paper was visible. Temptation prodded her to open it, but there was no time. *What more could Claude possibly want to tell me?* she wondered. Within seconds, her mind had fled back seven years in a feeble attempt to preserve the familiarity of the past. Lauren found herself reliving with uncanny vividness those first uncertain months when she had been thrust into the lives of her aunt Claude and the Hôtel Saint Germain. Lauren could still feel the tears that had burned against her eyelids and hear the thought that had escaped her lips as the horse-drawn carriage turned off the boulevard and onto the narrow side street. "God, why did you have to take *Papan* . . . He was all I had!"

19

She had approached the hotel with trepidation. The decadence of Paris was alive all around her, in every street and alleyway. She knew that she was an orphan now and had no one but her father's sister.

Lauren paid the driver and climbed down. "Are you sure this is it?" the driver asked curiously, letting his eyes rake over her young body. "This is a hotel for gentlemen."

"Oui, I know, but my aunt owns it," she replied, innocently unaware of his insinuation. She watched his face turn blood red as he dragged the two heavy trunks from the carriage and dumped them on the doorstep. Climbing into the rickety vehicle, he drove away.

Lauren adjusted her hat and the green woolen mantle that covered her shoulders and reached for the door knocker. Her hand trembled as she seized the brass ornament, and it banged louder than she intended. Embarrassed, she drew back and waited. The mahogany door opened and behind it stood a man with graying hair who looked as if his nose had been invaded with a foul odor.

"Oui, mademoiselle?"

"Is Madame Rousseau here?"

"And whom should I say is calling?" His focus lingered on her honey brown skin.

"I'm her niece." Biting her shapely bottom lip, Lauren struggled to suppress a nervous giggle.

"Oui, mademoiselle." His tone was patronizing. And while he wrestled with the impossibility of such a thing, he went to fetch Madame Rousseau.

Lauren stood in the open doorway flanked by the two trunks. In one she had packed her clothing and in the other she had put her few treasured belongings. Everything else had been sold to cover her father's burial expenses. She was not exactly sure how, but Lauren was determined to earn her own way. She would not be a burden to Claude.

Startled by what sounded like a commotion, Lauren's eye caught a glimpse of her aunt Claude as she swept into the foyer, her blue-and-white-striped skirt swishing over the polished floor.

"Madame," the man explained smugly, "there is a young colored person here . . . She says she is your niece."

"Where is she?"

"There, *madame.*" He beckoned toward Lauren, who stood shivering in the open doorway.

"Come in, child," she said, putting an arm about Lauren's shoulders. The older woman ushered her into the warmth of the room. "Justin, have Louis take these trunks to the third floor," she ordered impatiently.

Raising a discreet eyebrow, the elderly desk clerk rushed to do her bidding.

Turning her attention back to Lauren, she spoke hesitantly. "*Chérie,* you must be exhausted . . . so much . . . and you just barely seventeen. But you'll be fine here!" Putting her hand to Lauren's flushed cheek, she asked, "Have you eaten anything today?"

"I had lunch at school before I left," Lauren replied sadly, knowing that the door to a part of her life had been slammed shut.

"Well, let's get you to your room." Her aunt's voice, at least, was soothing, and Lauren felt the comforting arm warm the chill in her shoulders as Claude turned her toward the stairs.

Climbing the stairs to her new home, Lauren's focus was on Claude, the name shortened by its owner because she detested Claudine. Madame Rousseau was her married name, and her small, intimate hotel lay nestled among a cluster of more elaborate specimens of French architecture on the Left Bank of Paris. That was everything that Lauren knew about her one and only blood relative.

"Have you always lived in a hotel?" Lauren inquired with innocent curiosity.

"Good heavens, no, child," the older woman said, chuckling. "This was once a private residence. This was the home my husband brought me to as a bride; it had been owned by his family for years."

"How did it become a hotel?" Lauren asked, her tone still pregnant with curiosity.

"I started it as a boardinghouse some years ago when I found myself a young widow with no means of support. Men found the ambience appealing," she continued as though anticipating her niece's silent questions, "and soon the bar and club room made it an attractive after-theater refuge for single or unescorted gentlemen. They lingered until the wee hours, drinking, playing cards, and letting Armand enchant them with his antics at the piano. On their boisterous nights, they requested sing-alongs and all joined in singing words that would make a courtesan blush."

Pushing open a door next to her third-floor apartment, Claude ushered Lauren inside. "This room should suit you," she said. There was a long moment of silence between them in which Lauren noticed that her aunt's chatter had given way to a dolorous expression of empathy. "I'll leave you now to get settled," she added as she left the room.

"Merci," Lauren muttered softly. She did not dare say more lest she drown in a flood of tears.

Lauren's gaze fled over the room, taking in the brass bed, the billowy white curtains, and the flocked yellow wallpaper. Letting a long-imprisoned sigh of relief escape her lungs, she approached the two trunks that sat conspicuously in the center of the carpet. With nimble fingers she pried the lid from the smaller one and rummaged through it, searching for her treasures. Mixed with the odd things that most Parisians would have labeled junk, Lauren had packed her most valuable possessions: a blue hobby horse bought for her by her mother when she was three, the faded daguerreotype of her parents taken after they arrived in France, and her mother's tribal bracelet. Once she had unpacked the beaded bracelet and the faded photograph, she discovered the small table and lamp that sat next to the bed. Slowly, Lauren walked toward the piece of furniture, propped the picture against the gas lamp, laid the bracelet beside it, and then reached up to remove her hat and mantle. The moment her young body met horizontally with the mattress, she was asleep.

A month passed and Lauren began to settle into the routine of the Saint Germain. Determined to make herself useful, she filled her days with the chores that Claude assigned her, and at night she retired to the refuge of her room where the memories of her father were there to comfort her. In the kitchen, she helped Pierre, the hotel chef, and he painstakingly gave her lessons in cutting, chopping, and the art of stirring. "If the sauce is stirred improperly, you ruin the meal, *ma chérie,"* he insisted as his fingers pinched the edge of his moustache. Each time he said it, Lauren had trouble suppressing the restless giggle that rose in her throat. The rumor prevalent among the female kitchen help was that Pierre was Claude's lover, but Lauren could not muster up the nerve to ask her aunt to confirm it.

As Lauren helped press, fold, and stack away linens that would be soiled again in two days she knew that one day she would have to fill Armand's place at the piano but not for some time. The aging pianist was still a robust theatrical entertainer with ruddy cheeks and a jaunty spring in his step. "This piano is what keeps me young, *chérie,*" he would say and then tweek Lauren's honey-hued cheeks until they blushed burgundy.

But one Monday night, Armand did not show for his evening performance, and Claude received a message from his son saying that he had suffered a stroke.

Again, Lauren felt the pangs of loss and was very much aware of the implications to her.

"Mademoiselle," Louis said, approaching her in the pantry, "Madame Rousseau would like to see you in her office."

"Merci, Louis." Forgetting to remove her apron, Lauren fled through the foyer, trying in vain to smooth the wisp of springy curls from her forehead.

As her niece rushed into the room, the older woman rose from the desk and moved around to stand in front of her. Claude's tone was hesitant. "Lauren, I had thought to wait until you were eighteen . . . but fate has a way of thwarting the best of intentions." Her expressive white hands came up and clutched her own shoulders. "We need a pianist now. I might as well break you in."

Lauren felt the dryness prickle in her throat. She tried hard to swallow. "It's all right," she said, her voice cracking. "I have to start earning my way."

"You can start Friday . . . That will give you three days to look over Armand's music sheets and practice the songs."

When Friday arrived, Lauren was a wretched bundle of nerves. She passed up dinner for fear that her stomach would want to regurgitate it all over the piano. And now, alone in her room, Lauren climbed into the pink satin gown, realizing how many male eyes would be watching her. Nervously, she tugged at the décolleté, trying to cover the swell of her young breasts. She had not noticed before that it was so low. As she left her room and started down the stairs, her empty stomach grumbled and she felt light-headed enough to float to the bottom. Skipping dinner was a mistake, she thought as she collided with Bertrand, the hotel bouncer, at the bottom of the stairwell.

"Mademoiselle, you'd better watch where ya goin'" he grinned, catching her in gargantuan arms. "I don't wanta be the one to tell Madame Claude that you've hurt yourself."

He was a big man, clumsy in appearance, with the innate strength of an ox, and one only had to see the adoration on his face to know that Claude's wish was his command. His distorted face had a stupid, distant look about it, the remnant of flesh that had been battered too often, but there were few men foolish enough to go against him. Lauren had grown fond of him, and his presence made her feel safe.

"I'm sorry, Bertrand," she muttered sheepishly and then slipped away to the dining room.

The wood-paneled room, set with white linen tablecloths and polished silver, was beginning to fill with boisterous diners. Claude moved through the room in a burgundy taffeta gown, straightening leather chairs and adjusting the Impressionist murals that graced the wall. Her black hair was smoothed high off her forehead into an elegant pouf and pulled into a chignon at the nape of her neck. She had a way of sweeping into a room that made other women want to hide in a corner.

"Chérie, you should have eaten your dinner," Claude quipped perceptively as she swept by and saw Lauren stealthily holding her stomach.

"I didn't think I could keep it down," she replied. But now, with her nerves roiling like a storm in her belly, the thought lacked conviction. Finally, Lauren gave in and went to the kitchen for some food to appease her hunger pains. She seized the first thing that she saw, a piece of sugary pastry, and gobbled it down. After wiping her hands, she intended to slip away without anyone noticing her, but leaving the pantry, she bumped headlong into Pierre.

"Ah! So this is what becomes of young women who have no time for dinner. They end up with sugar on their faces," he teased, tenderly wiping the smudge from her chin. Blood raced to Lauren's cheeks, and her hazel eyes plummeted to the floor.

"The first lesson a lady must learn," he continued, "is to always eat dinner so that she doesn't have to scrounge in the pantry like a rat."

Over an hour had passed that seemed like only minutes, and then suddenly, the dreaded moment had arrived. Louis came and summoned her. *"Madame* says it is time for you to play."

As she followed him into the noisy club room, Lauren felt as though she were sleepwalking. She went to the piano, pulled out the leather bench, and self-consciously smoothed the voluminous satin skirt beneath her as she sat down. The palms of her hands felt damp and cold, but she took a deep breath and plunged into a forte. Mechanically, her nimble fingers raced through a medley of favorites that she had heard Armand play and then eased into a Chopin ballade, which, to her surprise, the men liked. When they had grown accustomed to having a female at the piano and had tired of staring at her exposed brown shoulders, they began to request their usual sing-alongs. Struggling not to blush at their naughty verbiage, Lauren complied.

As Lauren got up from the piano, an impeccably dressed man approached her, and to Lauren, his forty years seemed ancient. Sweeping his glossy high hat into his hand, he said, *"Mademoiselle,* do permit me to buy you a drink."

Flashing an innocent smile, Lauren replied, "I am sorry, *monsieur,* but I'm not allowed to fraternize with the gentlemen."

"I am a regular customer here, and I'm quite sure Madame Rousseau would not deny me the pleasure of your company, *mademoiselle."* His lewd emphasis on *mademoiselle* reeked with contempt at her rebuff, and getting no further response from her, he reached out and seized her arm.

"Monsieur, you're hurting my arm. Please let go!" But he tightened the grip on her arm, and his voice grew more insistent. Shaken and angry, Lauren was baffled as to how she should handle the situation until Claude appeared out of nowhere to handle the matter for her.

"Monsieur de Guy, surely you wouldn't force a mere

child to drink. Why, you're old enough to be her father. Why don't you have a drink on the house, and Lauren will play for us again. She's quite a talented young lady, you know." With a flip of her hand, she smiled and beckoned Lauren to return to the piano. He was calmed for the moment as he sat at the table toying with the drink. But as Lauren sat with her back to him, she felt his furious eyes burning two holes in her body. And then he left. Lauren relaxed to play the last request, envying the ease with which Claude had handled the disturbance.

Lauren finished the Chopin impromptu and slipped away to her room. As she climbed the stairs, weary from the ordeal, she sensed the presence of someone walking in her footsteps. Looking down the stairs to the next landing, she saw nothing. Continuing on, quickening her steps, she assumed that weariness had played havoc with her imagination. She approached her door, and a strong, sweaty hand lunged out of the darkness and clasped her mouth shut while another imprisoned her narrow waist. Lauren gasped. The hands spun her around, and hot, wet lips were planted against her trembling mouth. In her struggle, she saw that the beast in the darkness was Monsieur de Guy. She fought desperately, kicking at his shins and raking her nails over his face. Strange, grunting noises vibrated in his throat. Her fury managed to break his grip on her, and she lashed out at him.

"Monsieur de Guy, you're drunk!"

"Not too drunk to handle you! Who do you think you are, strutting around with all those grand manners as though you were a lady?"

"I *am* a lady," she snapped back at him.

"Huh! That's a laugh," he said, grabbing her again. "You're nothing but a mulatto whore."

"That's not true!" Lauren screamed. She fought him with the strength of her humiliation.

"Sure it is. I know all about you mulattoes. I've had many of them in Martinique. There's hellfire burning inside you, and you love nothing more than a romp in the hay."

Lauren saw that the man was half crazed. She wrenched her mouth free and screamed from the depths of her lungs.

"Who do you think is going to hear you way up here?" he asked in a mocking tone.

Determined not to give in, Lauren kicked, scratched, and bit his lips as he tried to kiss her. Her teeth marks drew blood. In his shock, he released her. She ran down the hall toward the stairs, but as she reached the landing, he seized her again.

Monsieur de Guy's wet, roaming mouth slobbered over the cleavage of her young breasts. His clumsy fingers fumbled with the front of her gown. An angry yank on the delicate fabric, and the sound of tearing satin ripped through Lauren's body as the bodice yielded.

"Delicious! Delicious!" he snorted, sounding more like a pig than a man. His greedy mouth lunged for her brown flesh, but she turned quickly and shielded her exposed body by clasping an arm across her chest.

On the landing below, she heard the pounding of heavy footsteps and looking down, she saw Bertrand taking the steps three at a time. He had heard her screams. In what seemed like a second, the massive man had snatched Monsieur de Guy by the collar and dragged him down the steps.

"Are you all right, Mademoiselle Lauren? Did he hurt you?" Bertrand's crooked mouth gaped open as he glanced back and saw the savagely torn gown.

"I'm all right . . . I think . . ." Her voice trembled. A mass of bushy curls spilled into her face as her eyes roamed over her badly mauled body. "Thank God . . . you came. I don't know how much longer—"

"Madame Claude'll be up right away," Bertrand called back, and he disappeared, dragging Monsieur de Guy behind him. She could still hear her attacker muttering insults at her.

Lauren stumbled into her room. Her fingers fumbled with the gas lamp until it flickered, and for the first time since she had been here, she locked the door. She climbed out of the torn dress and let it fall into a ragged heap on the floor. Her innocent body ached, her stomach retched, and tears swelled in her eyes as her hands traced over her swollen face. She splashed it with cold water and sank onto the bed, dazed and angry.

A soft knock penetrated the door. Lauren lay motionless, too weary to get up.

"Lauren. *C'est moi,* Claude. *Ouvre le porte.*"

Lauren stumbled to the door and opened the latch. Claude rushed in, took one look at her niece, and her face flushed in horror.

"I'm so sorry, *chérie*. He will not set foot in here again." The older woman put her niece to bed and nursed her bruises with cold compresses, comforting her with gentle words. Lauren lay still, but resounding through her brain were the abominable things he had said.

"Why did he call me a mulatto whore?"

"Not now, *chérie*. Right now I want you to sleep and forget this ugly incident."

Lauren knew she would never forget it. Claude left the room and Lauren fell into a deep, troubled sleep.

Days later, she learned that Monsieur de Guy was a very rich man with a notorious reputation. Seducing servant girls and other women beneath his station was his favorite amusement. Even though Claude forbade him to set foot in the Saint Germain and the matter was forgotten, Lauren did not forget the terrible names he had called her.

The door to their dressing room clicked open and its sound thrust Lauren back into the present. Roget emerged, making her senses acutely aware of his male presence. He had changed into a dressing gown, which subtly suggested that he intended to remain immured for the afternoon. Longing to shed her own restrictive clothing, Lauren followed his lead and entered the tiny alcove to change. After peeling off the heavy suit, petticoat, boned corset, and high-buttoned boots, she sighed with relief. It felt good to be free of those cumbersome underpinnings. As narrow as her waist was, wearing a corset seemed ridiculous. Wrapping her body in the white kimono, she let the silk slither wickedly over her skin. The silk robe unleashed a barrage of delectible images as she recalled the excruciating ecstasy of their wedding night.

Lauren stood in the doorway between the two rooms and gazed through opalescent eyes at the man who was now her husband. Her expression harbored a deep reservation.

"Does your family know that you're bringing me?"

"I sent word that I would bring my wife home. Whether they acknowledged it is another matter."

"What will they say?"

"I don't know," Roget replied flatly, "but I cannot imagine that they will be pleased."

"Didn't they expect you to marry?" Lauren continued reluctantly, however unprepared she was to hear his answer.

"Of course they did . . . but they expected the proper lineage. Marriages in our society are arranged."

Lauren looked away swiftly. Fear clouded her eyes as apprehension flooded her thoughts.

"It's a complicated story," Roget injected quickly. "We will be there soon enough, and then we shall deal with it. Right now, let's enjoy the few remaining days of our privacy." As he moved toward her, his solemn mood gave way to an amorous smile that curled his lips. "There will be precious little of it at home."

That evening they entered the dining room, still basking in the glow of an amorous afternoon, and Roget's words became reality sooner than she had dared to imagine. As Lauren's hand curled lovingly around her husband's arm, both their heads turned when a voice behind them bellowed, "Roget!" Roget's surprised facial expression acknowledged his recognition of the ebony-skinned man who smiled at them.

"Monsieur Duval, *madame*," Roget said, inclining his head in a gesture of respect to the older couple.

"Roget de Martier," the man chuckled, stroking the point of his goatee, "Fancy meeting you . . ."

"As you know," Roget interrupted, "I spent the past year in France. And you?" Roget's tone echoed his curiosity.

"We are returning from that infamous tour of the Continent that one must do once in a lifetime."

Roget touched his lips to Madame Duval's outstretched hand and the two men locked hands in the conventional manner.

"*Monsieur, madame,*" Roget said, intercepting the small talk, "I would like you to meet my wife, Lauren."

The older woman's fair skin flushed pink, and it would have been impossible for Lauren not to notice the way the woman's mouth flapped open when she was introduced.

Henri Duval lifted Lauren's hand from where it lay against her handbag and timidly touched his lips to her gloved fingers. His overly plump wife offered a limp greeting and exercised controlled civility as she mewed, "I am pleased to meet you."

Lauren responded coolly, her mind reacting to the unpleasant reception she had just witnessed.

"My dear, you *must* come to tea once you are settled," the older woman cajoled, but the half-hearted tone of her invitation resounded through Lauren's senses. It was a mere formality. The woman still struggled with her own private demons.

Sharing a table with the Duvals soon dissipated Lauren's desire to prolong her last few evenings alone with Roget. Throughout the meal Lauren only picked at her asparagus. Shortly after dessert, she feigned a headache and begged to be excused. But much to her chagrin, Madame Duval zealously agreed to accompany her. "I will be all right," Lauren apologized, "if I can just lie down for a moment. There is no need for you to leave."

"I will walk with you," she insisted. Following Lauren into the narrow hallway, they left the men to their brandy. Once out of their husbands' view, the older woman addressed the younger one with an unnerving condescension. *"Ma chérie,* where do you come from?

"I'm from Paris," Lauren replied.

"Are you French?"

"I was born in France."

"And your parents . . . are they in France?"

"They are both dead."

"But you're of mixed blood . . ."

"Obviously," Lauren retorted. "I'm the daughter of an African woman and a Frenchman."

"I didn't mean to pry," she said, noticeably recoiling from shock. "I was merely curious." But her voice dripped with sarcasm as she added, "Roget was always fascinated with such . . . beautiful women."

Lauren bristled. Instinct told her it was more than curiosity. She spun on her heel and left Madame Duval standing aghast in the narrow hallway. As she hurried off to her cabin, she wondered about the Duvals. He was black and she, nearly white.

Undressing rapidly, Lauren wrapped herself in the luxury of her silk kimono. Then remembering Claude's letter, she retrieved the ecru envelope from its hiding place. She examined it carefully. There was nothing on the outside that offered even a clue. Anxiously, she tore at the sealed paper until it lay open and extracted the sheet of her aunt's personal stationery. Four neatly folded five-hundred-franc notes scattered on the carpet. For a long while, Lauren could do nothing but stare at the money.

After some minutes, she gathered the notes and wanting an explanation began to read the letter:

Dearest Lauren,

Enclosed you will find two thousand francs. This is your dowry, so to speak, but I think it should remain in your hands and not your husband's. This is money your father left when he died. His instructions were to give it to you when you needed it most. It is my decision that you have it now. I realize that you are a married woman with a wealthy husband, but I sincerely believe that a woman should not be totally dependent on her husband's means. Knowing you and how fiercely independent you are, I felt that you should not be so far away without a penny to your name. You have the utmost faith in your husband, and I do hope you experience a happy life with him, but I will rest easier knowing that you have this money. It's not much, and perhaps you will never need it, but if you do, you'll be thankful for its existence. Well, *chérie*, if I'm to get this to you before your ship sails, I have to hurry.

Love, Claude

Lauren lowered herself onto the arm of a chair. That her father had left her anything was a surprise in itself. Carefully, she refolded the letter, placed it and the money in the envelope, and stood up to return the precious package to the ivory workbox. A more secure spot would have to wait until she was settled in her new home.

Chapter

2

Peering through the porthole, Lauren saw nothing but the ripples of moonlight dancing on the water. She toyed with the idea of a walk on deck, but then realized she was already shivering from the cold. Glinting like diamonds, the dancing ripples of water captured her imagination and brought to mind the glittering crystal pellets that dangled from the chandelier at the Saint Germain. Its beauty had eluded her until that winter day when the entire direction of her life had been changed. Still shivering from the night air, Lauren wrapped her arms about her shoulders. Her thoughts tred back over the gray, icy months, and she remembered that the winter of 1891 had been a brutal one.

Paris had just begun to emerge from its frigid, blizzard-torn blanket of snow when the untimely appearance of the sun made the air curiously warm for the first of February. Bounding from the entrance of the Saint Germain, Lauren slammed the heavy, brass-trimmed door shut behind her. "Why could Claude not understand?" she murmured, clenching her teeth in desperation. She merely wanted the chance to live her own life. Her feet met the sidewalk with an angry pace and she had covered several blocks before the cold air began to cool the fever in her brain. How could she possibly expect her aunt to understand? Claude had been married at twenty, and Claude certainly had never been in her situation.

Lauren crossed the bridge at Pont du Carrousel and paused just long enough to let her hazel eyes linger on the rippled waters of the Seine. On the other side of the river she passed through the Jardin de les Tuilleries, walking the same path she had walked as a child with her father.

The trees were bare, the flowers, the grass, and the foliage were not yet aware that spring was struggling to surface. The atmosphere was desolate, but the unusual warmth of the afternoon had lured an abundance of strollers from their winter hibernation. Lauren's gaze focused on couples walking arm in arm, nannies wheeling their children, children playing with their dogs as they nuzzled each other.

Twenty-four and unmarried, Lauren wondered if she was destined to become some rich man's mistress when her desire for love could no longer be suppressed. To live with a man and be heavy with his child without ever sharing his name was a fate she dreaded. Yet what chance did she have? Claude had warned her in so many subtle ways not to set her heart on marriage.

Men who patronized the hotel often found her attractive, and though her experiences with men were limited, female intuition warned her that their attentions did not include marriage. Mulatto women had a reputation for being lusty, sensuous creatures, and to that misconception Lauren attributed the numerous propositions she received each evening.

An obvious mingling of African and French, her skin was a rich honey brown, and her features vaguely resembled those of her father except for her mother's full, shapely mouth and perfect teeth. Lauren had a mass of hair that was neither straight nor kinky, but seal brown and rigidly curly. She was too far from the ideal to be beautiful and yet too exotic to be homely, but hazel eyes coupled with her mother's African mouth gave her face a sensuous quality that was quite pleasing to the eye.

Though her ample derriere had never required a bustle nor her hourglass waist a corset, she had always felt extremely tall and lean to be considered shapely by the day's standards. And by no means did she rank herself among the most feminine of women, that is, if feminine meant fragile, empty-headed, and docile. Long ago, she had conceived that these men were interested because she had African blood and therefore only to be courted for a night's amusement.

"Papan, you must have known that my life would not be a normal one," Lauren thought aloud as the familiar path brought back vivid memories of her father. *"Oh, papan,* I miss you," she cried softly. Her teeth chattered, and she pulled the worn woolen mantle closer about her body as she left the garden, but still she felt the insistent bite of winter cold.

Absently, guided by force of habit, Lauren walked along the boulevard until her restless spirit sought refuge in the Church of Saint Germain-des-Prés. She fled into the ancient church, her head a jumble of rampant thoughts, sank down into a pew, and then slid onto her knees. She had come here often over the last seven years. God had become her refuge, and out of desperation and loneliness she had begun pouring out her heart to a heavenly Father.

Her focus gazed up at the image of Christ, his body impaled to the cross, his head bleeding from a crown of thorns. Instantly, she felt the wave of hope that washed over her soul. "Jesus, if you could endure all that they did to you, in order to save us, surely I can find the strength to endure my life," she whispered.

Lauren rose from the pew, and within the space of a second, her lucent hazel eyes flashed opalescent with anger, an anger that railed at life for trying to defeat her, and at herself for almost allowing it to succeed. She forced her shoulders to her spine and walked briskly up the aisle. Pausing at the head of the aisle to genuflect, her thoughts again encompassed the image of her heavenly Father's son. "Father," she uttered with determination, "I promise that I will not get angry with Claude."

Turning away from the altar, she left the church and walked back to the Saint Germain Hotel, where she found her aunt already fussing over the dining room. The older woman looked up with alarm. "Where have you been so long?"

"Walking in the park," Lauren replied as she pulled off the woolen mantle. "I didn't realize it was so late."

Claude smiled warily and sent her off with a playful slap on the derriere. "Go and get your dinner. Pierre's been keeping it warm for you, and you know how dreadful fish is when it's overcooked."

Lauren ate the fish and green peas quickly, so quickly that Pierre promised she would have indigestion. "Is this why I labor over my cooking . . . so you can gobble it down in three bites?" he grumbled through his moustache.

"I'm sorry—" She began to apologize and then noticed his silly grin.

In her room, Lauren leafed through the closet, unable to decide on a gown for the evening; and then with hopeful anticipation she chose the emerald green satin. The low décolleté and enormous pouffed sleeves framed her honey-hued shoulders, and she marveled at the young woman who faced her in the mirror. She was considerably more poised than the girl who had been terrorized by Monsieur de Guy seven years ago.

"*Chérie,* you look lovely tonight." A twinkle danced in the older woman's eye as Lauren entered the dining room, a twinkle that meant she was expecting a lucrative night.

"*Merci, madame.*" Lauren feigned a regal curtsy. "And you, as always, look divine."

"My . . . what happened to that skittish young filly I took in some years ago? How the time did fly . . . You're a woman now." She perused her niece from the pouf of her hair to the high-heeled shoes on her feet. "And quite an attractive one, I might add." Claude beamed with pride.

"A lot of good it's done me," Lauren retorted sharply. Recoiling, she apologized. "I didn't mean to sound ungrateful for all that you have done."

"Not another word. Believe me, *chérie,* I do understand."

In the next moment, Pierre's voice bellowed from the kitchen. Claude touched her hand to Lauren's cheek and sighed, then gathering the voluminous folds of her skirt, she floated toward the chef's domain.

Claude and Pierre huddled over menus in the kitchen, and Bertrand kept a watchful eye on the foyer as waiters darted about, starched and pressed, looking much like tin soldiers. Lauren leafed through some unfamiliar sheets of music. Newfound confidence prodded her to try *Fantasie Impromptu* by Chopin, a piece she had never dared to play in public. Excitement swelled in her throat at the advent of something new, and Lauren smiled at her sudden recklessness. The crystal chandelier sparkled like a million diamonds, and Lauren wondered why she had never been caught by its beauty until now.

The dinner hour passed uneventfully. Then came the mad rush to turn a moderately sedate room into a club for carousing gentlemen.

They arrived alone and in groups, all wearing the elegant dress of the boulevards, dark tailcoats, white piqué waistcoats, and glossy black high hats, and before long the room was full with boisterous laughter, clinking glasses, and the stench of cigar smoke. Lauren loathed the smell of cigar smoke, and whenever time allowed it, she fled to the foyer for a breath of fresh air. As she stood in the shadows, her form obscured by the huge green fern that hung beside the door, a carriage ground to a stop and three young men emerged and entered the club.

Richly attired in high hats and fur-lined pelisses, they were well mannered despite their boisterousness. There was a white man among them, a Frenchman. The other two men were black. They laughed and joked among themselves in that cocky manner that men seem to affect when they are out alone. She noticed nothing about the Frenchman except a head of striking blond hair, which was contrasted sharply by the two black men. One was tall and muscular with a pleasant face, partially obscured by a bushy black moustache. The other man was taller than average but not nearly so tall as his companion. His body, judging by the fit of his clothes, was lean and trim, and he moved with a smooth, rhythmic grace. His face was turned away from her and toward his friends. A strange, quivery sensation raced through her as she watched them vanish into the thick, smoky fog, her eyes never leaving the body whose face she had barely seen.

With a self-conscious glance in the mirror, she returned to the smoke-filled room. Her hazel eyes scanned the area for some sign of him, but the fumes were blinding. A few seconds passed, and her eyes adjusted to the pungence, and it was then that she discovered the three men seated at a table in the far corner of the room, their luxurious overcoats draped recklessly over their chairs. Lauren had no feasible reason to go to that part of the room, except that suddenly she developed an urgent desire to talk with Pierre.

"Lauren, you know Claude doesn't want you near the bar."

"Oh, I know, Pierre"—she bit her lip in exasperation—"but I have nothing to do and I thought you could use a little help." Her gaze traveled to the corner opposite the bar. Just then, Claude swept by, her taffeta gown rustling as she walked and the low neckline baring lovely white shoulders that belied the fact that her aunt was a woman well into middle age.

"*Chérie,* I need you to mind the front desk for a while," she said as she caught Pierre's glance. "Justin isn't feeling well." Like a sow wading through mud, Lauren pulled herself away.

Sitting at the desk, she found a copy of *Harper's New Monthly Magazine* and began to flip the pages until a voice startled her.

"*Pardonnez-moi, mademoiselle.* I was told that you could supply us with a deck of cards." The voice was smooth and resonant, the French impeccable. Lauren lifted her head and stared into a pair of dark, mesmerizing eyes. They belonged to him—she knew instinctively.

His complexion was a deep, dark brown, the color of rich, luxurious sable, and the chiseled features could have been carved from a block of volcanic obsidian. Crisp, black hair covered his head like a carefully manicured hedge and trailed into clipped sideburns that framed his face. Never in her twenty-four years had she seen a face that captivated her like his.

"*Oui, monsieur.* I will get them for you." She rose from her chair and went to the closet where such things were kept. Suddenly she felt nervous and ridiculously clumsy. His sultry eyes seemed to penetrate her soul. She lingered behind the paneled door longer than it took to reach for a deck of cards, struggling feverishly to regain her composure.

As she turned to face him, raven black eyes caught her hazel ones, and the heart in her breast missed several beats.

"Here you are, *monsieur.*" Her voice strained with the effort it took to sound unruffled. She actually had to look up at him, which had rarely been the case with Frenchmen.

"*Merci, mademoiselle.*" His ample lips curled slightly. Lauren watched him move in long, easy strides away from her, and try though she did, her gaze would not leave him until he was beyond her eye's view.

"*Mademoiselle.*" Louis interrupted her reverie. "Madame Rousseau says it's time for you to play."

"*Merci,* Louis. Tell *madame* I will be there in a minute."

Her stomach felt as though a butterfly were trapped inside. Nervous anxiety played havoc with her senses. He would be listening. What if she made a mistake? She could not possibly face that scrutinizing crowd in her present condition, particularly when they would just as soon hear their bawdy café songs. But when she was finally seated at the piano, she played quite by habit, struggling to keep her wandering gaze from straying in his direction. *Fantasie Impromptu* would be her closing selection. If she should make an error, she could quietly disappear from the room.

Lauren felt perspiration drenching her hands, but she refused to be intimidated now. To focus her attention, she chose the Gaugin painting on the opposite wall. She began Chopin's composition, and like a great silent bird, a hush fell over the room. All their eyes were on her, all ears listened as her talented fingers danced over the keyboard, bringing life to Chopin's haunting melody. Her audience was enchanted.

Finally it was finished, and she had not made a mistake! Much to her surprise, he stood and led the applause. All their eyes were on her. She stood and took a bow amid raucous cries of "Brava!" Pleased, yet somewhat self-conscious, she took another bow and hurried from the room. Once free of their scrutiny, she headed for the door and stepped outside to get some air. She lingered there in the open doorway, breathing deeply and watching street lamps flicker like giant fireflies. Her ears listened to the rhythmic clopping of horses' hooves pulling their carriages.

If she never married, perhaps the life of a pianist would be an alternative.

The frosty night air forced her inside. On other nights she would have gone to her room, but tonight it was impossible to tear herself away. The smoke caused her eyes to tear as she wandered back into the barroom, and she found herself wondering if he smoked. Claude caught a glimpse of Lauren lingering by the door.

"*Chérie*, why haven't you gone to bed?"

"I'm not terribly sleepy tonight."

"I hope all the applause hasn't gone to your head."

"It was exciting, wasn't it? I hope that I wasn't too flustered."

"Your father would have been proud of you," Claude beamed.

A waving hand drew her aunt's attention to the other side of the bar.

"Promise me you'll soon go to bed."

"I promise. I'll stay only a few minutes longer."

Lauren knew very well that she had lied. The idea of leaving filled her with a sense of loss. It did not seem fair that she should see him for one fleeting moment and then he would be gone, especially when the mere thought of his presence sent flames racing through her blood. What would she tell Claude? Her aunt would think her ridiculous.

But Lauren decided that she did not much care what anyone thought. The copy of *Harper's New Monthly Magazine* that she used to occupy an idle mind did not serve its purpose notably well, but at least she looked busy.

Minutes later, voices invaded the foyer. One of the voices was his. Lauren got up and moved around the desk, leaving the magazine on the leather chair. The blond Frenchman boldly observed her figure as he passed her, and the black man glanced quickly at her face and looked away as his hand came up to smooth the edges of his bushy moustache. The two sauntered out the door while their companion paused. Again, his raven black eyes caused her heart to skip a beat.

"*Mademoiselle*, you play beautifully," he said, allowing his eyes to engage her in a subtle perusal. "My mother plays like that . . . at least there was a time when she did." An unconscious change of mood was apparent when he spoke.

"*Merci, monsieur.* I'm pleased that you enjoyed it."

"I did very much," he said, flashing a smile. His dark, clean-shaven face was in stark contrast to the voluminous beards and moustaches worn by Frenchmen, and something in his smile gave her the faintest hope that she might see him again. His friends called to him from outside, but still his gaze held her.

"Is there something wrong?" she questioned innocently. Feeling the strong urge to adjust the neckline of her gown, Lauren reached up and brushed a wisp of hair from her forehead instead.

"No, on the contrary. It's just that I am very partial to green, and you wear it magnificently." His friends called again and he turned to leave. "*Bonsoir, mademoiselle.*"

"*Bonsoir, monsieur.*" The door closed behind him, and Lauren climbed the stairs, two at a time, to her room. Sleep came easily that night.

The next morning a crisp breeze fluttered through the window, whirling periwinkle curtains about the room. A smile curled Lauren's lips as she awoke. Could she be certain that everything that had happened last night was not just her imagination?

Lauren climbed out of bed and padded barefoot to the window. As she stood staring down at the early morning activity, her thoughts drifted to the previous night. The onion hawker waddled by with his trundle cart and stopped at the side door, crying, "*Oignon, oignon,*" until Pierre came out and relieved him of his load. Would she ever see him again? What had made her think last night that it was remotely possible? Then she remembered his smile—his mouth—his eyes. No one had ever smiled at her like that. Lauren retrieved the pillow from the bed and hugged it to her body. Waltzing around the room, she held the pillow as an imaginary partner.

The street vendors sold their wares, and the hotel patrons had begun the morning calls for hot water and breakfast. Rumbling over the cobblestone street, the chair mender made known his skill in a loud mellifluent voice. Lauren heard none of it. She gazed at the warm sun shining on the bleak world below, and her optimism began to grow. Perhaps he would come again tonight.

Lauren dallied through the day, sometimes elated and other times sullen, her thoughts preoccupied with the approaching evening. The last pile of linens sorted, folded, and tucked away, Claude could no longer mask her concern.

"Are you feeling well today, *chérie?*"

"Quite well," she answered flippantly.

"One moment you're dancing on a cloud and the next moment you're depressed as if the cloud had burst. If I didn't know better, I would think you were in love."

"That's silly. With whom would I be in love?" Lauren looked away to avoid the older woman's perceptive gaze.

"Has something happened to make you behave this way?" Claude's eyes searched Lauren's face for an answer.

"No, I don't think so." Her feelings right now were much too fragile to be prodded by Claude's eternal wisdom. At just the right moment, Pierre's voice barreled out of the kitchen, summoning them for dinner.

"I'm not very hungry. Why don't you go on without me," Lauren insisted.

"Child, you have to eat. It's no wonder we can never put any weight on you." The older woman shook her head in resignation.

Later that evening, in the privacy of her room, Lauren closed the door and sighed happily that this moment had come. She took the yellow taffeta gown from the closet and laid it across the bed. Then, turning on the faucet, she filled the tub with water and several precious drops of her jasmine oil. Languidly she lay in the copper-lined tub letting the warm water cover her body. At that instant she would have given anything to be beautiful, so beautiful that he would be compelled to return.

The bath finished, Lauren dressed with painstaking care. Pulling her dark hair up from her face, she pinned it into a soft bushy pouf, allowing rigidly curly tendrils to cascade from her temples and frame her face.

She turned in the mirror, examining her image from all sides. Satisfied, she rubbed a dab of rouge discriminately on her lips and went downstairs to face a curious audience.

Claude, the only one with the right to question her motives, commented warily.

"Why so much splendor for a Friday night?"

"No particular reason," Lauren replied, masking the truth.

"You're beautiful, *mademoiselle!*" exclaimed Pierre and Bertrand almost in unison. They were like fathers, and fathers were inclined to be prejudiced.

Lauren glanced at the door every chance that she got. There is still plenty of time, she told herself. If he comes, he will probably come late. Every minute seemed like an hour, and the hours dragged on as she played the first repertoire. She prayed that tonight the men would not request one of their bawdy sing-alongs, for she doubted that her wavering composure could withstand the strain. Lauren felt ridiculous. She could not untie the knots in her stomach or loosen the lump in her throat. She felt as though she were seventeen again and facing this audience for the first time.

Time passed slowly, but it did pass. At long last she could play the final piece and seek the refuge of her room. Her fingers played mechanically with little feeling or animation while her eyes stared blankly into space. For a brief second, her gaze drifted from the piano and back again. She looked up, and there he was. Accompanied by the same two men, he walked toward the corner table. Her fingers continued to make music of the keys, but Lauren was scarcely aware of anything except the somersaults flip-flopping in her stomach. When she had finished, she escaped to the foyer for a breath of fresh air. The night air was cold and biting, a welcome relief from the thick, pungent air in the club room. She leaned heavily against the wooden door and looked up at the star-laden sky, struggling to calm the feverish thumping in her breast.

Coming in from the foyer, she was intercepted by one of the waiters who brusquely shoved an envelope into her hand.

"*Mademoiselle*, this is for you."

"What is it?"

"I don't know, *mademoiselle*. The gentleman there in the corner asked me to give it to you."

"Which one?"

"That one." Her eyes followed his outstretched arm. "The gentleman with his back to us, *mademoiselle.*"

"*Merci,* Louis." She tore open the envelope with fumbling fingers. The note read, "*Mademoiselle,* will you dine with me tomorrow evening? Roget de Martier." Lauren stared at the note, her thoughts running rampant. *He wants to dine with me!* Suddenly the joy faded from her face. Dinner with him on Saturday evening would be impossible. Saturday was the busiest night at the Saint Germain, and she would have to work. Life seemed eternally against her.

She sat down at the desk, and using hotel stationery, penned her reply. "Monsieur de Martier, I regret to say that it is impossible for me to have dinner with you tomorrow evening. Lauren Dufort."

Sealing the note, she caught Louis as he passed by. "Would you give this to the gentleman there in the corner." She watched until it was in his hands and then went slowly up the stairs to her room, but before she had reached the first landing, his voice called to her from below.

"Mademoiselle Dufort, may I speak with you a moment?" Her heart stood still as she descended the stairs and halted two steps above him.

"Why will you not have dinner with me tomorrow evening?" His dark eyes enveloped her curiously.

"Because I have to work tomorrow evening." Lauren's face flushed uncontrollably.

"Is that the only reason?"

"*Oui.*"

"Then why are you blushing? It's no crime to work. I work, too, even though it's frowned on to work with one's hands in my country." Again his lips curled into an intoxicating smile. "Will you dine with me on Sunday afternoon?"

"*Oui,*" she answered softly, "I would like that very much."

"Good. I will call for you here about three. *Bonsoir,* Mademoiselle Dufort."

"*Bonsoir, monsieur.*" Monsieur de Martier rejoined his friends, and Lauren proceeded to her room, unaware that Claude had witnessed the scene between them.

Lauren slept little that night. She turned on her stomach

and then twisted onto her back, and finally she lay awake, captivated by a foreigner who moved with the grace of a sleek jungle panther.

The next morning, long before the other guests had stirred from their sleep, there was a soft knock at Lauren's door. Claude entered, armed with freshly baked bread and steaming coffee.

"I see you're awake already." She feigned a cheerfulness that she did not feel.

"I didn't sleep very well." Lauren stretched lazily.

"Could the reason be that very intriguing young man you were talking with last night?"

"How do you know about that?"

"Your old aunt doesn't miss much." Claude smiled wryly. "I saw you talking with him on the stairs last night. He's quite attractive." Abruptly, her tone changed. "Lauren I know how cruel life can be. I've tried to protect you, but I can't watch over you forever."

"Claude, you worry too much," Lauren boasted, barely able to contain her excitement. "He's asked me to dine with him on Sunday. Surely that's respectable enough."

"It's not that, *chérie*," she warned. "You have to remember who you are."

"More likely *what* I am!" There was that ugly word rearing its head again. *Mulatto.* How she wished she had never heard it. With her glorious bubble of joy burst, Lauren collapsed against the pillows.

"I'm sick to death of warnings! I want to live like every other woman."

"Believe me, *chérie,* I do understand." Claude exited, taking the untouched breakfast tray with her. Lauren wondered whether she would ever be allowed to experience life as other women, or would she always be branded as a misfit? Determined not to let circumstances block her path, Roget wanted to see her, and that was all she intended to think about.

Lauren watched from the window as the horse-drawn victoria curbed at the main door and Roget de Martier stepped down. Wearing a pink wool day dress that had scroll embroidery framing the fitted jacket, she burst into her aunt's room.

"Claude, he's here." Her voice rang with nervous anticipation. "Have you seen my mantle?"

"Why don't you wear mine?" her aunt suggested tactfully. "This is the only thing that looks well with those leg-of-mutton sleeves," she added, placing her fur-trimmed cape on Lauren's shoulders.

"Claude, he's so handsome," Lauren purred. "Do you think he's rich?" she babbled absently, her mind engaged with placing of a small feathered hat on the crest of her poufed hair.

Claude glanced through the open window and then back at her niece with an unnerving skepticism and replied, "Poor men don't wear silk cravats, velvet-collared invernesses, and suede gloves."

Lauren greeted Monsieur de Martier in the lobby of the Saint Germain and dutifully introduced him to her aunt. Following the amenities, he offered his arm in gentlemanly fashion and led her to the carriage.

Tacitly, Lauren had questioned his instructions to the driver to take the long way around and travel along the Champs-Élysées, but now as the open-topped victoria cantered, through the Arc de Triomphe and down along the grand avenue, she saw the wisdom governing his request. It was a rare day along the boulevard. Wealthy Parisians promenaded in opulently designed carriages pulled behind fine high-stepping horses. The poor strolled with their offspring. Children darted about playing games, and the women of the demimonde twirled parasols overhead as they reclined in open carriages, blatantly displaying the wealth of their benefactors. Groups of young men and women on bicycles gathered to watch a mime, who had drawn a curious crowd as he made faces and strange motions trying to entice the rich to throw him a coin.

Roget's gaze remained fixed in the distance, his thoughts ponderously preoccupied. His hat lay conspicuously on the seat between them. Lauren had never been very adept at playing coy games, but she could no longer bear the excruciating silence. Her full lips curved apprehensively. "Are you wishing that I would disappear?"

"No," he answered pensively. "On the contrary, I've been looking forward to your company." He turned and caught her full face. Intoxicated by the sudden softness in his eyes, she pulled away.

"I did not mean to frighten you."

"You didn't," she answered quickly.

"Then why did you move away?"

"You were so engrossed in something . . . I felt like an intruder."

"I received some rather disturbing news from home this morning."

"And where is that?" she asked, attempting to sound only vaguely interested.

"Haiti." The name aroused Lauren's curiosity, but he seemed reluctant to discuss it further and the last thing she wanted was to appear over anxious. "Haiti is a long way from Paris," he added wistfully. "Let's not concern ourselves with it now."

The victoria turned left onto boulevarde de Italiens and ground to a halt before the gleaming glass exterior of Paillard's. As they entered the room, the dazzling splendor caught Lauren by surprise. She had heard numerous tales of Paillard's illustrious clientele but until now had never set foot in the establishment. This was definitely not ground for the working class. The haute couture of French fashion weaved through the room, the women exquisitely coiffured and reeking of expensive perfume as they languished on the arms of husbands, paramours, and benefactors. Lauren felt her two-piece wool dress grossly inadequate, but it was the best afternoon dress she owned and had been more than sufficient for afternoons in the sitting rooms of Claude's less affluent friends.

They settled at a round table that rested on Art Nouveau legs, their view partially obscured by graceful green palms and potted chrysanthemums. Perusing a menu that had neglected to list prices, Lauren was painfully aware that she was not very skilled in the games that other women played. She had had little practice. Already she had grown bored with polite small talk and with shameful interest longed to know everything about Roget—his life—and the home about which he was reluctant to talk. Laying aside the gilt-edged menu, she decided to tread on sacred ground.

"I've never known anyone from Haiti," she stated softly.

Roget looked up from the menu that claimed his attention. "But I'm sure you are well acquainted with one of her descendants," he commented sagaciously. Her hazel eyes questioned his wisdom. "Surely you've read *The Three Musketeers* and *The Count of Monte Cristo,*" he added, laying the menu aside.

"Dumas *père.*" Lauren's voice rose a full octave, echoing her surprise. "But he was born in France."

"Dumas *père* was, but his father, General Dumas, was born in Haiti, the offspring of a French nobleman and a Haitienne. Actually," he added as an afterthought, "Dumas was his mother's name and not his father's."

"I never knew that."

Openly charmed by her astonishment, Roget regarded her with a sultry gaze and inquired, *"Mademoiselle,* what would you like to eat?"

Having long ago decided that this was his world and most definitely not hers, she looked back at him and replied, "Whatever you choose will be fine. It all looks so delicious, I don't think I could make a choice." Her full lips curled into a tantalizing smile. "However," she paused sheepishly, "I do love asparagus and strawberries with cream."

"Garçon." Roget summoned the white-aproned waiter and then turned back to her. "How does poached salmon, mutton chops, lettuce salad, and asparagus sound?"

"Delicious," was the only word she could utter. He repeated the order to the waiter, adding a bottle of white Bordeaux wine.

Long, slender stalks of green asparagus arrived nestled in a frothy butter sauce. Lauren savored the last succulent bite of the asparagus, and with the flavor of the butter sauce still on her tongue, she sighed with deep-seated satisfaction. Roget smiled, baring the gleam of his perfect white teeth.

"Would you like more asparagus?"

"I would love more," she said shyly. Her hazel eyes met the snowy linen napkin covering her lap. "I'm afraid meals at the Saint Germain are not so sumptuous."

"Garçon!" Roget caught the waiter's attention. "Another order of asparagus for the lady."

"Ladies are not supposed to have second helpings of food," she said.

"Is being a lady so important to you?"

"Oui, I suppose it is. One always craves what is out of one's reach." Her attention lingered on the expensive gowns and dazzling jewels of the wealthy women to whom restaurants like Cubat's and Paillard's were a way of life. All at once, it occurred to her that she had never resented being working class before, and now simply because a man like Roget would marry nothing but a lady, she did. Women from her class, if they were fortunate, could be nothing more than mistresses.

After the meal, Roget ordered tea. The French rarely drank tea. Curious, Lauren said nothing, because a greater curiosity tugged at her brain.

"Where exactly is Haiti?" she asked finally. "What is it like?"

"It's an island in the Caribbean, a black republic." He sat back and allowed the waiter to place the silver tea service on the table.

"You haven't told me what it is like to live there."

"It is beautiful, ugly, tropic, barren, burning hot, and freezing cold." His voice trailed into nothingness.

"That's so contradictory."

"Haiti *is* contradictory. I see it the way it really is. It's my home, but I love it and hate it with the same breath. I sometimes think that I would much prefer to spend my life in France. When I'm here, it is hard to believe that France and Haiti occupy the same world."

"Why don't you . . . spend your life in France?"

"I have an obligation to my family and to my country." His somber expression told her that he had said too much. "Besides, I'm a farmer, and Paris is not exactly abundant with farms." His lips curled into a taunting grin, erasing the somber expression that clouded his dark, handsome face.

Ceremoniously, Roget lifted the silver teapot and poured steaming brown liquid into each of the cups. Placing one of the cups in front of his astonished companion, he proceeded to put one teaspoonful of sugar into his own cup and stir it gently. Lifting the cup to his mouth, he took a sip and put it down, never spilling a drop. Lauren doubted that she could match his finesse.

"How could you possibly be a farmer?" she uttered in amazement.

"Is it so difficult to believe that I'm a farmer? The de Martiers have always worked their own land, which makes us an anomaly, I suppose, but most of the revenue in my country comes from the export of our crops. Without them we could not exist."

"What do you grow?"

"Coffee."

"But you're drinking tea." She smiled curiously. "Parisians almost never drink tea."

"I know." His lips twisted into that provocative grin. "I suppose you could call me an anomaly as well, but I taste so much coffee at home that tea is refreshing for a change."

"Who runs the farm when you are not there?" Lauren continued the barrage of questions.

"My brothers." Lauren heard the strong hedge of futility in his tone. "I've been in Paris for the past year attending lectures at the conservatory. It's imperative that planters in Haiti learn to employ more modern irrigation methods, otherwise we will not survive. In the last fifty years, we've lost tremendous volume in our export crops." His eyes narrowed with skepticism.

Lauren sensed his reservation and interpreted it to mean that she had once again asked too much. Though she was anxious to hear more, she tactfully moved to a less passionate subject. "Do you come to France often?"

"Not lately." Roget shifted in his chair as though it were an uncomfortable restraint. "When I was younger, I attended school here, but running a farm does not facilitate being away. There are too many responsibilities. Knowing my brothers, I have no idea what condition our land will be in when I return home."

Watching him here in the midst of French elegance, surroundings with which he was clearly at ease, Lauren found it difficult to imagine him in another setting.

"And you?" he queried. A forced smile slowly replaced the intense grimace that had distorted his face. "I know nothing about you," he said, the smile giving way to an amused grin, "except that you are a talented pianist, that you eat second helpings of asparagus, and you have the most tantalizing eyes I have ever seen."

Lauren blushed. Taken aback by the genuine interest she heard in his voice, she was disarmed that anyone would be interested in the hapless details of her life, least of all him.

"There is not much to know," she replied. His ebony gaze imprisoned hers, making her feel ill at ease. Lauren pressed her back rigidly against the rungs of the chair.

"My mother was African," she began hesitantly. "She was born into slavery in French Guiana after her mother was captured and taken there. Her father . . . my grandfather, was left behind." Lauren felt the stabbing pain she had often experienced at being deprived of a family. "My father worked as an accountant for a sugar refinery. When my mother and father met and fell in love, the two races were forbidden to marry. They were forced to flee to France, my father's country. I was born a few months after they arrived here." She faced him with an odd expression of relief, realizing that she had known that story all of her life and had never repeated it to anyone.

Roget's dark eyes still held her captive. "And now?" he questioned with interest.

"My mother died when I was three . . . I don't remember her—and my father when I had just gained seventeen."

"Where did you learn to play the piano?"

"For the most part, in school."

"Such training in an ordinary school." His statement harbored a hidden question.

Indignantly, Lauren supplied an answer to what she perceived as an insolent question. "My father kept me in an exclusive school—far above his class and his means." Lauren looked away. Suddenly, she was at a loss for words, but the loss had gained her a sense of defiant courage.

"I hope you are not ashamed of the things that you've told me." He tread on the silence perceptively. "Slavery was a despicable crime, and we have all been scarred by it. We all pay in one way or another for the sins of our parents. Besides, *mademoiselle,* I like your honesty."

Lauren gazed up at him. "But I thought . . ."

"You thought that men expect women to play coy games," he broke in, finishing her statement. "But not every man is interested in playing games. They can be a bore." In a teasing tone, he added, "I find your honesty quite charming."

Lauren pulled away and focused her attention on the impersonal activity of the room. He made it impossible to think, especially when his gaze seemed to penetrate a part of her soul that she had carefully kept chained until now. Now aware that she was surrounded by the blatant displays of favor lavished on mistresses by their wealthy gentlemen, Lauren wondered why he had chosen this particular restaurant. That the cuisine was second only to Cubat's seemed an unimportant reason, just as the many fine ladies who dined here accompanied by their husbands seemed an equally unimportant fact. Lauren dwelt on the fact that Paillard's was infamous as a before- and after-theater resort for the *demimonde*. Considering that respectable women never mingled with *demimondaines*, reluctantly, she was forced to consider her aunt's warnings. Could Claude have been right? Did his interest lie in cultivating a mistress? And was this his way of introducing her to the life of the *demimonde*? Oh, God . . . she prayed not!

The return trip was endured in pregnant silence, and their few attempts at idle conversation were gratefully interrupted by the clopping of horses. Roget's subtle, perusing glances caused a skittish thumping in her breast even though she fought to ignore their effect on her soul.

Roget grasped the narrow curve of her waist between his hands as he lifted her down from the carriage. Futilely, Lauren struggled to hold the reins on her warring emotions, but his touch sent a stab of awakening desire piercing through her. When he had seen her beyond the door and driven away, the breath finally escaped from Lauren's throat, and she felt the locks that had held those chains intact slowly sliding open.

Claude grew increasingly alarmed at her niece's erratic
behavior. When confronted with the older woman's apprehensions, Lauren fluctuated between two responses. One
moment she shrugged them off indifferently, and at the next
confrontation, she flew into a paroxysm of angry frustration.

"Claude, I must see him," she pleaded. "Why will you not
try to understand? Has it been so long that you have
forgotten what it feels like to love a man?" Biting sarcasm
chewed through her tone, and Lauren bit her lip at its
impact.

"No," her aunt retorted. "Time has not afforded me that
luxury." Lauren's bitter sarcasm had cut deep, but experience made her understand that her niece had lashed out
with the pain and confusion of a young woman facing her
first and, in Lauren's case, clearly impossible bout with
love. "It's just that I have more experience than you do. I
know what men are like . . . particularly rich men. They
think of young women like you as their playthings, good for
a night's amusement."

"He's not like the men you've known, Claude. He's
different," she argued heatedly, not allowing her thoughts to
linger on the older woman's words.

"*Oui, chérie* . . . he's different until you find yourself with child, and then they are all the same. What do you know of men like him? For that matter what do you know of men?"

"I only know that I want to see him more than anything in life." Her hazel eyes had taken on an opalescent glow that testified to her excitement, and she was oblivious to the anguish that spread over her aunt's face. Lauren grabbed her mantle and escaped into the brisk midday air.

Crossing boulevard Saint Germain and the bridge that spanned the Seine, she barely noticed the steam-powered *bateaux-mouches* as they chugged up and down the river transporting passengers from one remote district of Paris to another. Lauren's feet carried her to les Tuilleries, but her thoughts remained back at the hotel with Claude. Her favorite path offered pitiful comfort now; she had been forced to face an agonizing reality.

Lauren ambled along, idly slapping a twig against the iron fence, until a voice invaded her reverie.

"Do you always vent your frustration on helpless fences?" She turned to discover what she already knew from the resonance of the sound and the quickening of the pulse in her veins. As she looked up, her light gaze locked with his darker one.

"What makes you think it's frustration?" she questioned sharply, unnerved that his keen perception had laid bare her secret thoughts.

"Because I have done such things myself when I felt defeated."

Averting her eyes from the deep penetration of his gaze, Lauren tried to shield herself from his scrutiny. She could not bear to have him toy with her vulnerable emotions.

"I was coming from the conservatory," Roget continued, "and noticed you walking here and decided to offer you my company."

Such arrogance! she thought. Her senses bristled with indignation, but the vexation was short-lived.

"Do you mind?" The sensuous contours of his mouth parted into a smile that melted all of her former resolve.

"No . . . of course not . . ." She hesitated, remembering the disheveled state in which she had left the hotel. In her haste she had not bothered to put on a hat, so that the loose wisps of her bushy hair that had managed to escape the pins were now blowing in the breeze. Her striped shirtwaist blouse and simple wool skirt were pitifully inadequate next to his elegant tailcoat and silk cravat. Lauren felt very much as she had during the years at school—like the scullery maid walking with her classmates.

"Do you ride?" he asked. She felt his eyes on her as if he were searching for an answer, an answer that she dare not give.

"I used to ride. I haven't ridden very often in the last few years." She lifted her head and paused slightly. "There hasn't been much opportunity," she added quietly.

"In that case, I will have to see that you get a gentle horse." His tone was blatantly teasing. "That is if you will go riding with me on Sunday? The bridle path circles the woods behind the Bois. It's a magnificent spot to ride on sunny afternoons."

"Let's hope that Sunday is sunny," she said. "I would love to go riding."

When Claude heard the news, she remained silent and allowed Lauren to enjoy her small taste of happiness. And to dispel her aunt's doubts, Lauren promised to invite Monsieur de Martier for dinner the following week.

Sunday arrived bright and partially sunny. The sun peeked out from behind gray winter clouds at frequent intervals and consumed the frigid chill that permeated the air. Lauren saw her breath as it escaped her mouth and formed a cloud of hazy fog before her face, but she was shielded from the cold by the warm glow that heated every nerve of her body. Mounting her horse, she felt poised and elegant next to Roget. Fortunately, her riding habit was not yet out of style. The burgundy jacket hugged her narrow waist, and the long skirt draped loosely about her hips. From the small black plume on her hat to her patent leather boots, she was dressed perfectly. The horses cantered off into the mass of barren trees, their hooves colliding with earth still hard from winter. Sunlight filtered through naked branches and danced off their sleek coats. Roget was at ease on his mount, and by the way he handled it, he rode expertly and often. Her own riding left much to be desired, but she had never been able to resist the challenge of a sprint.

"You had better ride easy if you're out of practice."

"I'm fine," she answered, forcing her chin up.

Their horses took off over the hard earth and seared past trees, under branches, over rocks and clumps of brush, until Lauren was gasping for breath. She loved the rush of wind in her face and the blinding speed of the animal beneath her but realized that she was in ill condition for this caliber of riding. She reined her horse in and stopped. No longer hearing the pounding hooves behind him, Roget reined in his steed and galloped back. Lauren, already dismounted and resting against the trunk of a bare chestnut tree, drew a deep breath.

"Are you all right?" He swung down from his saddle with an easy agility that was unencumbered by a riding habit.

"Oui." She smiled. "Just out of breath and out of practice."

"I warned you to go easy, didn't I? You forget that I was weaned in a saddle. The only way to travel a plantation is on horseback."

"You said you were a farmer, that you grow coffee?"

"I am. My family owns a coffee plantation."

Roget studied the skeptical expression on her face, and before she could reply, he reached forward and imprisoned her shoulders between his gloved hands. Lauren's knees trembled and threatened to buckle beneath her. Despite the well-defined features, his mouth was incredibly full and sensuous. For the first time in her life, Lauren stared at a pair of lips that she wanted desperately to feel on hers. He answered her silent plea. Their lips met. Softly at first and then wildly, passionately, she kissed him until her head spun and her heart leapt into her throat and strangled her breath. Other horses and riders thundered past them, but Lauren heard nothing except the raucous thumping in her breast. Roget's arms circled her waist and pulled her to him, and Lauren's body responded eagerly to the pressure of his touch. Everything in her cried out for him as she fought to control the spontaneous inferno that licked its way up from her womb and sought to extinguish itself in the warm, sultry lips that covered hers. Her arms ached to hold him, to feel the broad, muscular expanse of his back beneath her fingers. But if she yielded to her desires at this moment, she would be destined to be his mistress. Shocked by the things she was feeling, Lauren's head spun in circles. There were things she wanted from him, but improbable as it was, she wanted to be his wife and not his mistress, and she had decided to risk everything to that end. Sheer will made her pull away.

Roget released her easily. She was certain he had felt the surge of passion that raced through her, but he had also felt her unwillingness to release it. Lauren straightened her hat, nervously retrieved the fallen crop, and, gaining control of her warring emotions, allowed Roget to lift her into the stirrup. How would she quell the urgency that his touch had aroused in her. Silently, they rode back to the Bois. No longer able to endure the agonizing uncertainty of his silence, Lauren remembered the hastiness of her promise to Claude.

"My aunt Claude would like you to come to dinner on Monday," she said apprehensively, finally daring to let her gaze meet his.

"I would like that very much."

The moment she arrived at the hotel, Lauren informed the household that she had invited Monsieur de Martier to dinner. Pierre promised to do his culinary best, but Bertrand remained unduly disturbed by the entire matter. He was decidedly silent whenever anyone mentioned Roget.

In the week that followed Lauren spent every unoccupied second planning the dinner. She spent hours polishing silverware and shining Claude's modest crystal. She worried about having an appropriate gown to wear and if he would be impressed with Pierre's cooking. She wondered if they would like him and then told herself that she really did not care. Lauren had only to remember the feel of his mouth consuming hers and the burning brand his kiss had seared on her lips, and everything ceased to matter. Female instinct told her that he wanted her, too, but for what and in what way she did not dare think.

By Thursday, Lauren's nerves were completely frayed.

"*Chérie,* you should get out of here and breathe a breath of fresh air. Why don't you go to Madame Marie's and pick up those gowns for me?" the older woman suggested.

It felt good to be away from the hotel, Lauren mused as she lifted her skirt and climbed aboard the horse-drawn fiacre. Making her way to the second level of the double-decker omnibus was an adventure as she was pushed and jostled by grumbling passengers while they jockied for seats. But advantageously, as the crowded vehicle took the corner on what seemed like two wheels, she was thrown, derriere first, into a recently vacated seat.

On the return trip, however, Lauren felt no inclination to be bandied about while maneuvering two huge boxes, and so she crossed the avenue and decided to treat herself to the small luxury of a private cab.

She climbed into the victoria with an air of reckless frivolity and traveled with the wealthy along the Bois de Boulogne. Omnibuses were forbidden to mar the beauty of the grand boulevard, but horses cantering the bridle path behind the avenue made her instantly aware that the rich enjoyed their pastimes on weekdays as well.

The carriage approached the entrance to the bridle path, and her eye caught sight of two horses standing together, their reins held lightly in the hands of the riders who were dismounted. One of the horses appeared vaguely familiar, and as she looked again, she recognized Roget. Lauren felt as if her skittish heart had leapt into her mouth. He stood talking with a woman—a beautiful woman, a lady. The veiled stock hat threw deep shadows over the woman's face, but the way she tilted her head and laughed and the way she gestured ever so gracefully with her hand brought to Lauren's mind her classmates at Madame Poisson's school.

Roget and his companion talked and laughed intimately, as though they were very familiar old friends. His hand held her arm and she repeatedly touched his face with her gloved hand. Lauren looked away. Her throat swelled, and tears burned behind her eyelids. She ordered the driver to go faster, and the victoria bumped along on its thin, rickety wheels so rapidly that they should have broken. Who was that woman? Tears stung Lauren's eyes but she desperately fought them back until a few escaped and ran down her cheek. She rummaged through her handbag for a handkerchief. Was she the woman he would marry? Until she met Roget, Lauren had never resented her station in life, but now, being a lady seemed the only answer to her prayers. Would she settle for being his mistress if given no other choice? She didn't know—she couldn't think straight, her thoughts were blinded by the tears scalding her face.

As she looked up, her hazel eyes were assaulted by the bold, dark strokes and brilliant matt color of a Lautrec poster advertising the Moulin Rouge, and she realized that a world existed in Paris of which she knew nothing. Perhaps the life of a *demimondaine* was better than no life at all.

By the time Monday arrived Lauren had gained sufficient composure and stubbornly refused to crowd her thoughts with visions of Roget and that woman. As she stepped into her blue moiré gown and adjusted the ruffled sleeves that covered her shoulders, Claude entered the room, a pensive frown distorting her face.

"Chérie, I have some interesting information about your Monsieur de Martier."

"Claude, you've been spying on him!" Her lightning glance darted to the letter in her aunt's hand. "Why is everyone so suspicious?

"Chérie, be still for a minute and listen. I don't intend to tell you what course to take. It is your life, and you have to live it. I can only pray that you make the right decision." From a printed sheet of paper, the older woman rattled off a list of calculated facts. "He is the second son of an elite Haitian family, thirty-one years old, and unmarried. The family owns one of the few privately controlled coffee plantations that still exist in Haiti. He was educated, for the latter part, in France and travels in the most illustrious company. His father died twelve years ago, and the family has since been headed by the older brother. Going back some eighty years, there have been a number of deaths and misfortunes plaguing their ancestral home."

Lauren obstinately refused to share her aunt's doubts. "I could have told you most of that myself," she retorted.

Claude looked up from the paper. "Lauren, are you sure you know what you're walking into? Have you ever stopped to think of why he might be interested in you? There are numerous rich, beautiful women in France and in Haiti, too, I assume. Why you? Are you certain that he's not cultivating a mistress?"

"No, Claude . . . I'm not certain," she uttered reflectively. A vision of Roget and his breathtakingly beautiful companion crowded her thoughts. "But if he wants a mistress," she flared flippantly, "then a mistress I'll be! The life of a *demimondaine* is certainly better than no life at all." The dreaded words had escaped out of frustration. Lauren shifted her focus to avoid the older woman's expression of sympathy. Warily, Claude left her niece alone to finish dressing.

The hour arrived and along with it Roget. With light-hearted jubilance, Lauren ushered him upstairs to Claude's private dining room, made modestly resplendent for the evening with crystal and silver. Pierre had prepared a meal to rival Paillard's, and Lauren was more than pleased. Claude and Roget developed a polite rapport, while Roget and Pierre behaved like long lost friends after the younger man courteously commended the older's culinary talents.

The meal finished, the party moved to the small sitting room, where Roget amiably accepted Pierre's offer of a snifter of brandy and a narrow brown cigar, and Lauren became aware of Bertrand's reluctance to join them when he excused himself and left the room. Anxiously, Lauren went after him.

"Bertrand, why are you leaving. Is something wrong?"

The towering man lowered his eyes and curiously avoided the sparkle in her gaze. "I think he's deceiving you, Mademoiselle Lauren."

"Deceiving me . . ." Her stare looked askance as the words rolled off her tongue. The heavy footsteps halted, and he turned to face her.

"D'you remember the second time him and his friends came to the club? I heard his friends dare him to make your acquaintance. The two o' them had a wager that he wouldn't make good, and he said that he would. They put up five hundred francs each."

Suddenly everything became clear, as though she were looking through crystal. She was merely a wager between him and his friends. Hurt flared into anger. Her hazel eyes blazed amber. Painfully, Lauren flung open the parlor door and confronted her predator.

"It's very clear to me now, Monsieur de Martier. It seems I am nothing more than a bet between you and your friends." Anger churned with humiliation and raged through her veins as Claude tactfully maneuvered an exit, with Pierre close behind. "I hope you've had your sport!"

"Lauren, please let me explain."

She ignored his pleading tone. "Explain? What is there to explain?" she cried. "It's quite clear to me!" Her hazel eyes, lucent as the lip of a wave, sparkled with tears. Roget grasped her trembling shoulders with his hands. Prying his fingers from where they burned into her flesh, she twisted free of his grasp and came back sharply. "Please take your hands off me! I'm not your plaything!"

His gaze surrounded her, and he uttered with a tinge of remorse, "Lauren, there is something I must tell you. I could explain if you would only let me." He tried relentlessly to calm her fury, but his attempts fired her into a blind rage. She heard nothing he said. Through her fury, she remembered only his kiss and the humiliating wager of which it was a part.

"Lauren—" Roget tried again.

"The fancy lady you were riding with on Thursday . . ." her voice trembled, "she's the kind of woman that you take seriously."

"Lauren, please listen to me."

"There is nothing more to say. Please go!"

Reluctantly, Roget strode toward the wood-paneled door, and as his hand closed around the brass doorknob, Lauren vented her last bit of rage. Clutching the three dozen red roses he had sent earlier in the day, she hurled them, vase and all, at his fading back, but the closing door caught the brunt of her wrath. Lauren stumbled down the hall to her room. Reaching her own humble quarters, she fell facedown on the bed and surrendered her sob-racked body to the pillows.

Claude had been right after all. He didn't care for her. She had merely been a wager that generated laughs among his friends. Claude and Pierre had heard her outburst but did not question it, and she did not volunteer any information.

That week, Roget sent flowers every day with accompanying notes, but Lauren refused to open them. Religiously, she tore up his notes and threw the flowers into the garbage.

Finally, the flowers stopped. Lauren was distraught. She seemed not to care about anything—not him, not anything—or so she thought. She did not cry; she did not laugh. She barely spoke. She felt as though she were drowning in an ocean that appeared to be bottomless. Claude had tried to spare her the ugly truth, but she had been too headstrong to take heed.

Throughout that week, Lauren left the hotel only once and then because of her aunt's adamant insistence that she take a walk. Passing the ancient Church of Saint Germain-des-Prés, she went inside and knelt to pray. With hands folded tight before her bowed head, Lauren once again poured out her heart to God.

Another week passed. A letter came by personal messenger and with it two flaxen yellow canary finches in a gilded Victorian cage. Lauren was determined not to open this letter either until she held one of the soft, feathery creatures in the palm of her hand. The bird chirped, and she felt her heart encompass it as she placed it gently in the cage beside its mate. Time had softened her resolve, and compassion tugged at her will. Lauren opened the letter. It read:

My dear Lauren,

Since you refuse to answer my letters and will not consent to see me, I am forced to use this letter as an explanation. It is true, our meeting was because of a bet, bizarre circumstances to be sure, but how was I to know that I would be incapable of erasing the thought of you from my memory? When we were riding that Sunday, I wanted to tell you but could not find the words. Foolishly, I thought that perhaps you would never learn the truth. It seems I was wrong. I do hope you will forgive me my folly. You are not a plaything to me, I want to marry you. I'll be at the Saint Germain tomorrow evening, and I pray that you will agree to see me.

Yours always, Roget

Lauren read the letter at least half a dozen times, until finally the words penetrated her senses. *Roget had asked to marry her.* She showed the letter to Claude and then placed the birds by the window in her room. Lauren drifted into a sea of joyous delirium, biding the time until his arrival. No sooner was Roget through the door than Lauren was in his arms, totally oblivious to everything else that surrounded her.

62

Chapter 4

At twelve noon on February 28, in a private, uncomplicated chapel ceremony, Lauren Dufort became Madame Roget de Martier. As Roget slipped the gold and emerald ring on her finger, Lauren glanced up and caught a glimpse of Claude as she brushed a tear from her eye. Afterward, they shared an elaborate dinner with Claude and Pierre at Maison Dorée and then Roget whisked his bride off to see a production of *Othello* at the Odéon Theatre.

"Did you enjoy the performance?" he asked, offering his arm. Lauren tucked her hand timidly in the bend of his elbow.

"Oui. This time I did."

Roget glanced at her quizzically. Feeling his closeness and the strength of his body beneath the elegant evening clothes made those suppressed echoes of desire reverberate loudly through her soul. Finally, she found her voice and answered his silent inquiry. "When I was young my father took me to see it, but I was very upset when Othello murdered Desdemona, and for a long time I thought that was how my mother died . . . that my father had killed her."

"I hardly think it was a good choice of a play for a child."

"It was his favorite Shakespearean play, and I suppose he wanted me to see it," she said, defending her father against the attack.

"I enjoy the theater," he said in a lighter tone, "but unfortunately, I can only indulge my passion in Paris. Haiti has very little good theater."

Horse-drawn carriages lined the street in front of the theater, their gas lamps flickering like fireflies in the frigid night air. Roget lifted her into a victoria and then swung in beside her, placing his shiny black opera hat atop his head. "Boulevard Capucines, le Café de la Paix, *s'il vous plaît,*" Roget instructed the driver, whose gray hat was perched high on his head in imitation of the gentlemen whom he drove to and from the theater.

"Where are we going?" Naively, Lauren had assumed that they were going home. He turned and caught her expression.

"Surely, you're not ready to go home."

"I just thought . . ."

"Parisians rarely go home after the theater." Roget's voice held a teasing tone. *"Madame,* this is the hour when Paris comes out to see herself."

Lauren smiled sheepishly. It was the first time she had been addressed as *madame.*

"Besides, it's on the way," he continued. "I told Jerome and Alexis that we would join them for supper. They want to toast my blushing bride." Covering her trembling fingers with his hand, he reassured her. "It should not be so unpleasant. Marie and Eurydice will be with them."

Lauren shivered at the thought of facing his friends, especially at a moment when her stomach was already twisted in knots.

"Are you cold?"

"No," she uttered softly and wondered if he knew that his touch was capable of warming her to a fever.

Women adorned in fine jewels, furs, and low-cut gowns, accompanied by men wearing black tails, white piqué waistcoats, and diamond studs, occupied the throng of gilded carriages that converged onto the boulevard Saint Germain. Lauren thrilled at the spectacle. This was the Paris she had longed to see. As their carriage crossed the river at Pont de la Concorde, Lauren gazed down into the sparkling waters of the Seine. She had crossed the river many times, but she had never remembered it so brilliantly aglow with reflections from the nighttime lanterns, and it had never filled her with such feverish anticipation for the evening ahead.

The thin wheels bumped over the pavement, jostling their carriage along in the splendid midnight procession. As the driver swerved the vehicle to avoid hitting a dog that sauntered across the road, the jolt threw their bodies together. Now, nothing separated them, and despite the bulk of her red velvet gown and his heavy broadcloth trousers, she could feel the heat of a strong thigh pressing against her. The feverish thrill of his closeness, the excitement that was Paris, coupled with the frigidness of the night air, left Lauren breathless. She longed for nothing more than to throw herself in his arms and have the heat of his mouth consume the ridiculous fluttering in her stomach and the thumping in her chest. But she knew that was out of the question. She must be a lady.

High-stepping horses gleamed as their coats reflected the spots of light that flickered through the chestnut trees along the Champs-Élysées. The parade moved toward the Arc de Triomphe. All along the boulevard, café tables were filled to overflowing with people settled under the awnings, drinking absinthe to ward off the chill. As they drank, they reviewed the promenade, for even the sidewalks were alive to the midnight life of Paris. Boulevardiers, in their fancy clothes, strolled the pavements and the women of the *demimonde* were out to display their jewels and their benefactors. This was the Paris that Lauren had heard about but had never seen.

The driver made a loop around boulevard Capucines and ground the carriage to a screeching halt in front of the Café de la Paix. Parisians and some foreigners, mostly Britons, lounged at front tables drinking absinthe and grenadine. Lauren's stomach churned uncontrollably as she stepped down from the carriage and let her new husband guide her through the glass doors, weaving a path through the maze of tables toward his friends. The tall Haitian and the Frenchman, along with their female companions, were already seated at a round marble table.

"*Garçon!* Now it is time for champagne," the Frenchman called in a rather boisterous tone. "The bride and groom have arrived!" People at nearby tables who had heard turned to stare. Lauren was embarrassed that she was being put on display at such a delicate moment. It was not only her composure that had gone awry, but her pride had so recently been wounded by these two men who had been party to Roget's bet. *"Garçon!"* he called again impatiently, this time waiving his hand in the air.

"And these are my illustrious friends." Roget's tone was full of jest as he swept his arm in a wide arc that encompassed the occupants of the table. "The worst libertines you will ever meet," he added, and then broke into a wide smile. The tall, dark Haitian made a gesture of loudly clearing his throat and then smoothed his moustache as he rose to his feet.

"Mademoiselle Lyle," Roget continued, his dark gaze falling on the red-haired woman who clung tenaciously to the Frenchman's side, "and Mademoiselle Jourbert," he said, taking the hand of the beautiful bronze woman seated next to the Haitian. With an overtly gallant gesture he proceeded to kiss it.

"Oh, Roget," she uttered, sucking the air through her teeth. "Must you always be so formal? You are a true son of Haiti. Eurydice," she corrected, perusing Lauren from head to foot. Her slanted feline eyes were partially obscured beneath a large round hat, adorned with pink ostrich feathers, and a decidedly bored expression. "So this is the blushing bride." She smiled unwillingly and made a flaccid attempt to mask her displeasure. "It *is* a pleasure, I'm sure."

Lauren was not sure whether the displeasure was based on contempt or chagrin.

"Likewise," the Frenchwoman chimed in. Red hair piled high beneath a saucer-shaped feather hat crowned a skin that was white and translucent like porcelain. "And I'm Marie," she smiled. "It is a pleasure to meet the woman whom Roget finally married. He has been an elusive bachelor for too long and certainly not because others haven't tried."

Lauren flushed slightly; she was unaccustomed to being the center of female attention. Sensing her discomfort, Roget withdrew the attention by acknowledging the Frenchman, who had been preoccupied with the waiter and the champagne. "Alexis Vauxvelle and Jerome Sabardu," he said, nodding to the Frenchman and the Haitian, and then added flippantly, "the new Madame de Martier."

"Lauren," she injected quickly. It was the first time she had been addressed by her new name and could not quite believe that it belonged to her.

"A chair for the bride," Jerome said, making a gallant gesture of pulling out her chair.

Lauren sat willingly, knowing that in another moment her trembling legs would have crumbled beneath her.

Champagne flowed as though money were no concern. They were toasted and toasted and toasted. Inside her head, Lauren's brain fluttered like a weightless feather. A light supper of raw oysters and filet of sole helped to allay the flutterings in her stomach, agitated it seemed by the stench of the cigarette smoke as both men and women puffed incessantly on thin brown cigarettes. Despite her giddiness, Lauren managed to be amused by a butt-picker, stealthily winding his way to each vacated table to usurp the discarded cigarette butts at the end of his long wire. A roaming band of musicians strolled the boulevard playing a raucous brand of music on the street in front of the café. Alexis called for more champagne.

"I think we have had enough," Roget broke in, "at least I have." His dark eyes caught Lauren's amused expression, which seemed to suggest that as husband and wife, they were very much in agreement. Fire raced through her body as his eyes enveloped her and held her captive.

Involved in a lengthy literary discussion, the others were oblivious to Lauren and Roget, but suddenly, Lauren was aware that Eurydice drank in Roget's every move.

"How did you manage to hook him?" she asked blatantly.

"Eurydice!" Roget shot her a reprimanding glare as if to say that too much champagne had separated her from good breeding.

Not wishing to cause dissension among his friends, Lauren bristled quietly, but the champagne got the better of her tongue as well, and she retorted cleverly, "I was not aware that we were fishing."

67

Roget's raven brows arched in surprise. Recognizing that his wife was quite capable of handling things herself, he withdrew his defense.

"Roget, what do you think of Madame Rachilde?" Alexis inquired, pushing an unruly lock of yellow hair from his brow. "You are the scholar in this group. Do you think she deserves to be called Mademoiselle Baudelaire?"

"I haven't the slightest idea," Roget replied absently. His thoughts at that moment were on more serious matters, but he forced his attention back to the conversation. "She has opened a new path for the contemporary novel." Following the scholarly observation, he smiled rakishly, shrugged his shoulders, and added "Victor Hugo applauded her. Who am I to disagree?"

"I think the best thing she did was marry Alfred Vallete," Marie chimed in. "It was his publishing the *Mercure de France* that gave importance to the decadent movement." Her statement had but one purpose, Lauren noticed—to impress Alexis. Clinging to his arm, she gazed up at him seeking his approval, but her fragile porcelain beauty failed to hold his interest. His eyes had not left the tempting bronze cleavage resting above the décolletage of Eurydice's pink satin gown.

Carefully smoothing the edges of his bushy black moustache, Jerome pursued the discussion. "Has anyone read Oscar Wilde's story, *The Picture of Dorian Gray?*"

"Oh, let's talk about something exciting," Eurydice whined petulantly. "I am bored to death of literature and art."

Lauren imagined that her boredom served as a camouflage for a more potent emotion. She possessed the beauty, breeding, and haughty manner of a lady and the attention span of a two-year-old.

More than anxious to oblige her puerile fantasies, Alexis suggested, *"Ma chérie,* let us do something decadent like go to one of those bizarre artists' cafés in Montmartre. That one with all the cats . . ." He groped for the name, his hand sweeping back that same lock of hair.

"Le Chat Noir," Roget volunteered.

"Oui, that one. Let's go to le Chat Noir."

"That sounds like fun," Eurydice purred with interest. "Let's go." She rose from her chair and smoothed the voluminous folds of fabric in her skirt. Alexis waved his hand for the waiter, and Lauren noticed that the exquisite diamond and ruby ring he wore on his third finger was a miniature coat of arms.

"I think we will beg off on this one," Roget said. "Lauren and I have had a long day . . . and it *is* our wedding night."

Lauren was reminded that indeed this was her wedding night, the moment in her life she had been certain would never happen. Through the haze of intoxication that floated ephemerally in her head and the tiny bubbles that danced in her belly, she suddenly found herself facing the moment with ambivalent feelings of awakening desire and threatening anxiety.

Roget turned to her and uttered quietly, "Madame, it's late and I think you've had enough champagne. Shall we go?"

The hour was well past midnight when the hired carriage deposited them in front of the impressive five-story building that housed Roget's apartment on rue Fauborg Saint-Honoré. The gray stone facade was adorned with rows of magnificently sculptured window frames that echoed the stone balconies surrounding the upper floors of the house. Lauren was not prepared for the grandness of the structure or the opulence that greeted her as they stepped through the carved horseshoe-shaped doorway onto the main floor. As they climbed a wide marble staircase to the third floor, she smiled to herself, thinking that all these years she had thought the Saint Germain more than sufficient. Roget was about to turn his key in the lock when a short black man opened the door from inside and bowed his partially bald head in a reserved greeting.

"Bonsoir, madame . . . monsieur."

"Lauren, this is Walker.

"Bonsoir," Lauren replied awkwardly. She was not exactly sure how one greeted servants, especially when she was not far removed from that status herself. The small man took her wrap and scurried on short legs through the tall glass doors that led off the parlor. Lauren gazed about

the room, her eyes curiously digesting the things with which her husband surrounded himself. It was unmistakably a man's apartment. Despite the jacquard upholstery and the ornate mahogany furniture, the atmosphere had an unpretentious masculine elegance. As she was caught by the beauty of a smoked glass vase, Walker entered the room again.

"I moved all your things into the one armoire as you said, *monsieur*. The other is ready for *madame*'s things."

"*Merci*, Walker." Roget pulled off his tailcoat and began to loosen the stiff poke collar at his throat, as his narrow-trousered legs strode toward the glass doors. "Your things are in here," he said, looking over his shoulder.

Her head had cleared. All at once she was completely sober. Her two sturdy limbs had become rubber and moved as though they were wading through quicksand. Roget stepped aside and allowed her to precede him into his bedchamber.

"Is there anything I can get you, *monsieur?*" Walker called after them.

"*Oui*. A bottle of champagne and two glasses."

The room was almost dark, lit only by candles and an antique gas lamp whose glow illuminated the brass bedposts.

"This armoire is for your things," Roget said, inclining his head toward a chest of drawers that was obscured in the shadows. "I'm afraid . . . this *is* a bachelor apartment. There are not many provisions for a woman, but we will make do." Roget's soft dark eyes drank in the sinuous contours of her body. "Your dressing room is in there." With his bare arm, he gestured toward a closed door.

Inside the tiny room, Lauren stepped carefully out of her red velvet gown and looked about for a place to hang it. Her gaze lingered on the long, tight sleeves that burst into poufs just above the elbow and the soft folds that had draped across her breast, disappearing into a high snug collar at her neck. She had never worn anything so beautiful. It had been part of the meager trousseau given to her by Claude and Pierre, the remainder of which consisted of two nightgowns and one magnificent ball gown. She herself had paid for the eggshell wool suit she had worn for the ceremony, using the little money she had managed to save over the years. Because the scroll embroidery on the jacket was so simple, her frugal mind had reasoned that it could later be worn as a day dress.

Piece by piece she peeled off her other clothing and washed herself in the warm water that had been placed in the basin. Slowly, she inched the lace nightgown over her naked body. She lingered a moment before the mirror, slipped her feet into the satin slippers, and joined her husband in the bedchamber.

Roget, wearing only a white silk robe that outlined the dark muscled contours of his male body, stood leisurely pouring champagne.

"Champagne . . . *madame?*" He placed the crystal glass in her hand. Lauren was thankful for something to grasp that would steady her hand and keep her from making a fool of herself.

Roget leaned his weight languorously against the heavy mahogany armoire and shoved his left hand into his pocket, leaving the thumb exposed. His right hand raised the glass in a silent toast to his bride. Lauren reciprocated his gesture, her hazel eyes stealthily perusing the lithe, muscular lines of his body beneath the thin robe.

Timorously, she moved around and lowered herself into the plush cushions of an upholstered armchair. "I did not mean to be rude this evening," she said softly.

"Rude?" He repeated the word, gazing down at her with a close scrutiny.

"Eurydice . . . She seemed to have an apparent dislike for me."

"I wouldn't worry about Eurydice. She deserved no better." His lips curled with reckless mischief. "Besides, I rather enjoyed your clever retort." The smile faded, but his eyes never left her. "Eurydice is a Haitian expatriate, who has a doting old man for a father. She pretends that she has escaped the bonds of Haitian society, but one never escapes one's heritage." Shifting his weight, he moved across the room and refilled his empty glass. Returning to where she sat, he resumed the same casual pose. "You had very little to say this evening," he remarked leisurely, "especially for someone who kept me engaged with a barrage of questions only a few weeks ago."

Self-consciously, Lauren fidgeted in her chair. Finally she replied, "I was afraid that I might say the wrong thing. I didn't want to alienate your friends."

"I don't think there is any danger of that. Besides, which of them ever says the right thing?"

"You seem to." Lauren's shapely lips curved into a sly smile. "I didn't know that I had married a scholar."

Her tone was teasing, the same lighthearted jesting he had often used with her, but Roget's expression grew irritated as he inhaled a loud breath and let it out. "I am so sick of those *damn* literary discussions that lead nowhere. I have a plantation that may be in ruin, and they expect me to care about Mademoiselle Baudelaire." His hands went up in frustration.

Tact had rarely been one of her virtues, but at this moment it was necessary that she employ it to change the subject.

"Are they serious?" she asked, her insatiable curiosity providing a much needed diversion.

"Who?" he inquired, dragging his thoughts back from somewhere else.

"Jerome and Eurydice," she answered.

"Jerome would like them to be, but I doubt that Eurydice is capable of being serious about anyone."

"Except perhaps . . . you." Roget offered no noticeable reaction to her statement, but it was obvious to Lauren that she was not the only woman whose blood Roget set afire. "She's very beautiful," Lauren added, her long graceful fingers toying restlessly with the empty glass. "Alexis could not keep his eyes off her."

"Alexis harbors a disastrous lust for brown-skinned women," Roget commented flatly. "His family owns land in Martinique, and having sampled the pleasures of our women, he cannot seem to get them out of his blood."

"And Marie?" she questioned. "It appears that she rather fancies Alexis.

"It's unfortunate. Given Alexis's penchant for dusky-skinned women, I would say she doesn't have a chance. Her fragile, porcelain beauty is not what Alexis hungers for."

"And Eurydice is?" Her tone questioned him again.

"It seems that way," he paused reflectively, "at least for this moment."

"She is very beautiful," Lauren uttered again, almost as an afterthought, wondering why Roget was so obviously unimpressed with her beauty.

"No more beautiful than most of our Haitian women," he replied as if he had read her thoughts. "I sometimes wonder if she has anything between her ears—underneath all that hair." His expression was pensive, but his tone was decidedly sarcastic.

Roget mused as he observed Lauren's nervous fingers fidgeting with the empty glass. His eyes traveled from her hands up over the soft curve of her bosom to her mouth and lingered there. The cold bubbly liquid and Roget's easy, languorous, almost hypnotizing manner had calmed the flutterings in her belly, but her composure faded rapidly when Roget moved toward her and gently retrieved the glass from her hand.

"This *is* our wedding night," he said, his lips twisting into a lazy grin. "Are we going to spend it discussing my friends?" Taking her two hands in his, he pulled her to her feet.

"You have beautiful hands," he murmured as his lips brushed over her fingers. The butterflies in Lauren's stomach broke loose in a frenzy once again, and her rubbery limbs tottered under her weight. The day fleeted before her as unreal as a dream.

"Do you need anything?" he asked.

"No . . ." Her voice faltered as her mind raced over a thousand things she could have needed, but before she could inhale another breath, Roget pulled her into his arms and smothered her mouth beneath his, intoxicating her already giddy brain. His kiss rekindled the raging flame he had ignited that day along the Bois. His curious lips were demanding, and their demands grew stronger and more intense until her full, yielding mouth allowed him to invade its warmth. Pressed taut against the hard leanness of his chest, her breasts strained against the lace bodice of her nightgown. His lips played over her mouth, demanding more from her than she thought she could give, and yet she gave him more as her head spun and her lungs gasped for breath. Roget's mouth moved over her cheek to her ear, savoring every spot in his path. Taking the delicate lobe in his mouth, he nibbled it softly between his teeth, while Lauren squirmed with pleasure. His lips brushed over her neck, pausing to caress the hollow at the base of her throat, and finally discovered the pulsating cleavage of her bosom where the décolleté ended.

Feeling the wild surge of passion pent up inside her, Roget whispered in a husky, provocative voice, "Has anyone ever told you how delectable you are?" He caught her full face, his ebony eyes penetrating her soul.

"No . . ." Lauren's face flushed burgundy red. "I've never been in this situation with a man before."

Roget stared at her, a sudden flash of perception lighting his face. "You mean . . . I'm the first?"

"Didn't you expect to be?"

She asked the question with more naïveté than he had anticipated. It had not occurred to him that he would be deflowering a virgin.

"I assumed . . . that given your circumstances . . . living in Paris, working in that environment . . . there would have been someone before now. When I kissed you that day in the park . . . was that also the first?"

"Oui." Lauren's voice caught somewhere deep in her throat. Instantly, she understood what it meant to be awkward. Roget smiled slightly.

"So that was the reason you were reluctant. I could feel your desire, but you would not let go. Well, *madame,"* he teased, reaching to pull the ivory combs from her hair, "you can let go of it now. You *are* married." His mouth came down and met hers in a sultry union. This time her arms crept around his neck, and she uttered his name with her sigh as her lips responded to his challenge, savoring his mouth as ravenously as he had hers. Fiery torches balked and then yielded to a tantalizing game.

Roget's nimble hands slid over the delicate blue lace and

ran the length of her legs, the curve of her hips, her waist and up to the firm velvety skin of her back. He paused there, foiled by the tight drawstring of her gown. Lauren winced as his hand lingered there, the gentle fingers pressing into the contours of her back. Her body ached deep inside from the ecstasy evoked by his touch. Roget dropped to his knees, his hands still caressing her velvet-textured skin and a cold, piercing shudder trickled through her belly and down her legs as he came dangerously close to that private place she had not allowed herself to feel until now. Lauren trembled, wanting to take him in, longing to feel his maleness.

"I think it's time this came off," he whispered. He reached up, untied the drawstring and let the lace gown fall in a pool around her ankles. Rising to his feet, Roget removed his own robe and flung it aside. Her eyes feasted on his dark masculine skin, the lean, bare muscles that glistened in the flickering candlelight and gave off a sensual glow that sent desire raging like an inferno through her loins. Lauren felt every muscle in his body quicken as he lifted her willing form onto the huge brass bed.

Timidly, her graceful fingers crept over his male torso, her fingertips fondling the velvet smoothness of his skin and thrilling to the feel of hardness beneath it. The delicate touch of her hand exploring his body evoked a violent trembling that experience had not taught him.

Roget's mouth traveled over her skin, gently ravishing her as he drank in the nectar of her honey-colored flesh. His kisses teased her unmercifully, and Lauren wallowed in the pleasure. When another second seemed unbearable, Roget turned her as though she were a paper doll and exposed the smooth expanse of her back to the same blissful sensations. Her spine quivered beneath his touch, shooting rapturous sparks of pleasure through every nerve of her body. Involuntary contractions undulated through her womb. Her limbs trembled, unable to bear the excruciating pain of desire a moment longer. She had wanted to be discreet about his love, but her newly awakened body was on the verge of explosion. With little effort, Roget turned her until she was facing him. Lauren's shapely limbs were no longer under her control. They parted easily, allowing Roget's rigid maleness to penetrate the willing softness of her womanhood. Inside, her womb opened like a flower, blooming one petal at a time. Wantonly, ravenously, her body unfolded to caress the full expression of his manhood.

"Roget—oh, Roget!" she gasped as her head went back against the pillow and the breath smothered in her throat. From deep in her soul came a loud gasp of pain and then pleasure as she gave him her virginity.

Lauren felt her silken torso arch to meet him, drawing him deeper and deeper until the fullness of him assuaged the craving in her loins. Their entwined figures became one, as honey blended with sable, rising and falling with the same rhythm that spurred their breathing. Slowly, indolently, he moved with the elegant grace of a panther, purposely pacing his movements so that she would reach the summit before him.

Timidly her fingers caressed him, and what seemed to Lauren like a seizure grabbed his taut muscles and he began to tremble. Roget's maleness singed every nerve in her body, and she received him, extracting every ounce of pleasure he was capable of giving. Ecstasy rose to a crescendo. Lauren's breath quickened into short gasps and mingled with her sighs. A deep groan rose from the pit of Roget's belly as the essence of his manhood gushed into her. Her nails dug into the smoothness of his back, and a seething, rapturous fever surged through her womb as their throbbing bodies came together and exploded and then fell limp against the sheets. Their spent bodies languored in the afterglow of unexpected passion, each reluctant to move.

"*Ma chérie,* I thought you told me that you were a virgin," Roget teased.

Lauren turned her face away, embarrassed by his taunting smile. "I am . . ." Her voice faltered. "I mean, I was."

"You have nothing to be embarrassed about," he whispered softly, turning her chin with his thumb and forefinger. "But are you quite sure you were a virgin?" His dark eyes teased shamelessly.

"Of course," she retorted indignantly, "how could I not be sure?"

"I was only teasing," he rejoined, playfully allowing his fingers to trickle along her neck and down over the curve of her bare shoulder. Still, she trembled at his touch. "Besides, you are certainly not a virgin anymore."

"I know," she mumbled softly, again turning her face away. She was not yet ready to face the scrutinizing invasion into her private thoughts.

"At any rate, *madame,* you are full of surprises. I may have to keep you under lock and key. You could drive men wild." An odd smile lingered on Roget's face.

Finally allowing her eyes to meet Roget's gaze, she wondered if perhaps what Monsieur de Guy had said so long ago was true, but all she could think of now was that she wanted to feel Roget's mouth devouring her again. Lauren offered him the tempting fullness of her lips, and he drank their nectar for a moment, but exhaustion exercised a stronger claim on their spent bodies than passion. The new Madame de Martier fell into a deep slumber, the warmth of her husband's body still covering her.

Lauren awoke to a delicious surge of contentment flooding her body. Her hazel eyes were blinded by the sparkle of tiny emeralds circling the finger that lay close to her face on the pillow. She stretched lazily, reveling in the tingling pleasure of satisfaction that satiated her body. She no longer felt like a caged cat, clawing to be set free. Instinctively, she drew in her bare, outstretched limbs when her eyes focused on Roget who had looked up from his book and was now staring at her.

"Bonjour, madame," he said, with a teasing tone that echoed a familiar formality. "Did you sleep well?"

"Oui, monsieur," she responded, continuing the subtle charade. His eyes roamed leisurely over the contours of her body, making her suddenly aware of her nakedness. Prudishly, she yanked the sheet up around her neck. Roget swung his leg from over the arm of the chair and got up.

"Why so shy this morning?"

"A lady does not parade around naked," she flashed back indignantly.

Roget's two raven brows crowded into his forehead. "But I am your husband," he reminded her, laying his book aside, "or have you forgotten?"

Lauren turned from him and did not see the suppressed

smile that danced in his eyes. In long, easy strides he strode toward the brass bed, his fingers shoved neatly in his pockets, with the thumbs extended outward. A sharp thrill wiggled through her toes, up through her legs, and settled in her belly. A warm flush bathed shamefully over her face, for she knew that if he so much as touched her, her body would surrender to another wanton display of passion.

Roget did not touch her. For the moment, he had cautiously curbed the reins on his own desire. Instead, he inquired roguishly, "Are you ever going to get up?"

"I have nothing on."

"You had nothing on last night," he responded. Retrieving her nightgown from the chair over which it was draped, he let it fall on the bed as he left the room.

Quickly, Lauren climbed out of bed and pulled the lace gown over her head. She hated herself for behaving like a silly prude, but she needed time to think, time to sort out her feelings. Last night had taken her totally by surprise, and she had ambivalent feelings about the overwhelming passion Roget's love had awakened in her. A lady was not supposed to be a wanton hussy even with her husband. Perhaps what they said about mulatto women was true.

The door swung open, and Roget entered carrying a beautifully wrapped box adorned with bows and ribbons of the most enchanting colors.

"This is for you." He handed her the box. "It's your wedding present." He smiled apologetically. "I forgot to give it to you last night." Lauren flushed at his acknowledgment of the past night, but her embarrassment was short-lived. Her hazel eyes sparkled with impish delight.

"Merci, monsieur, but it's so beautiful that I hate to open it."

"What's inside may be even more beautiful."

Carefully she began to undo the delicate wrappings, trying not to destroy the ribbons but to no avail. Futilely, she gave up. She would never be able to see what Roget had hidden inside without destroying the cover. She lifted the lid and inhaled a long, labored breath.

"Oh, Roget," she uttered finally as she drew from the box a magnificent white silk robe, exquisitely embroidered with gold and silver threads to resemble the tail of a peacock. "Roget," she whispered softly. Her voice faltered and tears sparkled in her eyes. "It's beautiful . . . I've never owned anything so . . ."

"This seems to be your day for new experiences." He smiled, the inflection in his voice teasing her again.

Running the tips of her fingers lightly over the embroidery, she savored the luxurious feel of silk against her skin and marveled at the tiny gold butterflies that hovered around the peacock.

"Is it Japanese?" she queried. Roget nodded and replied, "A Japanese wedding kimono." Restraining the impulse to throw her arms about his neck and bury herself in the heat of his body, she clung rigidly to the edge of the bed for fear of the fire it would ignite. She merely said, *"Merci."*

"I cannot promise you anything so exquisite," he said, "but is there anything else you would like this morning?"

"Oui," she answered, "a bath." Lauren gazed into the dark mystery of his eyes and knew that her resolve was melting. Roget rang for Walker.

A light rap echoed through the door. *"Entrez,"* Roget called out.

Walker rushed into the room. *"Oui, monsieur?"* he said, inclining the top of his shiny head in Lauren's direction as if to avoid looking at her.

"Would you draw a bath for *madame, s'il vous plaît."*

"Oui, monsieur," he said as he scurried into the bathroom, nervously averting his eyes from Lauren's nightgownclad body. Walker was as unaccustomed to having a woman in the house as she was to being waited on by a servant. He was quite obviously a gentleman's gentleman, and her presence made him overtly uncomfortable.

When Walker was gone, Lauren peeled off her nightgown and stepped into the porcelain tub, a tub almost twice the size of the one she had bathed in at the Saint Germain. The warm bubbles tickled her now-sensitive skin, and the jasmine scent invaded her nostrils, lulling her into a sweet, languid repose. Sliding down under the water until the foam enveloped her chin, she laid her head back and closed her eyes. Startled from the reverie, she opened them to find

Roget observing her from the open doorway. A foolish sense of nakedness washed over her. "Roget, I'm taking a bath," she snapped. "Would you mind closing the door?"

His lips curled into a roguish grin as he pulled the door closed behind him. Lauren averted her eyes indignantly, but indignation forced her lips shut and into a provocative pose that Roget seemed to find irresistible. He strode toward her, untying his robe.

"Roget!" Lauren cried. "You wouldn't!"

"Why not?" His eyes danced with mischievous amusement. This was a mood she had not seen, and it intrigued her that he had yet another side.

"Lately, I've done many things I never thought I would do," he confessed. A long, silent pause ensued as his ebony gaze plundered her hazel one. "Besides, *ma chérie,* now I have you captive," he smiled, gazing into the water, "but my seeing you unclothed seems to bother you." His tone grew somewhat less playful. "You seem to forget, *madame,* that I know every inch of you."

Lauren cringed. His tone was taunting her again. She clamped her mouth shut, but it lasted less than a moment. Softly, his ample mouth enveloped hers, forcing the determined lips apart as he drank in the sweetness of her breath. The musky scent of his cologne mingled with the jasmine bath oil and formed a heady intoxication that numbed her senses. The white robe fell into a heap on the floor. His smooth sable body, the broad shoulders, the trim waist, and round muscular buttocks were honed to perfection. Lauren sucked in a sharp, jagged breath as her eyes devoured the sight of him in broad daylight. Lifting her arms out of the safe, foamy refuge, she wound them lazily about his neck.

Temptingly, Roget fondled the back of her neck, brushing his thumb over the sensitive nape. Writhing sensations of pleasure pulsed through her, melting away all of her reasoning and firm resolve. Lauren's weight on his shoulders threw his body off balance, and he was forced to grab the side of the tub for support.

"Do you want me to join you?" he questioned with a hint of skepticism. "Because if you don't, it will be impossible for me to remain like this without plummeting head first into the tub . . . against your wishes."

Realizing that pride would not allow him to force himself on any woman, not even his wife, she nodded sheepishly, thinking that if he did not soon join her and assuage the hunger he had aroused in her soul, she would surely go mad.

Roget climbed into the bubbly, perfumed tub, and the hard, wet feel of his body against her soft, yearning skin sent shivers racing up her spine despite the temperature of the water. Every nerve in her wanted him. Lauren surrendered willingly to the skill of his touch as her nimble fingers caressed him in ways that he had seldom experienced. No longer did she behave like the shy, prudish virgin, but like a woman eager to experience the delights of her husband's body. Roget's muscles tensed at her touch, and a deep, husky groan escaped from his throat.

"Is it all right?" she murmured, her voice full of naive intoxication.

"Perfectly all right," he groaned. Roget's agile hands prepared the way for their journey, and Lauren languished in the rapture of his love as they rode the crest of a wave to ecstasy.

With only a towel covering his narrow hips, Roget retrieved his robe from the floor and placed it on her naked shoulders.

"I must not see you undressed," he chided playfully as he turned away and strolled into the bedchamber. She followed him, the silk robe dragging loosely along the carpeted floor.

"Roget, you're making fun of me," she responded.

"Now you see how ridiculous it sounds." Turning her back to him, she let his robe fall from her shoulders and slipped her arms into the Japanese kimono. As she struggled with the long sash, Roget took the obi from her and wrapped the wasplike curve of her waist in Japanese fashion.

Taking another robe from the closet, Roget discarded the towel, shoved his broad shoulders into the armholes, and tied it securely about his waist. With his hands neatly in the pockets, all except the thumbs, he inquired, "What would you like to do for the remainder of your honeymoon?"

Before giving an answer, she sighed as though surrendering a long cherished belief, and then she began. "I want to see the Moulin Rouge, the Folies Bergère, and that artists' café in Montmartre where Alexis and Eurydice went last night."

"Le Chat Noir," Roget replied to her silent question.

"Oui, monsieur." Her hazel eyes glowed with a reckless bravado. "And all the exciting places in Paris that I have never seen."

"Those are hardly places for a lady," he chided her again, allowing his fingers to trail lightly over her arm.

"I don't care," she retorted. "No one thinks that I am a lady anyway." The scorching heat from his fingers was igniting a fire in her belly. "Perhaps I should have joined the *demimonde.*"

"Why do you say that?"

"Because men think that women of mixed blood are whores. Even you didn't believe that there had been no one else."

"White men think mulatto women are whores because that is what they want to think. I know different. Had you not been a virgin, I would still not think you were a whore. Why does a passionate woman always have to be branded a whore? Men complain of frigid, unresponsive women, and when they encounter one whose passion matches their own, they brand her a whore and assume she is giving it away to everyone. And I suppose," he paused reflectively, "after last night and this morning, *you* are branding yourself."

Lauren could not care anymore. Roget's hand caressed the luxurious silk robe that covered her body, stealthily arousing that insatiable hunger for his maleness that made her virtue questionable. Her body molded into him, and as he tilted her face up, she whispered, "I doubt that I'd be successful as a *demimondaine* . . . that is unless my benefactor were you." Hers was an insatiable desire, but it was for him—only him.

Lauren smiled up at him, her full, tempting lips slightly parted. Roget lowered his head and covered her mouth with his own.

Chapter 5

The remaining weeks of their honeymoon were spent on the rue Fauborg Saint-Honoré. Paris in 1891 was a gay, flamboyant feast of sensual delights, and Lauren blushed that she had been determined to taste them all. Any day, Roget expected a letter calling him home to Haiti, but until fate intervened, Lauren and Roget reveled in the pleasures of Paris. During the day they explored the city's many parks, went riding along the Bois, and indulged their passion whenever it arose. They even made love one rainy afternoon between the first and second courses of lunch. Conveniently, Walker always remembered errands he had not completed and left them alone for long periods of time. Evenings, they dined in intimate cafés, attended the opera, the boulevard theaters, and finally Roget relented and agreed to show her the Folies Bergère, the Moulin Rouge, and le Chat Noir.

"Are you sure you want to go there?" Roget prodded. "I promise you, the Moulin Rouge is not the place for a lady," he continued as the horse-drawn victoria plodded up the steep, dimly lit hill.

"Roget, you're making fun of me again. Will you never let me live that down?" Her hazel eyes smiled sheepishly into his darker ones.

"You got over being a prude, and now you have developed a wicked penchant for the bizarre and the decadent."

"This *is* the age of decadence, is it not?" She flung the statement off with a teasing gesture. "Just because I found le Chat Noir amusing—"

"Amusing," he broke in, repeating her word with a tinge of sarcasm. *"Ma chérie,* you were wide-eyed with delight."

"I was merely fascinated with all those paintings of black cats in such quaint situations."

"And with Bruant, it seemed." Roget's tone remained agitated.

"I thought Captain Bruant was charming."

"Charming!" he barked. "Bruant is an obnoxious lecher. But you, *ma chérie,* refused to be insulted at his lewd remarks. And yet, a few short weeks ago, you were covering yourself in front of me."

"Roget, *s'il te plaît . . ."* Lauren silenced him with her lips.

Before them loomed the brilliant red windmill, it's giant arms rotating slowly in a lurid glow of yellow light.

Inside the garden, Lauren's attention was drawn from one exciting spectacle to another. Men, escorting elaborately dressed women of the night, rubbed shoulders with refined American ladies and their husbands and they with French mothers and their daughters. All looked on, intoxicated with anticipation at the risqué spectacle of the quadrille. After the first show, Lauren sat back in her chair and sighed. There would be an hour's wait until midnight, when, she had been told, the real excitement began.

"Are you ready to go now?" Roget inquired. His full, sensuous mouth harbored an amused grin.

"No. Of course not."

"Respectable ladies are expected to leave now," he remarked lightly, his attention captured by the glow of determination in her eyes.

Lauren clicked her tongue against her teeth. "Oh, Roget!" Her tone was decidedly annoyed, but Roget remained captivated by the glow in her eyes that echoed that annoyance.

"Well, what do you think? Have your delicate sensibilities

been shocked yet?" he smiled, deliberately swirling the brandy in his glass.

"No, *monsieur*. They have not," she replied flippantly, draining the last drop of sherry from her glass.

"Would you like another sherry?"

"Of course." Already she felt light-headed and giddy but wanted to prolong the sensation.

"Don't you think you have had enough?"

"Roget, sometimes I think it is you who is the prude."

"Overindulgence in alcohol is considered bad taste in Haiti."

"We are not in Haiti; we are in Paris," she retorted boldly. Lauren glanced over her shoulder at the men in their shiny high hats and long dark beards that oddly resembled pictures she had seen of Toulouse Lautrec. Stretching her slender neck, she allowed her eyes to dart from man to man, hoping that she might catch a glimpse of the notorious artist.

At midnight the dancers divided into groups of four, and standing with feet apart and skirts hiked to show their ruffled petticoats, they took positions around the room. Spectators waited with bated breath for the music to begin. Lauren edged in close to the center of the circle, while Roget hovered close behind. He had little interest in the quadrille. He had seen it many times, but intrigued by the expression of puerile anticipation that lit her face and her abandon to its pleasure, Roget felt himself being drawn into the fervor of sensual excitement that permeated the room.

Kicking their black-stockinged legs high above each other's heads, the dancers circled on one foot and then dropped to the floor with legs wide apart to form an indecent split. These members of the fair sex assumed lewd, copulative movements to the beat of the music, egged on by the crowd's delirious orgy of chanting, clapping, and stamping feet. *Roget was right*, Lauren mused. *This is no place for a lady*.

In the frenzied crush of excitement after the performance, she felt the heat of Roget's hand against her middle as he guided her through the throng of people. Leaning forward, he placed his mouth within range of her ear and whispered, *"Madame,* are you ready to go home?"

Lauren opened her eyes and stared blankly into the darkness. After a few moments of confusion, she realized that the hour was quite early; Roget was not yet awake. Unwillingly, she contemplated removing herself from the warmth of the smooth, hard, masculine form that lay next to her. Hypnotized by the calm, even sound of his breathing, she lay there, her body still tingling from the vibrant thrusts of his passion. As much as she wanted to prolong the delectable feeling, nature prodded her to relieve her bladder.

Climbing out of bed at the last possible moment, Lauren had no time to search for her nightgown. The warm body next to her stirred but did not waken. Barefoot and shivering, she padded quietly across the carpet to the water closet that adjoined their bedchamber.

She returned and sidled gracefully back into the delicious nest of warmth. But inevitably, winter follows autumn. Startled by a knock at the door, Roget's dark eyes jarred open, and he growled in a husky voice, *"Entrez."* Walker entered wearing a robe and slippers.

"Monsieur, this appears to be urgent," he said, handing Roget a telegram. Roget shoved one bare, muscular arm outside the down quilt and seized the envelope.

"Merci, Walker," he uttered absently as the small man scurried from the room. Through sleepy eyes, Roget pondered the message, a dismal frown distorting his handsome sable features.

"I'm afraid this puts an end to our honeymoon," he said. "I have to return to Haiti."

"Do we have to?" she questioned hesitantly, her eyes studying the twisted contours of his face.

"Oui. It's my home." His voice harbored a strange remorse.

"But why . . . if you dread it so?"

Roget found the question curiously naive and her ignorance overwhelming. "I have an obligation to my family and to my country. I've been away for a year and there are problems at home—political problems. And some discord among the workers on the plantation."

Reluctantly, Lauren began to feel the pull of her husband's loyalty to duty. However, she was anxious to see Haiti—the mysterious island that would be her home.

Lauren shifted her gaze from the porthole, but her thoughts were still entranced by the ripples that danced over the water. Abruptly, the rhythm of Roget's footsteps outside the door invaded her reverie. At last, he had returned.

Roget turned his key in the lock and strode through the door wearing a jovial smile. Lauren assigned his unusual good humor to the brandy and the lusty male conversation of Henri Duval.

"I see that you survived Madame Duval," he quipped lightly, his mouth showing the hint of a smile.

Her hazel eyes searched the depths of his darker ones. "Roget, why was Madame Duval shocked when I was introduced to her?"

"Probably because I was promised to marry someone else." His reply was pensive and yet oddly fluent.

"Why should that upset *her?*"

"The woman I was expected to marry is her niece. The marriage had been planned for many years." Lauren remained speechless for more than a few minutes. Her gaze plummeted to the delicate embroidery covering her robe and lingered there.

"She was even more upset when I told her about my parents."

"Why did you tell her about them?"

"She kept prodding me with that haughty manner."

"I wish you had waited and let me handle it." Roget was now noticeably annoyed.

"The fact that I'm of mixed blood seemed to upset her."

"It shouldn't," he retorted with glaring sarcasm. "It is not so much your mixed blood as your African mother that unnerved her."

"Aren't mixed marriages common in your country?" she asked, remembering the Duvals.

"No. Only among the greedy upper class." Again he left her floundering in a sea of confusion.

"I don't understand." The tone of her voice questioned his reticence.

"You will. In due time you will. And Lauren, promise me," he added, "that you will not disclose any more facts until I've had time to break the news. This will not be easy, and you had best allow me to handle it. I'm more familiar with the enemy."

Slowly, Roget's vexation began to dissipate, and a suggestive smile curled his lips. He slid one strong arm around her middle, forcing her body back against the pillows as his free hand undid the obi that she had so carefully tied. Deft fingers eased the silk fabric down over her shoulders, exposing her trembling body to the nakedness of their desire. His hands caressed the smooth, soft flesh of her breasts and they grew rigid beneath his touch. Lauren writhed in blissful ecstasy as Roget savored her taut, sensitive skin.

"Your skin is like honey," he murmured, burying his face in the succulent valley between the swell of her breasts. "Rich . . . pure . . . and sweet."

Lauren coiled her arms about his back, caressing the hard muscles beneath her fingers.

The dark velvet night closed in on them, and somewhere in the midst of her passion Lauren wondered if she would ever fully understand this man that God had destined her to love. Their lips met, and his body fused into hers. Claude's warnings were, for the moment, forgotten.

The nine days it took for the ship to plough a path through the rough, icy waters of the Atlantic to the Caribbean were spent in idle pursuits of pleasure. Throughout the day, passengers strolled the windy promenade or lounged in deck chairs, heavily attired in winter clothing. Women were weighted down in heavy woolen suits, shawls, and warm mittens. Men moved about in long waterproof coats that warded off the spray from the waves as they crashed against the ship. Numerous meals were served to those with stomachs sturdy enough for the consumption of food. The uninhibited laughter of children playing echoed through the saloon deck and then drowned at sea.

Roget and Henri Duval spent the evenings sipping brandy, playing cards, and sharing anecdotes from home, while Madame Duval looked on with polite boredom. Several times, Roget had urged his wife to join him, but she declined in favor of reading the books about Haitian history that he had bought for her in Paris. Roget knew that Lauren preferred to avoid the company of Madame Duval, and he dared say that he could not blame her. However, two piano concerts and the promise from Roget that he would accompany her was incentive enough to lure Lauren from her seclusion. Overflowing with enthusiasm, she had enticed him to shed the company of the Duvals and join her in the Empress Saloon.

Roget strode along the corridor to the Empress Saloon, and with each rhythmic step a spark of anticipation sent warm blood racing through his veins. He told himself that he had suffered through those five evenings with Henri and Celestine Duval for the sake of proper decorum, but was that the reason? Or was it a subconscious attempt to pull the reigns on his passion? A passion he had never intended to exist to this extent. But now, as he approached his bride, he realized how much he wanted these last few nights with her.

It had happened so quickly, he thought. Two months ago he had not known Lauren, and now he was bringing her home as his bride. For his own selfish reasons, he was bringing Lauren into a situation that would be anything but pleasant. To say that his family and Lucienne's would be shocked would put it mildly. The Condé family could sue for breach of promise.

And this marriage—it had not worked according to his plan. He had meant the marriage to be a mere convenience, but since their wedding night there were times when he feared he was losing control. What he had failed to consider was that Lauren would be so appealing that he would not be able to keep his hands off of her—or not want to. She was different, different from any woman he had known, different in ways that had captured his imagination. She was more woman than he had imagined. But then he had never known a woman from her class. He remembered that night in Paris and how plausible it had seemed when he conceived the idea.

It was well past midnight when he and his friends poured boisterously from the Saint Germain Hotel onto the street. Jerome hailed a passing victoria.

"Messieurs, I will take my leave," he said, hoisting his tall frame into the carriage. "A lady awaits me." Grinning, he adjusted his high hat as the victoria pulled away.

Swiping the lock of blond hair from his forehead, Alexis turned to Roget. "So, you really do intend to make good on this bet," he said teasingly.

"Oui, mon ami," Roget replied jocularly. "You could not have thought that I would let you two rakes take me for a thousand francs," he continued, hoisting one raven black eyebrow, "or did you?" But in the split of a second, his tone grew wistful. "I only wish that all of life's games could be so easily won."

"Is something the matter, old man? You've not been yourself these past nights."

"Lucienne is here . . . in Paris."

"So, she came to drag the prodigal son home?" the Frenchman chided.

"No, she is beginning a tour of the Continent."

"Shouldn't that make you happy?" the Frenchman continued questioning, perplexed by his friend's troubled expression. "You are in love with the lady, and you two have been, ah . . . a bit more intimate than friends."

"I get your point," Roget said, cutting his dark eyes at the Frenchman's blue ones. "The problem is, she is pressing me to set a date. Once I return home, we will have to marry. I cannot evade it any longer; the families are getting impatient."

"Arranged marriages are hell." Alexis's blue eyes filled with empathy as he felt his friend's frustration. "And obviously you are still determined not to marry her."

"Now more than ever. My family is no place for a woman . . . certainly not a woman like Lucienne. They would destroy her. I watched it happen to Reinette . . . and to my mother. I will not watch it happen to her."

"How will you avoid it?"

"At the moment, I haven't the vaguest idea. All I know is that I love her too much to see her destroyed." It was then that the vision invaded Roget's thoughts—a vision of emerald satin shimmering against honey brown shoulders and the tantalizing eyes of the *mademoiselle* who had become the subject of their bet. He had always been partial to green. *She would wear emeralds well,* he thought. "Perhaps there is a solution," he added absently, his thoughts still flirting with the vision.

Climbing into a victoria, he and Alexis braced themselves against the chill and set forth into the shadows of the cold Parisian night.

The door to the Empress Saloon appeared as groups of passengers brushed past him, hurrying to secure their seats. Roget's thoughts jolted back to the evening that lay before him. Once inside the room, his dark eyes roamed over the two grand pianos to the rows of gilded chairs, and even through the throng of bodies that surrounded her, Roget noticed the hazel eyes that gleamed with anticipation. His stride carried him into the row, and he took his seat beside his wife.

"Roget, you came!" Lauren cried, her voice full of uncontrolled excitement.

"I said that I would," he replied.

During the next three days, their ship battled with a stormy sea, and the steel vessel thrashed about in turbulent waters. Lauren was laid up only once, and Roget suffered a bout of queasiness but was otherwise unaffected. While other passengers clung sickly to their berths, Lauren and Roget extracted their pleasure from the heaving, rolling motions of the sea. And just when it seemed that their passion would exist forever, the island of Santo Domingo appeared on the horizon.

Chapter 6

Within an arc of hazy blue, delicate mountain crests cut sharply out against a brightening sky. The black republic sat majestically between her tropical seas and maiden mountain peaks. Gliding slowly through Saint Marc Channel and around the tiny island situated in the bay, the ship chugged lazily into dock. Almost too massive for the channel, the ocean liner jostled rudely against the levee until it was secured by the anchor that plunged to the depths of Haiti's blue waters. The heavy metal dredged up a stench of stagnant pollution that rose from the water and hovered in the air, forcing passengers on the promenade deck to bring shielding hands to their noses.

While his impatient bride slipped away to steal her first glimpse of Port-au-Prince, Roget de Martier remained behind to attend to social amenities and to say their good-byes. Once Lauren was out of view, his handsome features twisted to a sullen frown as he took in the fleet of vessels that hovered on the edge of Haiti's waters. American ships, their masts ominously overshadowing the town below, disturbed him. Alarmed, Roget's unconscious gaze tallied their number. His country's freedom was facing a serious threat, and he realized that he had arrived home none too soon. He only prayed that it was not too late.

Anxiously, Lauren pressed her body to the railing and

stared at the city beneath her. A crush of people milled
about on deck, awkwardly craning their necks for a view of
Port-au-Prince as well, but Lauren was so immersed in the
new sights and sounds that echoed through her husband's
country that she was unaware of the surge of bodies that
imprisoned her. Even Roget's presence went unnoticed.

As Roget approached his wife to lead her from the ship,
he could hardly believe how much pleasure he had extracted
from those weeks spent with her in Paris. His eye caught the
delectable fullness of her mouth, and he was poignantly
aware of how much he had enjoyed making love to her, how
wantonly he had indulged himself. In Paris he had allowed
himself that indulgence, but he was back in Haiti now and
things would have to change. Paris was in the past, he
decided adamantly. Besides, he loved Lucienne. He would
always love her, his mind insisted.

"Well, *madame,* we have arrived," he said, drawing
Lauren's attention from the excitement of the city. "Before
you lies our capital, Port-au-Prince."

Startled, Lauren glanced quickly over her shoulder at the
sound of his voice and then turned back again, unwilling to
sever her attention from the exotic scene for even a moment.

"It's different from anything that I had imagined. Not like
Paris . . . or even Marseilles . . ." Her voice faded as she
groped for comparisons.

"I hope you didn't expect it to be," Roget broke in. "Like
Paris, I mean. I tried to prepare you, but you could not
possibly have understood. Haiti has to be seen to be
believed." His tone was suddenly wistful, and his ebony
eyes clouded with a moody expression she had seen often
since they left France. But the look quickly fled, and Lauren
soon felt his hands slide possessively around her shoulders
as he guided her toward the gangplank. "Come, *madame.*
Old Jean will be waiting for us."

Lauren stepped onto land for the first time in nine days
and was blatantly confronted with a sweltering inferno that
could only be rivaled by Hades. Like a great ball of fire
suspended in space, the sun hung overhead, and the sky,
deep blue and cloudless, offered no shade from its blistering
heat. The blazing brilliance of color assaulted her virgin

eyes, causing them to narrow and then close in blindness. Looking to the east, there was a glow of deep orange that made blue the brightest of blues and green the richest of greens, and against them, the white buildings glowed irridescent. Lauren was more than thankful that Roget had exercised a husband's authority and insisted that she buy batiste and lawn day dresses before leaving Paris. At the time she thought it frivolous, because she could not imagine that anyplace could be so hot.

A steaming seaport lay before her, the streets littered with debris and the air full of raucous noises, but tasting the salt air and inhaling the stench, Lauren was drawn into the excitement. The harbor was alive with people, and as the de Martiers picked their way through the throng of black bodies that pressed in on them, trying to sell their wares, Lauren felt not fear, but the revelation of belonging. For the first time in her life she did not stand apart, but blended amiably with a population that ranged in color from marble beige to ebony black.

Dark women swung provocatively through the streets, their hips swaying beneath the heavy baskets that perched regally on their heads. Bare midriffs gleamed in the sunlight as white skirts swirled about dark legs showing only bare feet and now and then a glimpse of calf. Printed scarfs wrapped proud heads, and earlobes dangled beneath the weight of fake gold earrings. Their supple, feline movements fascinated her, just as Roget's pantherlike strides had fascinated her long before seeing his face.

Moving in the same lithe manner, beads of perspiration gleaming on their bare chests, the men went about their business in straw hats and cutoff trousers that exposed half bare legs. Hawking their goods in a nasal patois, they shouted lewd remarks as they were forced aside to make way for disembarking passengers.

A wiry black man wound his way through the crush of moving bodies and approached the dock. Age had hunched his back, and Lauren guessed him to be near seventy years of age. His twinkling eyes danced as he thrust a weatherbeaten hand at Roget.

"*Soyez le bienvenu,* Monsieur Roget." The discerning eyes then rested on Lauren, and she shifted her gaze uneasily, as she felt the man appraising her. He was fond of Roget, and female intuition warned her that the wise old man would never accept her if she did not meet with his approval.

"Lauren, this is Old Jean," Roget said, intruding on their silent intercourse. "He's been our liveryman for as long as I can remember. Jean, my wife, Madame Lauren."

The old man observed her earnestly. But despite the unnerving perusal, Lauren could not help but notice the snow white hair that burst out from under his straw hat. Woolly like a sheep's, it lacked the carefully cropped, sculptured look of Roget's. Finally, he offered her a wrinkled hand and smiled. *"Soyez la bienvenue,* Madame Lauren."

The new Madame de Martier clasped the outstretched palm. "I'm pleased to be welcomed to Haiti by so charming a man."

Old Jean beamed with the delight of a schoolboy. "It's a good thing you come back now, Monsieur Roget," he rattled on in broken French. "Things is goin' crazy around here. You always was the only one with any sense, and with you away, things done gone haywire."

Roget's brows knit anxiously. "Has something happened?"

"Nothin' that wasn't caused by them American ships in the harbor. But you'll see what I mean when you gets there." The old man's answer was decidedly cautious. It was apparent that he did not want to discuss the matter in front of Lauren. "I'm glad you found yourself a nice wife," he continued, "but I can't imagine they'll by happy none about it." He grunted and stroked his straggly white goatee.

Just at that moment, a handsome, silver-harnessed carriage pulled up alongside theirs, and Madame Duval peered from the open window. "Remember, dear, do come to visit when you are settled."

Lauren drew a labored breath, not sure what had destroyed her composure. Was it the intense heat, Old Jean's last remark, or Madame Duval's cold, icy tone that chilled despite the heat?

"Madame's not dressed proper for this heat," Old Jean

said, studying her with concern. "We better get you to the house before you has a sunstroke."

Roget glanced her way with an expression devoid of sympathy. Any second she expected him to say, I told you so. Lauren climbed into the open carriage, grateful for what little shade its convertible top provided while Roget assisted Old Jean with the steamer trunks. Surreptitiously, he shouldered most of the weight himself, sparing the old man's crippled back.

Turning her attention to the raucous chatter that surrounded her, Lauren was puzzled when she realized that she could not understand their language. It sounded like French, and yet it in no way compared to the impeccable French that Roget spoke.

At long last, the carriage rolled through town, northward to the Cul-de-Sac Plain. Oriental bamboo trees lined the road, and vermillion red blossoms peeped out between green leaves and gave the air the sweet, musty smell of a greenhouse. Heaven had truly blessed this country if only for its beauty. On the outskirts of the city, gingerbread mansions nestled deep within stone walls. Obscure winding paths led to the entrances of these miniature castles, whose pastel exteriors were flanked with lacy iron balconies and intricately carved towers reaching skyward. Enchanted by the beauty of these villas, Lauren grew anxious to see her husband's family home.

But long, dusty, and hot, the journey droned on, sapping both her strength and her enthusiasm. She swallowed hard, trying to moisten her dry, parched throat. Roget hoisted an eyebrow at her discomfort.

"You look faint. Are you all right?"

"I'll be fine if I can just get out of this heat. It's brutal."

"I imagine it is." This time his voice was touched with sympathy. "I suppose it is hard to bear when you're not accustomed to it."

"It doesn't seem to bother you much," she replied, amazed at his ability to remain unruffled despite almost anything, including the heat.

"I was born here," Roget answered. "That does make a difference. But I also warned you to wear something less cumbersome, didn't I?"

"There's no relief from the sun. It's everywhere. There is no shade, no way to cover yourself." If only she had followed his lead, she thought regretfully. He wore white linen and a straw hat.

"You'll find the plantation more bearable. The trees provide a good deal of shade. That is, if my brother has not cut them down." His voice slashed the air like tempered steel. "Coffee beans need the shade."

"Oh!" she muttered in surprise. "I didn't know that."

"*Madame,* there is a great deal that you don't know about life here. I only hope that you'll not be as temperamental as the coffee beans." His sultry mouth curled slightly at the corners.

Lauren smiled through closed lips. "Don't think for one minute, *monsieur,* that you'll have an excuse to send me back to France." Settling back in her seat, she was determined to endure the journey in silent fortitude.

The carriage rumbled over a dirt road that was sheltered by palm trees and other foliage for which Lauren had no name. The exotic, green density of the foliage gave her the feeling of being enclosed in a jungle. Three young men working in the shade beneath the trees waved and called to Roget. Smiling amiably, he ordered Old Jean to halt the carriage.

"*Soyez le bienvenu,* Monsieur Roget." The tall thin one approached Roget's side of the carriage.

"*Merci,* Toussaint."

Another man, beads of perspiration trickling over his muscled ebony chest, studied Lauren intently and then questioned in broken French, "Is this your lady, Monsieur Roget?"

"*Oui,* Christophe, *c'est ma femme,* Madame Lauren." Inclining his head toward each in turn, Roget repeated their names. "Toussaint, Christophe, and Alexandre."

"*Comment allez-vous,* Madame Lauren." Replying in unison, proud of the paltry French, their voices blended like a boys' choir.

"*Bien, merci.*" Lauren smiled.

Following their meager attempts at French, they lapsed into a language she could not understand and exchanged what apparently were very serious words with Roget. It was strange to hear him speak the unfamiliar tongue. As the men returned to their chores, Lauren settled back against the leather seat.

"What language was that? Is it the same one I heard at the pier?"

"Creole," Roget replied, his fingers restlessly turning the brim of his straw hat.

"Don't they speak French?"

"Some do but not fluently. Only the house servants speak French well. Creole is the native patois, the remnants of African dialects mixed with French and a few other things."

Looking up at him curiously, she mused. She had discovered another fact about her husband she had not known. "You speak it so easily," she added.

"I work with them every day. I have to speak their language. But everyone here speaks Creole. French is spoken only among the upper class." He paused and flashed a perceptive grin. "You will learn Creole in time. I have no doubt about that."

Rumbling onto another dirt road, this one as wide as a Parisian boulevard, the carriage emerged onto a clearing that was a beautifully manicured labyrinth of foliage and sculptured hedges carpeted with lush green grass and brilliant red flowers that crawled along the ground. Old Jean pulled the horses to an abrupt halt.

"Is this it?" Lauren gasped breathlessly, overwhelmed by its size. "Is this your home?"

"This is Villa de Martier." Roget answered in a matter-of-fact tone as he leapt down from the carriage.

Lauren was spellbound. She gazed, entranced, at the massive structure, unable to tear her eyes away. Composed of rose-hued brick and golden stone, the villa's main entranceway had a carved triangular pediment supported by Ionic columns that suggested a Greek temple. Three stories high, the two main floors were graced with floor-to-ceiling windows, those on the second floor opening onto iron filigree balconies. Stone balustrades framed the triple flight of stairs that led from the garden to the main door. But in this lush, tropical setting, Lauren thought the grand structure seemed misplaced. Unlike the charming gingerbread mansions that had enchanted her along the way, Villa de Martier, despite its splendor, looked cold, austere, and uninviting.

Roget extended his hand to assist her from the carriage, and she stepped down.

"It is impressive," she uttered, finally shifting her gaze from the house to her husband. "But it seems to belong in one of the provinces of France."

"After acquiring his wealth, my great-grandfather went on a tour of the Continent and was enchanted by the chateaux in the Loire Valley. He returned to Haiti and spent the next seven years building a facsimile of one."

It was late afternoon, and the Haitian sky glowed a deep red as the sun began to wane. The new Madame de Martier lifted her skirts, climbed the triple flight of stairs, and entered the house with her husband close behind. A beautiful black woman, lithe and graceful, met them inside the doorway. Her turquoise skirts and headwrap were silk, and the bangle bracelets and dangling earrings were definitely gold. She was too young to be Roget's mother, and yet she stood pompously with one hand on the door, a "mistress of the house" air about her.

"*Soyez le bienvenu, monsieur.* Madame de Martier awaits you in her parlor." Her French was overly pretentious.

"*Bonjour,* Filene," he said curtly. Lauren noticed he withheld the easy smile he had given the others. His introduction of the two women was brusque and to the point. "Filene, my wife, Madame Lauren. Filene is our housekeeper."

"*Soyez la bienvenue, madame.*" The woman smiled and bowed her head but just barely. "You and *madame* will occupy the yellow rooms in the east wing as you requested, *monsieur.* I will have León take your things up immediately."

Roget uttered an abrupt "*Merci*" and guided Lauren through the main vestibule to his mother's parlor.

He knocked softly and a faint voice beckoned, "*Entrez.*" Reclining on a tapestry sofa, a snifter of brandy cradled in her hand, the elder Madame de Martier almost threw aside the crystal glass and sprang to her feet as she caught a glimpse of Roget. She rushed toward him and hurled herself in his arms. She embraced her son, her mouth kissing his face and murmuring intermittent sighs of joy.

Roget held her long and hard, burying his face in her silky chestnut hair. After some moments, he pulled away. *"Maman,* this is Lauren."

Madame de Martier extended a limp but well-manicured hand. "Lauren, I hope you will be happy here, since it appears you've stolen my son from me." Her tone was skeptical. Though she smiled as she voiced the words, Lauren knew that the elder woman was far from pleased with her son's choice of a bride but would tolerate her rather than alienate her son.

Clutching Roget's arm, she drew him to the deep red sofa and insisted that he join her for a drink. Lauren followed reluctantly.

"Ma chérie, please sit down." The older woman dismissed her presence with the flutter of a hand. "You must be exhausted by the trip."

"I'm fine," Lauren quipped, planting her weary body in the red Louis XV chair opposite them. "I'm not yet accustomed to your deadly sun. Paris is nothing like this."

"How well I know," she sighed wistfully. "Beautiful Paris . . . I remember it very well." The fond memories brought a glow of life to her face that could only be equaled by the light in her eyes when she set them on Roget. "What will you drink?" she inquired. "Is brandy to your liking?"

"I would prefer sherry," Lauren replied and then hesitated, "if that's no bother."

"Maman," Roget interrupted, throwing her a harsh glance. "Isn't it a little early in the day to be drinking?"

"Oh, nonsense, dear! You can be such a prude sometimes. Then perhaps your wife would rather have tea," she added stiffly.

"Sherry is just fine," Lauren retorted.

"I see she has spirit," she commented wryly, turning to Roget. "I wonder how long it will last? You will have a brandy with me, won't you, *mon chou,"* she pleaded. "Just this once."

"Just this one time, *Maman,"* he said sharply, knowing he had been baited. His mother had always been able to uncover that raw nerve in his heart that he otherwise kept shielded.

Much to Lauren's surprise, Madame de Martier's complexion was fair, like beige marble, and in the flesh, she differed greatly from the picture she had painted in her mind.

Madame de Martier handed Lauren a glass filled with golden wine and returned to sit next to Roget. Elegantly smoothing the folds of her peignoir beneath her, the motion of her arms drew attention to the ample bosom that sat imprisoned above the drawstring.

Putting the glass to her lips, Lauren let the initial sip trickle slowly over her parched throat, savoring the burning sweet moisture. The wetness washed the dust from her palate, and the alcohol was exactly what she needed to calm her jangled nerves. Catching only bits and pieces of their conversation, Lauren allowed her eyes to wander about the room. She could not fathom why anyone would want brocade draperies and tapestry chairs in such a warm climate. Inadvertently, her eye was drawn to the paintings, all French and all priceless, that graced the walls. At the Saint Germain, she was used to seeing merely reproductions of the Impressionist art that Claude loved so much, but these were the originals.

Inside, the house was cool compared to the inferno outside and offered welcome refuge from the heat. Not even the Haitian sun's powerful rays could penetrate those walls. Emptying the last drop of precious liquid from her glass, Lauren mused that if she were ever mistress of this manor, the decor would be changed to a style more in harmony with the country.

"Filene can show you to our rooms if you want to rest," Roget said, breaking into her reverie. "I'll join you in a while."

"But I've not met the rest of the family."

"Gaston is in Jacmel," their mother informed her. "He will probably not return until tomorrow."

"About the coffee shipments?" Roget inquired, a curious tone implying his question.

"No, dear, something about that Môle Saint Nicolas business," she replied, fluttering a diamond-ringed hand

and dismissing the matter as though it were no more important than a new gown. She lifted her glass and took another long swallow of brandy.

Roget's dark brow knit into a troubled frown.

"Antoine is out in the fields," she continued, only faintly aware of her son's distraction. "You will meet him at dinner."

"Then perhaps I will go up and rest," Lauren volunteered gratefully.

Filene led her to the top of the grand mahogany staircase that ascended from the main vestibule and down a long, wide hall of luxuriously carpeted parquet floors. At the end of the corridor Lauren was ushered into a suite of rooms with double French doors that opened onto a lacy iron balcony. Filene said nothing, and not knowing what she was expected to say, Lauren remained silent as well. Still unaccustomed to being waited on by servants and already aware of the intense animosity that existed between her husband and their pompous housekeeper, Lauren feared she would say the wrong thing. The ebony-skinned woman glanced at her new mistress from an oblique angle, baring both their discomforts, bid her good day, and hastily left the room.

Lauren felt a surge of relief as she noticed the bright yellow upholstery. She flung open the glass doors and drew a deep breath of the flowers that perfumed the air. Unbuttoning her shoes, she removed the kidskin boots and placed them neatly beside the bed. She then proceeded to peel off the heavy suit. Having removed only the jacket, she made the mistake of allowing her weary body to collapse, skirt and all, across the huge canopied bed. Promptly, she fell asleep.

Somewhere in her state of twilight slumber, that hazy area between being asleep and being awake, she heard Roget's low, resonant chuckle invading her dreams.

"Don't tell me Haiti has exhausted you already, *madame.*"

Gradually, evincing an obvious struggle, her heavy eyelids fluttered open. Her hazel eyes focused on her husband staring down at her, a delicious, amused grin curling the corners of his sultry mouth.

"I had León draw you a bath," he continued, "but you will have to get up if you want to take it." The amused chuckle still coloring his tone, Roget reached up and began to unloosen his cravat, as his long legs carried him to the adjoining room.

Dinner at Villa de Martier was a ritual with unbending rules. Roget, bathed and dressed, reappeared in their bedchamber. "I'll be out for a while," he said as he left the room. "I will see you in my mother's parlor about eight o'clock."

Dressing carefully in one of her new batiste gowns, Lauren brushed her bushy hair into a pouf at the crown of her head and pinned it with two ivory combs. With one long, slow turn in the mirror, she exited the room with the feeling that she could not get downstairs fast enough. Potted plants and flickering gas mantles threw lifelike shadows against the light walls. Lifting her skirts, she glided down the impressive double staircase and paused beneath the glittering brilliance of the crystal chandelier that hung in the vestibule to steady her composure. So far, on her journey through the house, she had encountered no one, not even a servant. With nervous fingers smoothing her skirt, Lauren urged her feet in the direction of Madame de Martier's parlor.

Roget had not arrived. Instead, seated opposite his mother's sofa was a tall, lean, young man whom she assumed to be Antoine. He rose from his chair and walked toward her, an amiable smile lighting his face. Taking both her hands in his, he said pleasantly, "You must be my new sister-in-law. Welcome to Haiti. I, for one, am delighted to have you."

Lauren smiled weakly. Disconcerted by his overwhelming enthusiasm, she managed to mutter, "I'm pleased to meet you Antoine." His eyes were openly pleasant, not mysterious like Roget's, and there was a gentleness about him that Lauren found appealing. Still clasping her left hand, he led her into the room and deposited her on the sofa next to his mother. She would have preferred a chair but decided to let discretion rule for this moment.

Madame de Martier was by now sufficiently intoxicated.

She maintained dignity and carried herself with poise, but behind that proud exterior, Lauren sensed more anguish than she displayed.

"I see you have recuperated, my dear." Her tone bordered on sarcasm. The dark chestnut eyes scanned her new daughter-in-law from head to foot. "Did you rest well?"

"Oui, madame. I did. Our rooms are quite comfortable."

Immediately aware of the discord between the two women, Antoine interrupted. "What will you have, Lauren?"

"Sherry will be fine," she replied. Rising from the sofa, Lauren smoothed her skirt and sat herself down in the red chair she had sat in earlier. She watched the younger brother as he filled the glasses. Just as Roget, he moved like a stalking panther, but where Roget's gestures were definitively masculine, Antoine's seemed somewhat effeminate. While his complexion made her think of roasted pecan shells and not the flawless sable of his brother, he had the same neatly sculptured head of crisp black hair.

"To you, sister-in-law." He raised the crystal glass in a toast to her. "It's good to have a young woman in the house again."

"I don't understand," she said, frowning with confusion. "Roget never mentioned a daughter in the family."

"In this family, no . . . but we once had another sister-in-law." His voice faltered. The gentle eyes clouded in that same moody gaze she had witnessed so often in Roget.

The door opened, and Roget strode in, brushing drops of water from his white linen frock coat. "It seems we arrived in time for *les Toussaints,"* he uttered with resignation. Glancing first at his wife, and then his brother, he commented, "You have met."

Like an apparition, Filene appeared in the doorway. *"Madame,* dinner is served."

Madame de Martier clung to Roget's arm as they left the parlor. Gallantly, Antoine took Lauren's hand and tucked it securely into the crook of his elbow and led her to the dining room.

Rain poured in torrents beyond the glass doors, but it was impossible to see out. The windows were shrouded in apple green moiré draperies drawn closed against the damp April night.

"How long does the rainy season last?" Lauren inquired of anyone who might be listening.

It was Antoine who supplied an answer to her curious question. "We will have rain every night from now until October."

"Does it just rain at night?"

"It seems that way." He grinned affably.

Two young serving maids under the watchful eye of Filene scampered about, carrying trays of poached red snapper, conch stew, and roasted yams.

As far as Madame de Martier was concerned, she and Roget could have been alone at the table. Bored and uneasy, Lauren ate mechanically, wondering what on earth he and his mother were talking about that could not include her. Was it always going to be like this? Madame de Martier was a pampered woman who refused to acknowledge the existence of her daughter-in-law, and Roget played into her hands.

Antoine attempted to ease Lauren's isolation, but his efforts failed miserably. Feeling deserted and angry, she merely wished for the torturous hour to be over. At least in the privacy of their bed, his mother could not come between them.

It was late when Roget, at long last, came up to bed, but Lauren lay awake, listening to the rhythms of murmuring rain outside the window. Earlier she had peered through the glass doors, but it had been too dark to see anything except the luminous silhouette cast against the sky by the arc of mountains that curled along the rear boundaries of the land. The rest of the plantation was a sea of shimmering wet treetops.

As she lay there watching her husband undress, the sight of his smooth sable skin stirred the reckless desire in her blood, but even the urgency of her desire could not quell her insatiable curiosity.

"Roget," she said softly as he slipped into bed, "Antoine told me that he had another sister-in-law. Why did you never mention her?"

He had not expected her to be awake. Startled by the sound of her voice as well as the impact of the question, he reacted sharply. "Because I would rather forget it."

"But why? Whose wife was she?"

"She was my brother Gaston's wife."

"What happened to her?"

"She died . . . in an accident . . . a terrible accident." Pain twisted the handsome features, but his expression was lost to her in the darkness.

"What happened?" Naively, Lauren persisted.

Her husband's temples pulsed. "Lauren, please! I don't care to talk about it now. We can discuss it some other time." His voice held an edge like tempered steel. She withdrew the question.

"Only if you promise to show me the plantation tomorrow," she teased, attempting to calm his irate temper.

The edge on his tone softened. "I will show you the grounds tomorrow, I promise." His irritation dissipated, and he grinned seductively. "Are you going to ask questions all night?"

The rain continued to beat down on the roof overhead, but Lauren's queries were silenced for the moment by her husband's sultry kisses. Pressed hard against the length of his lean, well-honed torso, her body yielded hungrily to the throbbing urgency of his manhood. In the heat of their passion, they soared into flights of ecstasy that carried them far beyond the discord that separated them. The problems that dwelt in the house lay quiet beneath them, at least until morning.

The empty space beside her in bed filled the new Madame de Martier with a lonely sense of desertion. Roget had already gone. Why had he not wakened her after he promised faithfully to show her the plantation today? Spurred by the aroma of fresh bread, Lauren dressed quickly and bounded down the stairs. Storming into the dining room, she encountered the elder Madame de Martier sitting alone in the small, informal breakfast room. Filene sauntered past her, giving off the strong impression that she hungered for nothing more than to be mistress of this house, while one very young serving maid percariously balanced a tray of fresh fruit.

"Bonjour, madame." In one continuous breath, Lauren blurted out her disappointment, not allowing the older woman to answer. "Where is Roget? He promised to show me the plantation today."

Madame de Martier's mouth spread in a placating smile. "My dear, please calm yourself. Sit down and have your breakfast."

Lauren pulled out a white lacquered chair and sat down, her senses struggling to smother her frustration. She had not thought about hunger until a plate of tropical fruit was placed before her followed by a basket of freshly baked breads. With the small silver knife, she cut into a juicy, ripe papaya, the only fruit she even vaguely recognized and mechanically ate the bright orange fruit.

"I have no idea where Roget is," his mother said, "but I assume he went to look over the grounds. He has been away for a year, as you well know."

"He was supposed to take me with him." Her throat swelled with bitter disappointment.

"He probably thought you were tired after the trip and did not want to wake you. They go out very early to avoid the noonday sun."

"That would not have mattered," Lauren replied. "I would not have cared how early he woke me."

"They'll return at noon for lunch. You can talk to him about it then."

Despite Madame de Martier's perfectly logical explanation, Lauren was unable to suppress that lonely feeling of desertion that crept over her. Why was she incapable of logic where Roget was concerned?

Finishing breakfast, Lauren wandered outside to the magnificent gardens surrounding the main entrance of the mansion. Resting the weight of her body against the rose stone balustrade, she wondered what in heaven's name she would find to do here every day by herself.

Roget returned at noon, as his mother predicted, and the moment he and Antoine entered the door, Lauren confronted him in the vestibule.

"You promised to take me with you today," she said heatedly. "Why didn't you wake me?"

"I should have warned you," he apologized. "We go out very early to avoid the noon sun."

"But I wanted to go with you," she said, her voice almost pleading.

"Antoine and I had a lot of ground to cover this morning, and I thought it best if we did it alone. There were details he had to fill me in on, things that have happened since I've been gone . . . things that could be of no interest to you."

"I'm interested in anything involving the plantation."

"I'll take you out this afternoon and show you the place leisurely. Besides, we have to choose a horse for you."

Disappointment faded as eager anticipation took its place.

Sitting opposite an outwardly amused Roget, Lauren managed to devour a healthy lunch. "After eating all that, I doubt that we have a horse that will hold you," Roget said, a suppressed chuckle still dancing in his eyes. "Change into your riding clothes and meet me at the stable. And remember it's hot out there," he continued as he got up to leave the table. "You will only need breeches and a shirt . . . and boots, of course. And do not forget your hat."

"I'll be wearing breeches. Does that mean I will not have to ride sidesaddle?" she inquired anxiously.

"Can you handle a horse the other way?"

"Oui." Thanks to her wild girlhood exploits, she could handle a horse both ways and secretly preferred the latter.

"I have no objections to your riding astride here on the plantation," he said. Leaving her in the vestibule, he strode toward the rear of the house.

Lauren asked directions from Filene and strolled along contentedly flicking the dry red earth with her crop. It would be fun to ride in breeches and not have to ride like a lady, she thought. Roget was waiting when she approached the stables.

"Madame, we have a lot of ground to cover," he quipped impetuously, as he ushered her inside. Old Jean began an illustrious parade of Thoroughbreds, beginning with a fine mare.

"Madame Lauren," he said in his meager French, "Monsieur Roget think that Miel be a good horse for you. She spirited but gentle, and she know the roads well." The mare was led out of her stall, and Lauren nuzzled her soft nose, liking her instantly. She was honey colored, hence, the name, with four white socks and a star on her forehead.

"She's lovely, Jean, but I would like to see the others as well."

"Oui, madame," he replied, his eyes darting to Roget for approval.

"Jean, she's a stubborn filly." Roget grinned, folding his arms across his chest. "You might as well show her the lot and let her choose for herself."

Lauren examined eleven beautiful Thoroughbreds, but none spurred her interest except one dark chestnut bay with an elegant neck and proud, skeptical eyes.

"What about this one?" she asked passionately.

"No think so, *madame,*" Old Jean hesitated. "That was Madame Reinette's horse."

"Madame Reinette?" Her face drew a blank stare.

"Gaston's wife," Roget interrupted. "I would rather you not ride that horse." His voice was firm. This was not a request, but an order.

The animal fired her imagination, and the fact that it had been Reinette's made the challenge more enticing, but she saw the hard determination in Roget's face. For the moment, she would heed her husband's wishes, but deep in her heart, she intended one day to ride that horse.

Lauren and Roget rode the horses out of the stable and turned left onto the main road. Feeling confident astride her mount, Lauren pivoted toward her husband. "Why was Old Jean so frightened when I wanted to ride that horse?"

"Perhaps he thought her too spirited for you."

"It was more than that," she insisted. "Didn't you see the look in his eyes? He was almost terrified."

"Lauren, these people have strange superstitions," he replied firmly. "You are better off not getting involved in things you do not understand."

Perturbed by his attitude, it had become quite clear to her that he disliked her inquisitive mind.

Miel and Bleu de Roi cantered along the shaded road side by side while their riders engrossed themselves in the atmosphere. The brilliant orange blossoms of the flamboyant, the red of the immortelle, and the snow white buds of the frangipani together formed a gloriously colorful bouquet. Around them the air hung heavy with a delicious perfume, and Lauren drew a deep breath to savor its fragrance. Orange and blue parrots flitted among the trees while iguanas and other small reptiles scooted along the ground, taking on the colors of fallen leaves. A large, furry black spider crossed the path ahead of them, and Lauren jumped, a chill snaking through her spine. Roget grabbed Miel's reins and held her at bay.

"What is that?" Lauren cried.

"A tarantula," he smiled, enticed by her innocent reaction of fear. "You have to watch for them, or they will spook the horses."

They ducked onto a narrow dirt road completely sheltered by trees, and as far as she could see were tall bushes nestling in the shade of their giant relatives.

"This is the de Martier fortune," Roget said. The sweep of his hand took in the tall bushes bursting with rich, green coffee buds. He urged his blue-black stallion into a gallop, and they rode past acres and acres of the eight- to ten-foot plants standing languidly along the mountain slopes. They grew in neat rows with paths between, as though the total design had been landscaped to fit a divine plan. Men working on the slopes stopped their work and raised a hand or called a greeting to Roget. They seemed pleased that he had returned.

Galloping forward, they finally emerged in a clearing. The mountains remained behind them, but the immense rose stone mansion was far in the distance to the right and almost invisible. Here, as around the house, all of the trees had been felled except a huge one with buttressed roots. Lauren pulled Miel to a halt.

"Why is this lone tree standing here?"

"It's a mapous, the sacred tree of the vodun."

"Is there *vaudou* on the plantation?" she inquired curiously.

"The practice is forbidden, but we are not immune to its superstitions." This time his reply was more thoughtful. "Many people believe that if a mapous is destroyed, disaster will befall the family. I doubt that there is any truth behind it, but we follow the tradition blindly. We have to keep our workers content, otherwise there would be no crops."

Lauren studied her husband and discovered a part of him she had not known. Astride his horse, stripped of the elegant French clothes, he was more competent than she had imagined. With his white silk shirt open to the waist and the eggshell panama pulled sideways to shield his face, he exuded a rugged, earthy sensuality she had not experienced before. But still, the perfect fit of his breeches and the custom-made riding boots reminded her of the man she had married. Now she knew that Roget belonged here more than anywhere on earth. And though he mixed easily with Parisian society, this was truly his domain. What dreadful reality would make him even consider forsaking his home to spend his life in France?

At the end of the clearing, they faced a wall of flamboyant, its brilliant orange blossoms forming a fiery boundary as far as Lauren's eye could see.

"Our property ends here." Roget motioned toward the flaming orange barrier that faced them.

"Who owns the adjoining plantation? Do they also grow coffee?"

"The Deffands own that property. The few remaining plantations on the Cul-de-Sac Plain grow coffee, but during the time of the French planters, the largest crop was sugar."

Somewhere in the distance a voice called Roget. They turned simultaneously to see a man riding toward them. Roget urged his stallion forward and met halfway the tall, brown-skinned man who approached them. Remaining behind, Lauren could easily hear the voices that carried on the wind.

"*Comment allez-vous,* Monsieur Deffand?" Roget and the older man clasped hands in a friendly handshake.

"*Bien, merci. Et vous?* We heard that you were coming home. So, you and Lucienne finally made it legal. Come and let me kiss the bride," he called to Lauren, "or are you shy since your marriage?"

"Monsieur Deffand," Roget interrupted as he beckoned her to join them. "I had better introduce you to my wife." Lauren reined Miel in, and the older man's countenance registered shock when he saw her. It was obvious he was expecting someone else.

"Lauren, this is our neighbor, Paul Deffand. He owns the plantation that you're so curious about. Monsieur Deffand, my wife, Lauren. And you may kiss the bride."

"*Bonjour,* Monsieur Deffand." Lauren smiled, meekly offering her hand. With a gentlemanly gesture, he leaned awkwardly forward and touched his lips to her hand. Trying hard to mask his discomfort, he bid them good day and abruptly rode on. This seemed to be the kind of response she could expect from her husband's friends.

Roget galloped Bleu de Roi far back to the base of the mountains and took the road that wound around the outskirts of the plantation and then led directly into the stables. Lauren and Miel followed close behind. "This is the shortest route back to the house," he said, "but you should not take it when you are alone." Shifting uncomfortably in her saddle, Lauren did not question her husband's warning. Her derriere reminded her painfully that she had not ridden astride for many years. Roget nodded slightly at her discomfort but resisted the urge to chide her. "We had better hurry," he said. "It will soon be dusk." The horses maintained their gallop until the Villa de Martier came into view, and as they approached the stables, Bleu de Roi trotted a few steps in front of Miel. Roget twisted in his saddle, the brim of the straw hat shading his face. "Now you have seen just about all of it."

"You mean there is more!" she blurted out, astonished.

"Only the section north of the house . . . le Petit Cul-de-Sac. Nothing but tenant farmers and workers' cabins."

She listened intently, but her mind had already begun to wander, and her thoughts drifted back to Monsieur Deffand.

"Who is Lucienne?"

She had caught him off guard. He appeared startled for a moment but then recovered quickly. As they rode into the stable, he answered her calmly. "The woman I was supposed to marry."

"Did you ride together on the plantation?"

"Oui. We did quite often. Why do you ask?"

"Because Monsieur Deffand thought I was Lucienne. Didn't you notice the expression on his face when he saw me?"

"Paul Deffand has known us since we were children. Everyone assumed that Lucienne and I would marry when I returned. No one anticipated my coming home with a wife . . ." His voice trailed away, and the conversation was bluntly terminated as he dismounted and his dark eyes detected the lathered horses standing inside the stable. He knew what Lauren had no way of knowing. Gaston had returned.

Arriving too late to join the family ritual in Madame de Martier's parlor, Lauren and Roget went directly to the dining room. Lauren had changed into a white lawn gown, simple but appropriate, that accented her narrow waist and enhanced her honey-hued shoulders, and Roget was resplendent as always in a pale linen jacket and a red cravat.

"My, you are a handsome couple," Antoine gushed as Lauren slipped gracefully into her seat. Roget exchanged a brief and not very cordial handshake with his brother Gaston. A strikingly handsome man with thin lips that twisted into a sinister grin when they entered, he was more massive in size than Antoine or Roget and towered over them both. Cold, discerning eyes pierced her flesh as she felt his gaze rake over her body.

"So, my little brother has taken himself a wife. I could say I do admire your taste, but then, you always had an affinity for the simple, more earthy things of life."

Instantly confronted with the blatant animosity that existed between Roget and his older brother, Lauren could only manage a weak smile as she was introduced to her brother-in-law.

When Roget had taken his seat beside her, she felt less vulnerable. Gaston made her flesh crawl. Throughout the long, arduous dinner, his eyes continually debased her while his subtle innuendos were designed to provoke Roget. The verbal attacks on her husband set her blood to boiling, and she decided that she disliked him intensely. All three brothers had the same dark, expressive eyes, but where Roget's were mysterious and Antione's kind, Gaston's were calculating and cold.

The entire family withered under his dominance. Madame de Martier became suddenly meek and quiet, picking listlessly at her food. Antoine was no longer the glib young man she had encountered the day before, but ate in silence, attacking his food with a noticeable vengeance. Roget withdrew into the depths of his own thoughts and very conspicuously ignored Gaston's hostility. Was there no love in this family? Only a stubborn charade of blind loyalty for fear the truth would come crashing down around them. Lauren was now beginning to understand what Roget had been evading these past weeks.

Lauren prayed for the dinner to end. The hostile silence was torturous. Gaston seized the moment and capitalized on her uneasiness by taunting her.

"I am afraid, dear Sister-in-Law, that you will find Haiti rather dull compared to the glamour of Paris."

"On the contrary," Lauren replied curtly, "I find it quite exciting."

"Do you?" His head tilted upward, gesturing the question. "That's interesting, considering that your husband prefers the refinements of France to the ruggedness of life here in his own country."

"I don't believe that's true," Lauren said. "Roget has tremendous loyalties to his family and his country." As she lifted her hand and placed it into her lap, Gaston's calculating eye focused on the stones glittering in her ring.

"Emeralds?" he said in a condescending tone. "De Martier men always give diamonds." His attention shifted to Roget.

"I chose emeralds." Roget replied with a final tone that said he would give no further explanation.

Madame de Martier's glance ricocheted from one of her sons to the other. "You know Roget has always chosen his own path," she said, as if her defense of him could smooth the friction between them. Instead it fanned the flames of his animosity.

"My dear brother is more a scholar than a land baron," he chided. "Why he even allows his wife and mother to defend his honor." He threw his head back and laughed mockingly. "This is a man's country and neither of my brothers is man enough for it. Here, the weak and spineless fall by the wayside only to be devoured by those strong enough to claim what is theirs. Our mother gave birth to three male heirs." He glared at Madame de Martier as though blaming her for her children. Shifting his gaze to Lauren, he continued the attack. "Your husband, *madame,* turned out to be a scholar, a man of the books, and his brother . . . an effeminate *commère.* Needless to say, neither is worthy of his heritage. I seem to be the only man in this household, the only one born with a true title to this land."

Lauren's face flushed burgundy red with indignation. His arrogance was appalling. She fought the impulse to lash into his egotism, to strike out in fury at his tyranny. A lump filled Antoine's throat as he swallowed, struggling to control his tongue. What power did he wield over them that she had not yet succumbed to? Roget—how could he take his insults and not be provoked? Lauren was incensed if only in defense of her husband. If no one else had the nerve to speak up, she would! As her lips parted to speak, she saw the anger flare in Roget's narrowed eyes. He was furious. She had never seen him so enraged that the muscles in his neck bulged against his shirt collar and his ebony eyes became hard, piercing daggers of hate. He had always kept a tight rein on his emotions, and she had envied his ability to remain unruffled no matter what the situation. Lauren was astonished to see him capable of such cold fury.

"Gaston, as you well know, I don't need my wife, my mother, or anyone else to defend me. I am quite capable of doing that myself. I've managed to live with you for a number of years and have survived extremely well, much to your chagrin. As for my mother and my brother, I hardly think it manly of you to bully those who have no defense. If you have a bone to pick with me, I would suggest that we take it up at some other time and not at the dinner table. In polite society, it is considered in very poor taste."

Shifting his position, Roget leaned his broad shoulders back against the chair. His tone grew less agitated. "If I were not a *scholar,* as you say," he paused, his steel-edged glare meeting his brother's head on, "this place would be in shambles along with the other plantations that once flourished in Haiti. They fell to ruin because their owners were too stubborn or perhaps too ignorant to accept modern farming methods."

He had played a trump card. Gaston's huge frame squirmed awkwardly as if he were too large for the chair.

"And regarding my wife," Roget continued, his tone dripping with sarcasm, "it may interest you to know that she has what the other members of this family do not: freedom from your tyranny. Lauren answers only to me. And she, *mon cher frère,* commands a spirit you'll find difficult to suppress."

Both Antione and his mother looked on Roget with the reverence of a saviour. Antoine smiled bravely, as though he had gathered strength from Roget. Their mother sighed weakly, her sigh condoning her faith in the son that she favored, thankful that he had returned to shield her from battles she no longer had the strength to endure.

Recoiling momentarily from Roget's effrontery, Gaston turned his attention to Lauren.

"I suggest we move this amiable party to the salon. We can become acquainted over some rum. I've been told that you are an accomplished pianist. The piano there should be worthy of your talent." He smiled arrogantly. "I would like to judge it for myself."

"Gaston, we have to talk," Roget broke in impatiently. "We need to discuss the Môle Saint Nicolas." Diverting his brother's attention from Lauren, Roget reminded him that there were more pressing matters than their personal animosity.

"I'm ready . . . as soon as you can tear yourself away from your bride." His gaze raked over the slender, sinuous curves of her hourglass waist and the fullness of her derriere.

"Now," Roget answered curtly, "would not be too soon."

Gaston's strong hand firmly gripped Lauren's arm and guided her through the vestibule and into the salon. Despite his size, he moved easily and wore his double-breasted frock coat well, but his touch was uncomfortable, and his closeness made her uncomfortable. Curling his wide lips into a taunting smile, he baited her.

"According to your husband, you're a rather spirited filly." His thin, wide mouth curled even more arrogantly. "In my opinion," he added, studying her face for a reaction, "spirited horses can be broken . . . by the right rider." Releasing her arm, he left her in front of the carved mahogany doors that led into the salon as he and Roget disappeared upstairs to the library. An icy chill squirmed down her spine, and Lauren shivered in spite of the humid evening heat. She yearned to be sheltered in Roget's arms and feel the flames of his passion consuming her.

Later in the seclusion of their bedchamber, Lauren sought safe refuge in the pleasure of his body. But with all her efforts to entice him, Roget remained moody and withdrawn. His body made love to her, but his thoughts were enclosed in some far-off, troubled labyrinth.

Lauren had never imagined the day when she would have nothing to do but amuse herself, and now that it was here, she felt useless. Exploring the villa, she discovered that Madame de Martier's bedchamber resembled her parlor, with one opulent material drowning out another. The gilt-edged dressing table glittered with crystal bottles, all containing perfume and all French, as though her mother-in-law had to be constantly surrounded by reminders of her wealth to convince herself that she truly did exist.

In Antoine's room, two flowered Chinese vases placed strategically atop matching chests, showed the inclinations of an artist.

Discovering herself in Gaston's bedchamber, Lauren noticed only briefly the contents of his room, and what she remembered of the black Chinese lacquer with accents of mandarin red exuded an unsettling ambience. Despite the opulence of the other rooms, she preferred the warm yellow atmosphere and simple elegance of the rooms she shared with Roget.

At the far end of the hall on the west side of the staircase, exactly opposite her own, was a room that she had not been able to inspect. It was always kept locked.

Lauren climbed the narrow, winding stairs to the third floor and discovered, along with servant's quarters, a nursery. The large airy room, still filled with little boys' toys, guns, soldiers, hobby horses, and trains, was where Roget and his brothers had played as children. Gaston—she could not imagine him ever being a boy. How could so virulent a man emerge from an innocent child, she wondered? She stooped to retrieve a toy soldier and was overcome by the strange feeling that a child had played here more recently than Roget or Antoine. Lauren pivoted in her footsteps and descended the stairs, leaving those memories quietly undisturbed.

Roget left mornings before she awakened and did not return until dusk. At dinner there was the usual stifling formality, after which Roget and Gaston sequestered themselves in the library until well after midnight. Sensing the serious nature of the Môle Saint Nicolas affair, Lauren wondered why Roget had not discussed the problem with her. The only time he seemed to belong to her was at night in their bedchamber, and she hated herself for relishing these moments as the sole relief from her solitary existence. One could easily be tempted to seek refuge, as her predecessor had, in a brandy bottle.

Lauren knew that his mother merely tolerated her, but one morning as she sat at the piano, her fingers skipping playfully through practice exercises in a futile attempt to amuse herself, Lauren looked up in surprise as Madame de Martier entered the salon.

"There was a time when I played like that . . . ," she said, her eyes dewy from restrained tears.

"Why did you cease playing?"

"I used to play for Roget and Antoine when they were boys. My Roget was fascinated by the instrument," she said, musing as though it had happened yesterday. "And once I found him inside trying to figure out its mechanics." Lauren winced at the way she called him "my Roget," but she continued her reverie, completely oblivious to her daughter-in-law's presence.

"He would climb over and under the piano wanting to see what made it work. He always wanted to know things . . . always wanted answers. Roget would sit for hours and listen to me play the piano," she murmured, her voice fading to a whisper.

"Why did you stop?" Lauren inquired again.

"My husband forbade me to play for his sons." Her voice cracked sharply. "He did not think that piano music was a masculine enough pursuit for his male heirs . . . and I, having no reason to play, lost interest." Clutching the half-empty glass as though it were the only life preserver on a sinking ship, she lifted it to her mouth. "You are fortunate," she said. "At least you can play for your own pleasure." She tilted the snifter and took a long sip of the amber liquid. "What *have* you been doing with your time?" she asked, letting the glass drift from her mouth. The question seemed more an afterthought than genuine interest.

"Mornings I practice, afternoons I ride." And then, lifting her eyes to meet the subtle perusal, she asked, "Do you ride?"

"Not much anymore," the elder replied listlessly. "There was a day when I was young and full of *joie de vivre* just as you are . . . When I was mistress of the house, that filled my day." She paused, struggling to suppress the anger that hid beneath her sigh. *"Mistress.* That's a laugh. I was not even mistress then. No woman has ever been mistress of this house. I've only lived here, borne my children here, and died here."

"How can that be—" Lauren blurted the question without thinking and then recalled Filene's pompous behavior.

"My dear Gaston decided that I was ill and needed rest and so relieved me of my household duties, making me no more than a guest in my own home. The duties of house-keeper were bestowed on Filene, and she has since become its mistress . . ."

"Madame, there is a room at the end of the hallway that is always locked . . . I was wondering . . ."

"Reinette's room." She answered before Lauren could finish phrasing the question.

"Why is it locked?"

"My son ordered it closed after her death, and no one has entered it since."

"How did Reinette die?" Lauren seized the opportunity to find the answers to some of her questions. "Roget said she had an accident."

"A horrendous accident . . . We have never discussed the circumstances."

"But why?" Lauren had difficulty believing what she was sure her ears had heard.

"Gaston forbade it." Her caustic tone divulged an inherent disdain for her eldest son.

"He certainly issues a lot of orders," Lauren retorted.

"You will learn, *ma chérie.*" Her voice had become sadly reminiscent. "I had spirit like yours, and so did Reinette, but this family of males has a way of taming fiery females."

Her glass was empty and she left the room, Lauren assumed, to refill it. As she closed the piano lid, Lauren felt that perhaps she had closed the gap, just a little, between Roget's mother and herself.

The topic at the dinner table that evening revolved entirely around the Môle Saint Nicolas, and invariably it embroiled Roget and Gaston into a feverishly heated discussion.

"First, the Clyde Steamship Company, and now this. What other scheme will they try to shove down our throats!" Gaston slammed down his knife and glared across the table at Roget. "That Negro statesman—an ex-slave they sent us—and you defend him."

Lauren cringed at his sardonic slur on the word *slave.*

"Ex-slave or not," Roget broke in, "the man is brilliant. Would you have preferred a man like Rear Admiral Gherardi, a white American who has no understanding and even less empathy for a people of African descent?" Roget pushed back his chair and folded his arms boldly across his chest. "You seem to forget, *mon frère,*" he began again, "that Toussaint *and* Christophe, as well as our illustrious ancestors, were ex-slaves."

"It's a loathsome fact I would prefer to forget," Gaston replied bitterly.

"It would serve you well to remember it . . . or we may find ourselves in that unfortunate position again, this time with the United States as our masters instead of France."

"And if so, Frederick Douglass will facilitate it."

"I find that hard to swallow."

"Of course, *mon cher frère,* you would always be on the side of the scholar even when he's against Haiti."

"I don't believe Douglass is against Haiti. He's merely caught in a precarious situation. Loyalty to his own country, vile as she may be, and loyalty to his kindred, a people of African descent, is placing him at opposite ends of the spectrum."

"And time will prove you wrong. His strongest loyalty is still to his ex-masters. He has already tried to convince Firmin and Hyppolite that the leasing of Môle Saint Nicolas would be in Haiti's best interests."

"The final decision still rests in Hyppolite's hands," Roget answered, a look of frustration crowding his face.

"Hyppolite is inclined to be more than favorable to the United States in granting this concession, because of the aid she provided in overthrowing Légitime."

"Perhaps, but I think he will be more inclined to be swayed by the wishes of the Haitian people. It was we who put him in office."

"And Douglass? Will he be swayed by the Haitian people? I think not. With his back to the wall, he will sell us, little brother," the older one replied with biting condescension.

"Give the man a chance," Roget flared impatiently. Pushing back the green moiré chair, he rose to his feet. "Just perhaps, that is what you would do with your back to the wall."

Filene hovered in the open doorway, giving hushed orders to two young serving maids, simultaneously taking in all that was said.

As Madame de Martier motioned to the housekeeper for another bottle of claret, Roget caught the subtle gesture. Flinging the linen napkin on the table, he said irritably, "Shall we continue this in the library? I don't see why *Maman,* Lauren, and Antoine must be subjected to our hostilities."

Roget and Gaston carried their argument to the second floor, where they argued strategies until well after midnight. Yet, Lauren understood little of the grim problem that had her husband and his brother clawing at each other's throats.

* * *

Still lying awake when Roget shuffled into their bedchamber and began to undress, Lauren lay in the dark and watched him move about his dressing room. But as his smooth, hard body slipped into bed beside her, she sensed that he was in no mood to satisfy her amorous desires, not after an evening with Gaston. Lauren stirred gently beside him, her long limbs brushing against his thigh.

"Are you still awake?" he whispered, his voice almost hoarse.

"I couldn't sleep. You and Gaston were so long." Her throat quivered. "Something is seriously wrong . . . Why haven't you told me?"

"I should have known that your inquisitive mind would not be kept in the dark."

"What is Môle Saint Nicolas?"

"The Môle is a seaport on Haiti's northern coast, and the United States wants to lease it as a naval coaling station."

"And that's the reason you were called home?"

"The most pressing one. There are others . . . problems with the workers on the plantation, but they all stem from that one threat."

"Why is Môle Saint Nicolas so urgent?" she questioned naively.

"People fear that President Hyppolite might be favorable in granting the concession to the United States."

He wanted to be angry at her ignorance but realized he had never taken the time to explain Haiti to her. The edge on his impatience softened considerably, and he answered her question. "As Haitians, we cannot help fearing that once America gets a foot in our back door, she will attempt to rule the country. Our ancestors liberated us from French masters years ago, and we do not intend to have Americans as our masters now."

Lauren lay silent for a moment, her mind weighing the implications of what her husband had told her and then hesitantly posed another question. "Those American ships in the harbor that you have avoided mentioning in the company of your mother and me . . . are they part of the problem?"

"A very big part. They're warships."

"I see," she said softly as weariness claimed her voice.

Anticipating her next query, Roget lay there pondering his own thoughts on the situation and wondering how much he should tell her. Haitian women were usually shielded from political affairs. After some moments of being lost in his own thoughts, Roget was suddenly aware of the steady, even flow of her breathing and realized he would not have to tell her anything just yet. Uttering a loud sigh, he turned over and drifted into a troubled sleep.

Lauren rose and gazed at Roget's side of the empty bed. She had hardly seen him these past nights. The few hours they used to have alone together Roget now spent with Gaston, arguing over the Môle Saint Nicolas issue. And when he did finally come to bed, he was too exasperated for anything but sleep. Knowing the seriousness of the matter that claimed his attention, she longed for his companionship, to be a part of his life, to share the burden of his problem, and she bitterly resented being shielded from reality as though she were a child.

Roget de Martier pulled the straw panama from his head and rubbed his forearm across his brow. His handsome, sable features squinted against the glare of the noonday sun. It seemed unusually hot this morning, he thought, but he had worked through many days like this without feeling sticky and irritable. Why was he finding it so damn difficult to concentrate today, today of all days when so many things needed his attention. His dark eyes traveled up toward the mountain slopes and lingered on the bare, sweat-drenched backs of the men laboring in his soil. He could never ask more of them than he did of himself. There was so much unrest over the Môle Saint Nicolas that the men were fearful and skittish, like unbroken horses. He called to Christophe in a lilting Creole that lingered in the still air. "Let's break for lunch, the sun is unbearable." Yanking the gold watch from his pocket, Roget glanced at its face. It was earlier than usual.

Christophe grinned amiably and said, *"Oui,* Monsieur Roget." The young man's grin was his secret acknowledgment of the extra half hour of break time. As he ambled off to signal the other men, his head bobbed with satisfaction. It felt good to have Monsieur Roget back. The men liked to work for him far better than they did for his mighty high brother. Roget treated them like they were human, even if they were not from his class. Not like Monsieur Gaston, who came around shouting orders and then left with the wind at his tail like he was afraid of putting dirt on his fancy clothes. He had seen Monsieur Roget unclog the machines with his own hands and even help to lift heavy sacks on the carts. Elite folks never did any work like that. And he even ate with the men sometimes.

Never, never would they forget when Jacobin's woman came to bear a child and fell to sickness and Monsieur Roget came for her and carried her in his fine carriage to the big villa and had the doctor to tend to her. His mighty high brother looked furious. And when Cicéron broke his leg and fell sick with fever, Monsieur Roget made the belly of all his children full. Some say he paid the money from his own pocket. It was good, good having him home.

Placing the soft straw hat back on his head, Roget strode to the satinwood tree where Bleu de Roi was tethered and freed the reins. The stallion reared his head high and pranced on two front hooves as the sun glistened over the blue-black sheen of the animal's coat. Wistfully, Roget turned his eyes up toward the azure blue sky and for some unexplained reason could only think of that rainy afternoon in Paris when he and Lauren had made love between the first and second courses of their meal. Though he wanted nothing more at this moment than to bury himself in the delicious warmth of her body and feel her female appetite responding to his maleness, there were too many things to deal with now that he was home and he could not afford to spend precious time satisfying his passion. Those few weeks in Paris had been more than he had ever bargained for. Instinctively, Lauren had given him a more exquisite pleasure than he had known. They had lived carefree days in France, but matters were pressing here, especially when Haiti's freedom was in serious jeopardy.

The damp shirt clung like glue to his back, and he felt a familiar tightening in his groin. Roget swung into the saddle and turned Bleu de Roi toward the mountain road.

"If I'm not back by two o'clock," he called to Christophe, "start the men on those bushes bordering the road. I want those weeded first. Besides," he continued, his brow knit in thought, "I will probably go straight to the warehouse."

"Roget," Madame de Martier gave a cry of delight as her son strolled into the vestibule. "How delightful to see you in the middle of the day."

Bending forward to touch his lips to his mother's cheek, he questioned impatiently, "Where is Lauren?"

"Don't you hear her?" she answered, dismissing the urgency of his inquiry. "She's in the salon." Capturing his face between her hands, the older woman pulled him to her and planted a gentle kiss on the side of his mouth.

"Maman, I'm dusty, dirty, and dripping with perspiration, please let me get bathed." Irritated and uncomfortable, he pulled away and strode through the vestibule to the salon.

"Roget!" Lauren looked up from the piano to find her husband quietly enjoying the strains of her music. "What are you doing home at this time of day?"

"Watching you, *madame."* He flung the words over his shoulder as he turned to leave. "I'm going to clean up. I will see you at lunch." He crossed the room in those same long, easy strides that had captivated her from the moment she met him.

Seeing him at lunch was an exciting diversion in her otherwise mundane day. Throughout the meal Roget said very little and what he said was directed at his mother. Several times Lauren felt his dark, moody gaze caressing her and was certain Madame de Martier had noticed also. As she looked up, about to put the fork in her mouth, his ebony eyes locked with her hazel ones. Unable to swallow another bite of food, Lauren shamefully lowered her eyes for fear that he and worst of all his mother would read her thoughts. Lauren wondered if the older woman had ever felt for her husband the burning desire Roget had aroused in her with just a look.

He had to be aware of how little time they had had together these last few days. Having lost her interest in food, she excused herself and walked stiffly upstairs to her bed-chamber.

"Mon chou, you have hardly eaten anything," Madame de Martier protested as her son left the table to follow his wife.

Lauren had barely closed the door when it clicked open again and Roget strode in behind her. The freshly bathed scent of him mingled with the musky aroma of his cologne and rekindled that delicious fire in her loins that had never been extinguished last night.

"You didn't eat very much," she commented with wifely concern. "Why did you come all the way home for lunch if you were not hungry?"

"I was hungry." Roget's mouth curled into a provocative grin. "Perhaps not for food." He moved in behind her, letting his hands span the narrow arc of her waist. His lips brushed the side of her face and trailed over her neck to her earlobe, leaving every spot in his path inflamed. Pressing his ample mouth against the velvet soft skin at the base of her neck made Lauren squirm with pleasure as tiny trickles of desire tingled down her spine. Gently forcing her head back, he smothered her mouth beneath his own, slowly savoring the sweetness of her full, shapely lips as they surrendered to his kiss. Enjoying the soft, velvety texture of her mouth as it entwined playfully with his, Roget instinctively pulled her closer, only to feel her resistance.

"What will your mother think?" she asked, absolutely convinced that they would break some unwritten code of decorum. Roget reached up and pulled the ivory combs from her hair, letting the tight curly mass fly free.

"She will think that her lecherous son wants to make love to his wanton wife in the middle of the afternoon. Why?" he grinned. "Are you still worried about your reputation as a lady?" His dark gaze confronted her teasingly. "Believe me, *ma chérie,* that went to hell long ago," he whispered, his lips still brushing her neck.

"And you were the one who sent it to hell," she chided. With one hand behind him, Roget turned the brass key in the lock. Unbuttoning the pleated front of her shirtwaist, his fingers traced the ruffled neckline of her chemise and brushed tauntingly over the smooth delectable valley of her cleavage before untying the satin bow. Lauren trembled with anticipation. Roget's touch sent a surge of reckless desire racing through her spine to linger deep in her middle.

"Why do women wear so damn many clothes?" he murmured impatiently.

"Probably to keep us from being ravished by impatient husbands," she replied. Coiling her arms about his neck, she allowed him easy access to her body. "At least I've eliminated one piece of feminine propriety," she added. "I've done away with my corset. Haitian society will most likely never forgive me for that indiscretion."

Roget's gaze followed the narrow, hourglass line of her waist where it blossomed into her derriere.

"You don't need a corset," he said softly, his arms molding her against him. Roget's hands spanned her middle and then slid over the skirt that covered the voluptuous curve of her hips. His sultry lips descended on the smooth, honey-hued cavern of her shoulder, while Lauren squirmed beneath the excruciating pleasure evoked by his kiss.

Rising to his full six feet, Roget began to strip his own clothing. With eager anticipation, Lauren unbuttoned the shirt down to his breeches and let her fingers fondle the smooth skin of his back and the power of the muscles that lay tensed beneath it. A piercing thrill crawled slowly down his spine and settled in the heat of his groin and he trembled with an uncontrollable desire. Lacking the assistance of León, his valet, Roget struggled with his boots until finally one of his legs was free. Lauren, wearing a satisfied grin, assisted with the rapid divestment of the other.

Reclining langorously across their yellow canopied bed, Lauren opened her arms and Roget entered them eagerly. Her honey-hued form molded taut against him and feeling the heat of her body searing into his, Roget thought for sure he would be consumed by the flames. Her hazel eyes gleamed and as his ebony gaze held her captive for one long suspended second in time, he realized her unabashed love for him. Lauren's lips parted and Roget sought them with an unbridled hunger, his sweet, sultry kiss plummeting them into a world beyond reality.

Skillfully, he feasted on the nectar of her skin. Slowly, as though he meant to remember each kiss, his mouth caressed and taunted her until they were both beyond any sense of reason. The scorching inferno he ignited in her loins burned through her like volcanic lava, and she gasped breathlessly with the painful pleasure of suspended fulfillment.

Lauren's graceful fingers savored and explored Roget's smooth, well-honed masculine form and then traced a path over the muscles of his back and along his spine to the hard muscles of his buttocks. Roget shivered with an involuntary fever. Her touch had set in motion a trembling in his belly that threatened to explode every nerve in his body. Lauren's fingers burrowed deep into the crisp, dark hair that covered his head as she drew him closer, and she felt herself being submerged beneath the undulating waves of bliss that ebbed against the walls of her womb, stimulated and sustained by Roget's searching kisses.

They had forgotten, for the moment, loneliness, isolation, the Môle Saint Nicolas, and the scandalous fact that it was midday in the de Martier empire. Roget could think of nothing else at this moment and he ceased to try, surrendering himself to the exquisite promise of pleasure that lay beneath him with arms entwined about his neck. Lauren's thoughts were consumed by the heat and power of his passion and the thundering wave they rode together to ecstasy.

Chapter

9

The torrid afternoons blistered feverishly in the tropical heat and seemed only to be tempered by evenings that brought torrents of cool tropical rain. Three days passed before the glow of that rapturous afternoon with Roget dimmed in Lauren's memory and then merely because other matters took its space. Gathering her hat and her crop, Lauren looked at her image in the mirror and thought of the afternoon they had made love in Paris. Even alone, her face flushed burgundy red at the thought of it.

Moments later, upon leaving her room, Lauren ran headlong into Gaston, his massive body stationed arrogantly against the balustrade at the top of the stairs. Startled at finding him there in midafternoon, she gasped aloud as her hand flew unconsciously to her breast. His mouth stretched to a broad grin, and a powerful hand gripped her arm.

"Don't tell me I frighten you," he said, his dark eyes staring boldly into hers. "Why would you be in such a hurry? Where would you have to go this fine day that is so urgent?"

Pulling her trapped arm free, she asked curtly, "What are you doing here at this hour? Is Roget—?"

"Your amorous husband is overseeing the grounds today." His bold, dark gaze raked her from head to foot, and twisting deviously, his wide mouth emitted a tone that continued to taunt her. "So, *ma chérie,* I'm enjoying an afternoon of relaxation."

Her body stiffening, Lauren drew back indignantly. It took all of her willpower not to lash him across the face with her crop. Turning abruptly to descend the stairs, she retorted, "If you will excuse me, my horse is waiting, and I find her more pleasant company than some people."

His dark glare pursued her down the stairs while his voice called after her, "You take well to britches, dear Sister-in-Law. Could it be you prefer them to gowns?"

The nerves in her bristled, but she denied him the satisfaction of acknowledging his lurid comment. Instead, she leapt two steps at a time to the vestibule below and bounded into the blazing heat. Pulling the straw panama snugly onto her head, she ran blindly to the stables. Old Jean obeyed her order and immediately saddled Miel, and she took off in a rage of fury toward the base of the mountains, the path Roget had forbidden her to ride. Galloping hard past acres of green coffee bushes, Lauren did not rein Miel in until they had reached the clearing.

Now she understood why Roget disliked his brother, and she agreed. Ahead she spied the wall of immortelle trees, their bright orange blossoms blazing in the sun as they saturated the air with a sweet, heady fragrance. Surrounded by so heavenly a sight, Lauren forgot Gaston, for God's beauty should not be wasted on human baseness.

Allowing mind and body to relax, Lauren surrendered herself to the omnipotence of nature. Miel flicked her tail and twitched her mane to ward off the pestering flies while her mistress nuzzled her nose and softly stroked her head, apologizing for the hard ride. Gazing overhead, Lauren let her eyes dance from tree to tree following exotic birds in their pursuit of nuts and wild berries. Her thoughts fled to the tiny canary finches Roget had given her, which she had left behind because they could not have survived the ocean voyage.

A voice rang through the thicket, and she looked up to see a young woman riding toward her. Her complexion was a rich chocolate brown and her hair black, judging from the bushy wisps that had escaped imprisonment beneath the wide-brimmed hat. Dressed in breeches the same as she, Lauren could not stifle the twinge of envy that pricked her soul as she noticed the way the other woman's voluptuous body filled her shirt and pants.

"Hey, *salut!*" the young woman called, reining her mount to a halt. "You must be new here. I'm Georgette Deffand." She extended a beautifully manicured hand.

"Lauren de Martier," Lauren volunteered, accepting the friendly gesture. "We seem to have the same unconventional taste in riding clothes."

"You're Roget's new wife. Paul told us he had met you several days ago."

"Are you Paul's wife?"

"Heavens, no! He's my father-in-law. I am married to his son, Jacques."

"He was rather surprised when Roget introduced me," Lauren commented.

"Oui, he was, but don't let it bother you. I am something of an outcast here myself."

"Outcast?" Lauren repeated the word as though its sound was painful.

"My husband was supposed to marry another woman just as yours was . . . some élite mulatto woman. Needless to say, his family and half of Haiti were more than shocked when he arrived home with me. I can certainly sympathize with you," she said, her gaze reaching out to Lauren with a knowing expression. "Things have calmed though. They are finally beginning to accept me, except for the subtle innuendos voiced every now and then."

"You are not Haitian," Lauren inferred as she dismounted and looped Miel's reins around a tree.

"Heavens, no! A Haitian woman would not be caught dead dressed like this. I'm from Martinique."

She slid from her saddle and tethered her horse to the same tree. "And you, of course, are from France. Ah, Paris," she sighed aloud, "my husband has promised to take me there one day."

The young woman's deep brown eyes smiled warmly, and for Lauren it was the most welcoming gesture she had encountered since arriving in her husband's country.

"Tell me," Lauren queried. "What do you do to occupy

your time?" It was a question asked half in jest but born of sheer desperation. "I'm going mad for lack of something constructive to do."

"Before Jacques's mother died, I had the same problem. Now I have the household to manage, but before that I read magazines all day."

Lauren nodded wistfully. "I have nothing to do in that house except amuse myself. I feel like a guest."

They stood for a while, their backs supported by the sturdy trunk of a frangipani tree and pondered the ironic similarity of their situations. With a sudden flicker of anticipation, Georgette twisted round and asked eagerly, "Would you like to go shopping tomorrow? I've found a wonderful dressmaker in Port-au-Prince, and I have to order a gown for the Condé ball in June. You and Roget are going, aren't you?" Her question put a fence around Lauren's wandering thoughts.

"I don't know. No one has mentioned it to me." Lauren imagined what fun it might be. She had never been to a ball.

"I hear from Jacques that Frederick Douglass has been invited," the young woman continued, attempting to share her concealed excitement with Lauren. "You know, that Negro American who is consul general here, the one in the middle of all the controversy."

"I know very well," Lauren nodded in recognition. "Roget and his brothers talk about nothing else every night at dinner."

As if she felt the dispirited tone in her companion's voice, Georgette pleaded, "Do come with me tomorrow. It would be a joy to have company for a change. I've not yet made any friends, except Jacques's of course, and their wives are terribly hincty." She gestured, raising her nose to the air and placing a finger beneath it. The two women burst into a hearty laughter. "Please say you will go. It is just not considered proper for an élite woman to be out alone," she said, repeating the haughty gesture. Again they laughed, this time with the heartiness of newfound camaraderie. Beneath Georgette's humor, Lauren recognized another woman as starved for female companionship as she.

"I would love to accompany you, but how do we get

there? Not on horseback, I hope. I doubt that my derriere could stand it," Lauren smiled. Accepting the offer of friendship, she felt as though she had gained an ally.

"My carriage will call for you tomorrow morning, about nine. We'll arrive in Port-au-Prince with time to lunch, that is if you are willing," she hesitated, "and then have the entire afternoon to shop." The question forming in Lauren's mind had long since flashed an inquisitive frown across her face.

"Elite women never do anything unchaperoned," Georgette said in answer to her silent question. "But, I've heard of a restaurant in town where a few daring ones have begun dining alone. If you're willing, we could try it." Her dark almond-shaped eyes grew wide with defiant excitement as she studied Lauren's face for acceptance of the idea. "I hear that in Paris women are eating in restaurants and even drinking and smoking in those naughty cafés. I can't promise you anything as decadent as Paris," she continued, a smile on her lips, "but I guarantee you a guided tour of the city."

Intrigued by Georgette's sense of defiance, Lauren threw caution to the wind and agreed to join her. "I would like that," Lauren said, remounting. "I merely snatched a glimpse of Port-au-Prince when we docked."

"Au revoir." Georgette waved as they rode off in opposite directions.

Hours after her delightful chance meeting with Madame Deffand, Lauren found herself once again surrounded by the de Martiers as they gathered in the main salon. Oddly, Madame de Martier always seemed out of place in this room. It was Empire in style and, except for the crystal chandelier that hung overhead and the crystal candelabrum that graced the commode, a masculine room. Her mother-in-law's overdone femininity clashed with the simplicity of gilded Empire chairs and the elegance of an olive, red, and black Persian carpet. Though Lauren preferred this room to many of the others, she herself was not totally comfortable here. It was not a room that invited women.

Gritting her teeth, Lauren sat placidly and witnessed the

three-way banter between Roget, Antoine, and Gaston about the Môle Saint Nicolas, a discussion that noticeably excluded her and Madame de Martier. Taking refuge in the brandy, their mother paid no attention, but Lauren's alert mind was not yet ready to be stifled by Haitian society's archaic conventions. If there was a crisis pending, certainly the women had a right to know.

Roget turned briefly away from his brothers and his eyes locked with her hazel ones in a silent communication. Roget's eyes lingered there, and then he let his gaze fall to the enticing pout that clamped the fullness of her lips together. Time was growing short. They would have to reach a decision tonight, if it took all night.

Roget knew he would have to concentrate. There was no time for frivolous thoughts of making love, even though, at the moment, he could think of nothing but the feel of Lauren's body as it molded into his. He would have to put a tighter rein on his emotions, this insatiable desire could not get the better of him.

Deliberately averting his gaze, Roget turned back to a discussion that had grown decidedly more intense.

"Hyppolite made the mistake of going to the United States for aid in defeating Légitime," Gaston ranted.

"But that does not mean he will agree to the leasing," Antoine injected innocently.

"Why do you think they lent their assistance—out of the goodness of their hearts? Don't be a fool, little brother!" Gaston bellowed impatiently. "He had to promise them something."

"Perhaps. Yet we still don't know if the Môle is what was promised."

"No matter what was promised," Gaston replied, his huge frame shifting uneasily in the rigid chair, "the problem is he left the door open. Having gone to the United States for assistance, they now feel justified to meddle in Haitian affairs."

"There is nothing to be gained by arguing what is or what isn't," Roget broke in impatiently. "The main issue is, what are we as Haitians going to do about it?"

"I'm in favor of telling them to get out once and for all

and to take their loyal Negro statesman with them," Gaston flared hotly. Rising from his chair, he paced the length of the floor.

Roget waited until his brother walked back toward him and then stated calmly, "That would be the wrong move. I'm against the leasing, not against Douglass."

"Douglass is favoring it as advantageous to Haiti," Gaston injected irascibly.

"From his point of view, he is probably right," Roget continued, "but from the Haitian point of view it would be occupation."

"At least there is something on which we agree, *mon frère.* We are both against an American naval base in Haiti."

"Agreed. But a power play is not the answer. A more discreet diplomacy is needed."

Gaston's condescending tone failed to get a rise of anger from Roget, so he mockingly cast a derisive glance at their younger brother. "And you, little brother?" he questioned, his animosity emphasizing the word *little* even though Antoine stood well in range of six feet.

"I'm opposed to letting the Americans gain a foothold in our country. But I agree with Roget; it must be handled diplomatically."

"And just what do you two diplomats propose?" Gaston retorted.

"I think we should meet with Hyppolite and Firmin and see exactly where they stand, then proceed from there," Roget suggested. "If we put enough pressure on him, let him know just how strongly the Haitian people feel, he has to succumb. Whatever hold the United States may have on Hyppolite, the Haitian people have a stronger one."

Gaston moved to the doorway and rang for Filene.

Filene appeared in the doorway, uttering an obediant *"Oui, monsieur."*

"Filene, have coffee and a decanter of rum sent to the library. And keep in mind that we do not wish to be disturbed."

"Oui, monsieur," she repeated parrotlike as she exited the room. In front of Gaston, her pompous airs were carefully subdued.

As the men rose to leave, Lauren knew instantly that Roget would be sequestered in the library for hours.

"Lauren, why don't you play for *Maman?*" he suggested and strode determinedly from the room.

Hours passed while Lauren lay in bed unable to sleep. Turning onto her stomach, she had finally begun to drift into twilight when she heard his footsteps come through the door. "Roget," she uttered his name softly as she turned over and strained her eyes to see through the velvet blackness that encompassed him. "I didn't expect you for hours."

"I managed to get my point across more easily than I thought. Gaston finally agreed to the idea of a meeting with Hyppolite." Just as Lauren was about to verbalize one of the many questions that had raced through her mind, Roget passed an idle comment that changed the subject.

"You were not the least surprised when Gaston announced our invitation to the Condé ball."

"I knew about it." Her lips curled into a self-satisfied grin, but the gesture was lost to him in the darkness.

"How did you know?" he questioned, the tone of his perplexity reaching through the darkness.

"Georgette Deffand told me this afternoon."

"Who?"

"Georgette Deffand . . . Jacques Deffand's wife."

"Oho," he sighed heavily. "Jacques married while I was in France, but I've never met his wife. So how exactly did you meet her?"

"I rode out to the clearing today. She was there, and we stopped to talk. We shared a similar problem: endless days and seeing our husbands only at night." Her tone injected a lighthearted teasing as she sidled into the curve of his arm and let her fingers caress the smooth hardness of his chest. His body quickened in an unconscious response to her touch but then bristled with irritation as his brain registered what she had said.

"Lauren, I told you not to ride the mountain road unescorted," he scolded irascibly. Through the darkness she felt the sting of her husband's displeasure.

"I know you did, but I was furious with your brother and

wanted to get away from the house as quickly as I could. It's a bad habit of mine, *monsieur,"* she said playfully, attempting to ease his irritation, "but I become defiant when I'm angry."

"I'm well aware of that," Roget mused in silent resignation.

"Anyway, she invited me to go shopping tomorrow in Port-au-Prince."

"Good. You can purchase a few items for me. I will leave you a list in the morning. I suppose it's as good as time as any to begin your wifely duties." At that moment, his thoughts turned suddenly serious. "Why did Gaston upset you?" He paused and then added in a voice full of sarcasm, "Not that one requires a reason."

"I'll explain it some other time," she whispered, not wanting to spend the precious moments with Roget thinking about the vileness of his brother.

Lauren's graceful fingers traveled over his hard male torso, savoring every muscle and sinew in their path. Roget shuddered with a trembling fever as he felt his body swell and grow rigid from her mere touch. Unable to bear the painful ecstasy a moment longer, he rolled over and imprisoned her between his powerful thighs. Roget's lips trailed a blazing path of sultry kisses along the length of her back. Beginning at her neck, he finished minutes later at the base of her spine, having slowly savored every delectable spot in between. Each time his lips met the sensitive nerve endings in her back, Lauren squirmed with blissful pleasure.

Slowly, deliberately, his hands fondled the softness of her body beneath the lace nightgown. Lauren let out a surprised gasp as she turned to face him and then moaned as his lips trailed from one tantalizing peak through the valley to the other.

"I do not want you riding that road again by yourself," he murmured, his mouth still savoring the nectar of her skin.

"I won't . . . but you must tell me why."

"Some other time," he whispered thickly, his lips blazing a trail along her neck to her mouth.

"Roget . . . ," she said hesitantly, her voice barely audible, "I have some other questions."

"Can they not wait until tomorrow?" he questioned softly. His ample lips smothered her reply.

Port-au-Prince at twelve noon was the same bustling metropolis Lauren recalled from two weeks ago. Café Bernis was a charming French restaurant patronized by the most daring of elite women, who lunched and chattered noisily, free for the moment from the bonds of male scrutiny. After ordering a meal of conch, salad, and a bottle of white Bordeaux wine, the two young women sat back to enjoy the ambience.

"I'm so excited about the ball," Georgette said as she lifted the crystal glass to her lips. "I'm anxious to meet Frederick Douglass. If something drastic happens with the Môle affair, he probably will not attend . . . but there would probably not be a ball either."

"What could happen?" Lauren asked. "Could there be war?"

"I suppose it's possible. Jacques and his father are very much alarmed at the number of American warships in the harbor. That is all they talk about lately."

"Roget and his brothers talk about nothing else either. However, Madame de Martier and I are carefully excluded from their heated *male* discussions."

Lauren's caustic emphasis on the word *male* brought a look of disgust to Georgette's face. Loudly sucking her teeth in a deliberately unladylike fashion, she replied, "Haitian men do have the ludicrous idea that women should know nothing about politics. They seem to think that we are frail, helpless creatures that must be sheltered from the realities of life. Perhaps their treasured light-skinned women are frail and helpless, but we black women have never been allowed that luxury," she expounded with an abundance of pent-up anger.

"It makes no sense," Lauren added thoughtfully. "If there is war, we women will have to live with it as well as the men. How will they protect us when American soldiers are tramping through our streets?" Lauren smiled wryly, and she pondered the senseless irony that governed human nature.

Georgette smiled, acknowledging that she as well was perplexed by their archaic attitudes. "Who said that men were logical?"

"How do you stand it? It makes me furious when they talk over my head. And then all I hear from Roget is what Haitian women do and do not do."

"It took me a year to make him realize that a woman is an adult human being, not equivalent to a child. But he's finally seeing my point," she grinned sheepishly, "with a little bedroom persuasion on my part."

A white-aproned waiter arrived with two steaming plates of conch swimming in frothy butter and smelling of shallots.

"After this meal, I don't think we will have a problem," Lauren teased. "I doubt that Roget and Jacques will come near us."

Georgette chuckled as she pierced a piece of conch with her fork and put it in her mouth. "Anyway," she continued, "how much do you know about the Môle Saint Nicolas?"

"Not very much . . . only what Roget has told me and what I pieced together from their discussions. Roget is in favor of a meeting with Hyppolite and his minister, Firmin."

"Jacques and his father are also in favor of a meeting as soon as they can decide on a spokesman. From what Jacques says, Roget could be a strong possibility."

Selfishly, Lauren resented any deeper involvement on Roget's part, especially when she was excluded from sharing the burden with him.

Their meal finished, they set off to attend the business at hand. Lifting voluminous skirts above their ankles to avoid dragging them over the debris, Madame Deffand ordered her driver to follow them. The streets were better maneuvered on foot than climbing in and out of a carriage. Awed by the exotic sights that lay before her, Lauren welcomed the freedom to explore each winding alley. Dark columns of Haitian soldiers crawled through the streets and American warships were visible in the harbor, but not even their ominous threat could daunt her sense of adventure.

Georgette led her through a labyrinth of winding, narrow streets, stopping now and then to peer into enticing store windows. Wooden planks, constructed like a landing stage, with one end resting on the street and the other on the corridor of the premises, allowed pedestrians to pass over while water and refuse from the houses ran in the gutter beneath them. Yet, some streets could not be crossed without descending to the gutter. With smug satisfaction, Lauren chuckled as she watched a lady, her complexion hidden under a crimson parasol, picking her way along them in Parisian boots and a silk dress.

There were shops displaying the finest imported merchandise, perfume shops full of French fragrances and crystal bottles, and dress shops that lured them with the latest copies of French originals. They gazed into Simone et Mailly, a lingerie shop, which displayed the most exquisite satin nightgown Lauren had ever seen. Still unaccustomed to being able to afford such luxuries, she thought, *Perhaps just this once.*

At Georgette's insistence, they entered the shop and Lauren tried on the gown.

"Madame," the saleswoman fawned in that utterly affected tone of French *vendeuses,* "this gown was made for you. I've not seen anyone wear it better." Made of the palest peach satin and cut completely on the bias, the gown merely slithered over her slender, sinuous body. Delicate beige lace formed minute cap sleeves and an Empire bodice that framed her shoulders and cupped her small, firm breasts.

"Ah, *magnifique,"* Georgette purred, clasping her hands together with delight. "Lauren, you must buy it. The color makes your skin glow. Your husband will love it!"

"Are you sure I'm not too lean for this type of gown?" Lauren interrupted. "I'm not endowed like you," she uttered enviously as her hazel eyes unconsciously perused the other woman's voluptuous bosom. "I've never worn anything so . . . so revealing."

"Lauren, believe me," Georgette pleaded. "This is perfect for you. Roget will love it."

Lauren remembered the silk kimono and the way it slithered sensuously over her body in much the same manner. "Perhaps I will take it . . . for some special occasion," Lauren laughed. "For us it's a special occasion when we get to spend an evening alone with our husbands."

Purchase in hand, they exited the shop, but Lauren could not forget the woman's outraged expression when she signed the sales draft: Madame Roget de Martier. They weaved through a gartantuan market in the center of town, filled to overflowing with strange tropical fruits and vegetables, baskets, handicrafts, and every other commodity a consumer could imagine. In and around more twisting byways, the two women arrived at Malraux's, a gentlemen's haberdashery, where Lauren was to make purchases for Roget.

She chose carefully, always mindful of his impeccable taste, and when she had finished, the proprietor gathered her choices to tally the bill.

"And to whom do I charge this, *madame?*" His icily formal tone stung like a frostbite in its frigidness. "I don't believe you have been here before."

"That is true, *monsieur,*" Lauren replied, affecting her best drawing room French, "but my husband has shopped here for some years. It should be charged to his account."

"And who might that be, *madame?*" His voice was still ridiculously formal.

"Roget de Martier," Lauren said flatly. With blatant shock, the mulatto face went pale. Regaining his lost composure, the man went about his task wearing a mask of nonchalance, behind which Lauren knew he was hiding his contempt.

"Please sign here, *madame.*" Light chestnut eyes scanned her from head to toe, and Lauren felt he was making a comparison. *Lucienne.* Would she ever meet the elusive woman whose name haunted her existence?

Mulgrave, the Deffands' Jamaican driver, leapt down from his perch and loaded their packages into the leather-lined carriage. Uneasily, Lauren turned to Georgette.

"Did you see his expression when I gave Roget's name? The blood literally drained from his face. It happened at Simone et Mailly," she paused reflectively, "when I signed for the nightgown."

"Don't worry. You will get used to snobbery." Lauren's hazel eyes caught hers with a questioning glance. "We are treading on elite territory," Georgette explained. "These shops are the exclusive habitats of the elite. Their proprietors are the lower rungs of the upper class, who are striving greedily for the cream at the top. Though they may boast blue blood, hold most of the government positions, and comprise the bulk of the professions, they have little real wealth."

"Blue blood." Lauren shot her another questioning glance and then proceeded to answer her own question. "You mean their claim that they are descendants of the French aristocrats."

"Exactly. Black families often control tremendous wealth and land holdings, which their mulatto countrymen strive to attain through marriage. Men from wealthy black families marry fair mulatto women, who bring prestige to their lineage, and in return he brings substantial wealth to hers. Both our husbands were promised to such marriages, and they do not take the rebuff lightly. Elite women are fair. If you're a woman and your skin is darker than pale beige, you are a peasant. And to them, *ma chérie,* you and I are peasants who have had the audacity to invade their realm."

Scattered thoughts raced through Lauren's brain as she labored to place things in proper prospective. Her face must have mirrored her turmoil, as Georgette took her arm and said soothingly, "I did not mean to depress you. I've survived," she quipped lightheartedly. "You will, too. Now for the last stop on this guided tour," she smiled, "we shall see Madame Fontenelle about my gown. You will like her. She's a peasant like us."

Knowing that Georgette's chatter was an attempt to lighten her spirits, Lauren smiled weakly.

Madame Fontenelle was a thin, sepia-skinned woman with an ample bosom suppressed beneath the tight bodice of a gray gown. Framed with kinky dark hair pulled tight in a chignon at the nape of her neck, her nearly pretty face smiled widely as she ushered them inside. The tiny shop barely had window space to display one creation, but that gown was testimony to her artistry with a needle. The decor was a poorman's French provincial, and though the furnishings did not ring of authenticity as did those at Villa de Martier, the atmosphere was decidedly more pleasant.

Motioning them to sit at a small table nestled among pink velvet chairs, the couturier offered tea. A skinny black woman with white kinky hair and several missing teeth emerged from behind a gray damask drapery. With wrinkled hands, she set a silver tray on the table and disappeared again behind the drapery.

Pouring the tea, Madame Fontenelle handed Georgette the first cup and inquired amiably, "What can I do for you today, Madame Deffand?"

"I've brought a friend, Madame Roget de Martier, but I'm sure she would prefer Lauren." Her gaze darted to Lauren for approval.

"Oui, bien sûr." Lauren smiled, taking the china cup into her hand. "I'm not accustomed to such formality." The woman nodded as if she agreed that the amenities of Haitian society were ridiculously ostentatious.

"So you're the new mistress at Villa de Martier. There's been a lot of talk. My best to you." Lauren caught the flicker of apprehension in her statement. "I had heard that there was something sadistic about their father, and Gaston de Martier is the mirror image of him. Perhaps it was an act of providence that killed his son. The boy did not live long enough to inherit his father's wickedness."

"Gaston's son!" Lauren gasped, quickly steadying her cup to avoid drenching her batiste gown. "I was unaware—"

"I'm terribly sorry," the woman apologized, her voice echoing her distress, "but . . . I assumed that you knew."

"No, my husband has never mentioned him," she said pensively. She was recalling the eerie feeling she had experienced in the nursery, that a child had played there recently. "How did he die?" she asked, annoyed at being made to feel foolish for having to ask such information of a stranger.

"No one really knows. The doctors found nothing wrong with him, but every day he grew weaker. One day, he died."

"How old was he?" Lauren's query was more than curiosity.

"Seven, perhaps eight. Some blame the housekeeper," she shrugged, "but who knows for sure?"

"Wouldn't she have needed a reason?" Lauren queried.

"Who knows," Madame Fontenelle sighed. "People conjure up all sorts of reasons for justifying their misdeeds."

Obviously intent on changing the subject, she placed the empty teacup on the silver tray. Clasping both hands together over her bosom, she said "Let us discuss something more exciting, like dresses."

Echoing her tone, Georgette chimed in. "I came in search of a gown for the Condé ball. I want you to make me the most ravishing woman there. I want those hincty mulattoes to squirm with envy." As Georgette paraded about the room imitating their haughty gestures, Lauren could not help chuckling at her companion's charade, even though she knew it was all being performed for her benefit.

The old woman reappeared to gather the tray. *"Maman,* this is Lauren de Martier, new mistress at the villa."

"New mistress. Huh," the old woman grunted indignantly. "As if she-devil let other woman be mistress of house. She evil that one. She got pact with the devil. You better watch step, Madame Lauren."

"Maman! That's enough of your nonsense."

"You can shut me up, but I say truth," the old woman continued in her paltry French. "Valery de Martier sold his soul to *lougarou* to get that place. No other way to get such land in old days. He made bargain with *baka.* No one but sorceress ever be mistress of devil's house." She took the tray and vanished as quickly as she had come. Lauren sat there speechless.

"I trust you won't take my mother's nonsense seriously. She's on in years, and you know how they get. Come," she said, patting Lauren's hand apologetically. "Let us choose a gown for Georgette."

Lauren's lips curled into a faint smile, and though a gown was the last thing occupying her mind at the moment, she was able to calm her ruffled nerves and let herself be drawn into the excitement of the ball. After all, these were only the babblings of a senile old woman.

With much effort, Lauren focused her undivided attention on Georgette's gown. After trying several styles, she had chosen a lavender moiré with huge pouf sleeves and a deep V décolletage, the color of which was perfect against her chocolate skin. An excellent choice, Lauren thought.

"That gown is marvelous on you," she breathed, her lungs

inhaling very little air. "Those sleeves are all the rage in Paris, *madame,*" she teased, immersing herself in their lighthearted banter. "You *will* be the belle of the ball."

Lauren's gaze skimmed over the intricately beaded bodice of the gown, making note of the way it accented her friend's full bosom and hugged her shapely waist. Struggling to suppress the nagging tinge of envy she felt for Georgette's voluptuous female beauty, Lauren turned her thoughts on Madame Fontenelle and the mechanics of fitting the gown. A few more minutes spent on measurements and details and the two young women were on their way, the day of shopping ended.

"Let's do it again soon," Georgette said, her eyes sparkling like Christmas ornaments. "I did so enjoy your company."

"And I yours, *madame,*" Lauren jested as Mulgrave handed her down from the carriage. "We must do it again and often, I hope. You're the only friend I have in Haiti." Warmly clasping her outstretched hand, Lauren stood silent for a moment, and then gathering her packages, she climbed the rose stone stairs that led into Villa de Martier.

The day had been pleasant until now. Perhaps the old woman's babbling had been nonsense, but Gaston's son was certainly real enough. Why had Roget never told her about him? The death of a child is not something so easily forgotten. And Filene . . . Her brain flooded with inquiries, Lauren grew anxious to talk to Roget and to try to pry some answers from her elusive husband.

At dinner Lauren was noticeably preoccupied and welcomed its approaching end. Feigning a headache, she begged to be excused and fled to her room, hoping that Roget would follow, and half an hour later, Roget bowed to her wishes.

"How did you manage to escape?" She smiled coquettishly.

"You provided me with an excellent excuse," he chuckled closing the door behind him. "I had to see to my wife's health. *Do* you have a headache?"

"Of course not. It was the only plausible excuse I could think of."

"I rather doubted it, but it was a possibility. You were so

quiet during dinner, even *Maman* noticed your listlessness. But headache or not," he smiled gratefully, "I was more than pleased to get away. *Merci, madame.*" Inclining his head as though thanking her for some great deed, he looked up again and Lauren noticed the playful mood that crinkled the corners of his eyes.

Dragging herself from his gaze, she turned slightly away, determined that her questions would not be silenced by his kisses. Foolishly, she imagined that the only thing she wanted from him tonight was answers.

"What did you buy in town today?"

"Oh, nothing extravagant. Just a nightgown."

"Just a nightgown," he echoed.

"It's really quite lovely," she said, pulling her attention back to the conversation.

"Do I get to see it?"

"Of course, *monsieur.*" Taking it from the box, she held the peach satin garment against her body for him to see and then moved stealthily to the mirror to steal another look herself.

"Exquisite," he said, expressing his approval. "I like the color against your skin."

"I thought I might save it for a special occasion." Lauren folded the smooth satin garment and laid it gently in the drawer.

"And when might that be?" Roget grinned as his dark eyes galloped over the honey-hued planes of her body.

"I suppose whenever the mood strikes me." Lauren fidgeted uneasily and then finally folded her arms across her breast.

"Did you purchase the items for me?" The glint had left his eye as he turned and strode into the adjoining room.

"Everything but the cologne. They were waiting for a shipment. I had León put them in your dressing room," she answered idly, her feet following him through the door. Moving the boxes from the ebony chest where León had put them to the day bed, Roget began to examine her purchases.

"Roget, why did you never mention Gaston's son?"

He reacted slowly, as though he needed time to collect his reply. Again, she had caught him with his guard down.

"Roget," she repeated impatiently.

"I heard you," he responded, turning away from her to gaze at the rain beating against the French doors. "We don't discuss it."

"Why not?" she demanded.

"What good would it do to talk about it? He's dead. That will not bring him back."

"No, but it seems odd that a child died here and no one ever mentions his name."

"Gaston wanted it that way. And you know as well as I that my brother is odd at times."

"How did he die?" Her tone softened considerably.

Drawing the yellow draperies against the dampness of the night, Roget moved away from the glass doors. "Heaven only knows. He became ill and never recovered." His voice broke, making his words barely audible. Lauren sensed that he failed to reveal all that he knew.

"Was Filene responsible?"

"It's possible," he uttered absently. His eyes were shrouded by that mysterious gaze she had seen so often. "Lauren, I'm in no mood to discuss this now." Angrily, he shifted his gaze to her. "Who has been filling your head with these absurd tales?"

"Madame Fontenelle mentioned it while we were having tea. She took it for granted that I knew. She couldn't have been more surprised at my ignorance."

"I see nothing has changed since I left." Lauren cringed at his biting sarcasm. "Women still spend their days gossiping about foolishness that in no way concerns them. Lauren, I hadn't imagined you to be interested in such nonsense," he said, his tone bitterly berating her.

"Nonsense! How can you call it nonsense when everyone has more information about my husband's family than I do? Surely, you could not have thought I would never find out."

"If I did—knowing you—then it was a gross miscalculation on my part." The caustic edge on his voice made her shiver, and she felt as though the dampness outside had crept through the glass doors and into her bones. Restlessly, Roget's fingers toyed with one of the unopened boxes and then proceeded to open it as if his hands were functioning independently of his thoughts.

"Could such an important fact merely slip your mind?" Lauren continued, acutely aware that she was treading on paper-thin ice. "How many other things have merely slipped your mind?"

His interest totally distracted from the package, he hurled it onto the daybed. Yanking out his cuff links, he threw them with a loud clank into the silver tray on the armoire, where León would collect them and put them away. He peeled off his pleated shirt and threw it over the door of the armoire as he stalked across the room to the closet. Lauren's eyes followed the smooth, dark outline of his sable skin and the grace of his stride. She bit down hard on her lip and turned quickly away, knowing that the right glance from him could melt all of her determination.

"Tell me something," she said hesitantly, once again allowing her gaze to linger on the broad expanse of his naked back. "In that language you speak . . . what is *baka* and *lougarou?*"

Roget glared at her with cold resignation and replied flatly, *"Baka* means evil spirits, and *lougarou* is werewolves."

"Werewolves," she gasped.

"Oui. Werewolves," he repeated caustically. "Just a few of the despicable things involved in *magie noire.* And since you are so anxious to learn all the wicked details, there is no need for me to shield you from the facts. But remember one thing along with your constant probing. The time will come when you'll curse the day you learned it. And where *did* you learn it?" Roget had never been so prohibitive. She had known him to be mysterious, distant, but never cold. Lauren's face registered her alarm.

"Madame Fontenelle's mother," she replied.

"Damn her! That old woman is a *mambo* and always babbling about something that is not her business." He was beyond anger; he had become coldly indifferent.

"What is a *mambo?*" She still dared to inquire.

"A vudun priestess," he answered curtly, not bothering to look at her. "Lauren, I'm surprised," he went on. Again he used that tone that made her feel unworthy even of his disdain. "I never expected you to be interested in those silly female occupations."

"Silly female occupations!" she ranted. "And just what do you expect me to occupy my idle time with, if not female occupations. You don't include me in your life. Your precious male occupations you keep to yourself. I am supposed to be your wife, and yet all I share with you is your bed. I know pitifully little of your business on the plantation and even less about the political crisis that threatens the country."

"Haitian women do not involve themselves in the running of plantations or in politics," Roget responded adamantly. "They are protected from such things."

"And how will you protect the frail little creatures from the atrocities of war?" she retorted with bitter sarcasm. "Today in Port-au-Prince we saw those warships in the harbor, not to mention an alarmed city crawling with soldiers." Lauren saw the anger flare in his eyes and realized that if he had been another man, he would have struck her. But Roget could hold a tight rein on his impulses, and glaring anger soon hushed to cold, quiet fury.

Now, desperately, she wanted to forget everything she heard and give in to the feel of his mouth ravishing hers and let his maleness assuage the nagging doubt that permeated her body. For the first time since their marriage, Roget turned his back on her and failed to offer the passionate refuge she sought in his arms. They fell asleep separated by an unsurmountable wall of silence.

Chapter 10

Haitian tensions escalated, as day by day, the unrest swelled to infectious proportions over the threatening possibility that the Môle Saint Nicolas might be leased to the United States. The arrival of two more American war vessels in their harbor had increased to seven the ominous number of watchdogs hovering over the capital.

The de Martiers and the Deffands had their hands full trying to quell the unrest that was disrupting the production in their coffee groves. Anxious over the dire imminence of the situation, the men had walked off and refused to work, fearing that they would soon be slaves of the Americans. It took all of Roget's eloquence and diplomacy to convince them that such was not the case and to coax them back into the fields. Though he had calmed them by a display of confidence and self-assurance, he prayed during the whole confrontation that they would not sense the doubt that flickered dangerously in the back of his mind.

During those three days, Lauren had scarcely seen Roget, and when she did, he was merely polite. He came to bed unusually late, always after she was asleep, and departed early the next morning before she awakened. Lauren ached from the loneliness. Roget had a way of making her feel alone, even though he lay by her side.

Lauren walked the short distance from the stables to the

main house unaware of the gloriously fragrant, brilliantly sunny afternoon that surrounded her, but she was very much aware of the ominous clouds of doubt that hung over her marriage, over the plantation, and over the country. Entering her room, she tossed her hat and crop onto the huge canopied bed and drew in a long, labored breath. Noticing the open door between the two rooms, Lauren wandered into her husband's dressing room, unconsciously drawn to the muffled sounds emanating from his bathroom. It was probably the maid, she thought as she paused to admire the pair of ebony armoires, so deftly inlaid with geometric figures of ivory. The two priceless pieces of furniture were testimony to Roget's impeccable taste. She was taken by surprise when he strode half naked through the doorway, his face lathered with soap and his hand menacingly wrapped around a razor.

"Roget!" Lauren stepped back suddenly, her reflexes reacting to impulse as though she feared what he might do with the razor. "I didn't expect you to be here."

"That's quite obvious," he said indifferently as he retrieved a towel with his free hand and retraced his steps toward the bathroom. Lauren shrank with painful contrition. She had seen him show more warmth to a stranger. Inadvertently, her hazel eyes followed him with silent inquiry, and as if he felt her query burrowing through his naked back, he turned and said, "I have a meeting with President Hyppolite this afternoon."

"Just you?"

"No." He paused. "Edmond Clerveaux is sharing the honor." His dark eyes narrowed.

Lauren felt the tension that hung heavy in the air.

"Time is running out . . . Something must be done one way or the other. This constant state of unrest is breeding lethargy among the men. I can't continue to convince them that there is no danger of the leasing," he paused, "when I am not sure of that myself."

Lauren knew he had not been talking to her so much as aloud to himself. Just then the door clicked open and León interrupted their privacy.

"Je vous demande pardon, madame," the stately gray-

haired man apologized, attempting to gracefully exit the room, backside first. "If I had known, I would have knocked, *madame,*" he continued in near perfect French.

"It's all right, León. Come in." Roget beckoned to the tall, sepia Haitian with his razor-wielding hand. "You can lay out one of my white linen jackets with matching trousers."

"The Prince Albert, *monsieur,* the one with the satin binding?"

"*Oui,* León," he answered pensively. "That *is* a good choice."

"And which waistcoat, *monsieur?*"

Roget's mind mulled over the possibilities before answering, knowing it was important that he choose the right thing. "The gray jacquard," he answered finally.

"Cravat, *monsieur?*"

"The gray pleated puff scarf."

León stepped efficiently to the ebony armoire and began laying out his master's clothes.

Feeling very much like an intruder, Lauren took a few steps backward, crossed the threshold to her room, and pulled the French doors closed behind her. Struggling with her boots, she was almost tempted to ask León to assist her when she decided that the ensuing struggle would keep her mind from Roget if only for a short while. The battle with the boots left her breathless and exhausted, and she flopped across the bed to catch her breath. Staring up at the looped fringe canopy that hung over the bed, her thoughts wandered back to the warm, downy brass bed they shared in Paris, where their lovemaking had not been marred by the impending danger of American warships.

Lauren lifted her body to a sitting position and began unbuttoning her shirt. Suddenly, she was intensely aware of her fear—fear at the outcome of the Môle crisis—and even more frightened that she would never bridge the gap between her and Roget. Hot, burning tears swelled in her eyes and dripped one by one onto her silk shirt. More than she had ever realized, she longed to feel Roget's arms protecting her and his sultry kisses telling her that everything would be all right, but she could no longer turn to him for solace. Sadly, Lauren knew she would have to face this as she had faced many other trying moments in her life—alone.

After washing off the dust and grime of the plantation, she slipped into the full skirt and lace-trimmed shirtwaist blouse and stood before the mirror, absently pulling a brush through her curly hair. Gathering it into a pouf at the crown of her head, she had just inserted one ivory comb when Roget's door opened and she heard him exchange a few muffled words with León. Anxiously, she forced in the other comb and ran swiftly to the door. She wanted to hold him, touch him, feel his warmth. Understanding the weight of the burden that had been placed on his shoulders, she wanted to share it with him, even though he had all but shut her out. Just as his long, easy strides approached her door, Lauren eased open the mahogany barrier and called after him, "Roget . . . good luck." In a voice no louder than a whisper, she added, "God go with you . . . my love," and swallowed the last two words in her throat so that he never heard them.

"Merci, madame," he replied somberly. His dark gaze raked over her swiftly as he made a gesture of tipping the hat that was not on his head but in his hand. Lauren's shapely mouth curled into a hint of a smile, acknowledging the familiarity of his habits. Stepping inside, she closed the door and resumed her toilette.

Moments later, as she was leaving the room, Lauren heard what sounded like the soft swish of a woman's skirts rustling in the hallway. She stepped quickly back and aligned herself with the doorjamb, for what reason she did not know, and peered like a nosy goose around the ornately carved door frame. Filene approached the top of the stairs, stealthily scanned the length of the corridor, and fled down the hall toward the west wing. Pausing before Reinette's locked bedchamber, she slid a key into the lock and, assuming the hall to be empty, vanished inside. What business did Filene have in there? she wondered. Perhaps she intended to clean it. Absurd! She had never seen Filene do any manual labor. She merely gave orders. Lauren quietly pulled her door closed and stepped into the hall, irresistably curious about Filene's purpose for being in that room, especially when Madame de Martier had firmly assured her that no one had access to it.

Slowly she made her way along the corridor, following the

balustrade to the west wing. Midway between the staircase and the massive mahogany door that matched her own, the brass doorknob turned and the door inched open. Stopping dead in her tracks, Lauren receded slowly, one step behind the other until she reached the stairway. Smoothing her skirt, she lifted her chin and assumed a nonchalant pose. Filene hurried across the parquet floor, her eyes searching from side to side and halted with a start when she glanced up and saw Lauren at the head of the stairs. A hand flew to her breast as she drew back in fear.

"Madame," she gasped. "I didn't know anyone was here."

"Obviously," Lauren arched an eyebrow perceptively.

"I thought you had gone riding, *madame."* Her agitated voice strained to make conversation. "You ride every afternoon."

Lauren could not help noticing the woman's discomfort and wondered if her own uneasiness showed so readily. Filene had always been restless in her presence, as though she expected her to betray a secret. But she knew of no secret except that Filene had a key to Reinette's room, and Filene was not yet aware of that.

Lauren studied the face of this woman whose eyes purposely avoided hers. Exotically attractive, her smooth dark skin was flawless like Roget's but considerably darker in tone. She had full, shapely lips and slanted doe eyes. There was a quality in her stature that said she thought of herself not as a servant, but as a lady. For a brief moment Lauren's heart went out to her, for she knew how unfortunate it was to have your life dictated by the hue of your skin. If not for the grace of God, she herself would be in the same position. Graciously, she allowed Filene to take her leave.

Roget de Martier and Edmond Clerveaux climbed the steps to the presidential palace side by side, their footsteps falling into a synchronized rhythm. The light-skinned man beside him attempted to make conversation, but Roget was too preoccupied to be anything more than polite. Edmond Clerveaux had never been one of his favorite people. Putting aside his personal prejudice, Roget realized that the Clerveaux family carried a lot of political weight. If his presence would guarantee their success, he was definitely in favor of it, and he would keep his personal feelings to himself.

"I hear that you married while you were in Paris . . . a French woman." His voice intruded on Roget's thoughts. "We had just recovered from the shock of Jacques Deffand's surprise marriage. And now you."

A faint smile spread over Roget's face, not strong enough to part his lips. Amused at the sly attempt to pry into his reasons, he carefully pondered his reply. He had no intention of providing the tongue-wagging fire with more fuel, even though it was perhaps Edmond's way of suppressing his nervous anxiety over the task before them.

"Oui, je me suis marie," Roget volunteered finally. "My wife is French and African."

"She must be quite a woman," the other man injected almost enviously.

But Roget never met his questioning glance, his attention caught by Haiti's blue and red flag fluttering freely in the breeze. Exactly one hundred years ago their ancestors, black and mulatto, had fought off Napoleon's army and declared themselves free. Violently, he disagreed with many of Haiti's customs, but as long as there was a breath in him, he would wage the battle to keep her free of foreign oppression.

Approaching the glistening white facade of the palace, the two men passed through an ornate main door, heavily guarded by soldiers in full military regalia of red, sky blue, and gold. Inside, they were ushered into an anteroom by an aide-de-camp, jauntily dressed in a gold-braided uniform, who relieved them of their high hats and gloves.

"Do you think we will be able to sway his decision?" Edmond asked, nervously washing his hands together without benefit of soap or water. As Roget was about to answer, the long gilded doors swung open, and they were escorted into the presidential office. Presented to President Hyppolite and his foreign minister, Antenor Firmin, they were welcomed graciously.

"Your Excellency." Roget lowered his head slightly as he took the president's outstretched hand.

"Monsieur de Martier, Monsieur Clerveux, *asseyez-vous, je vous prie,"* Hyppolite said, his hand gesturing toward the two Louis XV chairs facing his desk. As he seated himself behind the desk, the president began, *"Messieurs,* I understand from Minister Firmin that you are here about the Môle Saint Nicolas."

Seated opposite the ebony man who wore only a normal suit of clothes, Roget noted that he was not as imposing as the man he had seen on ceremonial occasions, resplendent with gold shoulder brushes, cocked hat, and saber.

"Your Excellency," Roget replied, confirming his statement. "I don't know if you are aware of how much unrest there is among the people over the Môle Saint Nicolas. They imagine themselves becoming slaves to the Americans."

"As Minister Firmin says," Edmond added, his glance acknowledging the foreign minister, "we strongly believe that concession of the Môle could spark a revolution. We work with these people everyday—they live on our land— we feel their vibrations."

Florvil Hyppolite leaned forward and rested his dark chin against a loose fist. "Minister Firmin has made me aware of that."

"Needless to say," Roget added, "none of us is anxious to have the Americans on our back porch . . . whatever debt you might owe them." This was the first time anyone had alluded to the president's precarious situation.

"There was never a debt to be paid," Firmin stated, flatly denouncing the slanderous rumor. "That tale is nothing more than Ligue propaganda." The small elderly man's glance darted from Roget to Edmond and then back again, but their stoic expressions offered him not a flicker of insight as to whether or not they were convinced.

With a deep cough, the president cleared his throat. *"Messieurs,* I have given this matter serious thought. It could offer innumerable economic advantages."

"Perhaps," Roget replied apprehensively, "but they are far outweighed by the disadvantages. I have had to quell two uprisings on my plantation alone, and my neighbors are having similar problems. If this continues there will be no coffee for export. Haiti has so few productive plantations. Are we to surrender our production and depend on an American naval base for support?" he inquired adamantly, his tone challenging the older and, he trusted, wiser man. "I don't think that is what our ancestors fought and died for."

"His Excellency and I have studied the situation from all angles," Firmin broke in heatedly. "Our ancestors died for the same cause."

"Messieurs," Hyppolite replied, "rest assured, I will only do what is in Haiti's best interest. As I said, I have given the matter many hours of serious thought. Minister Firmin has informed me of the dire consequences. Believe me, the Haitian people are my first concern. I am their servant."

After an hour of deliberation, Roget strode from the presidential palace not sure whether their mission had succeeded or failed. It was difficult to decipher Hyppolite's true intentions. He had been diplomatic and said all the right things, but that did not guarantee their success.

A pompously mannered aide-de-camp inched open the president's door and snapped to attention. "The gentlemen have gone, Your Excellency."

"Merci, Dantes," Hyppolite replied anxiously, turning to face the dour little man who was his foreign minister. "I'm aware that you've changed your position, but initially, you as well had considered its advantages. I can only submit the question to my cabinet members . . . and perhaps abide by what they decide."

"At this point, there is but one decision," Antenor Firmin said, tensely smoothing the wrinkles from his black frock coat. "Haiti could not possibly enter negotiations now; it would appear that we were yielding to foreign pressures. We would weaken our status as an independent people."

As the two younger men emerged once again into the stifling heat of day, Edmond turned to Roget. "Do you think we swayed his decision?"

Roget's features twisted to a thoughtful frown. "Whether or not we had any impact on his decision, only the future will tell."

The letter from Claude was a glorious surprise and provided pleasant relief. Roget had not bothered to impart the details of his meeting with Hyppolite the day before, and she stubbornly refused to give him the satisfaction of asking about *male* affairs.

Lowering herself into the cushioned yellow chair, Lauren read the letter for the second time. Claude made a point of telling her that her birds were doing well. Remembering the touch of their soft, downy feathers, she wondered if she would see them again. As she was lost in her daydream, Roget entered the room and caught her smiling to herself.

"From your aunt?" he asked as he strode through their room to his dressing room.

"Oui." Her hazel eyes sparkled with delight. She followed him to the adjoining room but paused just inside the doorway. "She says that the pianist she hired to replace me has come every evening with an excuse as to why she needs *just a little drink.* Claude says she can't imagine who will die next because each member of her family has died at least twice." Lauren's voice rose an octave with amused animation. "It seems Pierre and Bertrand have been secretly slipping her drinks, one not knowing about the other, so that when it comes time for her to play, she can barely hold herself on the stool."

Faintly amused, Roget suppressed his smile and turned away. "What else did she say?" he inquired as he pulled off his shirt and hung it on the knob that jutted out from the armoire.

"She had electric lights installed in the dining room and the foyer. But there seems to be an uproar about them. Some customers think it destroys the atmosphere, that it makes the room too bright." Distracted by the gleam of his skin glistening in the sunlight, Lauren's voice faded into her thoughts.

"That room did have a charming ambience," Roget added, a hint of resignation permeating his voice. "But I suppose modern technology is inevitable."

Lauren barely heard the words that left his mouth. She was too engrossed in the full, sensuous contours of his lips and the feel of them as they plundered hers. Not seeing him, she had not realized how desperately she longed to feel the warmth of his maleness. Determined, Lauren bit down hard on her lip in silent resolution. She would live without him if she must.

"Oh, Roget," she muttered softly to herself. "Loving you is not going to be easy. And I do love you."

Thinking he heard her speak, Roget shifted his gaze and caught her deliciously ample mouth clamped shut in silent determination. Smothering the desire to feel it's softness against his own, he solemnly averted his gaze.

"Send Claude and Pierre my regards when you write," he said and disappeared behind the door to his bathroom.

By April 22, public clamor had risen to such a height that President Hyppolite formally refused to grant the concession. So raucous was the outcry that he was forced to publish a ban saying that there would never be any such concessions granted to the United States.

Roget and Gaston rode into the stable simultaneously, each coming from a different direction. Having just received the news, Gaston paused before dismounting, his massive frame towering over Roget.

"So you were right after all, *mon cher frère.* Your diplomacy did work this time," he said, stubbornly refusing to admit that Roget's idea had been the best one. "I still think Hyppolite succumbed to the threat of revolution and not the persuasiveness of diplomacy."

"Perhaps," Roget replied calmly, "but no matter what tactics worked, we achieved the desired results."

One by one the American warships left Haiti's waters. An orgy of dancing and merrymaking broke out in the streets, causing pandemonium, and her landowners breathed a hearty sigh of relief.

Precariously celebrating the country's return to normalcy, the de Martiers—Gaston, Roget, Lauren, and their mother—had gathered in the parlor for the evening ritual. Antoine was noticeably missing. With a raucous thud, the youngest brother threw open the mahogany doors and strode in, victoriously waving a newspaper.

"Minister Firmin has finally resigned!" All eyes followed the tabloid that he held in his hand.

Gaston snarled. "A meager price to pay for having considered Gherardi's proposals."

"It's over at last," Madame de Martier whispered, throwing herself in Roget's arms.

Lauren bit down on her lower lip and looked away.

The whole messy affair ended with a startling abruptness, and the threat that had hung in the air for weeks suddenly was gone. Lauren thought the end of the crisis would be the end of Roget's indifference, but she was painfully mistaken. She still saw little of him. In that last bitter confrontation she had struck a stronger nerve than she realized.

The sharp blade of his indifference created an ever-present twinge of pain, but Lauren stubbornly refused to abandon her search for answers. She had every right to know about her husband's life, his country, and the family she had married into. If he denied her the information, she would be forced to seek it elsewhere.

With the crisis behind him, Roget's strong legs took the mahogany steps two at a time and then halted abruptly, midway between top and bottom, as if an invisible cord tugged at his back. *Maman.* Her name lit a spark in his thoughts, when he realized he had not spent a moment with her in days. He had been so occupied with the Môle threat and the trouble on the plantation that he had pushed everything else aside. Roget turned and descended the stairs.

Rapping his knuckles against the partially closed door, Roget called to her, using the affectionate term he had used as a boy. *"Maman beauté . . . C'est moi."* Why that term had escaped his lips at this moment he could not imagine, not having used it in years. There was no answer. He pushed open the door and walked in, his eyes rapidly scanning the empty room. Removing the straw panama, Roget rubbed a forearm across his dark sculptured brow and let out a deep sigh of relief. He reached forward and let his hat fall on the low table in front of the sofa, and the swish of air fluttered the lip of an elaborately engraved invitation. Grasping the elegant paper between his fingers, his eyes perused the invitation to the Condé ball while his thoughts fled to Lucienne. She would be furious, he knew, though he had done it to save her. The honorable way would have been to face her alone and tell her of his marriage himself without half of Haitian society looking on, but it was not to be. He sighed again, this time in resignation. Their first encounter would be a blatantly public affair. He had no doubt that Lucienne knew by now, because he could not imagine that Celestine Duval had wasted any time in writing to her niece after their impromptu meeting on board the ship.

He would have preferred to avoid the whole sordid ordeal, but now that they had so graciously extended the invitation, he would have to oblige or have it appear that he had done something to be ashamed of. Not for a minute was he fooled by their humble display of graciousness. His marriage was, on the one hand, a breach of contract and, on the other, a literal slap in the face, and it was within the Condés' right to ignore the de Martiers forever. However, he was well aware that they had not extended the invitation out of the goodness of their hearts, but because wronged as they might be, they had no intentions of closing the door to future alliances with the de Martier wealth.

Still clutching the gilded white card between his fingers, Roget lowered himself onto the dark red sofa, idly propping one dusty boot on the table. Allowing his head to rest against the sofa's plump, padded back, Roget let his eyes roam around his mother's parlor. This room was his mother more than any other part of the house. He took in the lavish Louis XV decor, too rich for his taste, and understood that his mother needed this artificial opulence to fill her emptiness. Lazily trailing his gaze from an Impressionist painting to the marble-topped commode, his focus was captured by a crystal decanter. His body winced as if suddenly pricked with a needle when his eyes took in the half-empty container of brandy. Roget's sturdy frame shuddered with disgust. He hated the way his father and this family of males had choked the life out of his mother. Knowing he had committed a brazen act of defiance, he would just have to make Lucienne understand that it was done to save her from the same fate.

In Paris when he had conceived the idea, he knew very well that he would only get away with it because the de Martier plantation desperately needed him. Hardheaded as Gaston was to admit it, the plantation would not be so successful without his progressive ideas and knowledge of modern cultivating methods. Still, Gaston's reaction had been mild. Roget attributed it to the overwhelming preoccupation with the Môle Saint Nicolas, but now that the crisis was over, he was certain he could expect a more violent backlash from his self-righteous brother.

Enmeshed in his own disturbing thoughts, Roget failed to hear Justine de Martier as she entered the room.

"Roget!" she cried, her face glowing with joy at the surprise visit.

"Maman." Roget looked up, startled, and attempted to correct his ungainly posture.

"Stay where you are, dear. You must be exhausted." One plump, beige hand forced him back onto the sofa. Fondling his face with her free hand, she placed a lingering, motherly kiss on his cheek. She rose with the idea of pouring herself a brandy and noticed the engraved white card lying beside him on the sofa. "It was gracious of them to invite us." She hesitated. "After the embarrassment you must have caused them . . . your hasty marriage. They could sue us for breach of contract," she added.

"They could, but I doubt that they will," Roget replied flatly.

Her light eyes searched her son's dark ones. "Why, Roget . . . Why did you?"

"Because I saw what happened to Reinette . . . and to you." His voice cracked as he responded, and he rose to his feet to dispel the thickness in his throat.

"Roget, my beautiful son," she murmured, her pale beige hand stretching up to caress the back of his weary neck. "You are mine, you know . . . more than the other two ever were."

Gazing down into her face, he said, *"Maman beauté,* I know."

"Gaston was always your father's child from the moment he was born. And Antoine . . . he is my youngest, and I love him, but I have never understood him." Gazing up at Roget, her melancholy gave way to a faint expression of pride. "You have always had a sensitivity, an innate perception, that your two brothers never had." Wrapping his strong arms around her, Roget buried his face in her chestnut hair. Madame de Martier clung to him passionately, as if he were the only reason for which she lived. It was not the passion of lovers, but of mother and son that spread a warm glow through them both. Lifting her face to his, she said, "Of course you know Gaston is not going to take this affront lightly. You and your choice of a bride have definitely incurred his wrath. I've been dreading the day when the Môle crisis would be ended, because now——"

"I'm well aware of it, *Maman,*" Roget said, interrupting her train of thought. He knew what she was about to say. "I did it," he paused reflectively, "and I will deal with Gaston."

Chapter

11

One month after the end of the Môle Saint Nicolas fiasco, the Haitian elite had to deal with yet another shock: an assassination attempt on their president. During the Fête-Dieu of May 28, while the festivities masked their actions, lawless bands of armed men descended on the prison, killed the soldiers on guard, and set free all political prisoners. Joining forces with the rebels, the freed anarchists attacked the arsenal and then the national palace, their prime intent to assassinate President Hyppolite.

Lauren assumed, after the assassination attempt, that the ball would certainly be canceled. She soon learned, however, that life in Haiti went on despite the political upheavals.

May came and went, and the weeks of blistering days and damp rainy nights changed nothing. Lauren felt alone and abandoned. Roget had a life that did not include her. As she was slowly finding out, the liberation of the industrial age had not yet reached Haiti. Haitian women were not involved in business or political affairs; their place was in the home.

Roget needed her for nothing except his pleasure and lately not even for that. Filene ran his home, León cared for his personal needs, and servants prepared his meals. She had never imagined that being his wife would make her feel so useless. She was nothing more than a legal mistress.

Having nothing to elevate her sagging spirits or purpose to occupy daily existence, Lauren allowed the Condé ball to loom very large on her horizon. It was hard for her to imagine herself so elated over a silly ball, but she was. She had never been to a fancy dress ball, this was her first, and to her own amazement she was excited.

On a recent trip to the city, she and Georgette had searched for and found the perfect stockings to go with Lauren's ball gown. Knit of ivory silk mesh, the delicate hose were embroidered on each side with a pale turquoise thread that matched the satin gown. After this purchase, Georgette led her to a "gem of a shoemaker," to put it in Madame Deffand's colorful words, where they both ordered shoes. At this tiny shop on the Grande Rue, Lauren chose a custom-designed pair of evening slippers to be fashioned in a turquoise kid, just two shades deeper than her gown. Feeling recklessly extravagant, she added to these costly purchases a pair of long white kid gloves and pearl drops for her ears. As she signed for the earrings, Lauren mused at life's irony. Having never been much interested in her husband's wealth, it seemed now to be the only part of him that she had.

Those two weeks fled by more rapidly than the entire month of May. Excited as she was about the event, she had developed a growing sense of apprehension. She would be scrutinized by the elite of Haitian society as the outcast that Roget de Martier had married, and she could not even depend on him for support should she weaken. Determinedly, Lauren pushed the disparaging thoughts from her mind. She had waited too long for this ball. Having spent weeks preparing for it and reveling in its gaiety, Lauren refused to let fear destroy her fantasy. Entering her room to bathe, Lauren wondered if what she sought from Roget was so wrong. Did Haitian women have no interest in sharing their husband's lives?

Roget dressed in his quarters, assisted by León, eliminating any reason for the discourse that might have passed between husband and wife. Although he said little to her beyond the necessary courtesies, that cold indifference appeared to have given way to some indulgence. Could she dare hope that he had forgiven her and that this evening would be the answer to her prayers? Lauren clung with foolhardy recklessness to the possibility.

"Will there be anything else, *monsieur*," León inquired as he watched the younger man adjusting the stiff white collar and tie that circled his throat.

"No. There is nothing more you can do for me. You had better see to my brother." Roget grinned knowingly. "He's probably having a fit."

"Very well, *monsieur*." Reluctantly, he obeyed the command and left the room to assist Antoine.

Roget straightened his tailcoat, adjusted his cuff links, and let his focus rest on the black-and-white image that stared back at him from the full-length mirror. He was not looking forward to the events of this night. The wife he chose was just not fitting into his plan. Erroneously, he had expected her to be like Haitian women, but it was going to be difficult to keep Lauren confined to a housewife's duties. Unlike Lucienne, she had not been raised a Haitian woman. Lauren was French, and as much as the Haitian elite espoused everything French, there remained blatant differences between the lives of French and Haitian women.

Lauren lifted her gown from the closet. Gazing fondly at the pale turquoise satin, she was pleased that finally she could wear the ball gown that had been Claude's wedding gift. *Claude, how I miss you.* Her fingers examined the aquamarine beads that covered the bodice and sleeves, tracing delicately over the pearl teardrops that bordered the neckline. It was so like Claude—her impeccable taste.

Lauren dressed with painstaking care and graciously accepted Madame de Martier's generous offer to have her maid do her hair. The woman's deft fingers swept her hair up into a fashionable double pouf entwined with pearls, leaving two wispy tendrils to cascade on either side of her face. Securing it all into place, she stood back to admire her work. Lauren pivoted in the mirror, perusing one side and then the other.

"C'est magnifique, Anna." Her hazel eyes glowed opalescent with approval.

"Merci, madame," the maid replied, demurely lowering her head. Spying the gown draped across the bed, she moved to retrieve it.

"Can I help *madame* with her gown," she continued as though wanting to practice her French.

"Oui, I would appreciate it, Anna," Lauren replied, grateful for the assistance.

"Will there be anything more, *madame.*"

"I don't believe so," Lauren replied, hastily dismissing her. Alone, she put on the pearl earrings and dabbed a jasmine scent discreetly behind her ears. Gazing into the mirror, Lauren barely recognized herself. The décolletage framed her bosom and exposed her shoulders while huge puffed sleeves camouflaged the fullness her body lacked. The bodice molded smoothly to her hourglass waistline, and the skirt draped into a glimmering satin bell.

One by one, Lauren worked her fingers into the long kid gloves and then stood there, frustrated, when she could not hook the buttons. As she wrestled with the gloves, Roget strode through the adjoining door fully dressed. From the tiny diamond studs in his white piqué waistcoat to the black satin stripe in his trousers, he reeked of masculine elegance.

"Are you ready, *madame?*"

"Oui . . . if I could get these"—she paused, deleting a word—"buttons fastened."

Roget hooked the buttons with a marked familiarity that indicated he had done it before. "We have maids to help with this. Why don't you use them?"

"I'm not yet accustomed to such luxury," she replied sheepishly.

Averting her gaze from his, she pivoted unintentionally in the reflection of the mirror. Certain that she had imagined the faint glimmer in his eye, she pushed it from her thoughts. But for the first time in her life, Lauren felt beautiful when Roget's lips curled slowly into a smile and he said, "You are lovely."

What Lauren had not known in the weeks of contemplating the ball and what Roget's brother Gaston was more than eager to share with her during the tedious carriage ride was that Lucienne de Luynes was the Condés' niece.

"So you will at last meet Mademoiselle de Luynes, a lady worthy of the name, the lady who was chosen to be my brother's wife. The purpose of tonight's celebration," he stated, smugly observing her reaction, "is to welcome the lady home from a six-month trip abroad."

Lauren's lips parted slowly, but anything that she might have uttered strangled in her throat. She stared at him aghast, her senses stunned by what she had heard. Rigidly, she pressed her back into the seat, a meager attempt to stifle the gut-wrenching sob that rose from her stomach.

"She was raised by the Condés," Gaston continued, very strongly aware of the impact his statement had on her, "and Lucienne has said many times that the Villa Condé is her home more than her father's home."

Lauren stared, speechless, unable to suppress the question in her eyes.

"Her mother's death left her father at a loss as to what to do with a puberty-aged daughter," he added, answering the silent inquiry, "and Madame Condé, having been blessed with no children of her own, offered to take on the task of raising her sister's child. She accomplished it magnificently, I might add."

"It will be delightful to see Lucienne again," Madame de Martier chimed in. "She was always such a stunning young woman."

Antoine turned his head and stared blankly through the window. Roget glared venom at his older brother but refrained from uttering a word. Lauren had never felt more alone in her life than she did at that moment.

In his devious efforts to antagonize her, Gaston had been more than willing to satisfy her thirst for knowledge. Lauren listened with ambivalence, knowing that he was baiting her but helpless to free herself. Her excitement about the ball had withered and died, leaving only the throbbing in her head, until the splendor of Villa Condé loomed into view.

Moonlight bathed the white exterior of the gingerbread mansion and set it illuminous in a frame of navy velvet sky. Latticework balustrades encompassed the four sides of the veranda and adorned tiny balconies jutting out from second-story windows. Narrow glass doors opened onto the porticos from each side, and two pointed towers of delicately carved filigree extended into the sky, giving the illusion of a small but enchanted castle.

Lauren was mesmerized. From within, the mansion was aglow with the flicker of silver candelabra, while metal firepots graced either side of the main door, the smoke a putrid repellent for mosquitos. An opulent crystal chandelier hung from the ceiling in the ballroom, and as she stepped onto a floor inlaid with squares of satinwood, ebony, and mahogany, it loomed forth like a colossal chessboard. Yellow cloisonné vases sprouted plants of camelia, hibiscus, and oleander in full bloom, and though the grounds were far less extensive than the de Martiers', the house was the most beautiful she could imagine. For the remainder of the evening she wanted only to revel in its beauty and allow its gaiety to penetrate her soul.

The men were directed to the cloakroom. Lauren and Madame de Martier followed a uniformed maid up the winding staircase to the powder room, where pretty young women and time-weathered older ones removed wraps and repaired wilted makeup. Young women chattered incessantly and sashayed about in lavish ball gowns, admiring themselves in the many mirrors that adorned the walls. Madame de Martier greeted several of the older women, not bothering with the formalities of introducing her daughter-in-law.

As they turned to leave the room, a striking young woman in a pink moiré gown and an exquisite diamond collar stepped into their path.

"*Bonsoir,* Madame de Martier."

"*Bonsoir,* Murielle. How charming you look tonight."

"Did Antoine come with you?" she inquired, lowering heavily fringed dark lashes.

"*Oui, ma chérie.* We left him downstairs with Roget and Gaston."

Murielle turned on high heels and fled down the stairs.

Gathering the train of her black brocade gown as she descended the staircase, Madame de Martier uttered proudly, "My sons do have a way with ladies."

"She's lovely. Who is she?" Lauren inquired.

"Murielle and Antoine have been promised since they were children, but it seems that Antoine will be headstrong like Roget." Lauren realized that the lamentation was solely for her benefit. "This evening will not be pleasant," the elder woman continued, "having to face all of our friends . . . particularly the Condés."

"Oui, madame," Lauren replied. Her voice was tinged with an edge of sarcasm. "Everyone has made a point of telling me."

French perfume mingled with the sweet tropical aroma of plants and the pungent odor of smoke. Before Lauren whirled a sea of faces caught up in swirling waves of satin, silk, taffeta, and Italian lace. Strains of music rose and fell over the constant chatter of voices. Elegantly coiffured women, wearing their wealth about their necks and their heritage in their graceful feline stature, were visible throughout the room.

The Condés emerged from the crowd to greet their newly arrived guests. An exchange of feigned embraces passed between the older women, while Madame Condé merely offered Lauren an icy smile. Lauren smiled graciously, accepting the frigid greeting, but not condoning it. The short, fair-skinned man at her side nodded and said gruffly, "You will find Roget at the bar."

Sipping idly at a glass of champagne, Roget looked up, startled, when she appeared before him. His reaction made it obvious that she had disturbed his thoughts, and she wondered what she might say to him that would elicit some warmth. What could you say to a husband who had barely spoken to you in weeks? Recalling how angry he had been that night they argued and how that anger had slowly become frigid indifference, Lauren shivered as the impact engulfed her bare shoulders.

"Champagne?" he asked flatly, lifting a glass from the silver tray that was offered to them by a waiter.

"Oui . . . s'il vous plaît." Her voice hesitated. Hoping instead that he would ask her to dance, Lauren was forced to drown her frustration in the tingling, bubbly taste of the wine.

Suddenly, there was a flurry of excitement, a buzz of chattering voices, until a dead silence swept the room and all heads turned toward the main door. A whisper resounded through the silence. "Frederick Douglass has just arrived."

Straining her neck to get a look at the famous statesman, what she saw was a tall, portly gentleman, whose bushy white hair flowed like a lion's mane over the collar of his dark cape. Recoiling to a more ladylike posture, Lauren felt the heat of Roget's touch branding her bare arm as he propelled her through the crowd to the reception hall.

"I'm sure you would like to meet the consul general from the United States." His dark gaze was faintly amused, indicating that he already knew the answer to his implied question.

"Of course I would!" she exclaimed, gazing at him through opalescent eyes. "I've never met anyone famous before."

"Oh?" Roget arched one raven black eyebrow. "Have you forgotten meeting Captain Bruant a few short months ago?"

Lauren sucked her tongue softly against her teeth. "It's not quite the same thing," she uttered indignantly. His hand on her arm had turned her knees to rubber, and she tried to hide her faltering poise beneath a mask of sophistication.

"He is famous, is he not?" Roget inquired.

"Oui, but he's a performer, not a statesman."

Inside the room, Chief Justice Condé stood dwarfed by his illustrious guest, as other guests filed by for an introduction. Roget seemed reluctant to join the line and appeared to be waiting for a more opportune moment. His moment came after the others had filed past and returned to the ballroom.

"Your Excellency, Monsieur and . . . Madame . . ."— their fair-skinned host hesitated as though the words were glued in his throat—"Roget de Martier." And then bounding into an unnatural glibness, he succeeded in disguising his distaste behind an elaborate introduction. "The de Martiers own one of the very few Haitian-controlled coffee plantations. Unfortunately, educated Haitians are not attracted to the land, and most of our agriculture is carried on by foreigners. However, the de Martiers have prospered with it for some eighty years." His voice cracked, betraying the fact that he had expected a share in that prosperity.

"Madame, it is my pleasure," the elderly man said, lowering his head to place his lips against Lauren's gloved hand. "An impressive introduction, Monsieur de Martier," the portly statesman continued, extending his hand to Roget.

"I'm afraid Justice Condé has been far too generous, *Monsieur Ministre,"* Roget bantered. Cordially clasping the outstretched hand, he added, "It is you who deserve the illustrious introduction."

Vilbrun Condé shifted his weight from one foot to the other, in an obvious gesture of discomfort. "Minister Douglass, I must see to my other guests," he said apologetically. Hastily excusing himself, he left the room.

Drawing the attention back to their discourse, the elderly statesman chuckled deep in his throat. "I've done very little."

"You've done a great deal," Roget corrected. "In 1889, you sent the first telegraph message from Haiti to the United States. We were introduced at the reception following the ceremony. And, *Monsieur Ministre . . .* you have not changed. Even then you professed to have done nothing."

"This appointment as consul general to Haiti has certainly been one of the high points of my life despite all the problems."

"And of course," Roget replied, "most of the Haitian people hold you in very high esteem. It's unfortunate that the Môle Saint Nicolas fiasco put an unjust blot on an otherwise brilliant career." Roget paused and then continued in a more adamant tone. "I put great faith in my country's need for intercommunication with the world, but as a Haitian, I will never condone the presence of armed American warships in our harbor. In that move your country was wrong. She obviously did not realize that Haitians are not easily frightened. We are still the same people who turned back Napoleon."

"I cannot disagree." The older man's reply was painfully acquiescent. "My country's ill-placed show of force has been a constant source of embarrassment for me in my dealings with your countrymen."

Lauren noticed the tired lines that creased his cheeks beside the broad nose and the aging skin that surrounded his keenly perceptive eyes.

"I'm aware, *monsieur,* that this was not your doing." Roget's tone had softened considerably. "A statesman of your talent and a man with your sensibility to the needs of the Haitian people would certainly know better. White Americans endowed with but incapable of wielding a power greater than yours, simply because they lack your insight, were responsible for this outrage."

"You understand the ways of the world, my son." Douglass smiled with smug recognition. "The sagacity and the graciousness of the Haitian people, both the men and the women, is a treasure of knowledge I will carry with me for the rest of my life." His gaze shifted fondly to Lauren.

"Monsieur, my wife is Haitian only by marriage." Roget smiled broadly, clearing the tension from the air. "Lauren was born in France."

"Ah-h-h . . . the land of Dumas," he sighed aloud. The twinkle in his eye precipitated his change of tone. "When we were in France, my wife and I visited the castle that inspired *The Count of Monte Cristo.* He paused a moment, placing a hand to his forehead. "Chateau d'If, I believe, is the name."

"You've been far more fortunate than I, *Monsieur Ministre.*" Lauren smiled. "I lived in France all of my life and I've never seen Dumas's inspiration."

"It may have inspired Dumas," he commented wryly, "but the old island prison, it seemed to me, was hopelessly anchored in the sea." Lauren chuckled at his wry humor, recognizing that he was merely passing a traveler's judgment. She was well aware of his reputation as a statesman, his eloquence as an orator, and his diplomacy as an ambassador. But at the moment she was battling the undignified impulse to fly into his portly arms and hug him as if he were the grandfather she had never known.

"Enough politics," he said, a smile dancing in his eye. "Monsieur de Martier, if you don't take your lovely wife in your arms and dance with her, I promise you this old man will steal her." The twinkle remained in his eye as his host reappeared and whisked him away to meet other anxious guests.

Still smiling at the stately old gentleman's last remark, Roget extended his arm and said, "Shall we?" Timidly Lauren tucked her hand beneath his elbow and let him lead her to the dance floor. Surrendering to the haunting melody of the music, she let her body whirl in abandon about the floor. Antoine danced by with Murielle coyly in his arms, and on the far side of the room her eye caught snatches of Georgette's lavender gown, but Lauren was in a world of her own, a world that for the moment encompassed only her and Roget. All the men were elegant in dark tailcoats and narrow trousers, but Roget was a rare mingling of genteel refinement and earthy sensuality. His nearness and the easy rhythm of his body as they danced mesmerized her, and Lauren deluded herself into believing that the moment would go on forever.

Sooner than she would have wished, the musicians ceased playing and the melody faded into nothing. Antoine joined them without Murielle, and precariously balancing a champagne glass in his outstretched hand, he bowed low and feigned a formal address.

"Monsieur *et* Madame de Martier." Wavering from having bowed too low, he waged a momentary struggle to recapture an upright position.

"I think you had better stay with rum punch for the remainder of the evening," Roget said with brotherly concern.

"Don't be a bore, big brother. I'm quite capable of holding my liquor . . . every bit as well as you and Gaston." Defiantly, he turned up the crystal glass and emptied it.

Roget raised one raven-black brow and shot him a questioning glance.

"Well, perhaps Lauren should dance with me, then *she* can attest to my capabilities."

"As you wish." Roget shrugged indifferently, handing Lauren over to his brother. In the last hour, Roget had spent more time with her than he had in weeks, and Lauren was reluctant to leave. It was like forcing herself to shut off the air that she breathed.

Prolonging her moment of departure as long as decorum would allow, Lauren took her brother-in-law's arm. Gazing up at her husband, she longed for him to reclaim her, but her silent plea never captured his attention. Suddenly, Roget's gaze locked in the distance. As her hazel eyes followed his, she saw the object of his attention. Gliding toward him, as though she had not feet, but wings, was an exquisitely beautiful woman, the train of her mauve silk gown rustling behind her, and her face animated with reluctant anticipation. Lauren's breath caught in her throat. Before her stood the most breathtaking beauty she had ever seen. *Lucienne de Luynes.* Lauren was not aware of how she knew, but she knew. Antoine's knowing glance darted from her to his brother to Lauren and back again within a split second.

"Roget . . ." she purred, her eyes focusing only on him. The rest of the world did not seem to exist. Roget took her hands in his and kissed them gallantly, displaying more emotion than one need put into such a gesture. Lustrous auburn hair cascaded against her slender neck, pulled to one side by two fresh white gardenias. The décolletage of her gown framed shoulders and breasts of beige marble, subtly exhibiting the ampleness of her feminine contours. Her face, an aristocratic one with high cheekbones and sculptured nose, possessed an indecently soft, full mouth, the only clue that African blood ran in her veins. Feline eyes gazed a deep velvety gray, and she moved with the liquid motion of a Persian cat. Her exotic mulatto beauty was unexpectedly cool, a perfect contrast to the scorching atmosphere in which she dwelt. Lauren felt drab and awkward in comparison. *She* was the woman he had been with in Paris.

When the two women were finally introduced, Lucienne smiled and offered her hand with the unwavering poise of a great lady. More gracious than her aunt before her, Lauren still detected that air of haughty indignation. Displaying all the composure she was able to muster, Lauren smiled bravely and touched her outstretched hand.

"It's a pleasure to meet you at last. I have heard your name so often."

"And I have heard a great deal about you, Madame de

Martier," she replied icily. Her haughty eyes rested on Roget.

Lauren ignored the stifled sarcasm. "Please call me Lauren."

"And do call me Lucienne," she smiled, feigning a warmth that did not exist. Turning her attention to Antoine, Lucienne allowed him to place a kiss on each of her cheeks and then engaged him in a few words of polite conversation.

Still in awe of her staggering beauty and awkwardly ill at ease in her presence, Lauren was relieved when Roget whisked Lucienne off to the dance floor. She doubted that her poise was secure enough to withstand Lucienne's proud indignation for any great length of time.

Her hand in his, Roget led Lucienne onto the satinwood floor and took her in his arms. Bodies touching, hips and legs moving rhythmically from side to side to the unmistakably African beat of the music, they performed a dance Lauren had never seen. A dignified, yet rather provocative dance, she learned from Antoine that it was a Haitian indulgence called the merengue. In no way did it resemble the very European Strauss waltz they had just danced.

They moved together as one, Lucienne following Roget's lead so easily that it was obvious they had danced many times before. The gentle, familiar way he held her, the way her hand rested intimately at the back of his neck, told Lauren that there had been more between them than just an arranged promise of marriage.

Sweeping her into his arms, Antoine cast a sympathetic glance at Lauren and whirled her onto the dance floor. Barely able to follow him, she felt ridiculous and clumsy but was grateful for the diversion. Several other men asked her to dance, but she would not attempt the merengue again, at least not without practice. Besides, she was sure that they were merely satisfying a bizarre curiousity. The chilly reception she had received warned her that it would be a long time before they accepted her, if ever. The men seemed tolerant enough, but the women behaved as though she had done them the worst possible injustice.

Antoine insisted that she accept the invitations, and blindly she obeyed him. Men danced with her, flirted with her, and talked at her, but she heard none of it. The only thing that burned an impression on her consciousness was the sight of Lucienne fitting so perfectly in Roget's arms. No longer able to tolerate the pounding in her eardrums, she opted for a breath of fresh air and the chance to look for the only friend that she had, Georgette Deffand.

Her eyes searched the swirling sea of bodies for Georgette's lavender gown. She found her wrapped in the arms of an elderly man, shorter than she, whose head continually rested on her bosom. Her expression pleaded to be rescued, but actually, the scene was funny, and Lauren found herself amused despite her bleak mood. She motioned to Georgette to meet her on the veranda, and Madame Deffand complied in haste the moment the music ceased.

"That old lecher," she complained, smoothing the bodice of her gown.

"Why didn't Jacques rescue you?"

"Huh!" she said, sucking her teeth. "He's the one who abandoned me with Monsieur Dugue. That man always maneuvers a dance with me just so he can rest his head on my breast. He does not fool me one bit, the little weasel. And Jacques finds it amusing." Her tone was genuinely annoyed. Glancing at Lauren, she added, "You seemed considerably amused yourself."

"I didn't mean to be," Lauren apologized, "but the look on your face was so comical." She was still suppressing a giggle. "I'm anxious to meet Jacques. He sounds like fun."

"And I have yet to meet Roget. Where are you hiding him?" She questioned puckishly.

"I'm not." Her reply was weighted with apprehension. "The last time I saw him he was dancing with Lucienne de Luynes."

"So you've met her! Have you ever seen such a beauty? She's like hot ice."

Lauren cringed. She wanted to scold Georgette's seeming disloyalty, but how could she? She was telling the truth. However, before she could even pretend to chide her, a tall, imposing man approached them.

"Lauren, my husband, Jacques. Lauren de Martier."

"So you're Roget's wife. I spoke to Roget a while ago and

invited him for a game of bezique in two weeks. He used to be quite a card player. Is he still?"

"I suppose so," Lauren replied hesitantly, recalling that the first time Roget spoke to her he had asked about a deck of cards. "I really couldn't say for sure."

"Jacques," Georgette interrupted, "Lauren's only been married a few months. You cannot expect her to know all of Roget's bad habits." She scolded him playfully, making their love for each other very obvious.

"You're still newlyweds," he said. "How delightful."

Lauren envied the attention that Jacques showered on his wife. His look said she was the only thing in the world that mattered.

Lauren liked him instantly. Charming, unassuming, and possessed of an innate kindness, Jacques was not strikingly handsome like Roget, but not unattractive either. Tall and brown skinned, he was heavier in frame than Roget but moved with the same graceful elegance and self-assured manner. His brand of love would be profound, secure, and lasting. Roget was passionate, exciting, and unpredictable but how faithful she had yet to learn.

"Why don't we dine together . . . the four of us?" Georgette suggested, breaking into her reverie.

"A wonderful idea," Lauren quipped, "if only I could find my husband."

"I'm warning you," Jacques teased. "When we were young, your husband was the center of attention at every ball."

"And a leopard rarely sheds his spots," she retorted sharply. Stepping back into the ballroom to look for Roget, she felt the green demon of jealousy slowly devouring her resolve.

She saw Antoine as he danced by with an array of different partners, and she had even encountered Gaston, but there was no sign of Roget. Before, she had seen him dancing with his mother, but now, Madame de Martier was engaged in conversation on the far side of the room, her brandy glass bartered for one of champagne.

Certain that Roget was nowhere inside, Lauren stepped through a pair of glass doors onto the veranda, and voices drew her attention to the rear of the house. In a far corner of the balustrade, completely obscured by the shadows, she noticed the vague forms of a man and a woman. Lauren's heart plummeted to the pit of her stomach, and her feet fused with the floor. Too engrossed in each other to be even faintly aware of her presence, they stood catercorner in the bend of the balustrade, their faces staring into the darkness while their backs shut out the world. Lauren had not meant to eavesdrop, but her feet were glued to the floor.

"How dare you show up with a wife! Everyone, including myself, expected us to marry when you returned. How could you do this to me after so many years? Why didn't you tell me of your plans the day we went riding in Paris?" Her questions were demanding and indignant, the sound of a woman scorned.

"I was unaware of them myself. It all happened . . . rather suddenly." His tone was strongly defensive. "However, it should not have come as a surprise to you. I have always told you that I would not marry you."

"Oui . . . you told me," she sighed, "but I never believed it. I didn't want to believe it. Considering all that was between us, I could not conceive of your marrying another woman."

"Exactly why I had to marry another woman . . . it was the only way to save us from ourselves. You know as well as I that it would have been disastrous. I don't think you ever truly realized how these marriages fill me with loathing. How they destroy people, particularly the women. I love you too much to put you through that torture."

"I suppose I didn't realize how strongly you felt about it," she said pensively. "Bringing home a wife was your way of avoiding our marriage. In other words . . . thwarting our families' plans."

"How else could I save you from my family? I couldn't bear to stand by and watch you destroyed like Reinette. It's been torture enough to watch my mother's destruction all these years . . ." His voiced faded into nothing.

"Are you sure it was not simply for shock value?" she chided sharply. "What better way of reproaching your family than to marry a woman far beneath your social class?"

"Perhaps it was for shock value—the woman I chose—but I had decided long ago not to allow your family's greed for our wealth and my family's hunger for your blue blood to destroy you as it has the others. That house has wreaked enough disaster. Unfortunately," he added softly, "rebellion always claims a victim, but I would die before allowing it to be you." He shifted his position, making the contours of his face partially visible in the moonlight. "I would have preferred to discuss this without half of Haiti looking on," he added reflectively. "I was surprised that we even received an invitation to this ball. I knew that the Condés would not so easily forgive my affront."

"It was I who insisted on the invitation," she replied with that haughty air of indignation. "I had no intention of crawling into a corner to hide like a wounded animal. I intend to fight for you. Perhaps," her tone softened as she gazed up at him with liquid eyes, "there is a way to have this marriage dissolved. Gaston said there is a strong possibility that it could be annulled."

"Lucienne," Roget breathed softly, attempting to silence any thought that she might change his mind.

Her marble skin gleamed in the silvery beams of moonlight, and her gray eyes gazed into his darker ones as she placed her hand against the side of his face. With a painful determination in her tone, she whispered, "My darling, I will never give you up. Wife . . . or no." Her shapely lips parted with invitation, and as if she were a cherished work of art, his mouth took hers with a tenderness and a reverence that made Lauren want to die.

He loves her. Lauren's brain echoed the words over and over again until she could no longer bear the sound of her own thoughts. Had he every intention of continuing their relationship, his marriage a mere formality, or would she convince him to have it annulled? Biting down hard on her lip, she fought back the tears that threatened to consume her. Lauren ached with pain and jealousy.

Lauren walked away in a blind stupor. Moving her legs like a baby learning to walk, she placed them timorously, one in front of the other, for fear a more complex motion would cause the shaky limbs to crumble beneath her. But each step grew heavier, and she was forced to stop. Swelling tears blurred her vision and burned against her eyelids, and her feet once again were cemented to the floor. She wanted to run, to get as far from Roget and his lover as possible, but her legs and feet refused to obey. So she stood there, dazed, wondering where she could possibly go to escape Haitian society's bitter scrutiny. Probably everyone had known except she.

Clamping her lips together proudly, Lauren gritted her teeth in silent determination and accepted the only viable choice: to return to the ballroom. She would not give them the satisfaction of gloating in the face of her pain. Smoothing the pale turquoise skirt of her gown with determination, Lauren braced herself, knowing that once inside, there would be no place to hide her despair. Gathering what remained of her courage, she turned abruptly to mount the steps and collided headlong with the portly chest of Consul General Douglass.

"Madame de Martier," he chuckled.

"Forgive me, *monsieur,"* she stammered. "I—I was looking for my husband," she lied.

"My wife is ill and had to remain at home." He paused thoughtfully. "She does not fare well in this climate. Since your husband is not around, perhaps you would honor me with a dance." His kindly eyes twinkled as he held her in the depths of them.

"I would be delighted, Minister Douglass. That is," she hesitated apologetically, "if it is not a *bal* or a merengue. I haven't learned the Haitian dances yet."

"Just between you and me," he whispered as though it were a secret, "I'm not very good at them myself. Why don't we do something very European, like a waltz? I think they are about to play one now." Placing his free hand over hers, he led her pompously onto the colossal chessboard that served as a dance floor.

Lauren gave herself up to the music and let him lead her effortlessly through the throng of whirling bodies that dipped and turned to the same melody. He offered the calming influence she needed in order to collect the wild dispersion of her thoughts.

When the music stopped, she gazed into his wise eyes,

eyes that were surrounded by a lion's mane of white hair, and smiled. He could have been the grandfather who was left behind in Africa. Her strongest impulse was to throw herself into his arms and hug him but under the circumstances that would have been undignified. Instead, she lifted her mouth and placed her lips against his tired, aging cheek.

"Madame de Martier, you are a very charming young woman. Your husband is a lucky man. If I were a much younger man," he chuckled, "Monsieur de Martier would definitely have competition."

Obviously, he had not seen Mademoiselle de Luynes, Lauren thought. *"Merci beaucoup, monsieur,"* was the reply that came out of her mouth.

The stately American diplomat escorted her back to where he had found her and bid her good night. "I must be getting home," he said. A part of her went with him, and she stood gazing after the tall, robust frame until the bushy white hair was no longer visible.

Lauren turned to walk away, unsure of where she might find a familiar face, and a strong menacing hand imprisoned her arm.

"I believe you owe me a dance. I have not yet danced with the blushing bride," the voice derided her. She recognized Gaston's malicious inflections. "And now seems the perfect opportunity." Seizing her in his Herculean arms, he left her no chance to reply or means to escape. Lewdly, he held her body to his while his fingers pressed into her back. The aura of him crawled on her skin like a maggot. "You never cease to be in a hurry, *ma chérie,"* he taunted. A disturbing smile began to curl his thin lips.

"Let me go!" she demanded, struggling to free herself.

"I'll say one thing for my brother . . . He certainly picks them with fire." His devious smile grew wider and more threatening.

"If you don't release me, I promise you, I will scream," she uttered with quiet desperation.

"Do you really think your husband will hear you, or is he too occupied with Mademoiselle de Luynes?"

Despair pricked Lauren's soul as she saw their kiss burning before her eyes.

"She is a beauty, is she not? *And* a lady."

"What do you mean?" she flared indignantly. Her hazel eyes glowed an opalescent yellow.

"You know exactly what I mean, *ma chérie,*" he said quietly. "She is what you are not. *She* is a lady. And *she* was meant to be my brother's wife. You are a fortune-seeking wench, but don't think for one moment that you can charm me the way you have charmed your husband and the senile old consul general. There had to be powerful reason for him to risk defying his family as well as Haitian tradition. He married you for some reason. I intend to find out what it is."

"You disgust me," Lauren lashed back at him, attempting to shield herself from the painful truth in his words. She felt as though he had put a knife to her rawest nerve.

The iron grasp weakened, and Lauren wrenched herself free. Escaping, once again she sought refuge in the ballroom, grateful for its bright lights and deafening noises.

At last she encountered Roget. Balancing precariously on legs made of rubber while her voice trembled with uncertainty, Lauren said softly, "Georgette and Jacques Deffand would like us to have supper with them."

"Of course," Roget agreed affably. "Then, perhaps, I will finally meet Jacques's wife. I don't know how she has managed to elude me all evening."

Lauren was tempted to retort, "Because you were not available long enough to meet anyone," but she bit her tongue caustically and said nothing for fear she would lose hold of the taut reins that held her wounded emotions at bay.

How she survived the remainder of the evening she could not imagine. It was a gray blur. Roget and Jacques confirmed their plans to indulge in a game of bezique two weeks hence. The succulent roast pheasant and pastries filled with rich butter cream that they dined on might as well have been dirt. Lauren's senses tasted nothing. Her mouth was merely going through the motions. Far removed from anything immediately before her, she was remembering Paris and Claude and all the questions her aunt had posed about her marriage to Roget.

By the time the family arrived home and she was alone

with Roget, her head was throbbing with uncertainties. Deeply immersed in his own thoughts, Roget was oblivious to her distress as he moved about the room methodically pulling off one piece of clothing after another, preparing himself for bed. Lauren approached the open door, the tremble in her lips causing her to stammer.

"You . . . you neglected to tell me that the ball was being given in honor of Lucienne."

"What difference could it possibly have made?" he replied bluntly. "You would have met Lucienne sooner or later."

"I'm sure," she answered curtly, "but I might have been a little more prepared."

"You also might have chosen not to go, and it was imperative that we go and that my wife be with me for the sake of propriety."

"You mean . . . you dragged me through this evening of humiliation for the sake of propriety?" Lauren bristled with anger.

"You're a strong woman," he stated soberly, "a fact you have pointed out to me more than once. I'm sure you will survive."

Enraged at his arrogance and his brash indifference to her pain, she had never wanted to lash into him with her fists as she did now, but curbing the violent impulse, she locked her clenched fists behind her back.

"You also neglected to mention that you had seen her in Paris."

"Paris?" Perplexity twisted his handsome features. "How did you know that I saw her in Paris?"

Lauren explained the day she had seen them on the Bois, privately reliving the anguish it had caused her. "The moment I saw Lucienne," she added finally, "I knew that she was the same woman. Why—why didn't you ever mention it?"

"I had no reason to mention it. I didn't realize that you had seen us. But again, why should it concern you?"

"Why should it concern me!" she raged in utter exasperation. "Could my feeling like a fool be reason enough? Everyone knows more about my husband's past life than I do. You and Lucienne were not merely engaged . . ." Her trembling voice cracked. "You were lovers." Her mouth had uttered the words before her brain had time to contemplate what they were saying.

"I saw no need to discuss my past love affairs with you. You must have known there were others. I was not sworn to celibacy." Roget's tone was caustic and irritated. "I've warned you that your meddling is going to bring you nothing but pain. Yes! If you must know," he added sharply, "Lucienne and I were lovers."

"Were lovers," Lauren's voice echoed. "Are you sure that's quite the right term? You spent most of the ball with her."

"I have not seen her since February, before I married you. There were things I had to explain."

"Of course! Things such as why you married me, a woman far beneath your class, with no money and most of all with no blue blood flowing in her veins. Did you inform her that our marriage was merely a joke, just as our first meeting was only to fulfill a bet? Or did your kiss tell her that?"

"So! Now you're spying on me!" he bellowed. The sound reverberated off the walls of their bedchamber.

"I didn't mean to," Lauren recoiled meekly, embarrassed at having blurted out her indiscretion. "It was an accident. I was looking for you because the Deffands wanted to dine with us. You were not inside, so I searched the veranda. You were there with Lucienne. Roget . . . why did you marry me?"

"At this moment, I wonder myself!" His answer was full of contempt. Angry words flared between them, and they argued bitterly well into the night.

Finally, Roget climbed into bed, turned his back to her, and, without the slightest hint of an apology, went to sleep. One by one, the scalding tears welled in her eyes and spilled onto her cheeks. As she lay there listening to the sound of his breathing, Lauren felt the wall of indifference created by the smooth, muscled expanse of his back. For her, that wall was insurmountable. He loved Lucienne. Turning her face into the pillow, Lauren no longer fought to hold back the flood of tears that threatened to drown her.

Chapter 12

Lauren lay in bed staring up at the intricately carved ceiling. For all the world, she did not want to face this day. The ceiling above closed in, and claustrophobia seemed intent on overtaking her. She gazed at Roget's side of the bed, long ago cooled from the heat of his body, and wondered where on this vast plantation he might be.

It was late. The heat of the day was already pouring into her room. Rising slowly, Lauren walked barefoot to the balcony doors and threw them open, letting heat and humidity rush in. Wrapping her arms about her shoulders, she attempted to warm the chill that made her shiver despite the fact that she was surrounded by scorching tropical heat. The most vivid image in her mind was Roget and how bitterly they had argued. Angry, frustrated, and wounded, Lauren remembered Gaston's lewd insults. And Lucienne—that icy beauty who would never relinquish her claim on Roget. Good Lord! Why did she have to be so exquisite?

Following a scant breakfast of bread with jam and a cup of coffee with cream, Lauren secluded herself in the salon and attempted to practice, but her brain would not concentrate and her clumsy fingers refused to touch the right keys. Bristling with frustration, she banged all ten fingers with rude force against the ivory keys and got up. Impatiently, she paced the length of the carpet.

Her hazel eyes traveled the confines of the room, comparing its masculine heaviness to the cool white feminine beauty of the Villa Condé. Cool, haughty, elegant, and magnificent, the Villa Condé was much like Lucienne. Lauren's thoughts flashed back to the scene on the veranda when Roget's lips had taken hers with such excruciating reverence that she wanted to crawl into a hole and die. Was it their last kiss or was it the beginning of a rekindled fire? A ride along the mountains might ease her tension. She was not foolish enough to even think that Roget would care if she met with some disaster.

Sauntering along the shadowed hallway, tapping her crop against the banister, Lauren looked up with a start as she noticed Gaston about to enter his bedchamber.

"Bonjour, ma chérie." He greeted her, employing his usual abrasive tone. "You're just in time to join me for a drink. Our Haitian rum is quite special you know. Or would you prefer sherry?"

"I don't drink so early in the day," Lauren replied curtly.

"Then perhaps the lady would prefer tea."

It took a supreme effort not to lash him with her crop. "I would prefer to saddle my horse and go for a ride."

"Madame, I don't think you understand me. There is something I wish to discuss with you, and we couldn't ask for a better time."

"We have absolutely nothing to discuss!"

"Oh, but we do, dear sister-in-law. When you hear what I have to say you will be very interested."

Lauren looked him squarely in the eye, trying not to be intimidated, but his size was overwhelming. Slowly her eyes scanned his face. Those dark, brooding eyes, so much like Roget's, on him were menacing, and the broad sculptured nose and wide mouth were cruelly insensitive. At first glance he was handsome. It took a good second look to discern the ruthlessness of his nature. His eyes on her created a feeling of nakedness, and Lauren longed for the shelter of Roget's arms, to feel the warmth of his body protecting her, but that was impossible now.

Gaston's powerful hand closed roughly about her arm.

"You and my brother had quite a battle last night. I'm sure you were heard throughout the house. In the future," he said, smiling mockingly, "I would suggest that you argue over his infidelities a little less loudly." His strong fingers dug into the flesh of her upper arm. "So, Mademoiselle de Luynes ruffled your feathers. And for good reason . . . She would have been the proper bride for this family."

Lauren winced from the pain inflicted by his taunts, but her flesh was numbed to the pain he inflicted on her arm.

"I wrote to France for your birth records and have just received some very enlightening information. Facts that will be of the utmost importance to you and your husband. And now, dear sister-in-law, am I correct in assuming that you have changed your mind about the sherry?"

There was a lump in Lauren's throat and a flush of terror in her belly as she preceded him across the threshold. Reluctantly, she stepped inside, and he closed the door behind them.

Lauren stood irresolute, her back against the closed door, the palms of her hands pressed anxiously against the mahogany barrier that blocked her path to freedom. He motioned toward a pair of chairs that flanked a black-lacquered table and ordered her to sit down.

"Do sit down and make yourself comfortable. I trust you're in no hurry to leave." His voice taunted her. Slowly, she moved toward the lacquered chair, her eyes never leaving his face, and lowered herself onto the edge of the silk cushion. Not moving an inch further into the chair or allowing her body to relax, Lauren sat there like one awaiting execution.

Gaston reached for a crystal decanter, uncorked it, and filled two glasses. "You do prefer your sherry dry," he said. His dark eyes raked her boldly. "Or am I mistaken?"

"No, that's fine," she answered abruptly, her voice choking in her throat.

He came toward her with the glass, much closer than was necessary for his long arm to reach. The menacing hand moved forward and she jumped, revealing the depth of her fear. Her hand trembled as her graceful fingers closed about the delicate crystal glass.

"Do I frighten you?" Masked beneath the sympathetic words, she heard his mocking tone.

Not trusting her voice to answer, Lauren put the glass to her lips and took a long sip of the golden liquor.

Gaston lowered himself into the opposite chair, leaned back in a reclining position, rested both arms along the arms of the chair, and stretched his long legs to their full length before him. His feet ended up just in front of her, where she sat still perched on the edge of her chair. Blankly, Lauren stared at the smooth shiny leather of his riding boots.

"I don't think I should be here. What if someone were to see us here . . . like this?" The words trailed into her thoughts.

"Come now, *ma chérie*. Surely you are not worried about proprieties . . . a woman with your background."

"What do you mean, *a woman with my background?*" Lauren demanded impatiently. "You have insinuated things since I arrived in this house." Her fear was forgotten for the moment.

"You're quite a spitfire when you're angry." He laughed. It was that taunting, mocking laughter that made her skin crawl and her senses seethe with fury. "Relax, and finish your wine . . . then we will discuss it. Agreed?"

"Agreed," Lauren repeated skeptically. He was Roget's brother, but she could not trust him. Some unthinkable horror lurked behind those eyes.

Lauren eased back against the chair and tried to finish the sherry. Gaston remained opposite her, his gaze never leaving her body. Lauren fidgeted in her chair, turning first to one side and then the other, afraid to relax her muscles for fear he might catch her with her defenses down. Diverting her attention to the majestic furnishings, she tried to ignore the feeling that his mind had stripped her bare and left her unclothed and vulnerable before his eyes.

For all the grandeur and vivid color present in his bedchamber, it reflected not warmth, but cold, sinister austerity. The lacquered Chinese chests and chairs cushioned in brilliant red silk should have reflected elegance. All of France delighted in Chinese silk screens like the one that covered the wall behind his bed, but none of it, even slightly, warmed the chill that permeated her bones.

Gaston emptied his glass and drew himself into a more respectful posture. His motion jolted her from her trance, and recoiling her senses, she swallowed the last fortifying sip of the sherry. No longer able to contain the curiosity, Lauren blurted out her anxiety.

"What is it you wish to discuss with me?"

"My, we are anxious, aren't we? You are a clever wench. You play at naïveté so well." There was that tone again.

Lauren was livid but knew she had to control herself. She had to try not to antagonize him until she knew what he was capable of doing.

"What clever trick did you use to get my brother to marry you?"

"Trick," she repeated. The inflection in her voice questioned him. "I—I didn't use any trick. Trickery had nothing to do with it."

"Come now, you know as well as I that a man in his position would never marry you unless he had a good reason, especially after you have read the information that arrived from Paris."

"What kind of information?" she inquired hesitantly.

"The information on your birth records." Lauren swallowed hard, strangling the breath in her throat. "It seems, *ma chérie,*" he continued, "that you were born out of wedlock. It's beyond my comprehension how such a fact could slip my brother's notice unless, of course, it was covered over in some clever way."

Lauren stammered in her attempt to answer. Blood rushed to her face, turning her honey-hued skin burgundy.

"That's not true," she replied, choking with rage. "My parents were married."

"But not at the time of your birth. Of course, you know what this means." He continued in a vindictive tone that stripped her of any possible defense. "Once your husband learns of this, he will have no choice but to denounce you. To save his face and the family honor, he will have your marriage annulled. We will allow no such blot on our family escutcheon." His words burned into her consciousness, but there was no recourse except to write to Claude immediately and find out where he had gotten the slanderous information.

Lauren rose from her chair and, painful as it was, forced herself to face him. "If that is all you have to say, I would like to go now."

Gaston moved in front of her, his massive frame obstructing her path. "Don't be so anxious to leave. I'm not finished." The bright glare in her eyes questioned him further. "I know how much you love your husband and how much you want this marriage. If you're willing to be cooperative, I could be persuaded to see that these facts never fall into your husband's hands. But I do mean very cooperative."

"I don't understand . . . What are you—?"

"Let's not play naive. Not with me. You know very well what I mean." The thin lips curled into a vindictive grin, and Lauren was suddenly aware of his intentions. His cold, dark eyes locked with hers, and a strong feeling of revulsion washed over her as his hand closed about her shoulder. "I intend to find out exactly what charms enticed my brother to marry you," he said, kneading her flesh between his fingers. "There must have been a damn good reason for him to even consider bringing a wench like you into our family."

Wincing at the word *wench,* Lauren jerked free of him and ran for the door but was trapped again before she could open it. Gaston imprisoned her against the door, his outstretched arms positioned on either side of her head like bars. His weight pressed firmly against the lean, sinuous curves of her body while his malicious gaze slithered wantonly over her bare neck and down the front of her high-necked shirt where the collar lay open. Lauren's heart thumped wildly in her breast. Filled with revulsion, she tried to break free of him, but her strength was no match for his. After some minutes, her captor relaxed his grip. In a split second she bolted out of the door and down the stairs to the stables.

Lauren urged Miel along the obscure road that skirted the base of the mountains. Feeling bitterly defiant, she picked her way through the dense green foliage. Whatever warnings Roget had issued about her riding this road alone, however adamant, could not possibly matter to him now. His husbandly concerns had been voiced long before he had held Lucienne in his arms again. And Gaston was determined to destroy the marriage even if he had to conjure up false information to do so. They had all made it clear that she did not belong here, that Roget belonged to Lucienne.

Deeply entrenched in her own perplexing thoughts, Lauren forgot the animal beneath her as she allowed the reins to slacken. Miel slowed to a halt. Where could Gaston have gotten that information? The thought hammered in her head. The nagging doubts grew to an alarming height, forcing Lauren to turn Miel around and press the willing mare into a fast gallop back to the house.

Pounding into the stable, Lauren dismounted in a frenzy, as Old Jean grabbed the horse's reins and held them.

"I'm sorry, lady," she said, hastily fondling the mare's wet nose. "Tomorrow we will stay out much longer." Old Jean gazed quizzically at his new mistress, wondering what had thrown her into such a fit. Calling over her shoulder to him, her tone was short and clipped. "Give her a long rub down and an extra apple."

The old black man wrinkled his aging forehead. Madame Lauren always was so kind and friendly. Never cool and uppity like some of the others. She always took time to ask about his grandchildren, he thought as he led the horse back to her stall.

Lauren bounded into her room, almost slamming the heavy door behind her, and rummaged through the writing desk for paper and pen. Impatiently, she sat at the edge of the escritoire and composed an urgent letter to Claude. But while her hand wrote, her brain began to doubt the assurance she had displayed in front of Gaston, especially knowing that part of his accusation was true. Her parents had not been married when she was conceived.

Finishing the hasty letter, Lauren scribbled a few lines to inquire about her canaries. Anxious to know how the tiny creatures were faring, she thought if she ever saw them again, she would give them names. Before being engulfed by the wave of fatality that encroached on her, Lauren sealed the letter and took it downstairs to be posted.

"You are coming, aren't you?" Georgette pleaded anxiously. "Lauren, you must come. The other couples are Jacques's friends, and I will feel so out of place if you don't."

"Georgette, I don't know if Roget is planning to keep the date or not." Lauren was apprehensive. She and Roget had talked little since the ball, and she was unaware of his plans. "Anyway," she continued, "he certainly did not ask me to go with him."

"Well, of course, you will come with him!" she said exasperated. "Why should he even have to ask? We invited both of you. The other wives will be there and so will I, so why shouldn't you be? Believe me, Lucienne would be there if she were in your place."

Lauren bit her lip at the bluntness of her statement. Her friend had no way of knowing that Lucienne de Luynes might very well be in her place sooner than she dared think.

Miel lifted her head and whinnied, a shrill sound that pierced the still air. The two young women untethered their mounts and climbed into their saddles.

"I will expect you Saturday evening. Both of you."

"You just don't take no for an answer, do you?" Lauren smiled precariously.

That evening, as they descended the stairs to Madame de Martier's parlor, Lauren posed the same question to Roget. Oddly, she felt as though she was still hearing Georgette.

"I made the date," he said, "I have every intention of keeping it."

"You had not mentioned it again," she hesitated, "and you didn't ask me to go . . ." Her words trailed off unfinished.

"Why should I have to ask you to go?" His irascible expression screeched like a violin bow against her tightly strung nerves. "The invitation was extended to both of us."

Pushing open the door, Roget gestured for her to precede him into his mother's parlor.

* * *

194

Madame Deffand was delighted to see her and welcomed her as she would an oasis in the desert. The other two women could have been Lucienne's sisters, Lauren thought. Fair skinned with doe eyes and silken hair, they flaunted a superior attitude that meant to inform Lauren and Georgette that they were stationed far above them in this society. Lauren realized now why Georgette had been so adamant about her coming. It would have been torture to spend the evening alone with these marble goddesses.

The two couples were introduced as André and Marianne Louis and Edmond and Françoise Clerveaux. They had all known each other since childhood.

"Roget," Françoise purred rather coldly, offering him her cheek. *"Soyez le bienvenu."*

Roget touched his lips to her marble skin and commented, "I didn't see you at the ball."

"I was not feeling well that evening. Of all nights to be ill," she sighed, "when Frederick Douglass was there."

"But you and Edmond," she said, glancing proudly at her husband, "accomplished a monumental feat in your meeting with President Hyppolite."

Roget shrugged as though the accomplishment were not worthy of praise. "We did what we had to do."

Almost as an afterthought, Françoise offered Lauren a frigid hand.

Their husbands vanished into the billiard room. Boisterous laughter, clinking glasses, the flick of cards hitting the table, were the sounds that filled the air coming from their enclave. Every time the door opened and closed again the noise rang in Lauren's ears. She envied the camaraderie.

Françoise put down her wine glass and fluttered a beautifully manicured hand toward her head. Gently smoothing her upswept hairdo, she directed her attention to Lauren. "I hear you met Roget in Paris. Did you know him long?"

"Only four weeks," Lauren answered.

"I suppose in other parts of the world long courtships are not the custom." Françoise sighed. "Edmond and I were engaged for eight years before we married. Roget and Lucienne were engaged for seven years . . . We all thought for sure they would marry when—" She bit off the words, pretending that she had just realized her indiscretion and then feigned an apology.

"That's quite all right, you needn't apologize," Lauren replied graciously. "I have had the pleasure of meeting Mademoiselle de Luynes." Lauren imagined that had they been men, Françoise would probably have challenged her to a duel.

Again, the door to the billiard hall opened and the blur of male joviality pierced the air, only to be cut off when the door closed once more. Certain that she could distinguish Roget's voice from the others, Lauren was aware of her husband's pleasure.

"Men and their gambling," Marianne sighed aloud. "Do you play cards?" she asked, turning to Lauren.

"I have played, of course, but very little."

"Roget was always so good at cards," Françoise said with marked familiarity. "Lucienne used to get so furious with him for spending hours hovered over a card table, but that was his one passion."

Lauren's impatience was creeping to the surface. Finally, Georgette rose and suggested, "Perhaps we should join the men in a game of bezique."

"I would never . . ." Marianne said, this time arching both eyebrows. "Gambling is such a dirty business."

"It's so unladylike," Françoise chimed in.

"I would very much like to play if I knew the game," Lauren replied briskly.

Georgette dropped her head but not before Lauren caught a glimpse of her faint, puckish smile. "I've played with Jacques and his father many times for fun." Her dark almond eyes focused on Lauren. "You've never played bezique."

"Played it?" Lauren retorted. "I only heard of it two weeks ago.

"You and Roget spent your honeymoon in Paris. I find it hard to believe that he never played cards."

"I never said that," Lauren replied curtly, her mind racing back to the bet and the deck of cards over which they had met. "I said that he never played bezique."

"My dear, what did you do on your honeymoon?" Françoise rejoined in a tone pregnant with sarcasm.

Lauren replied with identical sarcasm. "We did not play cards."

Suppressing a chuckle, Madame Deffand exited. Lauren sat stiff, straight, and proper, knowing that the slightest relaxation of body muscle would release the bridle on her composure. Their ill manners chafed at the bit of her temper, but she was determined to behave like a lady, no matter how strongly their good breeding reared its ugly head.

Georgette returned, smiling. "The men have asked us to join them."

Georgette caught Lauren's eye with a mischievous grin. Jacques granted Georgette whatever she wished. "Shall we join them?" she insisted.

Eagerly, Lauren followed her hostess, and the other two women joined them as if being forced against their will. Under her breath, Françoise commented to her companion. "Roget has certainly changed. He always said that Lucienne made him nervous when he was gambling."

The room was smoky and the round leather-topped table was cluttered with half-empty glasses, decks of unused cards, and piles of chips. Roget was the only one not puffing on a thin brown cigar when the women entered.

Pétion, the Deffand's butler, positioned more chairs at the table, and the women took seats beside their husbands.

"This is not my idea of pleasure," Marianne grumbled, her haughty eyebrows about to meet with the ceiling.

"Roget, you will have to teach Lauren the game," Georgette chided playfully.

"She couldn't have a better teacher," Jacques added. Grinning, he shot a glance to the pile of chips amassed at Roget's side.

Roget was patient and painstakingly instructed her in the secrets of the game. At times, she felt his dark gaze perusing her but assumed he was only checking to see if she understood. Lauren beamed with the joy of accomplishment when she managed to win a game.

"Don't tell me we are going to have two of you in one family," Jacques teased.

Georgette tauntingly matched wits with the men, and when she won, Jacques chided her victories with comments about lady gamblers. Lauren doubted that Jacques would ever give Georgette reason to be jealous of another woman.

Edmond dealt the last hand, the cards slipping from his fingers like liquid through a sieve. Jacques won, and they all decided to quit.

"You still owe my wife fifty gourdes," Roget said, chuckling. Edmond counted out the bills one by one and laid them in Roget's hand. Pocketing her meager prize, Lauren took pleasure in the small achievement.

Pétion announced that supper was waiting in the dining room, and the two mulatto women swept from the billiard hall, their noses tilted upward as though they feared some pungent odor would invade their nostrils. After the buffet, the evening was over, having flitted away like a restless butterfly.

Pétion appeared bearing their wraps, and Georgette gave each of the women a plate of pastries. Françoise and Marianne climbed into their carriages while Lauren said good night to her hostess.

"What on earth could they be talking about now?" Georgette commented, noticing the men in a huddle on the veranda. "Sometimes I think men gossip more than women." And then with a note of apology in her voice, she said, "I hope the evening wasn't too unpleasant for you. I hope it wasn't too selfish on my part."

"No, of course not. I enjoyed the evening in spite of the not-so-subtle daggers that were aimed at my back."

Lauren bid her friend good night and started across the veranda, balancing the china dish on her open palm. The jovial male voices of Roget and his friends carried swiftly on the brisk night wind.

"You shocked the hell out of us, coming back with a wife the way you did," André said.

"You always were the sly one," Edmond added, "but we never expected that. There was no doubt whatsoever that you would marry Lucienne."

"We were just beginning to recover from Jacques's bringing home a bride and then you come home with one, too," André continued. "I doubt that our society can handle two such upsets in so short a span of time."

Edmond smiled warily. "Granted Georgette and Lauren are charming women, but they are not . . ." He paused, clearing his throat.

"From our class," Jacques Deffand interrupted abruptly, completing his statement in a tone that said his patience was stretched thin.

"Our families are adamant about such things," Edmond replied.

"I knew the moment she floated into her father's office and he introduced us," Jacques said, "that there could never be anyone else. And I was willing to wage war against my family and tradition to have her. And on that note, *messieurs,* I will say good night."

As Jacques disappeared into the house, André's curiosity rested on Roget. "Lucienne is such a beauty, such a magnificent specimen of a woman."

"You might as well say it," Roget broke in, "and get it out of your gut. There are few women who can match Lucienne."

"If you felt that way," André questioned, "why didn't you marry her?"

"Let's just say, *messieurs* . . . I had my reasons."

Lauren hurried down the steps, her fingers numb where they clutched the china plate, and was helped into the carriage by Paul, their young driver. Placing the dish absently on the seat beside her, Lauren clasped her hands together attempting to revive the circulation. Terror yanked at her heart, and Gaston's threats lingered in the back of her mind.

How could she compete with Lucienne? Everything was in her favor. His family, his friends, and even Roget himself thought she was beyond compare. Gaston's malicious grin pulled at her senses, and Lauren wondered if Claude's letter would ever arrive. The thought of Gaston's cruel, massive hands on her made her cringe with revulsion. There had to be another way.

Roget climbed into the carriage and sat opposite her, flinging his inverness back over the leather seat. Neither of them spoke. Both stared blankly through the window, their thoughts lost in the velvet blackness of night. The moon was full, and its beams flooded the inside of their carriage as

Lauren looked away from the window and allowed her eyes to linger on Roget. The shadowy outline of his features was intensely captivating when light rays caught the planes of his brow and cheekbones.

Roget pulled away from the window and studied his wife thoughtfully. "Madame Deffand is everything that you and Jacques claimed she was," he said. "She is a beauty."

"I think so." Lauren's shapely lips curled slightly. "But I don't think Françoise and Marianne would agree with you."

"It's incredible that beauty can be so ugly sometimes," he commented wryly.

"Françoise?" The inflection in her voice questioned him. "Who else?"

"Unfortunately, beauty in this world is measured not by the heart, but by the eye," she replied wistfully.

Clamping her lips together, Lauren turned back to the obscurity of night and tried to lose her thoughts among the shadowed images of trees that whizzed by her window. She was poignantly aware of his reverence for beauty. She had only to remember his and Lucienne's kiss.

Lauren's decisively closed mouth captured Roget's attention. Perhaps he was being too harsh, he thought penitently. Certainly, it was not her fault that she had ended up a pawn in his chess game. But Lauren was far more difficult to keep in the background than he had foreseen. If only she would not interfere, not be so damned persistent, stay in the background and not make him so damned angry! His anger had never ridden so close to the surface with Lucienne. But probably he had no right to expect her to behave like a Haitian woman; she was not a Haitienne.

Unable to tear his gaze from the shapely contours of her mouth, his thoughts raced to other moments, moments that he had denied himself for weeks. But he would not wallow in mere animal passion, especially when this marriage was simply a ploy to protect Lucienne. Yet, why did Lauren's mouth have to be so damned appealing? Finally, Roget dragged his gaze from her and focused his dark eyes on the scene beyond his window.

His quiet, sombre mood penetrated her awareness, and inadvertently, Lauren turned back at the same moment he looked away. Had he been different with Lucienne? If she were with him, would he be sitting on the same side with her, his arms enclosing her shoulders, or would he have sat opposite her, as he did now, with his long legs spread loosely before him? Would they be laughing together about some silly thing, or would he be staring out the window, deep in thought, his irascible mood made obvious by the tightening in his jaw? A twinge of jealousy pierced Lauren's heart. Lucienne had been with them the entire evening. Lauren mused, remembering her peach satin nightgown. Perhaps this was the special occasion for which she had saved it.

Villa de Martier was quiet when they arrived home, like a great mausoleum in the middle of the jungle. The lush tropical foliage rustled in the breeze, imitating the swish of silk skirts, and trees glistened with silvery raindrops beneath a clear open sky, the color of navy blue ink. Upon entering the house, it seemed they would wake the dead, and for some unknown reason, Lauren felt compelled to walk on tiptoe.

After depositing the dish in the pantry, they ascended the stairs, his heels clicking defiantly against the hard mahogany wood and she on tiptoe. Roget threw open the glass doors that graced their yellow bedchamber and stood gazing into a darkness that shimmered in misty vapor. "Dear God, what a beautiful night," he uttered softly as though thinking aloud. A tinge of excitement dominated his tone. Was he thinking of nights like this spent with Lucienne, Lauren wondered as he strode past her and vanished into the privacy of his dressing room?

The doors of his armoire opened and closed as he undressed and assembled his barely soiled clothing for León to launder. The third drawer squeaked as he opened it; it always did. Lauren wondered why he had not told León to have it repaired. Perhaps she was expected to do it, but it had never been made clear to her what her duties were, if any. Perhaps no one had bothered to assign her duties because they did not expect her to stay that long. A feeling of despair crept over her, and she shuddered at the thought of being cast off like an unwanted toy.

Working her arms free of the tight leg-of-mutton sleeves, Lauren inched the bodice down over her hips and stepped out of the pink lace gown. She shed her petticoat, unhooked the corset, worn for the sake of propriety, and soothingly sponged herself with warm water. The pale satin nightgown slithered over her body, making her feel like Eve in the Garden of Eden.

Caught by the mirror, her eye gazed at the image reflected in it. The lace bodice pressed against her small, firm bosom, forming the cleavage that was indecently displayed by the décolleté neckline. Feeling luxuriously wicked against her skin, the delicate satin clung to her hips and thighs, defining the sinuous contours of an hourglass waistline and an amply rounded derriere. The gown gave her a fullness that she did not possess. Lucienne's voluptuously feminine figure flashed into her mind, and Lauren was forced to admit that a well-endowed bosom was beyond her reach. Once more she glanced in the mirror. The image perhaps was not beautiful or voluptuous, but it was appealing. It had aroused Roget's passion several months ago on their honeymoon, but was it strong enough to do so now that he had held Lucienne in his arms again? Lauren went cold remembering Gaston's wide mouth and the way the corners twisted into that lecherous grin.

"Roget," she uttered his name softly. Somewhere deep within him there was a feeling for her, a feeling that had lain dormant for many weeks. Minute as it was, it was her only chance. Lauren chewed on the corner of her lip as an idea invaded her thoughts.

The sound of the door told her that Roget had entered the room. He stood with his back to her, hands in his pockets, still staring out into the night. His lean, narrow hips and broad shoulders were clearly outlined beneath the thin silk robe. Lauren's pulse quickened, almost smothering the breath in her lungs, but gathering her courage, she drew a deep labored breath and stepped through the bathroom door.

Startled by the sound, Roget looked back over his shoulder, his ebony eyes studying her image. Two raven black brows arched in surprise as Lauren floated toward him imitating the grand manner of Lucienne de Luynes. Head held so high that she could barely see and fingers lifting her skirt ever so delicately, Lauren carefully placed one foot in front of the other and glided like a graceful swan over the carpet. Her husband turned full around, his attention fixed on her upturned nose as a faint smile curled his lips. His dark eyes danced with amusement. That was not her intention at all. Her attempt to be seductive, he found only amusing. His amused scrutiny was agonizing, and Lauren bristled with the humiliation. Whatever made her think that such a ludicrous scheme would work? She wanted to run, to hide; she wanted the floor to open up and swallow her, but she could not stop the charade now without letting him see her defeat. Mechanically, her feet propelled her forward, and she moved toward him as if she were a doll wound up and set in motion, compelled to meet her fate.

Ironically, the ridiculous gestures grew even more exaggerated. With her chest pushed defiantly forward, and her honey brown limbs wavering to keep their balance atop high-heeled slippers, Lauren's upturned nose threatened to meet with the ceiling, totally discounting the fact that her feet still had to negotiate the floor. Heartily enjoying the theatrics of her performance, Roget's gaze remained fixed on her upturned nose with a precarious delight. At that inopportune moment, fate blatantly ended the charade. The heel of a slipper caught the hem of her luxurious nightgown and sent her sprawling across the floor to land flat on her face at his feet.

His strong arms thrust forward to help her, but scrambling to right the failure of her ignominious blunder, Lauren refused to be tortured by the scorn she imagined would be in his touch.

"Are you all right?" he asked. Realizing that she was not hurt, Roget returned to his upright position, his dark eyes still suppressing his amusement. Lauren nodded, unwilling to let her eyes meet his stare. Tucking her legs under the soft cushion of her buttocks, she sat up. She felt like a clumsy schoolgirl, suffering her first crush.

An uncomfortable silence fell over them as Lauren fussed with the fateful heel of her slipper. And then suddenly, as if he were reliving the scene, Roget broke into a fit of raucous laughter. The resonant sounds of his laughter bounced off the walls and echoed throughout their bedchamber, probably throughout the house. Lauren had never seen him so racked with laughter that the muscled contours of his body shook. Obviously, nothing had ever struck him quite so hilarious as the sight of her sprawled on the floor at his feet. Lauren burned with humiliation. She did not relish being the object of his humor. Her hazel eyes glowed opalescent with restrained tears as she lashed out at him.

"Would you laugh so hard if Lucienne had fallen on her face?"

"I doubt very much that Lucienne would fall on her face," he replied, not yet fully recovered. "You and she are as different as night and day. I'm afraid, *ma chérie,* you will never be a femme fatale." His lips bore a faint smile, making his sensuous mouth all the more appealing. He infuriated her so—how could she still love him?

Minutes later, Roget's dark eyes still danced with the remnants of his laughter, and that raucous laughter still rang in Lauren's ears. He knelt beside her and let his hands circle her waist, intent on helping her to her feet, but when she indignantly refused his assistance, he could not release her. Much against his will, his hand moved in a caress over her back to the sensitive nape of her neck where he buried his fingers deep in the springy mass of her hair. Lauren's heart thumped wildly against her chest, heaving nearly bare breasts up and down in rhythmic motion as they strained to escape the delicate lace that imprisoned them. Trying to ignore the desire stirring within her and with a decided effort to escape his insolence, Lauren turned away from his piercing gaze. But Roget's open palm cradled the back of her head, gently forcing her resistant body against the taut, hard length of his. When his ebony eyes locked with her hazel ones, he was no longer laughing. His gaze held hers in a long, mesmerizing stupor that rendered them both immobile. He was so close that she could feel the warmth of his breath against her face and the quickening pulse that raced through his body. Despite everything, his touch still turned her spine to putty.

"Lauren," Roget whispered raggedly, his voice emitting a deep-seated sigh of resignation dredged up from his gut. And then suddenly he was kissing her—a burning, passionate kiss devoid of humor or even sympathy. Her first impulse was to pull away, but the plundering insistence of his mouth slowly flooded her body with desire until she was powerless to resist him. His free hand slid over the shimmering satin and caressed the firm, round, amply endowed derriere trembling beneath it. Humiliation and anger were forgotten, as her body melted into his and she surrendered herself to the feel of his mouth consuming her and his hands boldly inflaming the eager, sensuous flesh covered by the satin cloth. Languorously, her arms coiled one after the other about his neck as the weight of his lean, masculine form forced her to the floor. Her mouth was captive to the tantalizing games played by his, and Roget took full advantage of his dominant position. The delicious weight of his body pressed her onto the floor until Lauren was sure she could feel the mahogany inlays beneath the carpet.

With excruciatingly deliberate slowness, his hands stroked the thin, provocative gown that covered her, forcing the garment inch by inch over her body to rest in a cluster of shimmery folds. His dark gaze feasted on her naked flesh, boldly following the line of her waist as it curved into her derriere. Lauren felt the penetration of his gaze, and she shivered with anticipation as the pale, delicate satin left her body. As Roget's kisses discovered the enticing valley between her breasts, Lauren's nightgown lay discarded in a pool beside her head, the last barrier between her body and the pleasure of his love. Or was it nothing more than lust? Bewildered by his sudden show of passion, Lauren shrank from his touch.

"Roget, why now . . . after all these weeks?" Her voice quivered with apprehension.

"You meant to seduce me, didn't you?" His lips curled into a perceptive grin, carefully masking his own desire.

Somewhere long ago, she had meant to seduce him, she could not deny it, but did his tone have to be so damned full of assurance?

"Would you rather not?" he questioned, separating his body from hers.

"No . . . no." Lauren nodded meekly. She could not bear the thought of him not finishing what he had started.

"Shall we go to bed?" he asked, his tone more a command than a request.

In one graceful motion, Roget lifted her willing body from the floor and placed her on the bed. The faint rustle of trees stirred, agitated by a brisk breeze outside the window, while the yellow fringe looped over the canopy of their bed swung mildly to and fro, caught by the same breeze. Roget pulled closed the French doors and fastened the latch. Untying his silk robe, he let it slide from his shoulders to join her gown, which lay pooled on the carpet. Moonlight played off his sable skin and accented the virility of his manhood. Lauren drew a deep breath at the sight of him. It was not only she who harbored the need to be sated.

The gas lamp on the table beside the bed flickered and died at his touch, and the heart within her leaped at the same touch. Moonlight flooded the windows, illuminating various angles of the room while leaving other parts in obscure shadow. Over the length of her silken flesh, Roget's mouth blazed a trail of sultry kisses from her toes to the quivering hollow in the base of her neck.

Lightly caressing him, Lauren traced her fingertips over the muscled contours of his body, letting the feel of his maleness vibrate through her senses, and Roget's rugged, masculine torso trembled and went weak beneath her touch. In the darkness, Roget's lips found hers with little effort, and his mouth devoured her hungrily, passionately, until her head spun in dizzying circles. Shuddering involuntarily as she touched him, Roget drew a long, deep breath and held it as she caressed the sensitive inner side of his thigh. The core of his being melted into molten liquid. Lauren's breath quickened to short gasps, and the gentle tracings of her fingers became urgent clutches as the heat of his masculine body pressed possessively into her feminine one. The room whirled like a cyclone about her head, and she was caught in a whirlpool of delirious ecstasy.

Lauren's body responded wantonly to her husband's kisses and the pleasurable manipulations of his body. Her body curved and molded to his, soft blending with hard, honey blending with sable, until they were truly one. Roget held a tight rein on his own cravings, allowing her the lead in their climb to ecstasy, but the unbridled passion was overwhelming. Within them both was a need to be sated that went on until morning.

As dawn broke, their spent bodies lay entwined in a twisted maze of arms and legs and hands and feet. Shifting his weight, Roget buried his face in the curve of her shoulder, his nostrils drinking in the delectable scent of her skin. Lauren's fingers stroked his back and encircled his trim waist. Her fingertips felt the smooth sable skin and the strong muscles that flexed beneath it, no longer taut and rigid, but collapsed and resting in a languorous repose. The musky scent of his passion lingered in her head, and she gazed about the room that now lay motionless and quiet. Even the shadows were still.

Roget shifted his weight again, this time moving his head to her shoulder. Catching a glimpse of her face as he moved, he said quietly, "Your face is flushed."

"You embarrass me," she replied sheepishly.

"Why do you say that?"

"You make me feel like such a . . . wanton hussy."

"Why? Because I give you pleasure?"

Blood rushed to her face, turning it burgundy red, as she recalled meeting him every inch of the way. How could she have given herself to a man who did not love her? Shame swept over her with a gust of truth. Roget's love had aroused in her the inclinations of a whore.

"I just never thought . . . that I would . . ."

"That you would have such a capacity for pleasure." Roget finished her faltering revelation as if he were reading her mind. "To put it mildly," he added perceptively, sensing that her thoughts were not far from his own, "you've shattered the image you would like to have of yourself as a lady."

Lauren bristled. She hated the way he could read her thoughts and put into words exactly what she was feeling. Resentful, her mouth clamped shut as she turned her face from his scrutiny.

Wedging her determined chin between his thumb and forefinger, Roget forced her gaze back to his. "I see nothing wrong with being a hussy for a few hours a night," he said, tracing his forefinger teasingly along the lines of her full mouth. Unwillingly, the pursed lips relaxed. "What more could a man want than a lady in his parlor and a hussy in his bed?"

"Do you think of me as a lady?" she questioned.

"Sometimes," he replied. Lauren noticed the beginnings

of a smile. "You are a lady when it's necessary. But there are times when not being a lady is far more desirable." He grinned mischievously and then relaxed. "Like a few minutes ago."

Her face flushed as she remembered the past night, but then suddenly Gaston's threats pushed their way into her thoughts, and she recoiled painfully.

"Is something wrong?" Roget questioned, lifting his head from her shoulder.

"No . . . nothing," she lied, praying that he would not probe further. How could she tell him the truth? If she did, she would have to expose herself and then definitely it would be over. She was not ready to face the thought of life without him—not yet. One day she may have to but not now, not this glorious morning. She remembered the passion with which he had loved her. Had he forgotten Lucienne, or did his love for her still burn in the sacred corners of his soul? Was this the beginning or the last burst of life before death?

Fear weighted her heart with uneasiness. Instinctively, she drew him closer. Warming herself from the fire of his body, she let the heat of his passion thaw the chill that threatened to overtake her. As their lips met, the yellow fringe on the canopy swayed with the rhythms of renewed passion.

Chapter 13

The younger Madame de Martier opened her eyes and stretched like a lazy jungle cat, disinclined to get up. Her gaze traveled to the opposite side of the bed, and her heart twitched a little as she stared at the empty space beside her. He had gone.

But something moved on the balcony. She noticed the dusky line of Roget's silhouette, arms folded over his chest, his attention focused on some activity below in the garden. Then she realized it was Sunday, the one morning he did not leave before she awakened. How long had he been awake? It seemed they had only gone to sleep a few hours ago. She smiled contentedly, stretching her arms the width of the bed. Probably not very long, he wasn't dressed. He still wore the blue dressing gown from last night.

Roget took in the lush green mountains in the distance that served as boundaries for the de Martier property. Had his great-grandfather had any idea what havoc he wrought when he built this place, he wondered, or had Valery de Martier anticipated the selfish follies of his sons and grandsons? Lust was getting the better of him. True, he had intended to make the marriage work despite his love for Lucienne, but he could no longer allow this insatiable desire to rule his reason. If Lauren felt like a hussy, he felt dangerously as though he were losing control. Paris had been an idyllic feast, but that was over. Once he returned home, he had intended merely to play the dutiful husband. He abhorred the idea that he could succumb to nothing more than animal passion. Ironically, he was no better than Gaston or the other men in his family.

Roget threw his head back and sighed. Heaven knows, he had not meant last night to happen. He had struggled to suppress his laughter, but nothing had been so funny in years as the sight of her sprawled on the floor. Once more his lips curled with amusement. When her mouth clamped shut indignantly against his laughter, he was powerless. He ached to possess that mouth, to feel her in his arms again, to feel those silken honey limbs clutching his body as he pleasured her. Instinctively, she carried him to heights which he had not thought himself capable. Nevertheless, it could not go on. The fact that she was in name his wife was no excuse for wallowing in lust. He loved Lucienne. He would always love her. This marriage to Lauren was solely to protect *Lucienne*. He could not bear to watch year after year and see her magnificent beauty destroyed as his mother's had been.

Roget shifted uneasily and dropped his hands to the iron railing. But then perhaps Lucienne was right. Perhaps the proper thing to do was have the marriage annulled before it was too late—for Lauren's sake. Yet, all his noble convictions to the contrary, he thought last night if he didn't have her, he would die. From now on, he would have to exercise a tighter rein.

Lauren sat up. Her nostrils could still detect the faint, musky scent of his cologne. Looking about the room she saw that he had thrown her nightgown haphazardly on a chair. She climbed out of bed, went naked to the closet, and wrapped herself luxuriously in her Japanese kimono.

"Bonjour. It's about time you got up, sleepyhead," Roget quipped lightly as he came in from the balcony.

"Bonjour," Lauren smiled sheepishly. Gazing at Roget, so calm, so much in control, she found it hard to believe that he was the same man who had loved her with unrelenting passion a few hours ago.

"I don't know about you, *madame,* but I'm hungry. What do you say to breakfast?"

Hunger gnawed at her stomach as well, but stronger than her need for food was her reluctance to destroy the final remnants of their rapturous night. "Roget," she began hesitantly.

"Oui," he replied calmly, his fingers flipping the pages of yesterday's newspaper.

"Could we have breakfast here . . . in our room?"

He looked up from the paper, a flicker of interest lighting his dark features. "I can't see why not," he replied, realizing he was not yet ready for the moment to end. "It would be pleasant for change. Why don't you ring for Filene?"

Minutes later, there was a soft knock at their bedroom door, to which Roget replied, *"Entrez."*

Filene sauntered into the room. *"Bonjour, monsieur . . . madame."*

"Madame and I would like to have breakfast here this morning. Will you take care of it?"

"Oui, monsieur." Her glance sped from the peach night-gown lying carelessly on the chair and lingered on the rumpled, unmade bed that Lauren and Roget had recently vacated. Filene's mouth twisted curiously with distaste.

"Is there anything special you would like?" Roget inquired.

"Whatever they have is fine, but I would love some of the plantain relish that Emmeline makes."

"Oui, madame, monsieur." Filene lowered her almond eyes slightly and left the room.

Heat from the sun poured through the open doors and baked dry everything outside that lay beneath its rays, completely disputing the fact that rain had poured in torrents the previous evening. Two young serving maids appeared at the door, giggling among themselves, one of whom Lauren had spoken to several days ago outside the summer kitchen.

"Bonjour, Lisa." Lauren smiled at the young girl.

"Bonjour, madame." She curtsied, her eyes lowered respectfully. She had been quite friendly that day at the summer kitchen, and now it made Lauren uncomfortable to see her cower before her like a slave. Meekly the girl went about her duties.

The yellow moiré cloth was whisked from the table and

replaced with white linen. Silver platters arrived, steaming with savory aromas that escaped from under their lids. Sunday breakfast was a grand feast, and except for the sumptuous array of pineapples, mangoes, bananas, and figs, it was more English than French. When they had finished eating, Lauren put down her napkin and smiled across the table at her husband. She had clung to every minute of the precious morning spent with him.

Bathed and dressed, they emerged as moths from a cocoon. Descending the same stairs they had climbed together last night, she turned to Roget and asked, "When can I see le Petit Cul-de-Sac?" Her request penetrated like a dagger. Roget's face twisted into a noticeable frown.

"Why are you so insistent on seeing that place? There is nothing there that would interest you," he replied sharply. "Besides, I'm very busy at this time of year; I don't know when I can have an afternoon free. You will have to wait," he added sourly. Little did she know that her persistence gave strength to his convictions.

Blast her, he thought as he left her. She seemed determined to follow in Reinette's footsteps. Her quick mind and her unquenchable curiosity would not be curbed by Haitian customs. She wanted to know too many things, to unearth things he had wanted to forget.

Returning from the stables, Roget found the entire family in the salon with Henri Duval.

"Roget, it's good to see you again," the husky black man said as the two clasped hands. "I was just talking to your wife about Paris. She knows it quite well."

"After our honeymoon, probably too well." His reply held a subtle sarcasm that Lauren was sure he meant for her rather than Henri Duval. However, the latter cleared his throat and swallowed a sip of his drink as he changed the subject.

"I hate to spoil your Sunday with business, but I thought if you had a few minutes, we could discuss the J. B. Vital offer that you were considering. They definitely want part of your crop. It seems the Italians ordered more than they can supply this year. I'll be in Jacmel next week. I could begin negotiations and at least see what kind of terms they are offering."

"Most of our crop is promised to France," Roget informed him.

"But we are willing to talk," Gaston added.

"By the way, have you heard the news?" the older man inquired, not bothering to wait for a reply. "Frederick Douglass resigned."

"I'm sorry to hear that . . . It's a hell of a disappointment," Roget said, his tone full of regret.

"My brother was one of his loyal supporters," Gaston explained, gloating over the American statesman's defeat.

"So was I." Henri Duval sighed wistfully, emptying the rum from his glass. Filene appeared in the doorway.

"We will be in the library for a while," Gaston instructed the housekeeper as the men left the room. "Have coffee and a decanter of rum sent up."

Lauren felt an overwhelming sense of loss at the news, realizing that she would not see the consul general again. She remembered the portly arms that had rescued her when she had nowhere else to turn. He had become the grandfather left behind in Africa when her pregnant grandmother was dragged from her homeland and put on a slave ship.

Hours later, Lauren found herself seated in Madame de Martier's parlor, her fingers nursing a glass of sherry. Antoine sat beside her, uncomfortably twisting a glass of rum between his own two hands, as anxious to end this ritual as she. Gaston's eyes had raked over her, knowingly reminding her that he intended to make good his threats. She felt more unclothed now than she had felt last night when she was naked.

Their mother's tongue had succumbed to the loosening effects of the brandy, and clinging to Roget, she mewed, *"Mon chou,* I've hardly seen you all day." Roget squirmed uncomfortably. "Henri Duval kept you locked up in the library this afternoon and your wife managed to keep you upstairs the entire morning. You never even came down for breakfast."

Lauren bristled. "I did not tie him to the bed," she retorted acidly.

All faces turned on her. Madame de Martier's mouth flew open in a loud gasp. Lauren doubted that there would have been so strong a reaction if someone stripped naked in front of her, but she didn't care. She was glad she had said it. She was sick to death with the pretense of politeness and no one saying what they meant except in whispers behind closed doors. She caught a brief glimpse of Antoine's smile as it faded. At least he was on her side. Gaston glared at her with contempt, and Lauren was glad that she had given him a *reason* to scorn her. Roget was annoyed rather than shocked, but she could not tell in what way. Was it chagrin or shame?

"My dear," Gaston reprimanded, "such things are not said in polite company."

"No," she replied caustically, "they are only alluded to."

Antoine rose from his chair, hastily refilled his glass, and gulped it down in one swallow. The tall, lanky figure fortified, he filled the glass once more and sauntered reluctantly back to his chair. Idly, Roget's focus followed his younger brother as if an idea had suddenly taken shape in his brain. Roget drew a labored breath and concentrated on his youngest sibling.

"You should have some free time in the next few weeks. Lauren wants to see le Petit Cul-de-Sac. I can't spare an afternoon to accompany her there."

Antoine looked up from his glass, his dark eyes brooding, a wry grin on his lips.

"Sure. Why not?" Their eyes met swiftly, Lauren and Antoine's, and both knew Roget was skirting the truth.

"Surely you won't mind entertaining my wife for a day. Besides, you know the place better than I do."

"Mind?" Antoine looked surprised. "It would be an absolute pleasure."

Roget sighed heavily as the onerous burden lifted from his shoulders. "You can arrange it between you," he said.

Lauren followed him with her eyes as he strode from the room. She marveled at his cunning. It was no wonder that he was the one de Martier capable of holding his ground against Gaston.

They took the back road that led north from the house and veered left where the road ended at the base of the mountains. The sky was overcast, allowing the sun to shine through the clouds in snatches, making the temperature cool for the month of July.

"We've chosen a bad day for sightseeing," Antoine commented.

Lauren nodded in agreement but made no effort to turn back. It had taken her three months to get this far, and she had no intention of forfeiting the expedition simply because it threatened rain. Roget's obvious reluctance to take her there had fired her curiosity, and she was anxious to press on.

"What difference does it make if we get wet?" she questioned. "We will not melt, you know."

Antoine flashed a grin. "It's no matter if *we* get wet, but the horses could break a leg in the mud. Their hooves sink too far into it."

"Well, then perhaps we should hurry," she retorted.

Antoine urged his mount into a gallop, and Miel followed the blinding gait.

Their horses made short work of the winding path that skirted the mountains, and in no time they had reached the fork. The breeze blowing over the water was cool against their skin, and Lauren welcomed the relief.

"That breeze feels heavenly," she uttered, lifting her face to let its coolness penetrate her skin.

"It comes from the river, la Rivière Blanche." He motioned idly with his free hand.

"It seems little more than a stream compared to the Seine," she commented curiously.

"I've never seen the Seine." A hint of sadness colored his tone. "Did you live near it?"

"I crossed it every day."

"One day I hope to see it." Waving his hand toward the bare, sandy plain that faced them, he quipped, "And here begins le Petit Cul-de-Sac."

"But there is nothing here." A look of dismay clouded her face. "I thought the workers lived here."

"They do. Their village is beyond those trees over there."

"Is that still de Martier property?" Lauren was astounded by the vastness of it.

"*Oui.* All of it. We own more land than we will ever know what to do with."

"Roget led me to believe that this section of the land was small and unimportant," she added.

Antoine's dark eyes flashed with perception. "Roget hates this part of the plantation. He comes here only if he must. Why do you think he so cleverly arranged for me to accompany you?" His lips curled into a knowing smile. "If he had his way, you would never set foot on this section of the property."

"Why does he hate it so?" Lauren frowned with uncertainty.

"I don't know . . . He avoids even talking about it, but part of it, I'm sure, has to do with Reinette." He paused thoughtfully. "Shall we go on?" he continued, his dark eyes penetrating her thoughts.

"Oui . . . Oui, bien sûr."

They covered a desolate expanse of land on which no living thing could possibly exist. It was too hot, too dry, and too exposed. Off to the right and just before the green fortress of trees that enclosed the village, stood a lone tree, its buttressed roots uncovered like the one in the clearing. Lauren shivered for no apparent reason.

"Are you cold?" Antoine asked.

"No, it's that tree. It's identical to the one near the Deffands' property."

"The mapous," he said, urging his stallion toward the gnarled growth. Nearby stood another solitary tree, its branches heavily laden with a strange fruit that Lauren failed to recognize. Antoine stared at the large tangled growth, his eyes moist and his expression glazed with sorrow.

"This is where Roget found Reinette . . . somewhere by that tree," he said. "That is one tree Roget would like to see cut down."

Lauren's voice caught in her throat and left her speechless. "What is it?" she asked, finally recovering her speech.

"A machineel. And the juice of that strange fruit is deadly poison."

Echoing the uneasiness of their riders, the horses grew restless to move on.

What was called the village was nothing more than scattered clusters of African-style thatched-roof huts surrounded by palm trees. Barefoot children huddled around a litter of newborn kittens, while somewhere within the cluster of dwellings a family battle was taking place. They heard a scream, and a young woman bolted into the road. Desperately, she grabbed at Antoine's reins, pleading for help.

"*Monsieur*, please . . . you must go to help me!" she rattled in a stream of rapid Creole, a little of which Lauren understood but most of which escaped her. "Always, he's wanting to beat me," she cried, casting her eyes toward the thatched-roof hut. The dark eyes grew wide with fear. "Monsieur Roget said if he beat me again he would go to talk to him . . . to make him stop, but *monsieur* never comes here for me to tell him."

A man followed her out of the hut and lounged against the doorway. Lauren remembered speaking to him the day she arrived.

"I say to Christophe what Monsieur Roget told me, but he only falls to laughing. '*Monsieur* never comes here,' he say. 'How you going to tell him?' I say to him that someday I would go to the big house and tell him, but he fell to laughing so hard I thought he had a vomiting. Someday he will kill me."

"Ernée, no one is going to kill you. I'll see to that. I will speak to Monsieur Roget myself." Antoine consoled the frightened woman, his Creole rolling off his tongue as easily as Roget's. She was calmer now, but fear still lurked behind her wide eyes. Casting those eyes on Lauren, the young woman perused her from head to foot.

"This is Monsieur Roget's wife," Antoine said in answer to her silent question. "Lauren, Ernée's husband and his brothers work with Roget."

"I know. I met them the day we arrived."

"Ernée, I'm sure Madame Lauren will speak to her husband as well," Antoine reassured her.

"Most certainly, I will," Lauren promised. It was the first test of her newly acquired Creole.

Lifting her dark almond eyes, the woman examined Lauren curiously as though she were a specimen under a microscope. Lauren became aware of an unusual camaraderie between her and the ebony-skinned young woman, though she knew they had little in common. Ernée was her age, similar in height, with high cheekbones and long graceful hands, hands that could have played the piano. How ironic it was that she had probably never seen a piano. Pangs of sympathy clutched at Lauren's heart as she stared down upon the barefoot young woman. If not for the grace of God, she might be in her place.

Lauren and Antoine rode on. They left Ernée standing in the dirt road, her wide eyes trailing behind them, full of the promise that they would speak to Roget. Lauren knew that she would even though it would cost her Roget's good graces.

What remained of the village, their horses covered in a matter of minutes. There were fifty, perhaps sixty, of the meager two-room huts, having as their only shield against the blistering sun tangled clumps of palm rushes that formed the roofs. Occasionally, the appearance of a one-story wooden house interrupted the grim monotony.

Skinny, barefoot urchins darted about the mud huts, their black skin glistening in the rays of sun. A woman moved from door to door, a huge basket balanced atop her gaily wrapped head. With gossip and greetings, she bartered sweet potatoes, yams, cassava, plantains, and artichokes. Most of the dwellings had plots of land planted with vegetable gardens, and a few boasted flowers. Doors opened and closed, heads popped out and then in again amidst hushed whispers and the quiet jingling of cheap metal bracelets. Peering from behind every door, Lauren imagined that she saw Ernée's wide dark eyes, terrified with fear.

Leaving behind a trail of dust and curious wagging tongues, they plunged into the lush, green forest. Low-hanging branches and thick green foliage reached out like human fingers and attempted to behead them, forcing their heads low in order to evade the eerie grasp. Grass grew in wild, uneven clumps, sometimes reaching as high as the horses' flanks, and in other spots, the bare, sandy soil lay exposed and desolate. The atmosphere imparted a strange aura of wilderness and savagery. Dutifully, she urged Miel to follow Antoine's mount as she fought to overcome the shivery sensation that invaded her body. Her eyes caught glimpses of the huge cement slabs lying about the ground.

Suddenly one loomed in her path and Miel balked, refusing to move past it.

"You will have to lead her around it," Antoine said calmly. "The horses here have as many superstitions as the people." He chuckled softly, and though his words were making fun, she sensed an underlying concern.

"What are these slabs of cement?" she inquired innocently.

"They're to keep the dead from rising," he answered soberly.

Lauren gulped and drew in a deep breath. "Is this a cemetery?"

"I suppose you could call it that."

She waited for some sign to show that he was making fun, but there was none. "But why—why . . . ?" She was unable to put her question into words.

"Why are they there?" He seemed to have anticipated her question. "Because the people believe that the dead will be stolen from their graves and made into zombies. The heavy slabs make the grave robber's work more difficult."

"Zombies," she shuddered, unable to grasp the grotesque meaning of what she had heard.

"They believe that a sect called le Culte des Morts is capable of raising the recently deceased from their graves and turning them into living dead to be used as cheap labor in the fields."

"Antoine, that can't be true!" she cried. "Such a thing is absurd." And then pondering the idea for a moment, she asked, "Do you believe it?"

"No, I don't, but they do." His reply held the same puzzling uncertainty as Roget's when she had asked him about the mapous tree.

As they emerged from the forest, a long, low rectangular structure made entirely of wood caught the corner of Lauren's eye. Lewd, grotesque, primitive paintings in white paint decorated its exterior. Yanking Miel to a halt, she cried, "Antoine, what is that?"

He swung his head around to the direction in which she was staring. "A *houmfort,*" he said calmly. "Vodunists use it for their ceremonies." Pulling his stallion round, he headed for the foreboding structure.

Lauren followed eagerly, anxious to get a closer look. A chill rippled her blood as she noticed that the drawings were of animals in suggestive carnal poses. The simple wooden building lacked windows, and there was only one door. Antoine sat astride his pure-bred stallion, talking about the sinister primitive structure, his face totally devoid of emotion. He was indifferent in the very way that Roget was indifferent to the alien practices abiding in his country.

"Have you ever attended a *vaudou* ceremony?" she inquired.

"Who me?" he appeared surprised. "No . . . never. I've heard that they're rather unpleasant. I have no stomach for that sort of thing."

"Do they use human sacrifices?"

"As far as I know, that is against the doctrine of the true vodun. Have you seen enough?" he asked, anxious to move on. "Shall we go?"

Lauren nodded and started forward but found herself glancing back unwillingly, curiously drawn by the weird structure.

Miel's white-stockinged feet cantered happily alongside her brown male companion, trodding once more on familiar territory.

"What do Christophe and his brothers do with Roget?" she asked, unable to erase the desperate young woman from her thoughts.

"He has been training them to be overseers in the modern farming methods."

"I know very little about Roget's work. Your brother is extremely secretive." She smiled, letting her gaze meet his.

"You love him terribly, don't you?"

"Oui, I'm afraid so." For a brief moment, she averted her gaze.

"Roget is not an easy person to know. Even as a boy, he was very self-contained. He hates so much of what goes on here but feels powerless to change it. He mixes well with other people, he's charming and amiable, but no one ever gets close to him. Except, perhaps, . . . Lucienne." Pain registered on Lauren's face, and Antoine continued, determined to make amends by shifting to another subject. *"Maman* told me that when Roget was a boy, he had a little pony, and he would take his pony and be gone for hours, never once disclosing where he had been. She said he used to keep things . . . little mementos, rocks and things like that. He owned a silver box given to him by our grandfather, and in it he kept his private treasures."

For the first time, Lauren realized that Antoine loved his brother. "I would like to know more about the workings of the plantation," she said warily, "but Roget refuses to discuss it with me."

"Women here take no interest in how the fortunes are made," he grinned. "Their sole duty is spending them. Elite women run their households, raise their children, and indulge in the arts. Politics and business are left to the men."

Lauren bristled at being reminded of their archaic attitudes. This was the nineteenth century. "I have no house to run, and I have no children to raise," she ranted with exasperation. "I have absolutely nothing to do." Restless boredom pushed its way to the surface. "I'm used to working, to being occupied."

"Well, you're a lady now," he teased.

"Has it always been this way?" she questioned.

"Our ancestors were poor peasants whose wives worked beside them in the fields. But as they acquired more land and the plantation prospered, the family grew rich, and the men fancied that the fair-skinned, gentleborn mulatto woman brought more prestige to a man of wealth than the black woman who had labored beside him in the fields. These women became their wives while the black women had to be content as an occasional mistress."

"How did they accumulate such vast quantities of land? Wasn't it expensive? How did peasants grow so prosperous?"

"It seems our patriarch, Valery de Martier, was a very progressive man," he replied, amused by her ravenous appetite for information. "He was a soldier in Pétion's army, and in 1809 when the president had no money to pay his men, he paid them in land. De Martier prospered because he had the foresight to use ploughs and modern implements instead of the primitive hoes, mattocks, and shovels being used by the other farmers. Unfortunately, few

Haitians have been successful with agriculture, mainly because they are not particularly open to new methods. Farming is left in the hands of uneducated peasants, and they're too tied up in superstition."

"But the landowners . . . are they also governed by superstition?"

"To a great extent, they are. Roget is more like Valery de Martier than anyone, I think. That's why Gaston calls him the scholar. He is always open to new methods and untried ways. Roget is definitely a gentleman farmer," he said with a grin, "apt to use more brains than brawn. And this is where he and Gaston lock horns. It was his foresight that installed the hulling machines. He battled with Gaston for a year before he got his way, and although Gaston hates to admit it, it saves time, manpower, and crops and yields considerably more profit. The plantation could not survive in this modern age without his insight, and Gaston knows it." He thought for a moment and then added, "Roget is also good with the workers. He keeps peace. He treats them like human beings and not animals, and they respect him. It was difficult here the year he was away . . . utter chaos most of the time."

Lauren had learned more about her husband in one afternoon with his brother than she had learned in four months of marriage.

Thunder rolled across the sky. Overhead, the clouds grew dark and suddenly foreboding.

"We had better hurry or we will never beat the rain," Antoine said, forcing his brown stallion into a fast gallop.

Hypnotized by the pounding rhythm of Miel's hooves as they devoured the ground beneath her, Lauren remembered the machineel. A drop of rain fell like a teardrop on her cheek and another on her forehead, but she brushed them away absently. "Antoine, what happened to Reinette?" her voice called into the wind.

"She was thrown by her horse."

"There must be more to it than that. Why was she riding out here . . . alone?"

"No one knows," he said, shrugging his shoulders forlornly. "Roget thinks—" Lightning bolted across the sky and exploded.

"Roget thinks what?" she questioned anxiously. The sky burst open, and rain poured through like water escaping a dam.

"We're not far from the house," he yelled. "We can make a run for it." They took off over the mud, Antoine's voice trailing behind him. "Roget thinks she was poisoned." His reply was drowned in the storm, and the conversation was left unfinished.

Within minutes, everything was flooded. The horses ran through pools of mud, splashing themselves and their riders with sandy red muck. Lauren and Antoine laughed at their misfortune like gleeful children playing in the rain. The cold, wet rain felt good splashing against their bodies and slapping their faces as they rode into it. The animals sailed through blinding torrents, anxious to reach shelter, while Lauren and her companion wallowed in a joyous return to childhood. Giggling wantonly at the sight of their transparent clothing, they entered the stable in a flurry of mud, water, and dripping clothes, dismounted, and ordered Old Jean to rub down the horses.

Old Jean's eyes gave them a dire scolding as he led the mud-spattered horses away.

"Have we done something wrong?" Lauren asked. "Old Jean seemed annoyed with us."

"We should not have raced those horses through the mud as we did. The de Martiers do not take lightly to losing their horses." His expression was repentant, but then he smiled mischievously and added, "But it was fun, wasn't it?"

Lauren agreed, still suppressing her giggle. She had not laughed so heartily in years.

Entering the house by the back door, they received many curious stares from Emmeline and her kitchen staff.

In the main vestibule, they ran headlong into Gaston, who scolded them. "You raced those horses through the mud with your childish games. Do not allow it to happen again," he glared, his cold, dark eyes narrowed with scorn.

Behind the glare, Lauren felt him undressing her, though the transparent shirt and clinging breeches left little for his eye to remove. She covered herself with her arms and ran hastily upstairs to her room. The rain had washed her clean, and now she felt soiled again.

Shortly after her arrival, Roget came in, and he too was soaked to the skin. The drenched clothing clung to his lean form in much the same manner as the things Lauren had just stepped out of.

"I see you were caught in the rain along with the rest of us," he said, his eyes noticing the pile of wet clothes on the floor.

"Antoine took me to le Petit Cul-de-Sac, and we could not get back in time."

"You chose a perfect day for it." His tone was grimly sarcastic. "Are you happy now?"

"It was interesting . . . but strange."

"Very strange, I would say." His voice mocked her.

Realizing that this was not the time to bring up the subject of Ernée, Lauren ordered her bath instead. Sliding into the luxurious water, letting the soft, foamy bubbles cover her, she still could not erase the young woman's pleading eyes from her memory. The ground between her and Roget had been severely strained lately, and she wondered if she should risk antagonizing him further under the circumstances. But the sound of Ernée's desperate pleas echoed in her ears, and she knew that she must, whatever the price.

Emerging from her bath, Lauren found her husband freshly bathed and dried and, she prayed, in better humor. He stood in his dressing room naked, a towel covering his hard, round buttocks and narrow hips. She ached to be in his arms, to feel his mouth claiming hers, but it was impossible to forget Ernée.

"Roget . . . I want to talk to you about something."

"Oh?" He raised one raven black eyebrow. "What is it?"

"I met the wife of one of your men today. Her name is Ernée. Do you know her?"

"Oui." His eyes flickered with recognition. "Christophe's wife."

"She said that you promised to talk to Christophe if he beat her again. Well, he has beat her again, and the poor woman is terrified that he will kill her. I promised her that I would do what I could."

"Lauren, you have no right to promise her anything," he

said sharply. "This is not your business. I wish you would refrain from meddling in things that do not concern you."

She was well accustomed to that look of bitter annoyance he exhibited whenever she showed an interest in plantation matters. Undaunted, she persisted. "She believed you when you promised to talk to him."

"I can talk to him . . . That does not mean he has to listen. I have no control over what people do in their homes."

"Surely he will listen to you. Antoine says that they respect you. Can't you explain to him that a man should not beat his wife?"

Breathing a deep sigh of exasperation, he forced both raven black brows into his forehead and turned away. "Lauren, do you really expect the man to understand that?" he asked, turning back to face her. "What do I say to him? It's not nice to beat your wife? They don't understand our value systems anymore than we understand theirs. We are different classes of people, but it's necessary that we work together. I can keep peace in the fields and the warehouses. I can't govern their lives. Nor do I want to." His sensuous mouth twisted wryly while a quiet anger raged inside him.

"There must be something you can do." Lauren's voice scaled an octave. "Roget, the woman was terrified. Will you not at least try to talk to him? If you won't, I'll talk to him myself." Lauren knew very well that she was calling his bluff, yet it got the response she wanted. He glared at her acidly, and if a look could kill, she would surely have been dead.

"Lauren . . . if you dare try such a thing, I promise you I will—" His voice cut off bluntly, choked by the veins gorging in his throat. Lauren shuddered at the impact of his rage.

"What, Roget, put me across your knee and spank me?"

"It's not a bad idea . . ." His eyes glared. "Maybe Christophe is not so wrong after all."

"Why don't you? That seems to be the way other Haitian men handle disobedient wives." Her hazel eyes clashed with his ebony ones in a relentless fury. Two sets of ivory teeth clenched with stubborn determination and neither he nor she would back down. After moments suspended in time, Roget turned his naked back to her. When he faced her again, he held a tighter grip on his temper.

"All right . . . I will speak to him . . . this time. But in the future, I will thank you to leave the running of the plantation to the men. Women here do not meddle in business affairs; they have other things to occupy their time."

"I am not one of your precious women," she retorted with exasperation. "And I'm sick to death of the idle pursuits of women!"

"Certainly you can find something that interests you," he replied flatly.

"I only want to help you and understand what you do." Her tone pleaded for acceptance.

"Lauren, I don't need your help. From this moment on, I would appreciate it if you did not interfere." The words from his tongue hurt worse than if he had slapped her across the face. Lauren suddenly had the queer feeling that she had won a battle but lost the war. She had not helped herself, but perhaps Ernée would breathe a little easier.

Some nights later, Roget left the house following dinner and did not return until early morning, choosing then to sleep on the daybed in his dressing room. Lauren's pride forbade her to ask where he had been. Week after week, she watched as he spent countless nights away from home. At first, she had not been able to sleep without the warmth of his body lying next to her, but out of sheer desperation she had long since given that up. The few evenings he spent in the house were with his mother in her parlor or alone in the library, his head buried in a book.

Lauren had known since the first night that he had sought consolation in Lucienne's arms. When Georgette's tongue slipped and accidentally told her she had seen Roget riding with Lucienne, Lauren was not shocked.

"Lauren—I'm so sorry," she gasped in horror. "I did not mean to be so thoughtless. I can't imagine what I was thinking of." The penitance in her face rivaled her friend's despair.

"It's no matter, Georgette," Lauren consoled her. "I've known for some time." A sadness claimed her voice and kept imprisoned in her throat anything more she might have said. She could only imagine Lucienne's beautiful auburn hair combed into an elegant double pouf and the graceful sway of her voluptuous figure as he swept her into his arms. Lauren shook her head to erase the picture, but it refused to fade. Her husband was hers in name only, and if Gaston had his way, that too would soon be changed.

Chapter
14

In September, the Freemasons of Port-au-Prince lent their majestic, walled-in temple to raise funds for the Orphelinat Saint Joseph, and this year, President Florvil Hyppolite lent his impressive military band for the occasion. A group of elite women, who prided themselves on their generosity, lent their time, making the performance a major social event of the season. The landed gentry were expected to attend and bestow Saint Joseph's home for homeless children with generous contributions.

Lauren dreaded the evening. Since Roget had informed her of it a week ago, she had invented a plethora of excuses to forego it, but they were useless against de Martier tradition. Roget de Martier would be expected to escort his wife, and she, of course, would have to go whether she wanted to or not. The family code of honor insisted that she and Roget show proper face to their society. It had never been her society, they had not accepted her, and bearing their scorn seemed so fruitless now. Lauren envisioned herself smiling beside Roget, laughing and trading small talk with his friends and wondering if they knew.

As her foot paused on the last set of stone steps that led into the garden, her head began to throb and her hazel eyes narrowed with pain. "Why must I be tortured so?" Lauren murmured softly. Covering both eyes with the palms of her hands, she shielded them from the blinding sun and tried to turn off the thought that resounded in her head. How would she endure the moment when Roget's ebony gaze met Lucienne's across the room? "I will not go!" she cried, bringing her fist down futilely against the stone balustrade.

Lauren ambled restlessly among the brilliantly flowered bushes, vowing to find a way out of the ordeal. Yet she knew deep within her that in the end she would be forced to go— by the family, by her pride, or as a last desperate measure to cling to the hope that was slowly fleeting away. If only the letter from Claude would come, she would have some concrete evidence of the truth with which to face Gaston.

"Madame, monsieur say to tell you that they wait for you." The fair-skinned young woman stood in the hallway timidly peering through the narrow opening created by the door and its jamb. "Madame de Martier send me. She say that I'm to help you dress." Having accomplished pitifully little by herself, Lauren pulled the door open and, with a grateful smile, ushered her inside.

"It seems I could use some help," she uttered, spreading her arms in a gesture of helpless futility. From behind light eyes set in a rather plain face, the younger woman perused her half-dressed mistress and then shot a glance to the jade green and ivory gown still hanging in the closet. "Perhaps if you could do something with my hair . . ." Lauren paused, her eyes seeking the girl's name. "I can't seem to do anything with it." Her voice cut the air with a sharp edge of frustration.

"I'm Cybele, *madame,"* she replied, speaking her imperfect French with a decidedly English accent. She could not have been more than seventeen, Lauren thought, but her quick fingers worked with the skill of an older woman. Within ten minutes, she had the dark bushy hair brushed smoothly into a pouf and the knot at the crown of her head ringed with ivory feathers. And in the next five minutes, she had hooked her new mistress into the embroidered ivory bodice of her gown.

"Merci, Cybele," she said, smiling gratefully. Draping the feather-trimmed wrap over her bare shoulders, Lauren hurried downstairs to the waiting carriage.

Roget stood below in the stark black and white of masculine attire, impatiently rapping his fingers against the hard crown of his hat. Her gaze scanned him from head to foot. It had been weeks since they shared the same bed. Somehow, she would have to drown her feelings for him, or the evening ahead would be a torture she had not imagined.

"You're late," he said, his dark eyes clashing into hers. "What on earth took you so long?"

"I couldn't do my hair . . . Nothing seemed to work." Could she confess to him that no matter how she styled her hair, she could not rival Lucienne's beauty.

"Maman found a maid for you. Perhaps after this, you will cease being stubborn and use her."

"I will," she agreed reluctantly. Like a small child being scolded, she gazed down at the toe of her shoe. Roget's eye caught the graceful curve of her neck and the softness of her cheek as she turned into the light.

"We have to hurry," he said in a sharply clipped tone. Brusquely, his hand closed about her arm, and he steered her through the door. Old Jean helped them into the family carriage, and they settled in for the long journey to town.

"Lauren, you're very late!" the older woman scolded. "We will barely arrive before the performance."

"I'm sorry, *madame,"* Lauren apologized unwillingly. If she had her way, they could have gone without her.

"Well, I hope Cybele will prevent this tardiness in the future," she continued. "It is such bad taste to arrive after the performance begins. It leaves no time to greet friends."

Lauren looked away and focused her attention outside the window. For once, she was thankful for her mother-in-law's senseless chatter and even more thankful that she was not forced to endure Gaston's disdainful glare. The master of the house had gone to call for a lady. For the life of her, she could not imagine what lady would want him, but then he had de Martier wealth with which to woo her. The blue-blooded marble goddesses were probably waiting in line.

Roget, Antoine, and Madame de Martier traded meaningless small talk, but Lauren did not bother to join in. Suddenly the carriage jolted and swerved sharply to the right, throwing her intimately against the taut, lean length of her husband's body. Steadying her with his hands, he returned her to the opposite side of the chamois seat. "You had better brace yourself," he quipped. "Old Jean seems to think that we're in a hurry." He smiled vaguely.

The other two chuckled as well, but Lauren hardly noticed. Unable to suppress the tightening sensation that squirmed through her belly, she wondered how on earth she would get through this evening.

They arrived at the temple just six minutes before the hour, which left little time for social amenities beforehand.

Eventually Lauren felt the exhilarating rhythms of marches and flourishes along with the others. The beat of the drums, the cry of the bugle, and the zing of the cymbal, coursed through her veins catching her up in the fanfare. Lauren and Roget talked only when necessary, and she loathed the formality of it. One would think that he was a stranger she had recently met instead of her husband.

After the last thumping march came Haiti's national anthem and then a thunderous applause mixed with boisterous cries of "Bravo." Lauren applauded with great zeal. Stepping onto the rich Turkish carpet in the reception hall, she felt the pressure of Roget's hand burning against the flesh of her upper arm, and she was startled when he dropped a perceptive comment.

"So you enjoyed the performance after all."

Her usually glib tongue fumbled for an answer. "Much to my surprise," she said finally, "I did."

"When I first mentioned it to you, you seemed uninterested."

"I truly didn't want to come, but I'm glad I did. The president's band is superb." Would he also know that part of what she had said was a lie? As her foot sunk into the lavish blue, red, and gold carpet, her eyes glanced swiftly toward the door. She would only have to cross the floor, go out the door, and her ordeal would be over. But glancing back at the throng of people and at Roget beside her, she knew she had to stay and face it, however painful it might be. If she went through the door, her marriage would definitely be finished.

"Lauren." She heard a voice call her name.

"Georgette," she murmured under her breath.

"Did you say something?" Roget questioned.

"Nothing important," she replied. "I heard my name . . . I thought it must be Georgette." By the time the last word had left her lips, Madame Deffand emerged from the crowd dragging Jacques by the hand. She was so unpretentious, so refreshing. And stately as Jacques was, he followed behind her like a dutiful puppy. The two men clasped hands warmly, but Georgette greeted Roget with an expression of glaring disapproval.

"The band was fantastic, didn't you think?" With this comment she shifted her attention back to Lauren. "Last year the concert was not nearly as good, was it, Jacques?"

"As a matter of fact," he grinned in agreement, "it was terrible." His gaze met Roget's head on. "What do you say to another night of bezique?"

"Anytime," Roget agreed amiably, "you name it." The gleam in his eye reminded Lauren that her husband did enjoy his games of chance. He had strode into her life and turned it upside down only because he was determined to make good on a bet.

"Shall we say two weeks . . . Friday evening?"

Roget pondered the suggestion quickly and then agreed. "That should be fine."

Lauren threw her attention into the crowd, anxious to avoid Georgette's questioning glance. Almost immediately, her idle stare caught a glimpse of Madame Duval, who recognized them and came rushing over to join the festivities.

"Darling Roget," she gushed, offering him a limp hand to be kissed. Accepting her gloved hand, Roget touched his lips to it gallantly. Briefly, she acknowledged the Deffands.

"And Lauren," she added as if it were an afterthought. "How nice to see you again, dear." Her tone was as boldly insincere now as it had been aboard the ship. In spite of her contempt, Lauren took her outstretched hand and smiled pleasantly.

"It is good to see you again, Madame Duval." Memories wandered back of the great show of emotion with which Roget had kissed Lucienne's two hands the night of the ball. He had never offered her the courtesy, Lauren thought. Was this gallant gesture reserved for ladies only? Good heavens, why was her brain dwelling on such trivial things?

"My dear, I've been told that you are a remarkable pianist." The older woman's sardonic tone had mellowed considerably. "Certainly you would be willing to donate your talent to those poor, unfortunate waifs." Georgette shot her husband a derisive glance as the woman pompously spouted her attempt at charity. "We must help those less fortunate than ourselves, mustn't we?" Her voice still hinted at condescension, and Lauren was not sure whether the pun was directed at her or the children. "Roget, you wouldn't mind?" she inquired dutifully.

"Lauren is free to do whatever she likes with her time. It would be good for her to be busy at something."

"You will do it then?" she pleaded, her tone suddenly embracing the younger woman. "We do so need women with talent to offer."

"I suppose so . . ." Lauren hesitated, groping in vain for words that would allow her to refuse.

"Since you don't yet have a child to occupy your time, you could put yourself to good use."

Child. The word echoed through Lauren's head. She would probably never have a child.

"I agree wholeheartedly, *madame.* She needs something worthwhile to do." Roget grinned slyly and glanced at his wife. "Perhaps it will keep her from meddling in plantation business." And then glibly, he added, "She *is* a talented pianist. She plays a superb *Fantasie Impromptu.*"

Lauren fumed with indignation. The nerve of him! How could she possibly refuse after her husband had so generously offered her services. Not that she would have refused anyway, but she wanted the right to make her own decision. Her hazel eyes burned with vexation. Noticing the faint glint in his eye, it was obvious to her that he was pleased with any occupation that would keep her out of his hair.

"Good. Now that it's settled, I must borrow your wife for a while. I want her to meet the other women." Without another word, Madame Duval whisked Lauren away from the gathering.

Simone Gevres and Gabriel Fortier welcomed her cordially. No doubt they were unaware of her lineage. But then again, Madame Duval was not the kind of woman who kept any bit of gossip secret. Petite and rather pretty, Simone

Gevres was overjoyed at Lauren's willingness to share her task.

"You don't mind if I call you Lauren, do you? Call me Simone." Unleashing the rigid rein on her poise, Lauren liked her instantly. "We thought musical entertainment at one of the larger villas might be a good idea. Though I studied piano in France for several years, it's more than I could possibly handle alone."

"Oh," Lauren uttered with interest. "Where did you study?"

"Le Conservatoire de Musique et de Declamation."

"You must be very good."

"Are you familiar with it? Madame Duval told us that you came from Paris."

"It's one of the best," Lauren replied, impressed with her colleague's apparent ability. The two young women chatted amiably about France and music and the few things they had in common. Simone had been married less than a year and therefore had no children either. Though light skinned and lovely, she lacked that haughty, superior attitude embraced by the other women. Perhaps they would be friends.

Nevertheless, Lauren's thoughts never strayed far from the impending doom that hung over the evening. Once she looked up and stared blankly at a double-poufed hairdo and the pale beige shoulders glistening beneath it. Beads of cold sweat broke out on her forehead, her knees turned to rubber, and for the first time in her life she thought she would faint before realizing that the woman was not Lucienne. Waiting for the inevitable moment was like waiting to face a firing squad—knowing it would come but not knowing when or how. At least after the guns were fired, the prisoner was dead; she would still be alive.

Roget and Henri Duval abruptly terminated a heated discussion as their wives approached. "Georgette said that she will ride with you tomorrow," Roget said, recounting a message to Lauren. Lauren merely nodded her head in acknowledgment.

A crisply uniformed waiter marched by, a tray of crystal champagne glasses perched on his arm. Lauren reached for a glass along with the others and swallowed a long sip of what had been aptly called liquid stars. The flavor rolling over her tongue was refreshing, and the bubbles playfully tickled her throat. She chuckled softly, thinking that the expensive wine might refill the courage that was slowly seeping from her body. Lifting the glass, she swallowed another deep gulp. Her insouciant behavior drew a sharp, admonishing glance from Roget. What did it matter whether she behaved like a lady? Lucienne was a lady—that was all that should matter to him. Recklessly, she turned the glass up and emptied it and then looked around for a waiter so that she could retrieve another.

Finishing her second glass of champagne, Lauren placed it flippantly on an empty tray.

"Roget, here you are!" Françoise Clerveaux appeared from nowhere and swept into their presence, commanding undue attention. "Edmond said that he had seen you during the performance, but it's been the devil trying to find you. Madame Duval . . . *monsieur*," she purred, kissing the older woman on both pale cheeks. "Have you seen Lucienne?" she inquired frivolously, focusing on Roget. "I cannot find her anywhere. One would think she'd be easy to see with the gown she's wearing." Her beautifully manicured hands flapped arrogantly against the air as she talked. "Lauren, how nice to see you," she added with a nauseating sweetness. "I don't suppose you've seen Lucienne either."

Lauren felt a hiss of anger snake through her gut and give way to a sudden impulse to slap her face. For one split second, she wanted to smash that haughty, upturned nose with the brunt of her humiliation. But instead, she said pleasantly, "No, I'm afraid not."

"Has no one seen her?" Françoise continued.

"None of us has seen her this evening," Roget replied curtly.

"Oh, well . . . I must find my husband. *Au revoir.*" Putting her fingers to her lips, she blew a kiss at Roget and departed. Roget moved his head slowly from side to side as their eyes followed her into the crowd.

The minutes ticked by, and Lauren felt the last ounce of courage seep from her pores. Perhaps they would not acknowledge each other tonight. They had probably agreed beforehand to avoid an embarrassing situation. Why had she been so silly? Feeling lighthearted and lulled by the false sense of tranquility, Lauren reached for a third glass of champagne. As her fingers closed around the crystal stem, she glimpsed an ethereal fushia gown flowing regally across the room. Her hand trembled, spilling the bubbly liquid on the tray and the carpet, while the Duvals looked on, not uttering a word. Roget did not notice her clumsiness, but he did notice the fuschia gown. Unwillingly, Lauren's gaze was drawn the length of the gown to the bodice to the pale shoulders and auburn hair. She was breathtaking! Flinging her head away, Lauren took a reckless gulp of champagne and began to choke.

The coughing spell captured Roget's attention, and he scolded under his breath. "Madame," he whispered sardonically, "I think you've had enough champagne." Taking the half-empty glass, he placed it on a passing silver tray. "That is what comes from drinking like a wench."

Lauren cringed at the word. She had not heard him use it before. Gazing down at the toe of her satin slipper, she looked up again to find that his focus had been drawn back to the chiffon gown and the woman who wore it.

The Duvals were called away to join other friends, and Lauren drew a deep ragged breath, trying to hold onto what little of her composure remained. She could not look at Roget. She didn't dare. Lucienne came toward them, her arm entwined in that of a much older man, and their eyes met. In that brief moment, everything Lauren had dreaded came to pass. Roget's dark eyes glowed with a tenderness that she had not seen. In his eyes, she saw warmth, adoration, and love—unmistakable love. He still loved Lucienne. Their last night of passion had meant nothing—at least to him. His eyes devoured her beauty as one who drank in the omnipotence of a great work of art. Tears scalded her eyelids as she watched.

"Lauren, Roget . . . how nice to see you," she said as if it were just a friendly meeting. This time, Roget refrained from kissing her hand.

"Bonsoir, monsieur," he said, warmly grasping the older man's outstretched hand.

"And you must be the young woman Roget married. I've not had the pleasure of—" His voice was intercepted by his daughter's.

"Papan, this is Lauren de Martier, Roget's wife."

Offering her hand mechanically, Lauren uttered almost inaudibly, *"Bonsoir,* Monsieur de Luynes."

"We were certain that you and Lucienne . . ." The words trailed off. His confused expression bordered on senility.

"Papan, s'il vous plaît," Lucienne injected. He looked affectionately at his daughter and feebly patted her hand.

"I suppose you are right . . . We have no right to plan our children's lives," he said. Vacantly, his light gray eyes stared into space. "But its been tradition for so many years."

The champagne in Lauren's stomach rocked from side to side, like a storm-ridden boat. Her head whirled about the room, and she imagined the thick Turkish carpet coming up to meet her. Mumbling a few words of apology, she rushed frantically from the room before a worse disaster overtook her. In the powder room, she sat at the dressing table and stared in the mirror at the face staring back at her, as though it was a stranger. She made a pretense of repairing her sparse makeup, but the task was impossible. The tears escaped one by one and dropped on her bare chest, forming a stream that trickled into the cleavage between her breasts. She refused to cry. Stubbornly, she railed against the salted drops of water until their well ran dry.

Repairing her face, Lauren put on a rigid mask of composure and returned to the reception hall. Her vision scanned the vast room for Georgette, Antoine, or anyone with whom she could mingle in order to avoid Roget and his lover. In her search, she spied Gaston with his lady and moved hurriedly away before he saw her. It seemed there was nowhere to hide, and her traitorous eyes would see no one except Roget and Lucienne, who were standing alone by the staircase at the center of the room. Their bodies didn't touch. There was no need. Roget's dark eyes could caress in a way that touching never could. Lauren lingered on the auburn hair, swept up in an elegant double pouf as Georgette described. Diamonds glittered at her smooth, sensuous throat, accenting the voluptuous gown that draped Grecian style over her body. Lauren ached with envy. Could she blame Roget for loving her?

The remainder of the evening was a labyrinth of social amenities, and Lauren walked through it numbly, smiling mechanically and saying what was expected of her. Roget moved through the evening unruffled as though nothing out of the ordinary had occurred. Lauren prayed that she could face her future with the same unwavering confidence.

"There's a letter for you, *madame,*" Filene's voice rang after her. "The post just arrived." Lauren's hazel eyes scanned the ecru envelope as she took it from Filene's fingers. *Claude.* Her heart began to pound raucously against her chest.

"Merci, Filene," she uttered, preoccupied, not lifting her eyes from the pale, shaded paper. Clutching the precious letter to her breast, Lauren ran the length of the staircase, not halting until she was safely shielded by the privacy of her bedchamber. She fell against the closed door, letting the carved mahogany barrier support her while she caught her breath. For weeks, she had expected this letter. Why had it taken Claude so long to answer? No matter, she thought, it was at last in her hands, and she could confront Gaston with the truth. Her lips curled vaguely at the small victory. She would no longer have to live in fear of his slanderous accusations. He would have to find another way to dissolve her marriage to Roget.

Lauren tore at the paper, her graceful fingers fumbling as though they were used to flexing for nothing more than sport. Why had she not used the letter opener? It was lying right there on the desk, she chided herself as the envelope ripped raggedly in two. Wrenching the treasured piece of stationery free, Lauren unfolded it and began to read:

Dearest Lauren,

I must apologize for taking so long to answer your letter. Lauren, do forgive me. You should have been given this information long ago, but at the time you were too young, and when you were old enough, so much time had passed that I simply forgot. Lauren, it is true that your mother and father were not legally married at the time of your birth. There was some problem with your mother's citizenship that prevented them from being married when they arrived in France. However, they were married five weeks after you were born. Your father acknowledged you as his child and gave you his name, and from that moment on, the matter was forgotten.

Chérie, I pray these facts will not cause you trouble. Pierre and Bertrand send their love, and we all miss you.

Love always, Claude

Lauren's thumping heart plummeted like a ball of lead to the pit of her stomach, resounding its dire implications throughout her body. Like a sleepwalker, she went through the motions of refolding the letter and retrieving the torn pieces of envelope where they lay scattered on the carpet. From the armoire, she pulled out the inlaid pearl workbox, the one place she knew would elude Roget's possible discovery and stuffed every scrap of the letter inside. As despair sapped her last ounce of fortitude, Lauren sank into the upholstered yellow chair that graced the French windows, her shoulders rounded and her hazel eyes fixed blankly on the emerald ring that circled her finger. She wanted desperately to fight for her marriage, but she had no weapons.

The following days were filled with inner turmoil and the nagging anguish of secrecy. Terrified that Roget would learn of her illegitimacy, she had accepted the fact that he had every right to have the marriage annulled. Two weeks were between her and that dreadful meeting between Roget and Lucienne and one week had passed since she read the letter from Claude. The memory of both occurrences had dulled somewhat in her head, but their connotations lingered on unfaded.

Lauren's fingers played over the keys of the piano as she attempted to practice, but her brain would not concentrate. She was being consumed by a feeling of desperation and there was nothing she could do, nothing but wait, wait until the noose was around her neck and then try to die gallantly. Banging all ten fingers hard against the ivory and black keys, she rose, angry with her helplessness and started upstairs to change. Villa de Martier was quiet. Madame de Martier had taken a rare trip into town and would not return for hours. The men were overseeing the coffee production in the fields and warehouses. Except for the servants, Lauren was alone in the house.

Halfway up the stairs, she heard the main door open sharply and male footsteps clicked against the hard marble floor. As they approached the base of the stairway, Gaston stood grinning up at her. Gathering the folds of her skirt, Lauren moved quickly over the polished wooden stairs, but his long legs took the steps three at a time, and he soon caught her. A huge hand reached out and clamped on her arm.

"Ma chérie." He raised an eyebrow mockingly. "Surely you were not running from me. I can't imagine you being afraid of a man. I doubt that I've ever seen you run from my brother."

"Roget is my husband," she retorted sharply, struggling to free her trapped arm.

Tightening his iron grip on her arm, he replied, "And for how long do you think he will remain your husband?"

"I don't know." Lauren flushed. Her hazel eyes dropped to the floor. She could feel his gloating behind that wry grin and knew that she was powerless.

"From what I've seen lately . . . not very long. Perhaps there will be a new bride in the family very soon. You, *ma chérie,* must be feeling lonely," he taunted. "Your husband is not at home very much, is he? By the look of you, I think you could do with some male companionship. I was about to have a glass of sherry. Why don't you join me?"

"I—I would rather not," Lauren replied nervously. "I have to meet Georgette."

"Georgette can wait," he said, his fingers cutting into the flesh of her upper arm. "I daresay, if you wish to preserve your marriage a mite longer, it would be wise for you to join me. A few choice words from me, and the union will be quickly dissolved."

It was inevitable. There was no way she could escape his treachery after what Claude had told her. With his Herculean hand still controlling her arm, he prodded her toward his bedchamber. Lauren grew frantic with fear. Instinctively, she sensed that this time he would not let her go with just words. She wanted to run, but if she did, she knew what the alternative would be. Though she dreaded with all her being what awaited her behind that mahogany door, she had to face it or lose the one thing in her life that mattered. Perhaps all it would do was buy time, but she foolishly wanted that time. Lauren drew a deep breath, clamped her teeth together, and entered his room.

Once inside, Gaston strode on long legs to the black-lacquered commode and poured two glasses of sherry while Lauren stood frozen in front of the door. Handing her the glass, his look appraised her for one long moment. He turned the glass up, took its contents down in a single gulp, and set it aside. Lauren had barely swallowed a sip. His mouth came down on hers hard, smothering her breath and pressing the curves of her body flat against the locked door. Her glass spilled from her hand and spread amber wine over the carpet. She drew away, her body stiffening with revulsion, and tried to sever the contact with her hands. He sensed her revulsion and smelled her fear, and his power over her gave rise to a perverse excitement. His heart beating wildly against the massive chest, he crushed her shoulders beneath his hands.

"Dear sister-in-law, I do expect you to cooperate," he said. Lauren bit her tongue, denying him the satisfaction of her caustic reply. Anger flared in his veins and pulsated visibly against his temples. Roughly, he flung her body, limp as a rag doll, onto the red damask throw that covered his bed. Unbuttoning the front of his riding breeches, he eased them off. Slowly and with great pride, he displayed his manhood. Straddling her with his massive weight, he pinned her down and began to fumble with the buttons on her shirtwaist. Feverishly he pawed at her clothes, ripping them off piece by piece until she was naked. Lauren felt exposed and humiliated. His powerful hand fondled the smooth curve of her neck and then moved down to the hollow in her throat, where she felt his thumb pressing against her larynx, almost smothering her breath. Repulsed by the wicked gleam in his dark eyes, she averted hers.

"Don't ever turn away from me," he ordered. Burying his hand deep in her hair, he forced her gaze back to his. Lauren sensed that she had struck a raw nerve. The insensitive hands mauled and manhandled her soft, smooth flesh, the fingers groping roughly at places that were once intimate and private. Biting her lip, Lauren winced with pain yet exercised a rugged determination not to cry out. She would not give him the pleasure of hearing her pain. He enjoyed seeing her fear but grew increasingly irritated at her lack of response. At the onslaught of his abominable humiliation, Lauren's mind separated from her body. Her body grew tense and withdrawn, unwilling to accept his disgusting intrusion.

"*Madame,* I know your husband does not meet with such resistance. I'm sure that beneath Roget those silken thighs part willingly."

"But you're not Roget," she retorted, her tone dripping with sarcasm.

Outwardly, he laughed, but the dark eyes narrowed with disdain. "I see my brother has trained his pet well." Her insinuation that Roget was a more adept lover than he, brought his temper to the surface. He violated that sacred part of her, which, until now, she had given only to Roget. "This time, dear Sister-in-Law, I expect you to cooperate," he slurred, his voice full of contempt. "I want a taste of that wanton lust that you so eagerly give my brother."

Her honey-colored cheeks flushed burgundy with shame as he forced himself between her thighs. "I intend to see what possessed him to bring a wench like you—the grand-daughter of an ex-slave—into our family." Though she ignored the scathing tone, his emphasis on *wench* and *slave* still pricked her skin.

Gaston labored over her mercilessly, and Lauren clamped her teeth shut and ground her clenched fists hard into the mattress in an effort to control her rage. Humiliation festered to anger. It spread through her body like a raging fire, igniting every nerve in its path. It took all of her willpower to keep her nails from raking savagely over his smug, arrogant face. His greatest pleasure was in torment-ing her, and she could do nothing but lie there and endure his abuse.

Fiendishly, he tried to force a response from her that she was determined not to give. Still, Lauren lay there unflinch-ing. She wanted to scream, to cry, to lash into him with the fury of her fists. She longed to immerse herself in a tub of scalding water and burn his filth from her body. But as long as he held her captive with the facts of her birth, she could do nothing, nothing but lie beneath him and endure his lechery in pained silence.

At long last, lust succumbed to human frailty, and he fell aside, exhausted and spent. She had outlasted him with sheer perseverance and had not given him what he wanted most. Her body throbbed with abuse and humiliation.

"By no means am I finished with you . . . contemptible little bitch," he mumbled thickly, giving her one last venomous look.

Soon after she heard the heavy sounds of his snoring and knew that she was free. Dragging herself from the bed, she found the torn clothes and hastily put them on. She stared down at his inert frame, a thirst for revenge gnawing at her guts. If she had had a gun in her hand, she would have shot him for the abominable way he had used her. Instead, she fished the key from his pocket, unlocked the door, and let herself out.

Lauren hurried through the hall to her room, cautiously bolting the door behind her. Cybele would think it strange that she was ordering her bath at this time of day, but Lauren could not muster up the energy to care. All she could think was that she had to bathe. Reaching for the bellpull, she jerked it erratically and then rapidly peeled off the torn, unclean clothes and tossed them in the corner. Later, she would dispose of them. She never wanted to see them again.

Her bath was drawn hotter than usual, and Cybele hovered over her mistress fretfully, afraid that she would scald herself.

"*Madame* shall take a bad burn," she said in English-accented French.

"Don't worry, Cybele . . . I will manage," she assured her as she settled into the near scalding water. "You can leave me now." From the look of her wrinkled brow, the young maid had trouble perceiving that her mistress wanted nothing more from her than to be left alone.

"*Oui, madame,*" she said. Eyeing Lauren curiously, the pale-skinned girl backed out of the bathroom.

Relieved, she realized that there was no way she could go down to dinner that night. Facing Gaston would be unbearable with the rage still coursing through her veins, and she could not possibly face Roget. Lauren longed to pour out the whole sordid ordeal to her husband but knew she would have to bear her pain in silence or lose Roget.

As the soothing effects of heated water began to assuage her throbbing body, memories of his vile abuse dragged through her mind. She would not submit to Gaston's blackmail again even though it meant losing Roget. She would return to France if she had to. Good Lord, why had she let him use her that way? It solved nothing. Sooner or later, Gaston would tell Roget; he had no sense of honor. It was just a matter of time. Lauren shuddered, feeling that she would never be clean again. A tear escaped, rolled down her cheek, and vanished in the perfumed bathwater. Control lost its last ounce of strength, and the young Madame de Martier laid her head on folded knees and cried.

Chapter 15

Church bells pealed hauntingly from the cathedral tower. Somewhere on the outskirts of the city a rooster began to crow as the resplendent de Martier carriage swung off the dirt road and onto the Champ de Mar, making its way toward the cathedral. It was barely dawn.

Lauren slipped between the rows of cane chairs and knelt next to Roget and the elder Madame de Martier. She had not known that attending church service in Port-au-Prince meant relinquishing a night's sleep. Kneeling, she crossed herself, folded shaky hands beneath her chin, and closed her eyes to murmur a prayer. Roget quickly made the sign of the cross over his broad shoulders and sat back against the seat, leaving his mother and his wife reverently on their knees.

The first Sunday of each month, the president, guarded by the brilliantly uniformed *état-major*, officially attended services at the cathedral. Since Madame de Martier adamantly insisted on participating in the October festivities, it was Roget's duty as a son to accompany her. Though Lauren had yet to see the *jour militaire*, she eagerly accepted the invitation to join her husband for reasons of her own. For several weeks she had longed for the tranquility of a church so that she could pray. Her lips barely moving, Lauren murmured her confession.

"Lord, forgive me . . . for I have sinned. I should not

have succumbed to Gaston's debauchery, but out of desperation, I did. I wanted Roget's love so very much and at the moment it seemed that every hope had deserted me . . . that you had deserted me. I pray you will forgive my moment of weakness. And, dear God, please . . . *please* don't let me be pregnant from Gaston's depraved seed."

The delicate jasmine scent of her cologne mingled with the pungent odor of incense and invaded Roget's nostrils. Unwillingly, his eyes traveled from the curve of her neck, along her back, to the hourglass curve of her waist. What could she have done, he thought absently, that she felt the need to pray so fervidly? Rising from her humble posture, Lauren perched against the edge of the wooden chair and glanced behind her before moving fully into the seat. Hazel eyes met an ebony gaze, and her knees melted to liquid rubber beneath his dark, inscrutable stare.

"Have you been absolved of your sins?" he whispered.

A rush of repentant blood turned Lauren's complexion dark red. Did he know so soon? Of course not. He could not possibly know, she reassured herself. He would not behave this calmly. But then, what does he care? Her indiscretion would simply facilitate his getting an annulment.

Suddenly, there was a murmur of hushed voices, and without warning, gun salutes reverberated through that early dawn atmosphere. Attired in full state regalia, the president, preceded by the palace band, entered the cathedral. As Lauren devoured the excitement of the spectacle, her dire thoughts disintegrated amid the fanfare that accompanied Florvil Hyppolite's arrival. Ascending the dais opposite the archbishop's throne, the ebony-hued man stood at attention beneath a richly ornamented canopy that designated his seat until the female members of his family were seated. Once he took his seat, the mass was allowed to proceed.

The elder Madame de Martier and her peers frequently exchanged greetings and gossip between prayers. More than a handful of Haiti's elite caressed rosary beads and prayed stealthily for salvation behind fluttering fans and ivory-handled walking sticks.

At nine o'clock an illustrious congregation spilled from the church into a haze of early morning sunlight, but the low barnlike structure did not seem a very impressive cathedral for a city with the importance of Port-au-Prince. A military *tournée* followed, in which Hyppolite rode through the streets in an open carriage pulled by two American iron grays. Government officials and the silver harnessed carriages of the elite fell in behind, forming an impromptu parade along the Champ de Mar. Every soldier in the city and the adjoining arrondissements had a standing order to be on parade duty for the *jour militaire*, and for the remainder of the day the city wore a military uniform.

Paul, the de Martier's young coachman, leapt down from his perch and snapped to attention, imitating the soldiers. Bursting with pride in his new gray uniform, he assisted the two women over the carriage step, unaware that his salute had dislodged his hat. Grinning with amusement, Roget reached forward and straightened the boy's lopsided cap, and then with athletic agility he swung in beside his two women.

"Merci, monsieur," the young driver uttered sheepishly, with a shamefaced expression as he climbed to his seat.

"Paul, pull over behind that carriage," Justine de Martier urged, waving a hand at the Rousses.

"Maman, is it really necessary to participate in this pompous ritual?" Roget questioned, slowly pivoting the brim of his hat between his thumb and forefinger.

"Why, yes . . . of course, dear," she replied, positioning the lace parasol above her head. The inflection in her voice insisted that to see and be acknowledged by friends was the primary reason for attending. "I must greet my friends." Reaching up affectionately, she touched his face. Lauren cringed and looked away, not wanting to admit that his mother had more of his love than she ever would. Since he had chosen to sit beside his mother and not his wife, Madame de Martier languished next to her favorite son. Twirling the parasol above her elaborately plumed hat, the older woman nodded to acquaintances and preened as if she were a reigning queen.

Looking at the slender, ruffled object lying across Lauren's lap, she scolded, her voice a tone of bittersweet cunning. "Dear, you must open your parasol. How do you expect it to protect your skin resting on your lap?"

"Obviously, I don't," Lauren retorted. As an afterthought, she added, "There is nothing to protect."

"But just look at how brown you've gotten since you've been here." Madame de Martier cast a soliciting glance at her son. "A woman's skin should be fair and delicate, like a camelia."

"A woman's skin should be whatever color God made it," Lauren replied, her voice held at a stringent pitch. "My mother's skin was black."

"Roget, your wife should learn to use her parasol," his mother continued, conjuring him into making his wayward wife behave.

Roget had chosen to remain detached from their female squabble, but his mother's persistence and Lauren's stubbornness made the issue impossible to ignore any longer. With a slow, restrained tone of exasperation, he said, "Lauren, will you please open that parasol?"

Lauren's jaw tightened as ivory teeth clenched beneath her softly pursed lips. Polite as it may have sounded, it was a command and not a request. Madame de Martier turned away to admire a troop of foot soldiers whose pale blue and red uniforms marched past the carriage, leaving husband and wife grimly facing each other.

Using a low, deliberate enunciation meant only for her ears, he questioned, "Why do you insist on antagonizing her?" Lauren fumed. Her lips parted, but Roget glared acid as she attempted to voice her protest. "Lauren, not now," he growled under his breath. Fuming indignantly, she retrieved the ruffled umbrella and thrust it open, almost dislodging the blue feathered hat from her head.

Realizing that her mother-in-law would probably die of shock if she had the ill breeding to argue with Roget in an open carriage in the middle of Port-au-Prince, Lauren lost herself in the excitement of military pomp that filled the city. Throughout the morning she held her vexation in check until at last their carriage rounded the bend and started down the gravel driveway to the main door.

"Paul, let me out here," Roget called to the young coachman. "I want to walk the rest of the way."

Perplexed that anyone would choose to walk when they could ride, their young coachman ground the vehicle to a halt and let Roget leap down. Standing, Lauren attempted to exit the vehicle, thinking that a brisk walk might diffuse her suppressed rage.

"I would prefer to walk as well," she said.

"Lauren, you will stay in this carriage," Roget growled through clenched teeth. "Haven't you antagonized *Maman* enough?"

Lauren fumed. Refusing to sit down, she staunchly stood her ground.

"Paul, deliver my mother and my wife to the main door," Roget ordered. As the wheels jerked into motion, Lauren was thrown unwillingly back onto the leather seat.

A short distance up the gravel driveway, Roget watched the carriage halt again and his wife step out. Her eyes fixed straight ahead, she stalked toward the house, placing one foot rigidly in front of the other. His ire swelled like a tide as he lengthened his stride to catch her. Seizing her arm, he whirled her body around to face him.

"Damn it, woman! Must you be so stubborn?" he bellowed.

"And I suppose you've never noticed how stubborn you are," she flung back at him, her furious glare darting to the high hat he carried at his side. "Perhaps that's the reason your hat is more often in your hand than on your head."

"My hat does not upset *Maman,* your behavior does."

"Upset *her!*" Lauren sputtered through the pangs of injustice. "Has it ever occurred to you that she might antagonize me?"

"You are expected to behave in a certain manner. Is it so difficult for you to comply with her wishes?"

"I should have known that you would take her side," she retorted. Pulling her arm free, Lauren made a sharp detour from the road and tramped into the garden. "And my wishes. Don't I have a right to my wishes? Why must I comply with something that makes me feel ridiculous and uncomfortable?"

His long strides shortened to keep pace with her feminine ones, Roget followed her into the garden. "She has lived with these customs all of her life. At her age, she is not going to change."

"And, obviously, neither are you."

Trudging along between the rows of manicured hedges that graced the front of the mansion, Lauren saw red, a red as blinding as the flowers that nestled among the bushes. It was not enough that she had to be second to his lover, but he expected her to be second to his mother as well.

"Would it hurt you to appease her once in a while, to follow the social amenities that are expected of a Haitian wife?"

"Do you follow the social amenities expected of a husband?"

Roget's fingers tightened and curled against the brim of his hat.

"What I do matters little," she added, the edge on her voice growing dull. "I'm not the fair-skinned goddess she would have wished for you."

Lauren stooped to pick up a blossom and then held it to her nose, savoring its scent. Her full, pursed lips scattered Roget's anger to the peripheries of his soul. All of a sudden, he wanted to ravish that provocative mouth, smother it until she could not utter another word.

Looking up, her will clashed violently with his, and she saw only the intensity of his distaste. Roget turned and stalked from the garden, his boots pounding the gravel path that led to the stable.

The sound of a Lambi soloist wafted through the air and mingled with chants, creating an eerie disturbance in the dead quiet of the afternoon. Lauren's pulse quickened with each shrill note, and when she tried to swallow, her throat went dry and her tongue became a wad of cotton. Within seconds, the savage rhythm of drumbeats echoed through the trees. Startled by the sudden sound, the two women were almost unwillingly separated from their saddles. Letting her eyes follow the sound that assaulted their senses, Georgette glimpsed at the lewdly painted structure that stood secluded among the dense foliage of the trees.

"Lauren, do you see that?" Her voice was barely a whisper.

"Georgette, let's get away from here," she replied raggedly.

Lauren had the strange feeling that they had ventured

beyond de Martier property, and intuition told her they should not be here.

Georgette paused and asked in a somber tone, "Do you think it's a *vaudou* ceremony?"

"I don't know," Lauren replied hesitantly, "but I know in my bones we should not be here." Since her ordeal with Gaston, she was more aware of the existence of danger. "I don't want to imagine what they would do to us . . . if they found us here."

"Neither do I." The almond eyes widened with apprehension. "But I can't tear myself away."

"I know," Lauren sighed. "I feel it as well, but we must not stay here."

Lauren and Georgette urged their mounts forward, and the animals took off in a skittish gallop. In their haste to vacate the area, Lauren's horse stumbled over the roots of a tree that jutted into her path. Lauren was not aware of how she had missed it before, but as she hurried Miel around it, she recognized it as a machineel tree.

"Do we have to be in such a hurry?" Georgette quipped.

"These lone trees standing in the middle of nowhere make my skin crawl," Lauren replied. Her gaze surveyed the empty space surrounding her. "They must be here for a reason."

"They say the cults use the fruit of the machineel to poison their enemies. Years ago, the French colonists tried to destroy them, but they did not succeed entirely, and the few that remain on the island are guarded religiously. No one dares to cut them down, not even the landowners."

As they made their way along the river, each was deep in her own thoughts.

"I doubt that in a hundred years I could grow accustomed to this country," Lauren commented idly, her attention fixed on the wattle huts scattered before them. "One class living in huts, the other living in grand manors like Villa de Martier. Primitive spectacles of abandon coupled with elegant champagne balls." Lauren shook her head as if to awaken herself from a dream. "So much elegance living side by side with so much primitiveness . . . It's incongruous."

"Like that," Georgette said, wagging a finger from the

end of her extended arm. "Cement slabs to keep the dead from rising. It gives me chills just to think about it."

Lauren shifted uneasily in her saddle, feeling the skittish nature of the animal beneath her. "I was raised Catholic and believe that Jesus Christ is my saviour. I married Roget in a Catholic church. I had nothing to prepare me for this— the mixing of African religion with Christianity." She looked around and caught Georgette's gaze.

"Your mother was African?" Georgette's almond eyes gazed at her quizzically.

"But my mother never saw Africa; she was born in Guiana."

"Perhaps you and I truly don't belong here," the other young woman shrugged. "If I mention these things to Jacques, he dismisses them with disinterest."

"I suppose it doesn't seem strange to them; they were born here and grew up surrounded by it." Pulling off the white panama hat, Lauren fanned her face. "However," she began, her tone playfully teasing, "I don't know if my stomach could stand an encore of today. In the future, I think it would be wise if we stayed on familiar paths."

"There won't be a future for quite a while." Georgette's full mouth twisted sheepishly into a satisfied grin. "I'm pregnant again, and after my miscarriage last year, I want to be very careful."

Lauren's expression glowed with excitement once the impact of the words pierced her brain. "Oh, Georgette!" she cried, not bothering to control her outburst of joy. "I'm so excited for you! I know how much this baby means to you and Jacques."

"Of course you and Roget will be godparents." Her inflection posed a silent question.

Lauren shared happily in her friend's animated chatter about the expected arrival of her child. At the clearing, they parted. She was going to miss their afternoon rides. Lauren swung Miel around and headed toward Villa de Martier.

It was late. The sun had waned, and Lauren had barely managed to get back before dusk crept over the horizon. After Miel was cooled and wiped down, she went to her room. Her thoughts sped to the closed door between the rooms. Roget was in. She had seen Bleu de Roi in the stable.

Wrestling with her need to feel his presence, Lauren mulled over reasons sufficient enough to approach the formidable door. She would tell him about the Deffands' baby, she thought. Her feet moved forward as though governed by a mind not her own. Slowly, she coiled her fingers around the brass doorknob and let the cold metal calm her perspiring hand. Pausing irresolute, the blatant truth overtook her. *He loved Lucienne.* Aching with the desire to be near him, Lauren straightened her spine ramrod stiff and drew her hand away. She moved back into her room, the rigid posture acting as bolster to her sagging spirits. In her happiness for Georgette, she had forgotten her own dilemma, but it occurred to her that she might very well be pregnant. The thought of Gaston's child growing inside her made her shudder with revulsion. Wrapping futile arms about her shoulders, she tried to ward off the chill.

Once again Filene had taken the liberty of letting herself into Reinette's bedchamber. Lauren edged stealthily into the library and waited behind the heavy mahogany doors, intending to intercept the licentious housekeeper as she left the room. Motionless, she waited. The gilded case clock ticked away the minutes as she perused the family portrait gallery. Her ear pressed at the door for a sound, she wondered why there was no portrait of Gaston's wife or Yves, their son. Her ear caught the click of a key as it turned in the lock, and Lauren swung open the door and stepped into the hallway. The ebony skin stretched taut as the woman gasped at her unexpected presence in the corridor.

"Madame!" Her wide dark eyes dilated with apprehension.

"Bonjour, Filene."

"Bonjour, madame," she replied, her shoulders relaxing somewhat. "You startled me. Usually . . . there is no one about at this time of day." Her voice was hesitant.

"Madame de Martier told me that Madame Reinette's room was always locked. You seem to have the only key."

The stately black woman grew uneasy. "Monsieur Gaston gave me the key and said that I was to tell no one. He wanted the room kept as it was when she was alive."

Intuition told her that Filene was lying. It seemed unlikely that a man as insensitive as Gaston would harbor so strong a sentiment. Filene dropped her eyes to the floor, her right hand, nervously twisting the fingers of the left.

"Madame . . ." She paused for a long moment. "You won't tell anyone about the key." Her tone pleaded as if for mercy. "Monsieur Gaston would be furious with me if he knew that I had been careless."

Lauren studied the regal black face. She too lived in fear of Gaston. "Did you know Madame Reinette?" Lauren questioned curiously.

"Oui, madame. I knew her but not well. I had little contact with *monsieur*'s wife. I know nothing about her except that she was very beautiful . . . like a queen." Lauren heard the note of bitterness in her tone.

"I would like to see her room. Would you show it to me?"

"Oh, no, *madame!* I couldn't do that. Monsieur Gaston would punish me for sure."

"Monsieur Gaston need never know," Lauren said. "I would certainly never tell him."

"Please, *madame.* Do not ask me to do that. *Please . . ."* As if she knew what punishment awaited her, the pompous housekeeper cowered before her. With the pain of Gaston's wrath still drenching her memory, Lauren wondered in what way he had chastised Filene to invoke such fear.

"Filene, what do you know about *vaudou?"* Lauren meant the query to ease her tension, but ironically it made matters worse.

"Nothing, *madame,"* she answered, almost horrified. "Only what everyone knows. I wouldn't meddle in those things." She flung her head back indignantly, indicating that Lauren had insulted her intelligence.

"Is there anyone in the house who might know?"

The woman exhibited no outward show of emotion. "No, *madame.* No one in this house practices vodun. If they did, they would be dismissed." She spoke in a stiff monotone.

"Have you ever attended a *vaudou* ceremony?" Lauren prodded, undecided as to whether or not to believe her innocence.

Filene's wide eyes searched Lauren's face before she

answered. "No . . . never. It's not good to get involved in these things. Horrible atrocities befall outsiders who try to learn their secrets."

Lauren could not help feeling that there was a warning obscured in her words.

Lauren's heart pranced skittishly when Roget strode casually into their bedchamber later that afternoon. About to inquire why he had come, she spied the pale eggshell envelope held lightly between his fingers.

"Henri Duval asked me to give this to you."

"What is it?" she inquired anxiously. Her trembling hand reached forward and took the small note that dangled from his thumb and forefinger.

"I have no idea." He shrugged absently. "Probably an invitation of some sort."

Slicing the silver letter opener neatly through the edge of the folded paper, Lauren retrieved its contents. It read:

Dear Lauren,
    The women on the concert committee will be meeting at my home for tea on Wednesday. I do hope you will come. We have plans to discuss.

Yours truly,
Celestine Duval

"It's an invitation to tea," she informed him stiffly, returning the elegant paper to its envelope.

"Good," Roget replied emphatically. "You should go out more."

Of course, anything to keep me out of his way, she thought bitterly, her nails biting painfully into the flesh of her palm.

"They're meeting to discuss the concert for Saint Joseph's, the one for which you so generously volunteered my services." Her gaze raked over him hotly. "That's why I was invited." Socially they had ignored her, but now she had something they needed. How callous they were.

Much to her surprise, Roget made no effort to leave after completing his errand. Instead, he dropped his lean, muscled frame into one of the arm chairs and propped his dusty boots on the moiré footstool. A dirty smudge marred the front of his tan breeches. Lauren mused at the deliberate lack of fastidiousness that was sometimes a part of him.

"Alexis will be here next month," he said evenly. His dark gaze took in her mouth as the full, shapely contours parted slightly in astonishment. "He'll be in Martinique for a few weeks. He wants to stop here on his return to France. He seems to think I can show him the mechanics of running a plantation."

"You can . . . can't you?" she uttered, somewhat distracted. Memories trailed through her mind of the carefree role Alexis had played in doling out her destiny.

"In three days?" he rejoined, settling his weight into the frame of the chair.

Lauren's lips parted further with disbelief and then pursed to speak. Folding restless arms across his chest, Roget forced his attention through the glass doors and beyond the filigree railing. Acutely aware that he was oblivious to her presence, Lauren swallowed what she was about to say. Certain that he was thinking of Lucienne, her heart jerked a little, and her eyes plummeted to the olive green patterns of the carpet. Her yearning for him was unbearable. Unknowingly, he had done her a great service by avoiding her these past months. He had saved her from making an incredible fool of herself.

Roget heard her walk away, and his ears savored the rustling sound of her skirts as she went to deposit Madame Duval's note on the desk. He watched her move lithely across the room in much the same manner as she had maneuvered the streets of Paris. Recoiling his focus, he forced it back to the window while her free, limber strides played havoc with his senses.

Returning to sit opposite him, Lauren perched on the edge of the chair, clasped her hands, and waited. Realizing that not even her movements could disturb his thoughts, she decided there was nothing to lose as impatience nagged her to break the silence.

"Roget, what was Reinette like?"

Not one muscle twitched. He remained motionless, not acknowledging the inquiry. Thinking he had not heard her question, Lauren's pursed lips were about to repeat it when he answered.

"Much like her name suggests . . . like a queen."

"Was she beautiful?"

"Very beautiful," he paused reverently, "in every way." She had still not drawn his attention from the balcony, but the melancholy in his voice went through her like a saber.

"Did you like her?"

"Like her? I was probably a little in love with her. In many ways she was much like Lucienne, a work of art . . . flawless, priceless, magnificent . . ." His voice faded to an inaudible pitch. He was talking to her as he might talk to a stranger. *She* was not there. Lauren envisioned his sister-in-law looking much the same as his lover—scintillating, like a diamond—and envy pricked her heart at the core.

"There is no portrait of her in the library with the others."

"You won't find one," he said, his gaze finally shifting from the glass doors. "One used to hang there, a superb painting done by Henry O. Tanner, but my brother had it removed. Heaven alone knows what he did with it." Contempt colored his tone as he lifted his arms in a futile gesture and then dropped them to rest against the carved arms of the chair. "Gaston destroyed every trace of her . . . just as he destroyed her."

"Did she love your brother?"

"As unlikely as it may seem, she did." Looking up, he caught her in the depths of his eyes.

Lauren gazed down at the carpet and phrased her next question before daring to meet his perusal again. "Was her death really an accident? Antoine said," she paused, lifting her face to his, "that you believe she was poisoned."

"Antoine should mind his tongue!" he scowled. Roget bolted from the chair, flung open the glass doors, and stalked outside.

Seeking to smooth his ruffled feathers as he stepped back inside, Lauren approached another subject. "Do you realize this is the first personal invitation I've had since I arrived here?" She moved to the escritoire and absently fingered the eggshell envelope. "I doubt that your people will ever accept me," she said ruefully.

Roget noticed the long, graceful fingers as they played over the smoothness of the paper. She did have beautiful hands. Graceful, agile, a touch as delicate as a butterfly.

"Probably, they wonder what persuaded you to marry me in place of Lucienne," she continued, almost as if she were thinking aloud.

"My reasons are none of their business," he snapped. "You're my wife."

"Am I, Roget?" she questioned softly. Her hazel eyes followed him as he stalked through the adjoining door to his room.

Chapter
16

For lack of a more intriguing occupation, Lauren immersed herself wholeheartedly in the preparations for the concert. At last she had something to do that would fill the endless hours of idle time. The air in the salon was almost cool compared to the inferno that blazed outside, Lauren thought as she closed the door behind her and slid absently onto the piano stool.

Her nimble fingers played aimlessly over the keys and then broke into Chopin's G-sharp Minor Etude with an intensity of emotion she had not experienced in months. Pressing down on the keys, she stopped—the sound was abrupt and disconnected. Could her ear not be hearing right? She plunked it again. It was badly off key. Impossible. The piano had just been tuned a few days ago, and she had played it since then. Pressing her foot once more against the pedal, she felt its resistance. Using all of her weight, Lauren stepped down on it, yet it moved but half the range, as though something were holding it back. Dropping to the floor on hands and knees, she pushed against the metal protrusion with her hand. Something definitely was obstructing it. Too dark beneath the base for her to see, she ran her fingertips stealthily over the thick Persian carpet in an effort to search out the obstruction. A soft object brushed against her hand. Lauren stretched her long fingers to their full length and tried to grasp it, but it eluded her. Flattening her body to the floor, she extended her arm as far as it would go. Finally she had it! Graceful fingers clung tenaciously to the small leatherlike object as she withdrew her arm from under the piano.

Lauren sat in the middle of the floor, stunned, staring at the leathery pouch. The thing had fallen open to expose dead leaves, dried bones, and a tiny clay image. Mixed among the hideous things, she recognized a few tangled strands of her hair that could have been pulled from her brush, a broken piece of fingernail that strangely matched her own, and a small, ragged piece of the shirtwaist she had discarded after Gaston ripped it from her body. Petrified, her eyes stared at it, her brain unwilling to comprehend the terror of its meaning until awareness came through like water bursting a dam. It was some kind of *magie noire*. A hand flew to her mouth and muffled her scream. Swallowing hard, she stifled the sound in her throat, determined not to behave like an hysterical female.

Slowly, Lauren rose to her feet. Gathering her shattered wits, she walked to the kitchen, terror her companion with each step. She did not dare think what that horrible thing was or what it meant, or hysteria would overtake her rational mind. Lisa looked up and curtsied when she entered, but Lauren hardly noticed the sudden flurry of activity in her midst. The servants were not accustomed to seeing members of the family in the kitchen.

"Can I get you something, *madame?*" Lisa purred, her expression piqued with wonder.

"I need a towel . . . or something . . . I . . ."

"*Oui, madame.*" The young serving maid shot her mistress a curious glance and ambled toward the pantry. Returning, she placed a white linen towel in Lauren's trembling hands.

"*Madame,* are you ill?" she questioned, studying Lauren intently.

"No . . ." Lauren hesitated. Her voice cracked from the dryness in her throat, and then thinking quickly, she attempted to camouflage her fear. "There is a problem with the piano. It seems to be leaking oil." Reluctantly, Lauren tore herself from the comforting safety of the kitchen where the warm aromas of food reminded her of Pierre's kitchen at the Saint Germain. *"Merci,* Lisa," she called over her shoulder as she stepped across the threshold into the hall. With uncanny perception, Lauren felt the girl's eyes follow her through the corridor.

Entering the salon, she saw the hideous thing still lying on the carpet where she had dropped it. Lauren covered the vile object with the linen towel, and holding it cautiously away from her body as if contact meant imminent disaster, she scooped it up and transported it to her bedchamber. Her one conscious thought was to show it to Roget. After placing it unobtrusively in the washbasin, a numbing stupor seeped over her, and she planted herself in a chair to await Roget's return. Her hazel eyes stared vacantly ahead, seeing nothing. Terrifying images raced through her head. Clamping a hand over her eyes, she struggled to shut them out. *I must think about something else—cannot be afraid—must stay calm—cannot give in to fear.* Her mind rambled incessantly.

The time she waited seemed an eternity and it was still morning. She rose from the chair and paced back and forth over the carpet, wondering how she would survive six hours more without giving in to hysteria. Torn between the imprisonment of her room and the uncertainty that lurked on the plantation, Lauren eventually opted for the freedom of open space. Being locked up in her room for the remainder of the day would surely reduce her to a state of idiocy.

Where la Rivière Blanche disappeared into the sand, Lauren slowed Miel to a canter and let the animal move at her own pace. The sky above was a deep velvety blue and the sun's rays sparkled like diamonds between the leaves of lush green foliage that formed a blanket over the mountainside. *What a glorious place this is,* she mused. Filling her lungs with a long, deep breath of untainted air, she turned her face up to the sun. Why had Roget forbidden her to use this road? Standing face-to-face with the machineel tree, it no longer seemed a foreboding obstacle but an incongruity that a thing possessed of such utter beauty could be so deadly poison. A tarantula crawled lazily down from the tree's bark, and Lauren pressed Miel's flanks, urging her to a fast gallop that carried horse and rider swiftly onto the open plain.

Returning to Villa de Martier, she knew that Roget's arrival was less than an hour away, but exhausted and damp from the heat, Lauren shivered, remembering the grotesque omen that awaited her in the washbasin. The next hour spanned eternity, passing minute by minute by minute. She occupied herself by dressing for dinner.

At last, Lauren heard Roget's muffled footsteps striding across the carpet, followed close behind by León. She could contain herself no longer. Collecting the linen towel, she burst into his dressing room, not bothering to knock. As León tugged at his dust-covered boots, Roget looked up, throwing her a wicked glance.

"León, leave us alone. I'll send for you later."

"Oui, monsieur." The older man pulled the door closed behind him.

"What is so urgent it couldn't wait?" Roget growled, facing his wife. "I would like to get out of these clothes."

"Roget, I—I found this under the piano." Barely gripping the towel by the corners, she dropped it effusively on the chaise longue. Seeing the recognition flash across his face caused the strength to drain from her body, and all her former resolve melted like butter. Roget gazed down at the weird collection of items and moved his head from side to side in disbelief while Lauren stood shivering in ninety-degree heat.

"What . . . what is it?" she questioned.

"Lauren, forget it. I'll dispose of it."

"Roget, what does it mean?" she demanded weakly. The lump in her throat strangled what little breath remained in her lungs. "I have a right to know."

"I'm not sure," he replied hesitantly.

"You *do* know what it means. You recognized it the moment it fell open."

"Lauren, forget it . . . just forget it!" Abruptly, he turned toward the ebony armoire and began unbuckling his belt, needing time to collect his thoughts.

"Forget it!" Her voice penetrated his back with a terrifying rage. "What kind of mindless idiot do you think I am? I spent the entire day fighting hysteria, and now you tell me to erase it from memory as though it was no more than a bug you swat from the wall. I can't forget it! That thing," she cried, thrusting her finger at the chaise longue, "was put there for me! You know very well that I alone use the piano in this house, and so does the person who put it there. If you refuse me the truth, I will have to find it elsewhere!" Pivoting sharply on her heel, she started for the door.

Roget's dark eyes burned through her back as they followed her. "All right, I'll tell you," he said with bitter resignation. There was a noticeable silence in the room. Roget gathered the vile substances and tied them securely in the towel. "It's called an *ouanga* packet, usually composed of poisonous leaves, parts of the body, and other objects placed in a goat's uterus."

Clasping shaky arms about her middle, Lauren shuddered much against her will. "What does it mean?"

"It's used to cast a spell," he answered slowly as if the words hurt his tongue.

"Sp—spell . . ." she stammered. "Then . . . someone wants me dead?" Her tone pleaded for an answer.

"I wouldn't put much stock in it," Roget replied. "These things rarely accomplish what they are meant to. I think someone is merely trying to frighten you."

"But why?" she questioned.

"I would like the answer to that myself."

Unable to convince herself to accept her husband's seemingly logical explanation, Lauren's fear slowly grew into panic. She stood there welded to the spot, her body seized by a cold, shivery fever. Trembling uncontrollably, she felt her teeth chatter as icy fingers grasped her and sent chills racing through her veins. Suddenly, Roget pulled her shuddering body into his arms. For weeks, she had longed to feel him holding her, and now, her courage dissipated, she collapsed in his arms, letting the tears stream down her face.

"Lauren, you will be all right," Roget whispered. "It's nothing to be upset about."

How she abhorred sobbing, helpless women, she thought. Sobs dredged up from the bottom of her soul, wrenching her body into a chain of raw nerves as she surrendered her control to the arms that held her. All those shattered emotions that she had held together with nothing more than cosmetic glue collapsed, and her body went limp against the hard, comforting length of his.

"Why does someone want to kill me?" she sobbed, her words almost incoherent.

"Lauren, no one wants to kill you," he replied calmly.

"How can you say that!" she cried, drawing away from him. "Are spells not used in *magie noire* to do away with one's enemies? Why did it have my hair and my—"

"No one practices *magie noire* in this house," Roget interrupted, attempting to curtail her hysterical rambling. "Now please believe me, and calm down."

"If that's true," she said, still sniffling, "then where did the *ouanga* come from? It didn't find its way under the piano by itself . . . Someone had to put it there."

"One of the servants' children probably did it as a prank. You know how children are; they seldom understand the impact of their actions."

Burying a face stained with tears against his broad shoulder, Lauren felt her fear flow like water from a pent-up dam. His shirt dripping wet from the teardrops that streamed off her face, Roget responded to the devastating tremors of her fear. At that instant, huddled in his arms, she was small, frail, helpless.

Roget's strong arms lifted and carried her unresisting form to the yellow canopied bed in their room, the bed he no longer shared with her. Then Lauren watched his easy, rhythmic strides cross the room and disappear. From a decanter in his dressing room, he brought a healthy glass of ruby red port and forced it in her hand.

"Drink this," his voice commanded softly. "If nothing else, it will calm your nerves."

Tasting a tiny sip of the potent wine, her nose breathed the fumes. "But Roget—"

"All of it," he demanded. The first gulp gagged in Lauren's throat, and she choked, sputtering red wine over her face and down the front of her eggshell gown. Roget's stoic expression was relentless. Obediently, she swallowed what was left of the wine. As much as she welcomed his attention, she loathed the way it had been achieved.

Yanking a crisp white handkerchief from his pocket,

Roget took great pains in wiping every drop of red from her face and the slender, palpitating column of her throat. While his fingers nimbly undid the buttons of her décolleté gown, his gaze scolded her as if she were a naughty child. His hand on her bare flesh made her tremble. Once he had removed her arms from the huge poufed sleeves, he slipped the folds of the skirt over her hips and flung the ruined dress aside. Seeing her stripped to the lace chemise and bloomers, Roget rose quickly and moved away from the bed.

"Where are your nightgowns?" he asked abruptly.

"In the bottom drawer," she replied, her bare arm pointing toward the armoire. Roget opened the drawer and pulled out the first garment that loomed before him, a lavender one with tiny cap sleeves. Tossing it on the bed, he strode back to his room, leaving her alone while he bathed and dressed for dinner.

On his way downstairs, Roget detoured past the canopied bed, paused briefly, and covered her with a yellow quilt. Vaguely, Lauren heard the sound of his voice penetrating her stupor. "I'll have your dinner brought up."

Her heart sank as the door clicked shut and he was gone. Some time later, Filene arrived with a tray, and Lauren forced her eyes open and sat up.

"Is *madame* not feeling well?"

"A little under the weather," Lauren lied. "I suppose I had too much sun today."

"*Madame* should be careful in the sun. You're not accustomed to this heat. Anyway, I'm glad that you're all right."

"*Merci,* Filene." The queenly black woman deposited her tray of silver dishes and left.

The evening rain had begun to spatter the windowpanes, and Lauren listened as it danced against the glass doors that shut off the balconoy. Pleased as she was to miss dinner, she did not relish being in the room alone through the remainder of a long night. Knowing that Roget would spend it in his beloved Lucienne's arms, she merely picked at the food, and unable to awaken her lethargic appetite, she pushed the tray aside. Having waged a fierce battle against the drowsiness, Lauren's eyelids grew heavy and finally closed. She fell into a restless, fitful sleep, plagued by grotesque nightmares.

* * *

Roget undid the four-in-hand tie at his throat and yanked it off, the silk fabric snapping against his collar. From the open door, he heard Lauren's restless thrashings as she tossed from one fretful position to another. Treading through to the room he was supposed to share with her, he approached their enormous bed and frowned down at the narrow form that lay mumbling incoherently in her sleep. Her fear, as she shuddered in his arms, had prodded him to spend the evening in the house, but in her sleep, she was unaware of his presence. Divesting himself of his clothing, Roget wrestled with his falsely noble convictions.

Somewhere in a dream, Lauren imagined Roget's body sliding into the canopied bed beside her. It seemed an eternity since she had felt the hard length of his torso lying next to hers. The nightmares subsided, and for the remainder of the night, she slept somewhat soundly.

With the first light of dawn creeping through their window, Roget stirred and attempted to move his numbed left arm. When he awakened fully, he found Lauren huddled next to him, so close he could feel her heartbeat. Her hand rested casually on his stomach and one leg lay bent across his thigh. Her dark, rigidly curly hair had sprung free of the restraining combs and tangled wildly about her face, and her head nestled in the curve of his arm with the trusting innocence of a babe. Having her so close after months of abstinence wrenched a knot in his belly that threatened to choke him. Lauren stirred, and Roget's nostrils caught the mild jasmine scent of her hair. A liquid fire licked through his groin like erupting lava, singeing every nerve in its path.

Hazel eyes fluttered open. Groggy and blurred from the wine the night before, they surveyed the situation lazily until noticing the hand draped carelessly over his hard, flat belly. Her eyes widened like puppets at the end of a string. Realizing her vulnerable position, she recoiled, abruptly withdrawing the hand. Thinking that he had spent the night in his lover's bed before crawling into bed with his wife, Lauren inched away from him and smoothed the crumpled nightgown over her bare legs to her ankles, all the while hating her emotions for betraying her.

"I'm sorry." She apologized as if she were an intruder.

Roget noticed the same ignominious look she had had the morning after their wedding when she had been embarrassed by her passion. "Someone wants to kill me," she mumbled. Afraid to let her gaze meet his, afraid that her traitorous heart would long for the comfort of his arms again, Lauren toyed with the tiny knots on the bed cover.

"Lauren, you're being ridiculous." Roget raised up on his elbows. "I think you have attached too much importance to a childish prank."

Letting her fingers feel each satiny indentation on the quilt, she said, "Isn't that the purpose of a spell?"

"Not necessarily . . . It could mean a number of different things." Roget sat up and rubbed the muscle of his left arm. "There are *ouangas* for love, birth, protection—"

"I doubt that anyone is wishing me love," she interrupted, lifting her eyes to meet his.

"Perhaps not, but it gains its strength from your belief. If you ignore it, it has no power."

Lauren gazed at him with skepticism. "That sounds like an intellectual assumption," she replied. Yet she wanted desperately to believe him. Aching to shield herself in the warmth of his arms, she pulled away, clamping her lower lip painfully between her teeth. "I realize no one wants me here, but I never thought they would resort to this."

Roget swung his legs over the side of the bed and stood up. His attempts to diffuse the incident had failed miserably.

"Monsieur Roget, Monsieur Gaston is coming to have a big, big fever looking for you," Christophe said as he entered the dimly lit warehouse. "He is very much annoyed."

Roget heaved a burlap sack onto his shoulder, shoved it in the loader, and split it with his knife, letting thousands of burnished red beans flow into the tank of water.

"Why doesn't he come in?"

Christophe's droll expression answered the question immediately. "Monsieur Gaston don't like putting dirt on him none," he said in the nasal tone that was common to Creole.

"Where is he?" Roget questioned. Using the same nasal-sounding patios, he added, "Christophe, you and Aubin work this through the process, and make sure the cylinder in the pulper doesn't clog."

Brushing his hands on his breeches, Roget stalked outside. He found his brother leaning against a post, one booted leg crossed over the other, thumbs hooked in the pockets of his white trousers. A picture of the gentleman farmer to be sure, Roget thought.

"Isn't it a bit early in the season for you to be playing with your favorite toys?" he said, shifting his massive frame.

"Our chief crop comes in in November . . . just in case you've forgotten," Roget retorted. "There is no harm in being sure that the machinery is free of kinks." Shoving both hands in his pockets, Roget asked flatly, "What brings you here?"

"I searched the whole damn plantation looking for you. Antoine told me you were here. Everyone seems to know your whereabouts but me."

"I didn't realize you wanted to know," Roget replied, not resisting the urge to be facetious. "From now on, I will leave you an itinerary."

"I need your expertise." Roget shot him a look of genuine surprise. "The north mountain is flooding."

"Can't you handle it?"

"Irrigation is your specialty, *mon frère* . . . At least that was your excuse for spending a year in Paris."

"All right," Roget agreed, his tone bordering on vexation. "Give me a few minutes."

Entering the cool, concrete structure, he gave instructions to Christophe and then emerged, pulling the white straw hat snugly on his head. Some yards away, he untethered Bleu de Roi and swung himself brusquely over the stallion's back. The animal's blue-black coat gleamed in the blazing sun as he pranced forward to nuzzle Gaston's chestnut mount.

The half hour it would take to reach the mountain was an opportune time to broach the *ouanga* packet, Roget thought, but as they cantered side by side, he became aware that his brother had other ideas.

"There seems to be some discord between you and your wife lately." Gaston cast a derisive glance at his younger brother. "Could it be that you have finally realized she is not the proper bride for this family? Her heritage," he said mockingly arching an eyebrow, "leaves much to be desired."

"She pleases me," Roget retorted with calculated indifference.

"What pleasures you in bed, my dear brother, is of no interest to me. What does interest me is the family lineage. We all have our lascivious moments, but we don't marry them. Nevertheless your ardor cooled rather rapidly. Is that the reason for the late nights?"

"My marriage is not your concern," Roget replied acidly.

"It is my concern when the family honor is at stake."

"Honor," Roget repeated, his voice mocking Gaston. "Don't make me laugh."

"As a boy you defied our traditions. You have never respected the family heritage," Gaston scoffed.

"I respect truth, something the de Martiers know little about." Roget's glare met Gaston's head on, clashing like steel sabers in a matched duel. "You would sign a marriage contract with the devil if he came with a handsome dowry and a trace of blue blood."

"And your truth means carrying on an affair with a lady while you remain married to a loose wench."

"Lauren is my wife," Roget said sharply.

"For how long?" Gaston's mouth twisted to a wry grin. "Perhaps it's time for you to dissolve this mésalliance. Lucienne de Luynes should be your *wife* and not your mistress."

"Perhaps," Roget replied.

"She would give our family the distinction it deserves."

"Would she?" Roget's dark eyes squinted against the blinding sunlight. "No doubt the same distinction your wife brought to the family. I would not subject Lucienne to that. I love her. I will not see her end up like *Maman*."

Chopping weeds on the south mountain, a group of men, overseen by Toussaint, looked up from their work and stretched. Their bare black chests glistening with sweat, they called *"Bonjour, Monsieur Roget."*

"Bonjour, messieurs," he called back, jocularly lifting his

hat as he rode past them. Gaston shifted in his saddle. His eyes closed to slits and the wide nostrils flared with indignation, but Roget ignored the unspoken reprimand.

"Lauren found an *ouanga* packet under the piano. I don't suppose you know how it got there?"

"Why should I know how it got there? I don't play with toys."

"It had strands of her hair, a piece of her clothing, and a small clay image."

"Perhaps someone wants to be sure that your blushing bride does not conceive a child."

"Lauren is convinced that someone wants to kill her."

"Kill her." Gaston repeated the words, making the idea seem absurd. "It sounds like some child's prank."

"That's what I told her, but I doubt that she believes it . . . and frankly, neither do I."

"Who would want to kill your wife?" Again he flashed that perceptive grin. "There are other ways to rid the family of her." He paused and then added, "You may want to hear them one day."

"Reinette also found an *ouanga* packet," Roget continued, paying no heed to Gaston's blatant innuendos.

"Reinette's death was an accident."

"Was it?" Roget's tone suggested otherwise.

"She was thrown by her horse. What is that if not an accident?"

"Reinette was poisoned, Gaston, and you know that as well as I do. You will never convince me it was an accident . . . not the way she was broken and twisted, her eyes bulging out of her head. No fall from a horse could accomplish that much damage. Dr. Mauriac believes she was having convulsions, and the fruit of the machineel is capable of producing that kind of reaction."

"Since you're remarkably well informed on the causes of my wife's death, tell me, what was she doing in le Petit Cul-de-Sac? She was forbidden to ride there."

"Who knows?" Roget shrugged. "Reinette was stubborn and headstrong just as Lauren is," he said thoughtfully. "She did not take lightly to orders. And her horse . . . I don't trust that mare. I would swear she's the devil's consort."

Bleu de Roi's hooves lost their grip and began to slide as the animal plodded through scattered pools of deep red mud. Roget's gaze traveled up the mountainside. Water ran off the steep incline in small streams, the soggy earth too saturated to drink it in. Noticing the pools of muddy seepage collecting near the mountain base, perplexity twisted Roget's face as he entertained the possibility of flooding. Dismounting, he secured Bleu de Roi to the trunk of a bamboo tree and started up the slope on foot, his leather boots sinking deep beneath the soggy terrain.

Reluctantly, Gaston followed. Watching the way his brother cautiously placed his feet, Roget was reminded of a damsel eluding the litter in the streets of Port-au-Prince. His massive size made him decidedly less surefooted than his more agile sibling.

"This should not be happening." Roget's face tensed in a puzzled expression.

"But as you see, it is." Gaston's tone was clipped.

Winding his way among the neatly engineered rows of green coffee bushes, Roget's focus rested on branches that drooped with near ripe berries. "This area was well shielded from erosion when I left last year." Dwarfed by plants that stood seven feet taller than either he or Gaston, the two climbed further up the incline, Roget still perplexed by the sliding mud. Reaching the top, Roget stared in disbelief at the bald plateau where hundreds of rosewood trees had once grown. Disgusted, he ground his teeth in bitter resignation. "Why were these trees cut down?" he demanded.

"I was offered an excellent price for the wood."

"And you may one day be offered an excellent price for a plantation—one that no longer exists. The day will come when the entire plantation will be swept away in a flood." Roget stretched down and scooped up a handful of the soggy dirt, looking for a brief second as if he might smear it on Gaston's face. "I left instructions not to fell any trees on this mountain. We still have heavy rains ahead of us," Roget snarled, kneading the mud between his fingers. "How in the hell do you intend to keep this mountain from sliding onto the plains?"

"That is your problem; you're the family scholar," Gaston responded, squirming uncomfortably. Watching the mud ooze through Roget's fingers and plop to the ground, he imagined his skin covered with crawling maggots. "You were the one who spent a year attending lectures at the conservatory."

"All the world's schools won't help if you refuse to heed their advice." Yanking a white handkerchief from his pocket, he started down the slippery path. "The only thing I can do is have trenches dug and pray the earth will soak up more water. We may lose the crop on this hill, and it's a shame," he said futilely, reaching up to cup a cluster of the burnished berries in his hand. "It's a handsome crop."

Roget's bitterly admonishing glance cut right through his brother's arrogant facade. "You're exactly like our father—unable to accept change even though it's crucial to your survival."

"Our father adhered to family traditions just as the de Martiers before him."

"Custom doesn't make it right. It's asinine to blindly follow a tradition that will inevitably destroy you. Progress has to happen."

"Never!" Gaston bellowed. "As long as I am lord of this manor, it will remain as it is. Neither you nor anyone else will change it's traditions." His voice resounded through the thick, hot air.

Roget flinched at the truculent sound and lost his footing. Cursing silently, he struggled to regain a slippery balance.

"You're as bullheaded as our father," he said, scowling.

"Father controlled what belonged to him. He would not have allowed a scholar to disrupt his domain."

A caustic glance shot from one pair of dark eyes to penetrate the other. "Mother was one of the possessions that Father controlled and destroyed. That, too, is a custom that your precious tradition would not change." Roget's stare challenged him. "Have you taken a good look at her recently . . . talked to her? There is only a skeleton of the woman she used to be."

"She has led a privileged life. What more could she want?" he said indifferently.

"She spent a lifetime in a house and on land over which she had no autonomy or control."

"She is well provided for," Gaston said, his attention

fixed more on his muddy boots and sliding feet than his mother's welfare.

"On her sons' property," Roget retorted.

"That's a woman's lot when she marries into this family."

"A destructive one to be sure." Roget lifted an eyebrow with skepticism. "To be handed from your husband to your children . . . would you like it?"

"I am not a woman," Gaston replied as they neared the base of the mountain. At last, he was able to concentrate on his brother's verbal attack. "This is man's country," he said, an arrogant smirk spreading wide across his face.

Stifling the urge to let one blow of an angry fist silence his brother's tyranny, Roget took a broad leap off the slope and onto flat ground.

"A man does not destroy everything around him nor does he destroy his women."

"You're so occupied with the causes of women and other weak creatures," Gaston said, scoffing as he untied his chestnut stallion, "could that be the reason you're in no hurry to discard that wench?" His tone harbored a challenge. "You know, little brother, you would only have to say that you were not the first and we could easily be rid of her. Your marriage would be annulled."

"I'm well aware of that," Roget retorted, his lips curling to a sardonic grin. "But ironically . . . I *was* the first." Glistening beneath the open shirt, his sable chest bared as he swung his body up to meet the saddle. Roget flanked the black stallion and headed for the warehouse, Bleu de Roi's hooves pounding the sand to a whirlwind of dust at their backs.

With the terrifying week behind her and the sight of the *ouanga* packet less vivid in Lauren's memory, Roget resumed his late nights. During that week, he had shared her bed as he would have shared it with a sister, and after that first night, Lauren was careful not to stray from her side of the bed. When again he began sleeping in his dressing room, it was clearly evident to Lauren that he had returned to the pleasures of Lucienne's arms.

Chapter

17

Day after day, the reality of the concert grew nearer, inflating Lauren's apprehensions to a fully blown state of anxiety. She was not convinced it was the advent of the coming performance that had strung her nerves to the tautness of a bass fiddle as much as the fact that her monthly cycle was two weeks late. Desperately needing diversion from her own thoughts, Lauren agreed to accompany Georgette to a fitting at Madame Fontenelle's.

"It's good to see that your talent will finally be put to use," the couturiere said, her teeth dangerously clamping a pin. "There could be no better cause. Those children need help so badly." Drawn by the rustle of silk taffeta, their attention fled to Georgette as she emerged from the fitting room draped in a pale green gown.

"Madame Duval convinced me to play the concert . . . or should I say, coerced me into it," Lauren added wryly.

"For once they didn't allow arrogance to get in the way of good sense," Madame Fontenelle said, her hands pinching and tugging at the excess fabric. Lauren threw the woman a questioning glance. "I doubt that they've accepted you as one of them. Believe me, they won't swallow easily the bitter pill your husband has forced down their throats. They'll harbor the resentment for years."

"I believe you," Lauren answered reflectively.

With nimble fingers, Madame Fontenelle pulled the green silk snug about Georgette's middle and pinned it securely with the silver pin that protruded from her mouth.

"I see we have a little one on the way," she said, noticing the signs of the younger woman's condition. Georgette grinned sheepishly, letting her hands spread over her thickening waist. But while Georgette basked in the joy of her pregnancy, Lauren dreaded the possibility of hers. A picture flashed before her eyes of Lucienne in Roget's arms and drowned out all other thoughts. Standing abruptly, she circled the small room, hoping to stifle the wave of despair that rolled over her.

"Do you think I will meet with their approval?" Georgette teased mockingly, her hand fluttering in a facetious gesture.

Returning to the pink cushioned chair, Lauren lowered herself slowly, her attention fixed on the other young woman who pirouetted pompously in her new gown. "I should think so," Lauren replied, forcing a smile.

"Such grand ladies, all of them," Madame Fontenelle broke in scornfully. "Priding themselves on their good deeds by raising money for charity. Any one of them could easily donate the money needed, but no, they give fancy concerts and benefits. Which of them would go to Saint Joseph's and give those children their time or attention? Which of them would take a child into her sumptuous home? What those children need are homes and love, not a few meager gourdes tossed at them from a safe distance."

Georgette let out a loud sigh. Lauren said nothing but decided there might be someone who needed her after all. She knew what it was to lose one's mother, especially in childhood. Fortunately, she had had Claude. How she wished she could talk to her aunt Claude now.

"Good luck," Simone Gevres whispered, squeezing Lauren's hand as they crossed paths behind the drapery. "They're all yours." Lauren slid onto the gilded bench, her apricot satin gown rustling as she smoothed it beneath her. The ballroom at the Fortier mansion bulged with the Haitian elite, and somewhere among the sea of stoic faces were her husband and her few friends, Georgette, Jacques, and Antoine. Lucienne, too, would be there perusing her, probably not far from Roget.

Lifting her fingers above the keys of the grand piano, she lowered all ten in a strong forte. Her first notes resounded in the air, penetrating the buzz of chattering voices, and a hush of silence shrouded the room like a cloak. Every pair of eyes, it seemed, had focused on the palpitating heart that pounded between her bare shoulders. The perspiring hands, the knot in the pit of her stomach, were poignantly reminiscent of the first time she attempted *Fantasie Impromptu* at the Saint Germain—the night she met Roget.

Grateful that Simone had agreed to play first, Lauren had used the much-needed time to muster her courage. The memory of that hideous charm had left an ugly scar on her. Following her solo repertoire, she and Simone would play several duets, and then each would play a closing selection. For her final piece, she had chosen *Fantasie Impromptu*.

Losing herself in the melodies created by her fingers as they flew lithely over the keys, Lauren became oblivious to her audience. Only once did she allow them to penetrate her secret world, and when she did, she caught a glimpse of Lucienne's magnificently coiffured auburn head turned toward Roget. She missed a key. Perhaps her audience had not noticed, but determinedly, Lauren grit her teeth and vowed not to let her eyes wander in their direction again.

Roget sat almost mesmerized as her fingers danced from one key to the next, transporting him back to the Saint Germain and the memory of that silly bet. Then, as now, the enchantment when he heard her play had invaded his soul with the giddiness of a child.

"Roget, your wife plays beautifully," Lucienne whispered, muffling her voice with the white ostrich fan.

"Oui," he replied. "She does."

Awkwardly, Roget stretched his leg and adjusted the fit of his trousers, but Lucienne had heard the faint expression of pride that crept into his tone and envied Lauren her ability to enchant. She had played for most of her life and very often for Roget, but her skill could not match his wife's talent.

With the last notes of *Fantasie Impromptu* still vibrating through the air, Lauren stood amidst the clamor of clapping hands and curtsied to the floor, her heart about to burst from her chest. As Roget rose to join his wife's standing ovation, Lucienne heard him utter a resounding cry of "Brava!"

The handsome carriage rumbled along rue Republicaine, rounded the bend, and clattered onto the sandy dirt road that bypassed Port-au-Prince. Old Jean sat protectively at the reins. Lauren leaned back against the soft chamois seat and sighed. It felt good to have somewhere to go.

"I'm pleased that you decided to join me," she said to her companion, her voice dragging with uncertainty. "I need your support."

Georgette Deffand gazed at her skeptically. "I doubt if traveling on these roads is a good idea in my condition," she said, bracing her back firmly against the seat. Georgette looked across at the hazel eyes that perused her. "So, the vultures have convinced you to join in their two-faced philanthropy." Her tone was cynical, almost chastising.

"I need something to do beside wander about the house all day. What could be better than helping unfortunate children? Perhaps they need me . . . no one else seems to . . ." Lauren's voice vanished into the clattering noise of turning wheels. A sadness passed over her face and faded away. "Please, Georgette," she pleaded. "I'm sure it will not be as unpleasant as you think. I wouldn't be surprised if you came away wanting to help as well." Lauren's lips suppressed a knowing smile.

"I've seen enough of orphanages, waifs, and poverty to last a lifetime," she answered coldly. "And rich ladies who dabble in charity give me a pain." Georgette pressed a hand against the small of her back to relieve an obvious discomfort. "Madame Fontenelle was absolutely right. What those children need is love, not a few measly gourdes tossed at them from afar."

The de Martier carriage rumbled to stop before a rambling white residence, an archaic mansion that long ago had forgotten its better days. Old Jean reined in the horses, and the two young women stepped from the carriage to the surrounding grounds, sparsely dotted with coconut palms, raggedly trimmed hedges, and a balding carpet of green grass. Five children, working in the garden, abruptly interrupted their chores and stood numbly in awe of the fine silver-harnessed vehicle. Ten wide, awestruck eyes followed the women as they picked their way along the crumbled concrete path to the front door. Dingy curtains flickered behind open windows, as small black faces peered from between the folds. Obviously, they had not seen such an impressive vehicle parked here before. Lauren felt their curious stares fixed on her from every direction, and her heart ached for their deprivation. Madame Fontenelle had not been wrong. The elite had not bothered to give their time.

Desolate was her sole description of the remaining grounds—acres of space with no sign of civilization. Lauren was appalled. These children were shut away here, isolated from society as though they were its outcasts. A stab of pity plunged through her breast. She knew too well the pain suffered by victims of circumstance.

Walking beneath the sign that read Orphelinat Saint Joseph, they rapped at a wooden door that was badly in need of repair. The huge door swung open, and the two women stood face-to-face with two sisters of the order. Dressed in voluminous white robes with starched white headdresses binding their dark faces, they smiled curiously at their two visitors.

"I'm Lauren de Martier, and this is Georgette Deffand. We have come to see if we can help with the children."

"Oui, mesdames. S'il vous plaît entrez." The older nun stepped aside allowing them to enter. "I am Sœur Dominique and this is Sœur Clarice. What is it you wish to do?" she continued, her tone rigidly formal.

"Madame de Martier?" Sœur Clarice could not suppress her sudden look of surprise. "You are the lady who played the concert," she said. Lauren nodded amiably. "You said that you would come. However, I never believed . . . The others donate money, but they rarely come." Clasping her arms to her breast, the young nun tried to contain her joy. "Oh, *madame!* Would you play for us—the children, I mean?" She rambled on excitedly, no longer clasping her shoulders in surprise but clasping her hands with delight. "The children would love it. They have little chance to hear music. We have an old piano, but there is no one who can play it."

"Of course," Sœur Dominique said reflectively, "you would be Madame Roget de Martier."

How odd, Lauren thought. People knew of her, her life, her actions—people she did not know existed. "Do you know my husband?" she questioned curiously.

"He came here some years ago, inquiring about a child. At the time, he was a young man. He would be considerably older now."

"How long ago?" Lauren asked, silently wondering whose child he had been searching for.

"Eight, perhaps nine years ago," she replied. "But come! Let us show you the place. We've seldom had ladies visit the home. Rarely does anyone visit us out here. But thank the Lord," she said breathing a heavy sigh, "we were fortunate enough to have this house donated to us. Otherwise, the children would be in the street."

"But it's so isolated," Georgette added, her gaze caught by the doleful stares of tiny urchins peering from the doorways.

"We are delighted to have someone take an interest," Sœur Clarice broke in. "The children need exposure to other people." Her soft, young voice was sad, wistful.

"The wealthy families always send money, of course," the older nun added quickly, not to appear ungrateful. "Without it we could not exist. But there are too many little ones for us to have time for each."

"That is exactly why we came," Lauren said, her attention focused on her reluctant companion.

"We will help if we can," Georgette volunteered. As she met Lauren's glance, a feeling of empathy bridged the gap between them.

From a wide main hallway, they followed the nuns up a palatial staircase. At least it had been palatial in its day. Age and neglect had taken their toll on the grand mansion. Having never been inside an orphanage, Lauren was unprepared for the cold, institutional atmosphere of the place. She assumed that the sisters were doing their best under the circumstances, but two women to care for sixty, perhaps seventy children. It was abominable!

"This is where the children sleep," Sœur Clarice said, her robes trailing on the floor behind her. There were ten bedchambers, each about the size of the one that she and Roget occupied at Villa de Martier. Six or seven rickety frame beds formed a row along the walls, and over each bed, jutting out from a stark white wall, was a wooden peg holding the child's meager articles of clothing. The room housed nothing more except a small table on which stood two copper washbasins.

Lauren was overwhelmed by a feeling of remorse as her own luxurious bedchamber flashed into mind. Her huge canopied bed, the yellow moiré chairs, the rich Oriental carpet, the fine porcelain washbasins hidden in a separate room. If nothing else, she and Georgette could bring color and warmth to the drab, impersonal existence of these children. The Deffand and de Martier fortunes could certainly finance so modest an undertaking.

Downstairs, they were escorted to what was once a ballroom.

"Our piano is here," Sœur Clarice beamed proudly. Her dark hand motioned toward an impressive grand piano. Elated, Lauren lifted the folds of her skirt and moved swiftly toward the majestic instrument. But as she approached it, she realized that as imposing as it might have been, it was pitifully dilapidated. Choking back her disappointment, she sat down and ran her fingers over the keys. It was badly out of tune. Soon, small faces appeared from nowhere, lured by the sound of twinkling keys. Lauren sighed heavily. Disappointing them now was more than she could bear.

Hordes of children were summoned from other parts of the house and assembled in the vast ballroom. Doleful, wide-eyed faces stared up at her as her fingers danced playfully over the keys. Lauren searched her memory for light, gay tunes that would appeal to young ears and executed them with an ethereal touch. Sixty boys and girls sat cross-legged on the floor, their cherubic faces fixed intently on her as she created for them a fantasy. She had never enchanted a more appreciative audience.

One small child of two or three, as yet too young to enjoy the fantasy, toddled to Georgette and tugged impatiently at her skirt. An older girl rushed forward to pull the baby away, alarmed that its small, grubby hands would soil Georgette's exquisite lawn gown. They could only manage if older children took charge of the younger ones, and apparently this child was her responsibility. Apologizing for the baby's behavior, the girl gently slapped its tiny hands away and scolded, "You mustn't do that! You will ruin the lady's dress."

"Please," Georgette broke in, her arms reaching for the child. "You need not worry about my dress. Why don't you sit and enjoy the music, and I'll mind the baby," she said. As the older child fled from her side, Georgette called after her, "What is her name?"

"Ceci," she called back. Happy to be relieved of her burden, the girl edged in close to the piano and lost herself in the music. Several times, Lauren looked up and found Georgette bouncing the contented baby on her knee.

When she had finished her idyll of make believe, the young spectators clamored round the piano, all trying to plunk the keys and tread the pedals simultaneously. They climbed over and under it like a swarm of ants, pulling and plucking at anything that protruded. It was no wonder the instrument was out of tune. From the corner of her eye, Lauren noticed the girl standing shyly at her side, the same one Georgette had spoken to minutes earlier. She seemed reluctant to approach the massive piano, yet her eyes remained curiously entranced by the keyboard.

"Would you like to play?" Lauren asked, looking up at the gangly young girl. She barely nodded. Tall and thin for her age, she had marvelously long, graceful hands. Pianist's hands, Lauren thought. "Do you have a name?" Lauren questioned softly.

"Madeleine," she answered, almost inaudibly.

"Do you know how to play, Madeleine?" The girl shook her head no. "Would you like me to teach you?"

"Oui, madame," she replied, showing the first signs of animation.

Lauren rose from the stool and motioned her young protégé to sit down. Placing her fingers on the keys next to Madeleine's, she painstakingly taught her the scales. The forlorn face brightened with delight as she played the simple exercise over and over again. Her fingers moved with delicate precision across the black and ivory rectangles. Lauren had never fancied herself a teacher, but it would be sinful to let exceptional talent go undeveloped. She would teach Madeleine to play, but she would need a new piano. This one was beyond repair. Dwelling on that thought, Lauren motioned to Georgette that it was time to leave. After retrieving their feathered hats and kid gloves, Lauren and her companion climbed into their carriage for the bumpy ride home.

Old Jean urged the horses around the bend and his passengers stared straight ahead at the sprawling Deffand villa that dominated the end of the road. Suddenly Georgette laughed. Stunned by the outburst of laughter, Lauren turned and faced her.

"Do you realize how ridiculous we are?" Georgette said. "Our husbands are among the richest men in this country and we sit here scheming to buy a piano."

"Surely, you would only have to ask Jacques," Lauren said, "but Roget . . . I don't know . . . We've hardly talked. How could I possibly ask for a piano?" Darting her hazel eyes toward the window, Lauren fought to divert the tears that stung against her eyelids.

"Lauren, I'm certain I can get it from Jacques." Georgette's tone attempted to comfort her. "I will get it, I promise you."

Staring fixedly at the lush green foliage, Lauren did not answer. And then, unexpectedly, her forlorn expression brightened to one of enthusiasm. "I could use the money my father left me," she said.

"Lauren, that's all you have in the world that is really yours. You may need it one day." Georgette's soft, almond eyes filled with empathy. "Please let me donate the piano," she pleaded with a deliberate persistence.

Lauren questioned the obvious change of heart. Was she doing it simply because she sympathized with her precarious situation?

"I'm sure that Jacques will agree," Georgette said. "And if not, I will convince him."

Lauren stiffened. She did not want pity.

"You have your talent to give," she continued. "There is nothing else I can give." Sincerity colored Georgette's expression, and Lauren softened.

"All right, if you insist," she said, her lips smiling reluctantly. But she knew that despite her friend's generosity, she would also approach Roget. She had always stood on her own two feet, and she would now.

That same evening, opportunity beckoned. Roget had not gone out after dinner. Perhaps he planned to spend the evening at home. Quickening its beat, her heart thumped wildly against her breast as she listened for his footsteps in the hallway. Anxiously, Lauren paced the carpet like a restless panther waiting to leap on its prey. At last she heard the rhythm of his heels clicking against the hard parquet floor. Drawing a deep breath, she squared her shoulders and waited, but the sound stopped short of their bedchamber. Sequestered in his favorite refuge, he would more than likely remain there for hours. She would have to go to him. Was the humiliation more intense because deep inside she realized her longing for him gnawed not only at her gut, but at her pride as well?

Dragging forth her store of courage, Lauren raked the silver brush over her hair, wrapped the silk kimono about her body, and padded through the hall to the library. Knocking softly at the closed door, she turned the knob and pushed it open, heeding his invitation to enter.

"May I come in?"

"Please do," he said, perusing her curiously. Roget rose from the chair and laid a book aside on the table.

"Roget, I have to talk to you." Suddenly, Lauren was aware of the thumping in her breast. She had never had to beg for anything, at least not in this manner and not from a husband.

"Oh," he said calmly, hoisting one raven black brow. "About what?" His face lacking any definite expression, Roget motioned with his hand. "Sit down."

Lying open on the small rosewood table was the copy of Oscar Wilde's recent novel that they had purchased together from one of the bookstalls along the Quai before leaving Paris. Lauren brushed past him, and the musky aura of his cologne seeped into her nostrils. From the beginning it had been the same intoxicating scent. Abruptly, Lauren stifled her train of thought. Remembering the joy that brightened those little faces when she played for them, she strengthened her conviction that their cause was more important than her own.

"I want to buy a piano for the orphanage," she stated with fierce determination. Lowering herself into the cushioned armchair, she looked up at him and waited for his reply.

"So now you intend to fight the cause of Saint Joseph's. You know Lauren, I think you missed your calling. You should have been a crusader."

She could not distinguish whether his tone held sarcasm or amusement, but before uneasiness gained a hold on her tongue, she continued her plea. "The children were so enchanted when I played for them. Their sad eyes seemed to come alive with the sounds of the music. When I had finished, they hovered around the piano, plunking at the keys with their small, awkward fingers trying to produce the same sounds." Roget saw the tears swell in her eyes and watched her turn away to divert them from his gaze. "I could teach several of them to play," she continued, "and then they could play for the others. There is one girl, Madeleine, whom I think may be exceptional . . . But the piano is old and badly out of tune, beyond the point of being repaired. It would be impossible to train a pianist on an instrument in that condition, even a mediocre one." Realizing that she had talked for some minutes without giving thought to Roget or herself, Lauren relented and sat silently awaiting the verdict. However, determination remained stubbornly on her pursed lips.

Roget had listened intently, but now his gaze had fallen to her mouth—so poised, so determined. He turned brusquely, took a glass from the sideboard, and filled it with rum. He had also seen the opalescent glow in her eye and knew that when she was so fiercely committed to something, she would fight him through heaven and hell.

"Sherry?" he asked, his inflection indicating the question.

"Oui, s'il vous plaît," she replied, hoping the wine would give her resolution to continue.

Roget filled a glass with golden sherry and handed it to the determined woman that challenged him. As Lauren reached for the crystal glass, her fingers collided with his and sent a surge of blood racing through two sets of veins. Recoiling as if she had put her hand to a flame, she felt her body weaken. Roget savored a long swallow of rum and then reached up to loosen the elegant cravat at his throat.

Lauren took a mouthful of the sherry and swallowed it in a single gulp. "Roget, I mean to buy a piano for those children," she stated firmly. The persistence was still evident in her voice as her hazel eyes clashed with his ebony ones.

Fiercely, Roget clenched his jaw. At times he could not believe her audacity. A Haitienne with much more in her favor would not defy him the way she did. And yet, why could he think of nothing at this moment but his desire to smother her sultry, defiant mouth with his own.

"Since obviously you're determined to give them a piano, you will find a way. So, before you sell your soul to the devil ... buy it." His consent was calm and indifferent, lacking any outward sign of emotion.

"What do you suggest I buy it with?" She was annoyed at having to remind him of the fact. "My monthly allowance is hardly enough to purchase a piano."

"*Tonnerre*, Lauren!" he bellowed, emptying the glass. "I am well aware that you cannot pay for it. Buy it and have the bill sent to me." Roget turned to refill his glass, clearly dismissing her when he said nothing more.

Lauren left the room feeling oddly cheated. Battling with him was decidedly better than no communication at all, yet she had come prepared for a battle and he had given her none. Getting her wish had been almost easy.

It was a rare evening on the Cul-de-Sac Plain. The rainy season had subsided several weeks ago, and nights were warm and dry with the nectar sweet aroma of ripening fruit permeating the breezes. For Lauren it had truly been a glorious day. That morning she had awakened to clearly visible signs that she was not pregnant from Gaston's seed. Lifting her hazel eyes toward heaven, she had said a prayer, thanking God for not deserting her.

The de Martiers had gathered in their mother's parlor before dinner, and for once all three brothers were present.

Drawing a hasty sip from his glass, Gaston turned to Roget. "So, the newly married de Martiers have donated a piano to Saint Joseph's. Surely, there must be other necessities of life more urgent than a piano." News traveled with the speed of a telegraph in Port-au-Prince.

"Lauren is teaching several of the children to play," Roget replied. "Orphans, as well as anyone else, need beauty and pleasure in their lives. Should they be condemned on all counts?"

"Well said," Antoine joined in.

"I should have guessed that your meddling wife instigated the matter. She becomes more like Reinette every day. The unique difference is that Reinette was born with the right."

"Must one be born to a certain class to gain the right to help those less fortunate?" Lauren inquired indignantly. "Forgive me. I was not aware that human kindness was partial to class."

"Only when one's own class wavers precariously on circumstance . . . destined to fall at any moment." Taunting her, Gaston alluded to their dreadful secret.

Antoine shifted in the red damask chair, uncrossed his legs, then rose to join Roget before the mantle. "I consider it a very humane gesture," he said, raising his glass in a toast to his benevolent sister-in-law. "The de Martiers could use more of it."

"Reinette was always involved in such matters," Madame de Martier added. "Her heart could have encompassed the world."

"And since Reinette," Antoine said cynically, "this family has been devoid of compassion."

"Lauren needed to employ her talents; it was as simple as that," Roget said. "I should have known that she would do nothing halfheartedly; it's not her nature. However, I consider the matter closed," he stated flatly as he strode from the mantle to join his mother on the sofa.

"And what is her nature?" Gaston questioned, his glance darting to meet hers. Again he was baiting her, and she was powerless to retaliate. Would he one day boast of their illicit encounter to Roget when all else had failed?

"Not dissimilar to Reinette's," Roget retorted. "Lauren

should have been a crusader." A hint of a smile parted his lips.

"She should learn her place!" Gaston scoffed arrogantly. "She forgets that she was not born to the same privilege as Reinette. Reinette was a lady. Beauty and breeding such as hers will always be indulged." Inclining his head to one side, he lifted his empty glass to Roget. "Just as you, my dear brother, indulge Mademoiselle de Luynes."

His words penetrated Lauren's soul like a dagger. Clapping her lips tightly together, she avoided letting indiscretion rule her tongue.

"Our women are in a class by themselves," he continued, "not to be challenged or equaled by status seekers."

"But their exclusivity does not prevent them from being killed," Roget replied with biting sarcasm.

"What can prevent being thrown from a horse except perhaps better skills?"

"I thought she was an expert horsewoman," Lauren countered.

"She was a superior equestrienne, to be equaled by none."

"Your women may be superior, but I hardly think that none can equal their skill. Whether you realize it or not, I, too, am a very capable horsewoman."

"Capable, perhaps, but never superior." The stench of his condescension filled the room.

Lauren bristled. Blood raced to her face, coloring her dark skin, but her tightly pursed lips remained closed.

Roget stared at her intently. A smoldering flicker of desire lingered in his gaze, but no one noticed. "Lauren rides superbly," he said, "and is equally as stubborn."

"I doubt that her skill would have matched Reinette's. There was not a woman alive who could handle Côtelette other than she."

"I have never been granted the opportunity," Lauren retorted. "Roget has forbidden me to ride her."

"Oho! Because he knows you could not handle her."

A soft rapping sound penetrated the door, and at Gaston's invitation, Filene stepped inside. Her long ebony fingers curled around the brass doorknob as she announced, *"Madame,* dinner is served."

Chapter

18

Unable to resist a challenge thrown at her so blatantly, Lauren's desire to ride Côtelette became urgent. Somehow, she would have to find a way to get around Old Jean. Roget had given strict orders that she was not to ride that horse, and Old Jean obeyed him as though he were lord and master. There had been times when he had succumbed to her charm if for no other reason than the fact that she was Monsieur Roget's wife. Little did he know that Monsieur Roget cared less about his wife than he did Mademoiselle Lucienne. But what did it matter? Lauren doubted that Old Jean would ignore his master's orders, but she was left with the remainder of the morning to devise a scheme.

Lauren approached the stables still undecided as to how she would get the horse saddled and out of the stall, but fortune seemed to smile on her. Inside, there was no sign of Old Jean. The de Martiers' young coachman was the lone person in attendance.

"*Bonjour*, Paul," she greeted him, flashing a beguiling smile.

"*Bonjour, madame.* You want me saddle your horse for you?" he questioned in a lilting Creole.

"*Oui*, Paul, but today perhaps I'll ride a different horse. Miel was a bit ploddish yesterday." Her voice taking on a disinterested tone, she nuzzled Côtelette. "Why don't you saddle this one?"

"But, *madame . . .*" The boy hesitated.

"*This* one, Paul," she demanded firmly.

"*Oui, madame.*" The boy dropped his head and moved away.

Lauren felt the tension mounting. Her heart began to pound like a mischevious child who was disobeying orders. *What can be taking him so long?* she thought, her feet pacing the ground impatiently. The boy returned and heaved the saddle onto Côtelette's back. The chestnut bay reared up, arching her proud neck, and Lauren saw the wild, reckless gleam in the animal's eye. Excited by the challenge, she would prove to the de Martiers that she was as fine a horsewoman as Reinette.

Anxiously scanning the area, her eye caught a glimpse of Old Jean's fuzzy white head coming toward the stable. She had to hurry.

"Paul, isn't she ready yet?"

"*Oui, madame.* She ready now." He handed her the reins and held the stirrup for her foot. Lauren swung into the saddle, not in the controlled way she was used to, but like someone being pursued. As the boy moved from her path, an ominous fear registered in his dark face. Old Jean stood in the door blocking the horse's exit. Côtelette reared back on her hind legs, her front hooves flailing wildly at the obstruction, but Lauren urged her flanks into a gallop and the animal bounded forward as if Satan himself were at her tail.

"Madame Lauren, come back!" the old man cried after her, as the bedeviled beast thrust past him. "You shouldn't be riding that horse! She's full with the devil!" The last thing she heard was Old Jean bitterly scolding the boy for his disobedience.

Driven by an unknown force, Côtelette's hooves beat against the dry earth with a power more fierce than lightning, and she headed straight for la Rivière Blanche. Lauren's breathing grew labored, and she gasped for air as the wind gushed into her nose and mouth. Lauren had given the horse her head, but suddenly she felt the need to slow her gait. She pulled at the reins, but Côtelette did not stop, she only lunged ahead faster. Lauren yanked the reins in tighter, but to no avail, the animal would not heed her commands. Yet she must stop. She could barely breathe. Desperately, she fought to control the wild creature, but the animal still pounded forward as if in a frenzy. This horse had a mind of its own, Lauren thought, driven by a command more powerful than hers.

The fork in the road loomed ahead, and Lauren knew she should avoid the path that skirted the mountain. Employing all of her skill, she attempted to rein the chestnut bay in and turn her onto the other road, but the horse did not miss a gait. Côtelette lunged forward in an uncontrollable fury. Dust spun from her hooves like a tornado, enveloping horse and rider in a reddish brown blizzard. Lauren coughed and gagged on the sandy dirt, fighting to catch her breath. Jerking feverishly at the reins, her attempts to slow their pace merely sent them plunging ahead faster. Despite Lauren's expert efforts to divert her, Côtelette raced head-long down the forbidden mountain road and aimed straight toward le Petit Cul-de-Sac.

Orange-blossomed trees whipped by her like a blazing inferno, the leaves and branches tearing savagely at her skin. Air was completely shut out of the sand tornado that engulfed her. Dust clouded Lauren's eyes and filled her mouth and nose. She could not see, nor could she breathe. Yet staying with the horse was a matter of life and death. If she fell at this speed, she would be finished. The leather reins had fused into one with her hands. Aching with blisters, she was unable to free her fingers. Unaware that this agent of the devil was carrying her to hell, Lauren fought to hang on. Seconds later, a low-hanging branch cracked like thunder against her skull. Lauren slumped in her saddle and drowned in a black wave of unconsciousness.

Gagging on the bitter liquid being forced down her throat, Lauren regained consciousness. She tried to open her eyes, but they refused to obey her. Finally, the lids parted. Everything looked blurred and hazy as though she had been wrapped in gauze like a mummy. Her mouth felt as if she had swallowed a wad of cotton, and something wet and bitter trickled down her throat. Growing accustomed to the foggy haze, she managed to decipher a human figure standing over her with a decanter. The ghostlike figure once again forced the decanter of bitter liquid to her mouth. Struggling to turn her head away, Lauren realized that she could not move. Her body would not heed her commands. She was paralyzed!

Her body, her arms, her legs, were without feeling. The only sensation she felt was a wavering dizziness that lingered over her body and the odor of dung from live animals seeping in her nostrils. Strangely, the room smelled like a barn. As she lay there, somewhere in the distance she heard drums. Gradually, the dizziness faded, and in her stupor of immobility, the sound of the drums grew stronger. Why were they so loud, so close?

Lauren's eyes scanned the ceiling and then wandered to the sides of the room. Her vision had cleared. Primitive oil lamps flickered like torches, casting supernatural shadows into the corners of the room. Slender white candles, copiously dripping wax on the surface below, stood in a perfect row atop a crude wooden table. The walls were hard clay and painted with lewd serpent symbols. Snakes and hideous sea creatures imitated human copulation with decidedly human expressions emanating from their monstrous faces. Lauren shuddered at the strangeness.

As involuntarily as the shudder, a flicker of awareness invaded her stupor. Why was she here? Why was she lying on a table in a place like this? Lauren tried to move her hands, flex her fingers, feel the surface beneath her. It took several futile attempts, but her fingers finally obeyed her will and rubbed the table that supported her. It was stone! Cold, rough stone. Her body trembled with fear, but still she was unable to move it. Her arms and legs lay paralyzed and useless against the hard stone slab.

Shadows and forms and people moved about the room speaking only in Creole, but Lauren's knowledge of the peasant patios was not fluent enough to understand their rapid tongues. How long she had lain there she had no idea. To her it seemed like hours. The sound of the drums drew closer and hammered at her ears until she realized that they were in the same room, and then they stopped. The people ceased talking and moved toward the far side of the rectangular room. Suddenly, Lauren felt her body being moved. Two young men, one on either side, lifted her to a sitting position and left her propped, half dazed, against the wall. Fear shot through her soul like a bolt of lightning, yet she lacked the strength to resist. They left her and returned to the others. Lauren's eyes dropped to her body, and she saw that she had been undressed. All of her clothing had been removed—boots, breeches, shirt, everything! She was naked except for a peach nightgown. Peach nightgown, peach nightgown. The two words kept resounding in her brain. Looking again at the thin piece of material covering her, the truth dawned on her senses.

"My nightgown!" her brain cried out in silence. An overwhelming terror possessed her as she shivered beneath the pale shimmering satin.

The *Rada* drums began to echo their throbbing rhythms again, and Lauren's frightened gaze searched the room for an answer. The long room was dark except for burning candles and crude oil lamps that blinked in the darkness like torches. The quivering candlelight allowed her to see the low, wide altar that was hidden beneath a lace tablecloth. From a pole in the center of the altar, a wooden serpent dangled in the air surrounded by Christian crucifixes of gold and silver and primitive necklaces made of snake vertebrae. On either side stood huge earthenware jugs. A dazzling array of French wines and expensive food delicacies that would make King Christophe seem poor in comparison, graced a table nearby.

Rada drums pounded out their quick, steady rhythms, like the pulse of the jungle. Lauren imagined black ancestors doing primitive dances to those same rhythms years ago in Africa. She drew a deep breath and felt the hammer of her heart against her chest. Then, as unexpectedly as they started, the drums stopped. A hush fell over the dwelling. All eyes faced the center of the room. A powerfully built black man, clean shaven and adorned with a red turban and bright embroidered stole, stepped before the altar. In front of the low table, he made a sign on the earth. With a long polished stick he drew a line and, coming from it, three circles. As the people chanted, *"Wangol mait la terre"*

[Wangol is the master of the earth] he poured oil, flour, and wine in the first circle. In the middle circle, he spread rum and ashes with the people chanting, *"Queddo, ou mait la ciel"* [Damballa Queddo, thou are master of the sky]. And finally in the third circle, he poured water from an earthen jug as the congregation chanted once again, *"Papa Agone, il mait la mer"* [Father Agone, he is master of the sea].

The man stood with hands raised solemnly before the altar and gave a sign to the woman hidden in the shadows. With this sign, she emerged into the light, her body draped in a scarlet robe and a headdress of red and black ostrich feathers. A shrill chant rose from her throat and penetrated the silence, ending in the sound of a sharp, prolonged hiss like that of a threatened snake. The woman drew and expelled breath through her teeth until her smooth black face was like a rigid mask. Her face became alternately bony and skull-like as she inhaled, and then as she exhaled, it puffed out and covered with flesh as though coming alive again. The disciples joined her with their chanting until the hissing faded into the air. The chanting died. She whirled three times around the floor and fell prostrate to the ground, her lips flat against the earth.

An altar servant came forward with two red cocks and handed them gently to the priest. Using flour, he marked crosses on their backs and fed them finely crumbled pieces of sweetcake. After each bird had eaten the cake, the priestess seized it in her upstretched hands and rose, dancing wildly, its head and feet bound by her grasp. As she whirled, the drums throbbed in quick, steady, tangled rhythms. Then with a sudden frenzied twist, the scarlet-robed woman took off the cock's head.

Lauren gasped. She could think now, though not too clearly. The drugged stupor still clung to her senses. It was as if she were dreaming, and everything moved in slow motion. Lethargy had drained her power and left her brain so feeble it could not command her body to move.

She was a captive audience as a voluminous white turkey became the priestess's victim in a feral death dance. The turkey spread its white wings and flapped frantically as she whirled with it in her state of frenzy. The billowy white wings surrounded the woman, enclosing her, until it seemed that the giant bird would easily overpower her frailty. Grabbing the head between her knees, she tried to break its neck, but the bird attacked ferociously, clawing at her legs and beating her face and breasts with its omnipotent wings. The frail black woman, enfolded by the great white wings in this mythical embrace, painted a savage scene that was not devoid of beauty, Lauren thought. When she tried again, the turkey attacked, once more enclosing her in its savage embrace, but with a sudden twist, it too was dead. As the people writhed in agony, confessing fears and sins as though all the blood letting would cleanse their souls, Lauren's stomach retched. Strong as she was in the stomach, nothing had prepared her for this savagery.

Struggling to turn away from the savage ritual, her attention was dragged back by a long wooden trough carried coffinlike and placed in front of the hall. The servants surrounded the earth around the trough with wooden bowls, china cups, and a gleaming saber. A beautiful white she-goat with limpid brown eyes was led into the room by four men. Bleating and balking, she finally surrendered and stood still. The woman entwined the horns of the little she-goat with red silk ribbons, and its hooves were annointed with oils and fine wines. A symphonic female howling arose from the throats of women who were robed in white and echoed throughout the dwelling. The head of the goat was marked with a cross and a circle. Grass and a green leafy branch made an involuntary meal, while it was poured over with some liquid that drugged it into submission. Lauren watched the helpless thing munching at the leaves, and somewhere in the back of her brain, her senses flickered and her heart went out to the animal. She knew what its fate would be.

Then without warning, two altar servants approached her where she sat huddled against the cold clay wall. Lifting her body from the stone slab, they placed her before the altar. Lauren's head swam in a sea of fear as her legs crumpled beneath her. She could not hold herself up. Two women, draped in diaphanous white robes, lifted the thin gown from her body leaving her naked before the altar. Lauren shivered. She felt herself sinking into a pit of unspeakable horror. The tall black priest forced a drink of rum into her mouth that burned her throat and chest as it went down. Lauren's nauseated stomach retched violently. Supported on either side by the two women, she employed her only means of defense by allowing apathy to take hold of her faculties. She was no longer on the ground, but hovering above the scene, looking on, uninvolved.

Forced down upon her knees before the lighted candles, her head was wound with red silk ribbons just like the little goat's. The priest tied other ribbons on separate clusters of her hair, but it was too curly and they would not hold as tightly as on the goat's horns. The priestess uncorked two bottles of fine French wine and poured them slowly, one at a time, over Lauren's head and body. Wine ran off her face, over her bare breasts, and at last trickled down her legs. Fumes from the alcohol invaded her nostrils, and as she inhaled, her head cleared considerably. She was now back on the ground. A feeling of sick fear grabbed her stomach, but she could not shake the cobwebs from her head. It was spinning beyond her control. Nor could she control her limbs. She tried desperately, but there was no communication between her body and her will. What on earth was she going to do? Another substance was poured over her head and body that rolled off her chest. It appeared to be thick and colorless. Extending her tongue, Lauren tasted it. It was oil. The liquid dripped off her nose and lips, so she caught it with her tongue and swallowed it. It felt good going down. The oil soothed her insides against the sharp sting of the rum. At that moment a voice in the background began a weird song of lamentation, and Lauren was left on the ground facing the little goat.

Staring dolefully into the goat's glassy eyes, she realized that she and the animal would share the same fate. She *had* to escape, she had to! She must will her body to move. With all the strength she could muster, Lauren tried flexing her fingers slowly, easily, so that no one would notice. At first she felt nothing, and her spirit sank further into despair, and then at last—they moved! She tried the other hand. It moved, too! Something in her brain stirred, sharp and clear. Most of the dizziness had passed, her head no longer whirled in phantasmagoric circles. The stupor remained, but it had ceased to be overwhelming. And then the song ended.

The drums began to throb again in quick, frenzied rhythms, and Lauren was pulled to her feet, supported by the two women. Her brain balked, sensing the inevitable threat to her life. *You must run—must make yourself run—when the drums stop.* Lauren cringed with the thought. *Not now!* her brain scolded. *You cannot think about that now—must escape.*

The only entrance to the dwelling seemed to be in the anteroom where the animals were kept. She had looked before and not been able to locate another door. As she tried to remember, the dizziness returned momentarily, causing her thoughts to waver. Why could she not clear this fog in her head? She had to remember, had to escape, there was not much time. A picture of the *houmfort* she had seen that day with Antoine dragged through her memory. That entrance had been through the anteroom. *Would this one be in the same place?* Lauren wondered. She had to take the chance; there was no choice. Her only hope was that her legs would support her until she could get to a horse. Côtelette had brought her here. She must be tethered somewhere outside. Lauren recalled that demon of a horse that brought her to this hell, yet that horse was the only chance of her leaving here alive. The women had loosened their grip on her, and Lauren realized that she was almost standing by her own power. Instantly the drums stopped. The little she-goat bleated, and again the smell of death permeated the air.

The woman came toward her, carrying the headdress of red and black ostrich feathers regally on her head and a gleaming silver knife in her right hand. Lauren drew a long, labored breath as her heart sank to her stomach. The woman moved past her and stood facing the goat. With one quick slash of the silver, she had severed the animal's throat. Lauren's body trembled unwillingly. She would be next. She had to go *now.* "Dear God, please give me strength," she prayed. And with a strength fired by desperation, Lauren willed her limbs to move, twisted free of her captors, and ran blindly toward the anteroom. She clawed, half crazed, at the door, but it refused to open. Her heart stopped beating and hung suspended in her chest. "It must open, it must!" she cried. With a strength she had not known she possessed, she pulled once more and the heavy door swung open. A heavy male voice behind her yelled, "Stop her! She can't leave here alive." Scrambling through the door, she grabbed a sack lying near the doorway and hastily covered her naked body.

By now it was dusk, and the descending sun had turned the sky a reddish gold. An eerie haze was creeping over le Petit Cul-de-Sac. If that was where she was. She could not be sure. Nothing looked familiar. Frantically, her eyes searched the area for Côtelette or any horse that would carry her from danger. There was none. She ran to the other side of the dwelling. There she spied Côtelette bound to a tree. Lauren raced toward her like one approaching an oasis in the desert. Holding the cloth against her body with her arms, Lauren fumbled with the reins until they came untied. As she shoved her foot in the stirrup, the metal cut a deep gash in her bare ankle, causing the flesh to bleed. Wincing with pain, Lauren swung into the saddle, and the horse took off in the same wild frenzy as before. Raucous voices filled the air behind her, but she never bothered to look back. The horse raced forward, flinging sand in her face but she did not care. Breathless, dizzy, and sick to her stomach, she would welcome the sight of Villa de Martier.

Côtelette pounded forward, trees and bushes whirring by, until Lauren felt as if she were floating. The machineel loomed up ahead, and she heard the horse's hooves bounding toward it. Suddenly, there was a sharp jolt. She felt her weightless form fly through the air and then succumb to blackness.

Lauren opened her eyes to the thundering of horses that rumbled the ground on which she lay. They had caught her, she thought, she had not escaped after all. Attempting to move, to get up, to run, she discovered that her limbs were immobile again. Perhaps her escape had been a dream. She lay there terrified, lacking the will to command her battered body. Things moved in slow motion, but through the haziness of her stupor, she saw the horses jerked to a halt. The two riders leapt from their saddles and strode rapidly to where she lay paralyzed on a bed of dead leaves. One figure knelt beside her and the other loped toward the heap that lay sprawled on the ground some yards away. A feeling of sick fear wrenched in her stomach as she drew in a deep breath and held it. A male voice uttered her name. "Lauren, can you hear me?" It was Roget.

Her tension easing, she tried to answer. "Y-yes," she stammered.

"Can you tell me where you're hurt? Can you move?"

"N-n-no . . . I—I can't move." She saw the pained expression that contorted his face.

Bending over her, Roget let his hands roam her body as though he were searching for something. The pressure of his touch was excruciatingly painful, but still she could not move. Her husband rose from her side and walked toward the other man who was staring down at the huge chestnut mound sprawled on the ground. The two men exchanged a few words in Creole that were unintelligible to her and then moved back to where she lay. Seeing her, the younger man gasped in disbelief. Lauren did understand, however, when Roget ordered, "Touissant, go back to the stable and tell Old Jean to bring a wagon out here as fast as possible. Also, have him send someone for Dr. Mauriac. I want him at the house when I get there."

"*Oui*, Monsieur Roget. Right away." Toussaint climbed on his mount and beat a path of dust back to the stable.

Drugged and delirious, Lauren watched Roget pull a rifle from his saddle and hook it under his arm. Her heart leapt to her throat as he walked toward her. *He's going to kill me,* she thought, *and when he's rid of me, he can have Lucienne.*

Cocking the pin, Roget aimed the rifle at the wounded animal and fired. Two shots blasted the silence, but she felt nothing. No pain, nothing. Perhaps she was dead. Roget replaced the gun in his saddle and knelt beside her, but Lauren had drifted into delirium.

Old Jean arrived with the wagon. Covering her with blankets, Roget made a bed on the wagon and he and Old

Jean lifted her into it. Carefully, Roget transported her back to the mansion, driving the wagon himself. Dr. Mauriac was there when they arrived. Lauren was examined for broken bones, and miraculously, there were none. She was bathed and put to bed. Roget recounted to Dr. Mauriac, as best he knew, what had happened when he found her. Lauren came to at intervals but immediately slipped back into her haven of unconsciousness. For several days, she vacillated between a conscious and semiconscious state, all the while tottering on the edge of delirium.

On the fourth day she returned to the world. Lauren opened her eyes, flexed her fingers, and even delighted in wiggling her toes. The paralysis had gone but not the horror of the ordeal. Cybele, her maid, was sitting by her bed when she regained consciousness and ran off to tell someone. Heaven knows who, Lauren thought. Some minutes later, she heard a soft knock at the door. *"Entrez,"* she replied almost in a whisper. Madame de Martier entered the room clutching the voluminous folds of her peignoir.

"I'm pleased to see you feeling better, my dear. We've been worried about you. My poor Roget has hardly slept these last three nights."

Roget worried, she mused. Lauren found it hard to imagine Roget upset about anything, least of all her. And yet she wanted to see him. "Where is he?" she inquired anxiously.

"He will be along later. He has not come in from the fields yet."

Lauren turned away quickly, thinking that he was probably with Lucienne.

"Dr. Mauriac will be here to see you this evening as well. They're both anxious to know what happened out there. They think it may be the same accident that killed Reinette."

"Accident." Lauren threw her a skeptical glance. "It was no accident."

"My dear, you don't realize what you are saying."

"Yes, *madame,* I do." Then it dawned on her that she had disclosed too much, so before unburdening her tale on the wrong ears, Lauren quickly severed her reply. *"Madame,* I'm very tired. Would you mind if I slept now?"

"Of course not, dear. I will come back later." She swept from the room, the expression on her face wrapped in confusion.

Lauren ate her first meal in several days, and after devouring two bowls of mutton soup, a baked yam, and some boiled plantain, she felt considerably stronger. Filene had just collected the empty dishes and left when Lauren heard the distinct rap of knuckles against the door that adjoined her room.

"Who is it?" she inquired, knowing very well whose knock it was.

"C'est moi." She recognized the resonant whisper of that familiar voice. A voice that, after all that had happened, could still arouse her senses to a state of giddiness.

Roget strode in still wearing the clothes he had worked in all day. The graceful stride was less confident than usual, and he looked tired. With weariness governing his motions, he pushed the yellow coverlet aside and sat on the bed. Lauren looked up and, for a fleeting moment, was caught in the perplexing depth of his eyes. Had he really been worried about her?

"Did you have a good dinner?" he asked.

"Oui. I was quite hungry." She smiled, nervously fondling the coverlet.

"Now I know you've recovered." His sensuous lips curled into a teasing grin.

Lowering her gaze from his, Lauren plucked at the satin quilt until the shimmering satin alluded to something she could not remember. Roget saw the fear tremble through her body as she remembered the nightgown.

"You're shivering. What's the matter?"

"Roget, they had my nightgown!" She bolted upright. "They wanted to kill me!" she cried as her ranting became incoherent.

"Lauren, calm down!" His fingers digging into her shoulders, he shook her violently. "I cannot understand what you're saying. You've had a bad accident, and you are not fully recovered. You need rest." Roget's arms slipped around her pulling her against his rapidly heaving chest.

300

Lauren clung to him, terrified, and tried to bury her fears in the warmth of his embrace. As if performing a duty, he held her until the tremors ceased, but even he could not deny the tightening in his belly.

"Roget, why doesn't anyone believe me? It happened . . . and I am not delirious." She bristled with irritation.

Brusquely separating her body from his, Roget knew if he held her a moment longer, he would never be able to quell the turmoil that raged inside him.

"What happened to you is what usually happens to stubborn women who disobey their husbands' orders and ride horses they have been told not to." His tone admonished her severely, but the softness in his eyes almost betrayed his thoughts.

"But, Roget, it was not an accident." Her body shuddered again at the reminder.

"Dr. Mauriac will be dining with us this evening, and he wants to talk with you. You can tell both of us what happened then. For now, try to rest." Roget had no trouble easing her into bed, and after covering her with the sheet, he left. Lauren drifted into a world of recurring nightmares.

Hours later she awakened with a start. Roget, accompanied by Dr. Mauriac, had entered the room. The doctor, a tall, fair-skinned man with hair the color of dead leaves and a tight curly texture not unlike her own, seemed young to be a practicing physician, but his voice was pleasant and comforting.

"*Bonsoir,* Madame de Martier. It's good to see you feeling better. You gave us quite an upset."

"Yes, I suppose I did," Lauren smiled sheepishly, pulling the coverlet over her breast.

"Your husband told me that you don't believe it was an accident. I'm inclined to agree with you, *madame.* I've discovered some interesting things that I'd like to look into further if only for medical purposes."

Lauren sighed, relieved that at last someone did not think she was hallucinating.

"Roget tells me that he found you in much the same condition as Reinette de Martier, sprawled on the ground, unable to move. The difference was that her neck was broken and she was dead." He paused thoughtfully, rubbing his chin. "You had no broken bones, but you were paralyzed, is that true?"

"Oui. I couldn't seem to will my body to move."

"When she told me she couldn't move," Roget added, "I was afraid her neck was broken also. They had been riding the same horse."

"You were covered with a sticky substance," the doctor continued, "that made dust and sand cling to your skin. We had a hell of a time getting it off." He grinned and looked at Roget, as though there was some private joke between them. Lauren cringed, realizing that her naked body had been viewed by almost everyone. "Do you have any idea what it was?"

Lauren pondered the question a minute and replied pensively, "It was oil and wine. They poured oil and wine over me." Her teeth chattered as she relived the moment, while puzzled glances shot between her husband and the doctor.

"They. Who are they?" Roget questioned with an intense curiosity.

"I don't know. I could not see them clearly. They forced something bitter down my throat and then everything was hazy."

"Try to tell us, as best you can, what exactly happened," the doctor said.

"I will try, but it's not terribly clear. My brain was in a stupor, and my body was immobile."

Lauren's eyes drank in the bright yellow atmosphere of her bedchamber. The warmth seemed to calm the icy chill in her bones. As best she could remember, Lauren recounted her nightmare. When she had finished the bizarre tale, she looked up and studied the expressions on the two very different faces. Dr. Mauriac merely shook his head in disbelief, whereas Roget's emotions ran the gamut from disbelief to anger and finally disgust.

"Surely you cannot think that was an accident," she said.

"No, *madame,* I'm afraid you're right. There's more to it than meets the eye." The doctor looked at Roget hesitantly, seeking his approval to continue with the information he had to report.

"What did you find out?" Roget questioned anxiously.

"As you may know, *madame,* we had to pump your stomach. I found what I suspected. Poison. A plant poison that renders one helpless, even paralyzed, until a slow death overcomes. However, it was a different chemistry than the one I suspect killed Reinette. I believe that she was given the same poison as the horse. It's a shame there was never an autopsy." He shrugged in resignation.

"Why not?" Lauren questioned.

"Her husband forbade it, *madame.*" Scorn filled the doctor's voice.

"I see," she commented and said nothing more. Silence hung over the room.

"Your horse," Dr. Mauriac began, "had massive doses of poison in its bloodstream also. Its effect was similar to that of the machineel."

Lauren gazed at him surprised. "That's why it was impossible to control her!" She paused for a moment and gathered her thoughts. "But . . . why the horse?"

"I'm certainly not sure, but seemingly it was a perfect way to deliver you into their hands. Roget noticed strange marks on the carcass when it was brought back to the stable, so I had it tested."

Perplexed, Lauren glanced from the doctor to her husband. "How would the horse know to go there?"

"That horse was ill trained from the moment Gaston bought her," Roget said. "She would go in one direction: le Petit Cul-de-Sac. Whoever trained her trained her well and for their own purposes. I've wanted to get rid of her for some time."

"But Reinette rode her," Lauren said, her voice questioning his statement.

"Reinette was able to control her sometimes, but more often than not, the horse controlled her. She said she enjoyed the challenge."

"Why do they want *me* dead? Why did they kill her?"

"We don't know." Dr. Mauriac shrugged. "We don't even know who they are."

"I told you they were vaudouists," she expounded as exasperation raised her voice an octave higher.

"Lauren, true followers of vodun do not offer human

sacrifices," Roget broke in as if to let her know that she should know better. "It would not have been the *Rada* or the *Petro,*" he continued, shifting his gaze to the doctor.

Dr. Mauriac turned back to his patient. "And you were under the impression that you would be killed like the goat."

"Oui," she answered weakly. The doctor's conclusion echoed what Roget was thinking.

"I suspect it was a clever plot to make it look like vodun. However, we should let you rest now," he said. "For a while, I was not sure you would recover, but you inherited your mother's strong African blood and a desperate will to survive. That and a blessing from heaven pulled you through."

"Blessing," Lauren repeated the word, her tone wrapped in confusion.

"Oui, madame, a blessing. You had swallowed some oil. It mixed with the poison and slowed down the absorption into your bloodstream. The poison had not circulated enough to do any permanent damage. If it had, you would not possibly have moved like that, even for a few seconds. And, *madame,"* he paused briefly, "the next time you go riding, I suggest you heed your husband's wishes and stay close to home." With this, he smiled and left. Roget remained just long enough to see that she was comfortably bedded down for the night, and then he strode through the door to his dressing room.

The following evening she had to face Gaston and his ridicule.

"So, *ma chérie,* I see that you were not able to handle Côtelette after all."

Lauren dropped her eyes and spread her fingers over the satin quilt. What good would it do to explain to him that it was not her fault. She remained silent.

Just as Gaston was about to bait her with another of his malicious taunts, Roget strolled through the door, stifling his attack. "Gaston," he nodded, pushing the door closed behind him.

"I was reprimanding your wife for causing the loss of a good mare."

"It was no great loss," Roget replied with bitter sarcasm. "That horse should have been shot several years ago, after Reinette's death."

"I find it touching that you're so concerned about revenging my wife's death, but that does not alter the fact that we've lost a prize mare."

"The horse had broken two legs. There was no other choice, so I shot her." Bristling with exasperation, Roget pushed aside the sheets and sat close to her on the bed.

"My, what a tender scene," Gaston scoffed.

Roget glared acid at his brother's ridicule. "If you don't mind, Lauren needs her rest."

Unwilling to tangle with his brother's belligerence, Gaston relented. He would catch her at another time.

"Bonsoir, ma chérie." He turned on his heel and left.

When she was well and on her feet again, Roget's attentions gradually diminished, and along with them, the secret hopes she had harbored slowly faded.

One day, after searching every drawer for the peach satin nightgown, she realized it was nowhere to be found. She forged, unannounced, into Roget's room and found him dressing to go out.

"Roget, that really was my nightgown! I've searched my drawers and it's gone."

Roget looked up and continued tying his cravat. "León, leave us alone for a few minutes," he said, dismissing him.

"Oui, monsieur."

When the older man had left, Roget met her apprehensive outburst with obvious vexation.

"Didn't you realize before that day that it was missing?"

"No."

An eyebrow arched in surprise as he struggled with the bones in his collar.

"You've given me no reason to need it." Her voice stabbed with resentment. "That means that someone with access to our bedchamber gave it to them." Instantly aware of the implications, Lauren gasped loudly while her husband, noticeably unaffected, continued to fasten his cuff links.

"Roget, someone in this house wants to see me dead," she said. Getting no response, she cried shrilly, "Roget, you're not listening to me!"

"*Ma chérie,* I cannot help but listen. You're yelling in my ear."

"You still don't believe me, do you?" she asked, her voice almost a whisper.

"Lauren, I believe you, but there's nothing I can do about it at this moment. There's no evidence and no proof. Besides, the entire incident would not have occurred had you not disobeyed me and stubbornly gone out on that horse. I've warned you to stay away from that place. If you refuse to heed my warnings, then I cannot be responsible for what happens to you." He had meant to give her comfort, he thought, not scold her like a naughty child, but lately the mere sight of her seemed to churn the ire in his gut.

"Roget," she interrupted softly, "I went because I was curious, and no one would tell me anything. I wanted to know about your country."

"Well, you see what your curiosity has gotten you. The next time you may not be so blessed." His scorn cut through her like a dagger. "If you need me, I'll be at my club."

It seemed the only time they talked was when they argued. Lauren wondered if he was really going to his club or if he was going to be with Lucienne tonight. Anyway, her marriage was over. Since all she ever did was make him angry, her only thought was to leave and return to France before someone succeeded in taking her life.

Chapter 19

Harvest time descended on the Cul-de-Sac Plain like a swarm of locust that would devour every burnished bean in its path. The fragrant coffee bushes would be left bare to blossom and seed again and grow a new crop of fruit for the coming year. The tender beans that they had nurtured and coddled these past months had at long last ripened into the deep red berries that would become Haiti's black gold. Processing the crop demanded many hands and backbreaking hours of work that kept Roget and his brothers away from the house for long stretches of time. It was an exciting panorama of plantation life in which Lauren had no part.

Wandering aimlessly through the tedious days, Lauren was elated when her husband assigned her her first household duty. She was to see that one of the guest rooms was prepared for Alexis Vauxvelle's intended visit. It was a meager chore, but having a duty to perform made her feel useful again.

In a flurry of activity, she had the maids changing linens, polishing furniture, and dusting armoires. She had even arranged for fresh tropical flowers and potted plants to be placed in the room each day of his visit. For Lauren, it was a poignant reminder of being back in Paris at the Saint Germain.

In truth, Roget had simply told her to see that Filene

carried out his wishes, but having decided to do it herself, she noticed that the pompous housekeeper kept at a distance. So when Filene appeared at the door and announced that *madame* had a visitor waiting in the vestibule, Lauren was somewhat startled. Arriving there, she found Paul, anxiously stubbing his toe against the marble floor.

"Madame de Martier, you the only one who can help me."

"How can I help you, Paul?"

The skinny young man lowered his head in shame. *"Madame,* please, you must go to help me." He was pleading, the words barely audible from his bent head.

Lauren felt an overwhelming rush of sympathy, but she had no idea for what.

"I would like to help you, Paul, but if you don't lift your head, I will not be able to hear you." Her Creole had improved sufficiently, enabling her to piece together his story.

"I sorry, *madame* . . . I do not mean to bother you, but Paul don't know what else to do."

"It's no bother, Paul, but the suspense will kill me for sure if you don't tell me what it is."

He blurted the words at her in a stream of broken French mixed with breathless Creole. *"Madame,* Monsieur Roget say to Old Jean that he no want me to work in the stable anymore. He angry at me for letting you take that horse. I say to him that I try to stop you, but he does not want to listen. He say I don't follow orders good and should not work with the horses. Madame Lauren," he said, his eyes finally meeting hers, "I only saddle that horse because you order me. I follow your orders and Monsieur Roget fell to anger with me and send me back to the fields. All my life, I only want to work with horses like Old Jean. Please don't make me go back . . . I be so unhappy. If you talk to Monsieur Roget, he listen to you. Tell him Paul kill hisself if he have to leave horses. Please, *Madame* . . . please tell Monsieur Roget give Paul another chance. Please. . . ." His eyes grew big and round as saucers, and Lauren empathized with the boy's despair.

"I will talk to him, but I can't promise that he will change his mind. He's angry with me as well, but I will do my best," she said, uttering a sigh. "And don't do anything silly like kill yourself; it's not worth such drastic measures." The corners of her lips curled into a wry smile. Her husband's wrath could be painful as she well knew.

Confronting Roget about the matter, she found him stubbornly adamant about his decision. Undaunted, she pleaded further on behalf of the helpless young coachman, since his dilemma could be blamed entirely on her impulsiveness.

"Roget, it was not the boy's fault," she argued. "He did nothing more than obey my orders."

"And disobey mine."

Instantly she was aware of his antagonism, but the sense of responsibility made her determined to win her point.

"How can you expect a stable boy to appease both of us?"

"I do not expect him to appease both of us. I expect him to obey my orders, regardless of whether my wife comes behind me and changes them." Wrapping a towel around his narrow hips, Roget proceeded to lather his face. "I gave strict instructions that you were not to ride that horse. Knowing that my wife would not heed them, I at least expected that my servants would."

"Then you're giving the servants license to disobey my orders?"

"Yes, if they contradict mine."

"Ohhhh!" Lauren clenched her fists together in a huff, fuming with exasperation.

Roget felt the heat of desire snake through his gut, and he wanted to grab her and silence that temptingly petulant mouth.

"You know, Roget, I wonder why you didn't leave me out there to die. Obviously, I do nothing but irritate you."

Damn her, he cursed silently as the razor gouged his chin. Smashing the razor against the bathroom wall, he stalked past her to the closet. "Perhaps I should have," he growled acidly.

"How did you stumble over me there anyway?" she questioned, following him to the closet.

"Old Jean sent Paul to tell me that you had gone out on Côtelette. Toussaint and I wasted the entire afternoon searching for you. Heaven only knows why," he scowled.

"So Paul redeemed himself," she added persuasively, playing on his sense of justice. "Couldn't you give the boy another chance? After all, what decision would you have made in his place?"

The adamancy of his mood softened. "All right . . . I'll tell Old Jean that the boy can remain in the stable for now, but if he ever flouts my orders again . . ."

"You still have soap on your face," she remarked. Her lips threatening a smile, Lauren lifted the folds of her skirt and left.

With Lauren's task finished and the blue suite ready to be occupied, Villa de Martier awaited the arrival of her visitor. Realizing that he could not spare the time now for a day's trip into Port-au-Prince, Roget relented and asked his wife to go in his place. Because she was the only person other than himself who knew what Alexis Vauxvelle looked like, she could hardly refuse. Needless to say, the young Madame de Martier was not overjoyed at facing him. She had not forgotten the humiliatingly fateful part he had played in her life. But his ship had to be met, so on Wednesday morning, accompanied by Cybele, she climbed into the carriage behind Old Jean to make the trip to Port-au-Prince.

Alexis Vauxvelle reached up to push the wayward lock of hair from his face, and Lauren recognized him immediately. His white complexion and shocking blond hair beneath the gray hat stood out like a beacon amidst the throng of dark faces that crowded the harbor.

"Monsieur Vauxvelle," she said, approaching him.

"Madame." He looked perplexed. Then gathering his wits about him, he remembered her. "Madame de Martier," he said, gallantly sweeping the high hat from his head as he kissed her hand. "And Roget?" His blue eyes questioned.

"He should arrive home about the same time we do. We have a long trip ahead of us." She smiled, and the Frenchman noticed the magnificent contours of her mouth. Those lips were made to be kissed. It seemed Roget got more than he had bargained for, he mused.

"The carriage is this way, Monsieur Vauxvelle. Old Jean will get your baggage."

"Alexis," he said, his voice competing with the shrill sound of the ship's whistle. Lifting her skirt above the debris, Lauren blazed a path through the crowd, and the impeccably dressed Frenchman followed.

Rumbling along rue Republicaine toward the outskirts of the city, he plied her with numerous questions about Haiti. Eagerly, Lauren supplied him with information about those things that she knew but then suggested that he keep the more complex inquiries for Roget. "Roget is far more adept at answering questions about his country than I am. There are things that I'm still learning," she said with a tone of apology. Cybele's French was not at all fluent, so she could be of little help.

Perusing the fair-skinned servant accompanying Roget's wife, Alexis wondered why she was here.

"I doubt that I will ever grow accustomed to the social practices here," Lauren commented as though reading his thoughts. "Their women are ridiculously sheltered. I abhor being chaperoned, but elite women are never left alone with men who are not family."

"Strange custom," he uttered absently.

Arriving at the villa, Old Jean pulled the carriage up to the main door, and its travel-worn occupants stepped out. Just minutes before, Roget had dismounted, and leaving Bleu de Roi to be groomed, he strolled lazily toward the house. Pulling off the damp panama, he entered through a rear door, and as weary legs carried him to the vestibule, he was besieged by the raucous commotion that took place on the front steps. Filene stood behind the open door as if she were mistress of the manor and not merely its housekeeper, while Old Jean struggled alone with the steamer trunks.

"Filene, call León and Felix," Roget barked impatiently. "Have them take care of *monsieur*'s baggage!"

Drawn by the resonance of the voice, Alexis looked up, and the two friends stared at each other.

"Roget, old man, I daresay you look a bit older." The corners of his blue eyes crinkled.

"I am . . . by about a year," Roget retorted. Grinning, he added, "And you're still a rake."

"Now I don't feel bad calling you old man," the Frenchman teased, drinking in the sight of his friend.

Clasping hands and then shoulders, the two men embraced, Alexis's white skin in shocking contrast to Roget's deep sable complexion. Lauren was amazed that two men so utterly opposite had become friends.

Throughout dinner the de Martier's were polite, but Haitians did not warm easily to strangers. Madame de Martier engaged him in social chatter about Paris, whereas Antoine drank in his flamboyant manner and the ruby ring he wore on his little finger. Lauren warmed to him considerably, but Gaston made it subtly clear that a friend of his brother's would have nothing in common with him. Alexis did not relax until he and Roget were alone.

Accompanied by a decanter of Haitian rum, the Frenchman and the Haitian passed the night in the library, boisterously reminiscing about their days in Paris. Alexis, the black sheep son of an old, aristocratic family in the south of France, met Roget when they were young men at school in the suburbs of Paris. Immediately, they had become friends. Even though Roget's strong sense of honor and duty was in utter contrast to Alexis's lack of it, they had stood by each other through the blessings of heaven and the ravages of hell. Roget was the only person he had ever truly trusted.

As dawn approached, they sat sprawled in their chairs, legs stretched before them, collars open, staring at the inlaid pattern of bone, rosewood, and ebony that composed the walls. Alexis hung one leg over the arm of his chair, and the conversation took on a more serious tone.

"You left so suddenly, old man, we never gave you a proper bon voyage."

"The Môle crisis had suddenly turned serious. There was no time," Roget replied.

"I know. I followed it in the newspaper. The French scandal sheets played it up royally, and yet they have no great love for the Americans either." He paused to light a long, dark cigarette. "This is incredible country, old man, but according to your laws, a white man is not allowed to own land here. Much to my chagrin," he sighed and imbibed another swig of rum.

Roget grinned. "Is it the land you're interested in . . . or the fruits of it?" Two raven black eyebrows arched as he set aside the glass. He knew very well the Frenchman's fascination for brown-skinned women.

"You know me too well," Alexis grinned. "However, I thought if anyone could show me what's involved in running a plantation, you could."

"Don't tell me that you have decided to become a gentleman farmer," Roget chuckled.

"I've been thinking about it. My grandfather, the old goat, left me that piece of land in Martinique."

"But you hate farming." Roget's tone was skeptical.

"I know . . . At least I always thought I did."

"Besides, how could you exist without the decadence of Paris," Roget said with a teasing grin.

Without warning, Alexis's tone grew urgent. "They're pressuring me. You should see the dog they want me to marry. Her nose would stab you." He chuckled with a false air of insouciance. "Some noblewoman they have chosen for me," he said, flicking his wrist. "If I don't, I will be cut off without a *centime* . . ." His voice trailed into a bitter sigh.

Roget noticed that the carefree motion of his wrist was a dire contradiction to the desperation in his voice and knew that he was in pain. Alexis had never taken life this seriously.

"How the hell did you get away with it?" he asked, his blue eyes searching the darker ones.

"I know my family, or I should say, I know Gaston. This plantation needs me, and he would never cut off his nose to spite his face. He's much too greedy." Roget drew his legs in and stood up. "Besides, the laws of inheritance set down by our patriarch are of considerable consequence. Our land can only pass through de Martier offspring, never to those who marry into the family." Stretching his arms to a wide arc, Roget stifled a yawn, and then reaching over, he clasped the Frenchman's shoulder in a comforting gesture.

"We had better get some sleep. Tomorrow will be a long day," Roget said, flinging the white linen jacket over his shoulder. "I have to teach you to be a farmer," he grinned.

Pushing the lock of yellow hair from his face, the Frenchman retrieved his jacket and followed the Haitian from the room.

Warily heeding her instincts, Lauren reined Miel into a trot and then a walk, her attention glued to the shoeless men and women who labored beneath the coffee bushes. She was lost. Not having been here before, she was not sure how she had strayed onto this road. But Lauren's initial apprehension calmed as it occurred to her that she should seize this opportunity to see the harvesting.

Wandering past the groves of lush green bushes, she watched men furiously shaking the trees until piles of deep red berries covered the linen sheets that were spread on the ground. Once the sheets were full, women gathered and dumped the ripe berries in baskets and hauled them to the waiting carts. A parade of mules pulled the heavily laden carts, bumping and creaking over the road, until they vanished around a cluster of bamboo trees and out of sight. Her curiosity pricked, Lauren decided to follow the animals and their precious cargo. Who knows where it might lead, she mused. Smiling to herself, she urged Miel in behind, but no one was more surprised than she when she found herself surrounded by the bustling activity at the warehouses.

Men were unloading wagons, dumping baskets, heaving and carrying sacks in every direction. Overwhelmed by the enormity of the operation, Lauren slid from Miel's back and indecisively started toward the group of buildings. Men, with their chests bared to the sun, stopped their work and boldly stared, whereas the women tittered behind dark, callused hands. They had never seen a woman wearing breeches.

"*Bonjour,* Madame Lauren." A voice came over her shoulder. She started and whirled around to find Christophe staring at her as well.

"*Bonjour,* Christophe," she said, withdrawing her open hand from her throat.

"You look for Monsieur Roget?" His eyes curiously questioned what she was doing there.

"*Oui* . . . is he . . . ?"

"He is in the big, big warehouse." Her focus followed his arm to the end of a pointed finger.

She entered the low concrete structure, not knowing what she should expect to find. Inside, it was cool and surprisingly dim, with few windows and a ceiling supported by heavy wooden beams. Women in white dresses with brilliant handkerchief turbans knotted African style around their heads sat on the floor amidst mounds of burnished red berries. Sifting through the beans, they threw some aside and placed the better part of them in giant cylinders. Her mind curiously devouring the surroundings, Lauren failed to see Roget when he strode toward her.

"Lauren, what the *hell* are you doing here?" His voice emitted a tightly controlled rage.

"I lost my way." She shrugged, feigning an apology. "But I've never seen this part of the plantation." She smiled beguilingly.

"Now is not the time to explore. Not in the middle of harvesting. I have no time to accompany you back."

"I don't need anyone to accompany me back. I found the way here by myself; I can return by myself. I'm not a child."

"But you *are* a woman."

"And of course that is equivalent to a child in this society."

"No, but you should not be on those roads alone, particularly now when there are so many transient workers milling about."

"They hardly noticed me."

"That is beside the point."

"If I'm not mistaken, those are women." Her eyes flashed as they darted toward the many female hands sorting beans.

"There is a difference. They are workers."

"And what am I?"

"Lauren . . . not now." His ebony eyes glared. "I haven't the time to argue with you. I will not be going back for several hours; you'll have to wait. You can wait in the office," he said, the motion of his arm directing her to the small secluded room.

"Monsieur Roget." A young man rushed in spouting a colorful stream of Creole. "One of the vats is clogged and the berries they not going through the pipes. They backing up all over the place.

"Where is Christophe?" Roget questioned the ebony-hued boy.

"Don't know, *monsieur.*" He shook his head.

"Find him!" Roget ordered. "And have him take care of it."

"Oui, monsieur." The wiry young man fled as Roget breathed a sigh of exasperation.

Stubbornly reluctant, Lauren moved toward the room. At last she could see how he spent his days, and she did not relish being shut up in a cell. Sauntering in the direction of the room, her eye was drawn to a metal cylinder that oddly resembled a huge nutmeg grinder, and she detoured to peer into it. All heads lifted and all eyes scanned her from head to foot, lingering on the riding breeches. A hum of chatter rose from the women's mouths and invaded Roget's ears, and he spied his wife, backside up, watching the rasping action in the pulper. Roget strode toward her. Clamping his hand roughly about her upper arm, he dragged her to the room as hundreds of eyes followed them.

"You're causing havoc," he growled, forcing her inside. His voice almost hissing, he ordered, "Stay here. And try to refrain from disrupting my workers."

In a querulous tone, she retorted, "If I had something to fill the endless days with, I would not have to disrupt your workers." Leaving, Roget slammed the door behind him.

Fuming with rage, Lauren stalked to one end of the small cubicle and then back again. Her fists clenched, forcing the nails into her palms. Her teeth ground together, and her face flushed burgundy like a child, "How dare he treat me like a child," she cried, banging an angry fist against the wall. "I'm not one of his precious Haitiennes." Pain seared through Lauren's arm, and she cupped the stinging fist in her other hand.

Through narrow slits, Lauren unwillingly explored his desk, and her lucid gaze discovered the gray gloves that lay crumpled among his ledgers. Taking a small doeskin glove in her hand, she saw that it was a riding glove—a woman's riding glove. So this is where he meets Lucienne, she thought. No wonder he does not want me here. Hot tears welled up and singed her hazel eyes.

With leisurely strides, Alexis ambled in from the adjoining building. "What's all the disturbance, old man? Wasn't that your wife I saw a moment ago?"

"*Oui*. She lost her way and managed to find her way here," Roget replied sarcastically.

The door opened, and Lauren stormed from the room.

"Lauren . . ." Roget scowled.

"I'm going back to the house. I refuse to be locked up here like a prisoner with your mistress's clothing," she said, tears still stinging behind her eyes.

"Lauren," Roget snarled under his breath, "I cannot go back now."

"I don't need you to go with me. I'm quite capable of finding my way alone."

Lowering his voice to a controlled whisper, he dug his fingers into her arm and pulled her aside. "Damn it, woman! I don't want you to go alone."

"Unfortunately, one does not always get what he wants," she replied, flinging the words at him flippantly.

His insides quietly consumed with rage, it took his last ounce of control not to strike her.

"I'm about ready to leave," Alexis volunteered, perusing their dissension. "I think I've had enough farming for one day." In an attempt to lighten the air, he turned to Lauren and made a jest of bowing gallantly from the waist. "If *madame* will accept me as an escort, I will be happy to accompany her, that is if *madame*'s husband has no objections." He grinned, seeking Roget's approval.

"None." Roget's lips curled slightly. "In fact, I would appreciate it."

Lauren's temper railed at being bandied about like a piece of chattel. Roget cared little whom he entrusted her to, she thought, so long as they kept her from interfering in his life. His concern for her welfare was nothing more than his duty to make certain that a de Martier wife did not tarnish the family honor.

"There is one problem, old man," Alexis said. "How do I find my way through this maze?" Roget strode into the office, took paper and pen, and drew a hasty map while giving the Frenchman directions.

"Follow this road to the fork and bear left, that will put

you at the clearing where our property meets the Deffands'. Lauren knows the way from there."

Throwing her husband one last glare of indignation, Lauren stalked out of the warehouse.

Silently, the two riders climbed into their saddles. Their attention fixed on the hulled brown berries that lay drying in the sun, they said little. Spread on barbeque trays that spanned acres, the drying beans gave off the aroma of roasted coffee. As they rode, Alexis inhaled the lush, tropical beauty that flowered around him, and Lauren remained locked in her thoughts. Eventually they reached the clearing.

"This is magnificent," Alexis breathed as they came upon the wall of bright orange flamboyant that separated Deffand and de Martier property. He drew in a deep breath that Lauren thought for sure would strangle him because he was so long in releasing it.

Unaccustomed to Haiti and her jungle terrain, the Frenchman's untrained eye failed to see the tarantula that frightened his horse. The sleek brown stallion reared suddenly and sent the Frenchman flying from his back. Lauren moved quickly. She swung Miel into the animal's path to head him off, slid from her saddle, and reached up to grab hold of the dangling reins.

"There boy, there . . . It's all right," she purred in the stallion's ear. Talking him down, Lauren ran her fingers gently over his head, fondling his neck and nuzzling his nose until she had stroked him into submission. The stallion calmed. She tethered him to a tree and turned to the animal's disheveled rider.

Alexis lay on the ground, his weight propped on one elbow, watching her performance. *"Madame,* where did you learn to gentle a horse like that?"

"Here one learns quickly, there are so many things that spook them. Are you hurt?" she inquired.

"Only my pride," he quipped, brushing the red dust from his shirt.

"I thought not." She smiled to herself, thinking that the fall would bring his aristocratic arrogance down a peg. And then noticing his discomfort, she said, "It could have happened to anyone."

"But not to a Vauxvelle." His tone had not lost the echo of arrogance. "Where I come from, we are known for our equestrian skills." Rising to his feet, he attempted to brush the red dust from his impeccably tailored fawn breeches. "The white knight is supposed to rescue the damsel in distress, not the other way around. Now, I am cheated out of my reward." The twinkle in his blue eyes teased her.

"And just what reward are you referring to, *monsieur?*" Lauren knew very well that she was baiting him, but still fuming and humiliated over the bitter confrontation with Roget, she thought, *Why not?* and turned to nuzzle Miel.

The Frenchman's eye followed the curve of her narrow waist and full, rounded derrier as she attentively stroked her horse. He knew women in France who would give a fortune to possess an hourglass figure such as hers. With biting resignation, his thoughts fled to Alis de Comte and his impending marriage. He pictured her thin, lifeless mouth; the long nose, and the narrow, fleshless hips. Painfully, he grimaced at the thought of making love to her. He had always had a fascination for dusky women, and Lauren was utterly delicious. That skin, that mouth, and the firm, round protrusion of her derriere in those breeches were unbearable, he thought.

Alexis reached up and touched the soft, bushy texture of her hair. Delighting in the sensuousness of it, he buried his fingers deep in its mass and pulled her to him. Lauren was startled but not in the least repulsed by his intrusion. His touch was gentle, soothing.

Enchanted beyond control, his other hand spanned the slender, sinuous curve of her waist and then slid down over the deliciously ample derriere. The scent of her honey-hued skin in his nostrils sent an inferno of desire racing through his loins as his lips moved hungrily over the velvet of her palpitating throat. His lips touched hers, and Lauren responded by pressing her body to his and winding her arms languourously around his neck. If she could love other men with the same passion that she had loved Roget, a life in the *demimonde* might not prove so unfortunate.

His mouth claimed hers hungrily, feasting, tasting, savoring, with an all-consuming passion, but to Lauren it was merely a pleasant sensation, one she could easily live without. There was not the dizzying surge of phantasmagoric pleasure that consumed her when Roget's mouth plundered hers.

Lauren pulled away, unresponsive. "Oh, God," she uttered, tears brimming in her lucid eyes. She would never forget Roget's kisses, though she would probably never know them again.

"Lauren, I'm sorry . . . I have no idea what demon possessed me . . . I . . ." The glib voice was agitated. He gazed at her through repentant eyes, searching her face for assurance. "I don't pretend to be honorable," he went on. "I have always been a libertine, as Roget says . . . but you're Roget's wife . . ." Alexis stifled his train of thought. "Above all else, I value Roget's friendship," he said, knowing this indiscretion could force a wedge between them.

Reflecting on his actions, he wondered why she had first responded? He consoled himself that it was probably a silly feminine ploy to thwart her husband. Whatever her reasons, and however much he may have been tempted, it was not worth risking Roget's disdain.

"It's Roget, isn't it?" he questioned softly, attempting to calm the ripples. "You're in love with him."

"*Oui.* Unfortunately, I am." Lauren looked away, not wanting him to see the hopelessness she felt.

"Roget has a captivating charm when it comes to women. He could have had his pick of the litter, but he was always extremely selective. He does not dally frivolously."

The truth of his statement plunged through her heart like an arrow. Lifting her foot to the stirrup, Lauren swung herself over Miel's back. "We should not be dallying here like this. The neighbors will talk." She smiled slightly and urged the horse forward.

"Tonnerre!" Lucienne cried. Effusively, she flung her hat and sent it sailing across the marquetry commode and onto the floor. Riding skirt and all, she flopped prostrate across the sofa, propping her dusty boots on its upholstered arm. *I am not always the lady he thinks I am,* she mused, the corners of her shapely lips curling upward.

Yesterday was the first time she had seen Roget since

harvesting began two weeks ago. Yet his obstinance had annoyed her so that she had run off, leaving her gloves, and now it would take weeks to get the calluses off her hands. She realized he was exhausted, but his refusing to make love to her because an abandoned mountain cabin was not the proper place for a lady was pure hogwash. Sometimes Roget was so damn prudish that she imagined him a British schoolmaster instead of the earthy, virile male she knew he was. Strangely, she could feel him slipping away from her.

She had grown up having everything. Beauty, position, wealth, *and* Roget. She had been spoiled from the beginning. Having known the joy of being adored, she had always assumed it her right. But under the circumstances, the one thing she wanted most was eluding her grasp.

They had come blissfully close that day in Paris. She had even suggested a wedding date. She should have insisted on their marriage before he left Haiti, but Roget was not easily pushed. He did nothing until he was quite ready to do it. She was well aware that he would never have risked what he did in marrying Lauren had he not loved *her* so deeply and want to save her from what he thought would be a disastrous union. Yet, she could not help thinking that the conqueror was becoming the conquered.

She and Roget had not made love since he left Haiti to live in Paris, and that was a year and a half ago. She had known from that one aborted attempt that he was simply going through the motions. Being adored and put on a pedestal like a goddess had brought her to this!

Her body racked with frustration, Lucienne flung her crop across the room and buried her magnificent face in her hands. She could certainly find another man to marry given her beauty and social position, but another man like Roget . . . Exhaling her breath, Lucienne released a long-suppressed sigh.

It had been another tiring, exacting day as Roget and Alexis dismounted and walked their horses the remaining steps to the stable.

"Does farming invariably require such backbreaking work?"

"Most of the time," Roget grinned, giving him a sidelong look. "But it's not imperative that you do it yourself. You can hire a manager and overseers; others do. The Haitian elite are not fond of getting their hands dirty."

"Why do you?" Alexis questioned, swiping the lock of yellow hair from his face.

"You could say we are an anomaly," Roget shrugged. "Valery de Martier believed that working his own plantation made him prosperous. No doubt he was right. Over the years, it has become our tradition."

Absently, Roget's interest in their conversation waned as his attention was drawn to his wife's lathered horse, who was patiently being groomed. Why had she just come in at this hour? Flipping the gold watch from his pocket, he glanced at the time. Seven o'clock. A noticeable rage wrenched his gut as he relived yesterday's confrontation with her. Why was she so damn obstinate! He had always been capable of controlling his emotions, even with Gaston, but with her, they seemed to be totally beyond his control. She could provoke him as no one else could.

Alexis felt the change of mood that pricked the needles of Roget's ire. Perusing him intently, the Frenchman pulled off his gloves.

"It seems it's become more than that impulsive bet we had." The blue eyes crinkled in amusement. "She's a lot of woman, old man. I think you've got yourself a prize filly."

Disgruntled, Roget scowled at his friend's perceptive insinuation. "I think I've made a grand mistake," he said curtly. "Lauren will never learn to behave as a Haitienne should."

"Do you want her to?" The Frenchman looked up at him. "I'd gladly take her off your hands."

"I would gladly give her to you," Roget replied as Alexis gazed at him intently. "I promise you, you would not keep her."

Perhaps Roget was not yet aware, Alexis thought, but he had not meant a word he said. "That sounds like love, old man."

Roget snorted and in a huff folded his arms across his chest. "I *love* but one woman."

"That may be." The Frenchman grinned, lifting a skeptical yellow eyebrow. "But as Shakespeare put it, 'I think thou doth protest too much.'"

The next day Alexis had gone. Roget returned to the demanding tasks of the plantation, attempting to regain the time lost by putting in longer hours. Lauren dreaded the return to mundane days and fitful, sleepless nights. With Alexis there, Roget remained at home nights, which provided her with a much-needed respite.

Days later, Lauren came home from Saint Joseph's pleased with the rapid progress that Madeleine was making as a pianist. Either she was a better teacher than she had ever dreamed or the child had more innate talent than she had realized. She smiled with satisfaction as she climbed the rose stone stairs. As she approached the door, she was busy working her fingers free of kid gloves, and not until she looked up, did she see the Deffands' coachman anxiously pacing the marble floor of the vestibule.

"*Bonjour,* Mulgrave."

Bending slightly from the waist, he replied, "*Bonjour, madame,* I have this for you." He handed her a small envelope. "I have been instructed to wait, *madame.*" A clipped Jamaican accent colored his French.

"*Merci,*" she uttered curiously. Hastily opening it with her fingers, Lauren read the scribbled note.

"Oh, no!" she gasped, turning her face from him. It read:

Lauren,
Georgette has suffered a miscarriage. Please come.
Jacques

"I will need a moment to change," she said to the perplexed coachman as she fled up the stairs.

Barely ten minutes had passed when Lauren sidled into the carriage. She rested her back against the seat, but her mind refused to comply. Palm trees and bright tropical foliage whirred by the open fiacre, and her mental ponderings whirred just as rapidly. Inside, she felt like a deflated balloon that had not had a chance to fly. She did not want to imagine how Georgette must feel.

Arriving at the Deffand villa, Lauren hardly waited for Mulgrave to assist her from the carriage. Leaping from the step, she clutched her skirt above her ankles and trudged to the door. Vaguely nodding to Pétion as he opened it, she fled up the winding white staircase and rushed into the lavender bedchamber. Georgette looked up from a bed of fluffy white pillows.

"Lauren." A weak smile illuminated her face.

"Oh, Georgette . . . I *am* sorry," she said. Affectionately, Lauren touched her lips to each of the smooth dark cheeks.

"So am I," Georgette replied, a sadness creeping over her. "I feel so empty . . . such a sense of loss . . . It had no chance to live."

"Georgette . . . ," Lauren said, groping for words that would comfort her. "What can I say . . . except that I understand . . . and that God knows best." Reaching out, Lauren clasped her friend's hand in hers. "There will be others."

"Of course there will," she replied bravely, clinging to the comforting hand.

The two women spent the day chattering, ogling French fashion magazines, and gorging themselves on Georgette's favorite pastries. Lauren labored to keep her friend amused and preoccupied, and by evening she had succeeded in reinflating Georgette's spirits.

Minutes before dinner, Jacques appeared at their bedroom door. The usually pleasant face was worn and haggard, and Lauren noticed the grooves of tension that distorted the smile.

"May we come in?" he inquired.

A luminous ray of pleasure spread over his wife's face. "Please do," she replied.

Roget stepped into view, and the two women's gazes locked in surprise. Acknowledging his wife with a private glance, he strode immediately to Madame Deffand's bedside.

"Georgette, I'm very sorry," he said ruefully, kissing the two sides of her face.

"Merci, monsieur," she replied quietly.

"You are certainly in better spirits than I left you this morning," her husband quipped.

"Lauren has kept me amused."

"I rather thought she would," he said. He gazed at Lauren, silently expressing his gratitude.

"I merely told her that she would probably end up with a houseful of children one day," Lauren teased. Imagining the beautiful Madame Deffand with numerous little grubby hands tugging at her fashionable skirts, the four broke into laughter.

Leaving the Deffands alone, Lauren and Roget descended the stairs together and walked toward the salon.

"I didn't expect to see you here," Lauren said.

"*Maman* gave me your message," Roget replied. The musky odor of his cologne seeped into her nostrils.

"Roget, I want to stay a few days with Georgette. Would you have Cybele pack some of my things and send them to me?"

Roget nodded his head in agreement. "Jacques wanted this baby badly," he said.

"Georgette did also. She was so happy when she told me she was pregnant. It must be painful . . . what she has had to endure." She looked up at him, and their angry gazes, quelled for the moment, locked. "I feel dreadful for her, especially after the miscarriage last year."

"Jacques is more than a little worried," Roget said thoughtfully. "The Deffands need an heir."

She watched his long easy strides cross the floor with that rhythmic grace that seemed inherent to Haitian men.

Returning home alone, Roget entered their bedchamber. His ebony gaze fell on her kimono, and for some unknown reason he took the embroidered garment in his hands. The jasmine scent of her wafted through his nose, and tugged at his groin. Flinging the silken thing aside, he rang for Cybele. Loving one woman and wanting to bed another made him no better than other de Martier men who married elite women and then had their pleasure with mistresses or *placée* wives. He refused to be consumed by this lascivious passion. But there were times when he thought he would explode if he could not feel her female warmth enclosing him.

"You need me, *monsieur?*" The plump young maid appeared.

"Oui. This is from your mistress." He shoved the list in her hand and left.

Lauren lay awake, tossing in the strange empty bed. She recalled the endless nights she had lain awake and longed for his maleness to assuage the aching in her loins. Except this night, he was not asleep in the next room. *Where is he?* she wondered. Turning on her stomach, she buried her face in the pillow and tried to blot out her visions of Lucienne.

Chapter 20

Lauren stayed a week with the Deffands before returning to Villa de Martier. Having arrived home and settled in on Saturday, Sunday morning whispered quietly by except for the soft swish of skirts trailing on parquet floors. The plantation harvested an abundant crop, more than they had expected due to the flooding, and the brothers were now willing to discuss J. B. Vital's offer to purchase. Gaston had made the long journey to Jacmel to negotiate with the Vitals, and Antoine had not been home the entire night. Frantically, the elder Madame de Martier paced the floor of her parlor, sipping a snifter of brandy.

"It's unlike Antoine to stay out the entire night. Something dreadful must have happened to him."

"*Maman*, Antoine is a grown man," Roget said. "Stop coddling him. He must assert himself at some time." He succeeded in allaying her fears for the moment.

Without warning, there was a raucous thumping at the main door, and the sound carried vaguely into the parlor. A female servant appeared bearing an impressive envelope.

"This is for the master of the house. Monsieur Gaston not here," she said, "so I bring it to you, Monsieur Roget."

"*Merci*, Marie," he said, his eyes curiously perusing the crisp white envelope that bore an official gold insignia.

Walking away from the two women, Roget tore it open and read its dire contents.

"What is it? Is it about Antoine?" One hand clutching her glass and the other pressed against her breast, Madame de Martier moved to where he stood. "Roget, what is it!" she demanded. Giving in to hysteria, she grabbed for the letter, but her agile son raised his arm overhead, removing it from her grasp.

"Maman!" The harsh tone of his voice admonished her. "Calm down, and I'll tell you but I cannot talk with you barking at me."

"Where is he, Roget? Where is Antoine? Why did he not come home last night?"

Lauren had rarely seen her mother-in-law make such an effusive display of emotion.

"It seems," Roget began slowly, "that Antoine is being held in custody in La Coupe."

"That means he has been arrested, that he is in prison."

"Something like that," Roget replied ruefully. He yanked at the bell cord, and Filene appeared.

"Have Old Jean prepare a carriage. I'm going to La Coupe."

"Oui, monsieur." The pompous housekeeper hastened to do his bidding.

"Roget, what has he done? Why has he been arrested?" Her doleful tone had become demanding.

"I don't know, *Maman.* I shall tell you when I return."

Lauren realized that his reply was a convenient half-truth, since apparently he needed time to decide how much to tell her.

"Lauren, stay with *Maman* and try to calm her," he said. His handsome face still distorted by a frown, he strode through the door.

Lauren was left alone to placate her not too sober mother-in-law. *"Madame . . ."* Lauren attempted to comfort the older woman, but somehow she could not bring herself to call her mother. "Antoine will be all right. Roget will take care of it."

Toward that evening, Madame de Martier had sunk into oblivion and no longer cared about anything, least of all Antoine's being in jail.

Roget returned from La Coupe with a noisily repentant Antoine in tow, and the family dressed and sat down to a late supper. Antoine ate absently, his hands and mouth moving in mechanical fashion as though he were a doll someone wound with a key. His soft dark eyes, painfully aware of the suppressed curiosity of the others, rarely looked up from his plate. Madame de Martier, now bordering on the edge of sobriety, remembered the plight of her youngest son.

"My poor darling." She literally cooed. "It *was* a mistake, wasn't it?"

"*Oui, Maman.* It was a mistake," Antoine replied, never lifting his eyes from the damask tablecloth.

"Was everything settled?"

"*Oui, Maman,*" he said calmly. "Roget handled everything."

"I suppose that Roget is right," she gazed at him wistfully. "I must stop treating you like a child. All of my children have grown into men," she sighed, her voice trailing to melancholy.

Sometime later, the two brothers' voices bellowed out from behind the heavy mahogany door of the library. Their mother, Lauren assumed, was too intoxicated to comprehend the implications of their rantings. From the beginning, she had sensed Roget's intention to shield his mother from the truth. Antoine's desperate pleas filled the hall surrounding the library, and Lauren's heart ached for him.

"Antoine, how in hell did you allow yourself to be caught in such a situation?"

"It was totally innocent, Roget. I did nothing they accused me of . . . I swear."

"Then how did you come to be in that room with him?"

"As I explained to you in the magistrate's office, I was in the bar having a drink, and the fellow came and sat next to me. I had only intended to have one drink," he explained with gripping remorse.

"That one drink will cost you dearly," Roget commented thoughtfully.

"He became friendly and started a conversation, and I offered to buy him a drink. He insisted on returning the favor, and before we knew it, we were laughing together."

"And you had not the slightest idea that the boy was barely sixteen?"

"N-n-no . . . I didn't," he stammered. "He seemed older . . . about my age." Antoine stared at the floor, embarrassed by his naive deception.

"Go on," Roget prodded.

"He told me he had a room in the hotel and suggested we buy a bottle and go there, where we could be more comfortable. I saw no reason not to continue the acquaintance, since it's not often that I meet someone who amuses me. We left the bar, I bought a bottle of rum, and we took it to the squalid, shabby room and sat there with me trying to smother my aristocratic distaste." A hint of a smile appeared on Antoine's lips. "I remember opening the bottle and pouring two drinks . . . Shortly after, my head began to spin. I felt sick and stumbled to the bed and fell across it. Then I must have blacked out. The next thing I remember is the police coming in the room, dragging me down the stairs, and shoving me into a closed carriage with bars on the windows."

"What did they say?" Roget questioned, pensively cradling his chin between his thumb and forefinger.

"They say that I was charged with sexual molestation of a minor."

"And you never did it?"

"No! Nothing happened. I never touched him, Roget, I swear to you!"

"Did the boy know who you were? Was there anything missing from your person—money, papers?"

"I don't believe so," Antoine hesitated, "but it seemed that my pockets had been ransacked."

"If what you say is true, my dear brother, *you* have been had by the oldest trick in the book. It sounds to me as if it was very well planned. We will have to pay, you know that, to avoid a public scandal."

Antoine looked at Roget with a blank stare.

"It's blackmail, little brother, blackmail." Roget's tone was penalizing but not condemning.

Antoine shuddered as comprehension took hold of his senses. "I'm sorry," he apologized ruefully. "I didn't know.

I am not as worldly as you. *Maman* never let me go to school in France as you and Gaston did."

"A mistake on her part," Roget sighed. "At any rate, I will have to go and see this boy and make a bargain for his silence. I'll pay him from my personal account. Otherwise, Gaston will surely hear of it."

The mention of Gaston's name caused Antoine's lean muscled frame to shudder violently. Terror filled his eyes. "He does not have to know, does he? Please, Roget, you won't tell him . . . please . . . He will make my life miserable," the distraught young man pleaded. "I beg you, Roget. I'll do anything . . . *anything,* but *please* do not tell him!"

Empathizing with his younger brother's hapless plight, Roget agreed. "All right, I'll buy the scoundrel's silence, and when you're granted your inheritance, you can return the money to me."

"*Merci,* Roget. *Merci,*" he muttered, his dark eyes tearing with gratitude.

"Don't thank me yet; the matter is far from finished. I can't promise you that Gaston will not learn of it. I can only promise you that he will not hear it from me. He may very well get it from other sources. There is very little that escapes the devil," he remarked wryly, his brow knitting in thought.

"Roget, if there is anything . . . ?"

"There is one thing. You've been released in my custody. Do me a favor and stay out of common bars." Antoine saw a faint hint of a smile. "You might do well to remember that the snake who wants to live, does not travel on the highway."

Roget did what had to be done, and the skirmish was hushed over. Antoine breathed a sigh of relief and thought the matter finished, but his older brother was not so confident.

Lauren was in their bedchamber when her husband returned, weary and irate from his mission. The austerity of his manner and the elegance of his attire told her that he had come from somewhere other than the coffee groves. Gazing at him, the incredibly handsome, compelling man she had married months ago, she wondered if it had not been part of a dream.

"I didn't mean to startle you," she apologized, her hand toying with the emerald band that circled her finger.

"You didn't." he replied, his eye trailing along the curve of her middle.

"Did you pay the blackmail?"

"Oui. I bought the rascal's silence," he replied disgruntled.

"How much did you pay him?"

"Twelve thousand gourdes . . . and a lot of blood."

"Will that keep him quiet?"

"It had better," Roget growled, his ire rising. "I forced him to sign a voucher. If he utters a word of it, I'll hang him, the thief. However, I must admit he is a clever rascal."

"Is he really only sixteen?" Lauren inquired curiously.

"Oui. Sixteen going on sixty." His mouth curled wryly. "Antoine was right about that. He appears much older than he is. I would have taken him for twenty. He sat there glaring at me with a cocky grin that I was tempted to erase with my fist," he expounded as if thinking aloud. "He's discovered a laborless occupation: victimizing wealthy young men who harbor a penchant for the experiences of the flesh."

"Do you think Gaston will find out?" Lauren questioned anxiously.

"For Antoine's sake, I hope not, but I seriously doubt his optimism. Gaston will learn of it sooner or later."

"What will he do?"

"Heaven only knows."

Gaston did, of course, learn of Antoine's folly. Who the informer was no one knew, but they had definitely released the ravages of hell. His vile, angry eyes glared with contempt when he summoned his youngest brother to the library. There with the portraits of ancestors peering down in judgment, Antoine was issued his sentence.

"It seems, dear brother, that you are entertaining perverse desires."

"Gaston, I did not—" He was sharply cut off.

"Do not interrupt me!" Gaston bellowed, snapping his fingers in Antoine's face. "You will listen—and listen well—and then do as you are told. You have no choice in the matter, none whatsoever."

Antoine fidgeted from one foot to the other, unaware that he was wringing his hands. Gaston's powerful legs stradled a corner of the desk as he lit a thin dark Havana cigarette. Purposely he prolonged the action, knowing that the most effective part of torture lay in the victim's mental anguish while anticipating the unknown.

"It's time for you to grow up, little brother."

Antoine stiffened. He knew the derisive tone of voice too well. Gazing helplessly around the room as a prisoner gazes at the confines of his cell, he searched for an escape.

"If nothing else will make a man of you, perhaps marriage will. I've decided it is time to arrange your wedding."

Antoine looked up, his soft dark eyes pleading. "I don't want—" Again he was truculently cut off.

"Remember," Gaston snarled, tightening the reins of power over him. "You *have* no choice. That is, unless you wish to be turned out without a *centime.*" He took a long puff on the cigarette, watching the smoke curl around his head, and said in a taunting tone, "You will learn to appreciate the pleasures of women once you've been exposed." The thin wide lips broke into a smug grin. "Christmas is next week, a perfect occasion to have the Rousses for a festive holiday dinner and decide on the date. Emile Rousse shall be delighted to see one of his daughters married, and Murielle, I'm sure, will be a willing bride." Gaston smiled, pleased with his plans, and strode from the room.

In the week that followed, Antoine remained unobtrusively out of view. The elegant, charming young man had been reduced to a sullen, despondent recluse, drowning in a well of despair. He pleaded with Roget to talk to Gaston, and Roget did intervene, but he, too, got nowhere. In desperation, Antoine pleaded with Lauren to help him, but there was little she could hope to do.

"Lauren, please talk to Roget. Ask him to try talking to Gaston once more. There must be a moment . . . in your bedroom, at night, when he'll listen to you."

"Antoine, he has not shared my bed in months." Laying her hand against the hard muscle of his biceps, she said, "I wish I could help you, but unfortunately there is nothing I can do." His despair was as real to her as her own, both victims of an unkind fate, she thought.

Antoine even appealed to his mother, but Madame de Martier's comprehension quite frequently was dulled by the overindulgence in alcohol. She only replied, "How wonderful, dear! It will be good to have another young woman in the house."

It was an onerous chore for Lauren to imagine Christmas without frigid winds whipping through her back and slapping against her face. The past Christmas, a snowy blizzard had covered the streets and rooftops with a lacy white ice that made Paris a place of fairy tales. January through March, however, was considered winter in Haiti, and it was crisp and dry and less scorching than usual, but not by much. After attending mass at the cathedral, the family exchanged gifts late in the morning. Thrilled with the luxurious rope of matched pearls Roget had given her, Lauren's gift to him was an emerald cravat pin.

The green and white dining room at Villa de Martier sparkled with the glow of fine china, exquisitely polished silver, and Belgian crystal. The mansion was bedecked in a splendor Lauren had not witnessed before this holiday, and however improbable, the occasion had enticed Gaston to employ a trio of musicians to entertain following the sumptuous meal. By late afternoon, the Rousse family had arrived. Parades of French and Haitian delicacies wended their way from the pantry to the parlor on the arms of de Martier servants, while French wines and liqueurs flowed copiously. Amid all the grandeur, Gaston, attired in a superbly tailored black frock coat and narrow trousers, preened like a peacock.

At the dinner table, Lauren found herself seated next to Edmond, the Rousses' son, a modest, scholarly young man who would leave in a few months to study law in France. With fair skin and dark hair, he was not as imposing as his father but certainly attractive enough.

"Madame de Martier," he said in a decidedly formal tone. "You were born in Paris, is that true? Do you think I will like it? I've never been there."

"I can't fathom anyone not loving Paris," she replied, her

lips twisting slightly upward. "But it's my home and I'm inclined to be prejudiced. My husband is fond of it, though, and he would probably be better equipped than I to advise a young man on life in Paris." Her parted lips grew into a full-blown smile.

"Merci, madame," he replied, smiling sheepishly. "I forget sometimes that men and women do not lead the same lives."

Roget chatted amiably between Yvonne Rousse on his right and her younger daughter, Coco, on his left. At seventeen, the little Haitienne was already a coquette, and she had seduced Roget's dark eyes to drink in her beauty. Smooth charcoal black hair like her mother's framed a pert uptilted nose that rested pleasingly between feline gray eyes. Her skin, like her sister's, had the glow of beige marble. At her tender age, she had succeeded in holding Roget's attention longer than was deemed necessary for polite conversation, and more than once she had provoked him to laughter. It seemed he was enchanted by a beautiful woman no matter what her age, Lauren thought as jealousy tied a knot in her stomach.

Just then, a pair of serving maids, their hips swaying from side to side, sashayed through the door, bearing trays of rosy baked ham and succulent brown turkey. The meat rested on beds of green watercress, surrounded by honeyed yams.

"Oh, I adore English ham," Yvonne Rousse said, drooling effusively, lifting her nose to savor the delectable aroma. "From Yorkshire?" she questioned, shifting her gaze to the elder Madame de Martier.

"My husband always insisted on Yorkshire ham for Christmas dinner," the older woman replied, "and wild turkey, of course, is native to Haiti. Over the years," she paused wistfully, "the two have become our traditional holiday dinner."

"No one makes ham like the British, but imported, it is dreadfully expensive." Madame Rousse's expression imparted that she was overjoyed to have a daughter marrying into a family that could afford these luxuries.

As she contemplated the huge roasted bird, Lauren's stomach turned a queasy somersault. She had not eaten turkey before, but debated seriously if she would be able to swallow it without reliving the part it had played in that horrendous ritual. She shuddered involuntarily. The aroma, however, invaded her nose, and finally tempted by the hunger in her stomach, she tasted it. Much to her surprise, it was delicious.

Throughout the sumptuous meal, Antoine and his intended bride were seated side by side. Reticent and withdrawn, a stranger would have assumed that he was sitting in for someone who had asked to be excused for a moment. Toying with the savory meal laid before him, Antoine talked when spoken to and answered simply enough to appease Gaston's scornful scrutiny. Meanwhile Murielle chattered incessantly and emitted animation sufficient enough for them both.

"Oh, Antoine, isn't it exciting!" she exclaimed, hugging her shoulders with anticipation. *"Papan* says that I can order gowns from Paris for the wedding. From the House of Worth. Can you believe it? It will be the most beautiful wedding ever!" Antoine struggled to smile but managed only to nod in defeat.

Their appetites thoroughly sated, Gaston suggested that they move to the salon and relieve their overstuffed gullets with a dance or two. Roget offered Coco his arm, and she slipped a delicate hand coyly beneath the bend of his elbow, cleverly not releasing it once the party had reached the salon.

As they sipped aperitifs, Gaston motioned to the musicians to begin playing. Their first tune was a mellow, very European waltz that wafted melodiously through the room, inspiring no one to move. Changing their pace considerably, the musicians' next selection was a faster-paced merengue, which stirred the group's Haitian blood to motion. The African-inspired beat pounded its rhythm until every sedate hip swayed in a frenzy of animated motion.

Gaston began the pairing off by approaching his intended sister-in-law. "Would the future Madame de Martier honor me with this dance," he asked, gallantly holding her hand as she rose from her seat.

"Oui, monsieur," Murielle replied, giggling. What a pity, Lauren mused, that Murielle lacked her sister's clever wit.

Emile Rousse, following his host's lead, swept Justine de

Martier onto the floor and whirled her in time with the music until the older woman gasped for air. "Emile, I don't remember when I last danced like that," she laughed, struggling to catch her breath.

Coco clung to Roget's arm in such a manner that his not asking her to dance would have been considered a slight. *"Mademoiselle,* would you do me the honor?" Roget said, a twinkle of mischief dancing mysteriously over his face.

"Monsieur, I would love to, that is if your wife does not mind," she purred, throwing Lauren a calculated smile of innocence.

Lauren nodded, feigning an amiable smile that she did not feel. She watched Roget slip his arm around the girl's back and watched her coil her hand intimately around his neck, while the low-cut red gown displayed her high young bosom to great advantage.

"I thought red would be perfectly festive for Christmas," she said, employing a worldly tone that drew his attention to the dress.

"A beautiful choice, *mademoiselle.* Its beauty is surpassed only by that of its wearer." Roget's sensuous mouth smiled approvingly.

Blushing, she lowered her eyes with a well-practiced coyness and proceeded to admire the elegant cut of his white linen jacket and trousers.

He is openly flirting with her. Lauren looked away, fuming. The emerald cravat pin that she had poured her heart into choosing for him was being fingered and fawned over by that little vixen. Bristling with anger at the little coquette's gall, Lauren had not noticed that Edmond had approached and was standing beside her chair.

"Madame de Martier," he said, his voice modestly flustered, "would you like to dance?"

"Lauren," she corrected him.

"Lauren," he repeated, his fair skin blushing a tawny red.

"I've just learned the merengue, and I'm not very good at it."

"That doesn't matter," he said, his tone growing bolder. "I can teach you; I'm quite good at it."

Smiling up at him, she rose and took his outstretched hand.

"How could I refuse so generous an offer."

Antoine, who had remained sullenly on the side, nursing his drink, finally decided to join in the festivities by partnering the only female left sitting, his future mother-in-law.

The music throbbed with decidedly African beats, and partners were changed often. But Coco pursed her lips petulantly when Roget danced with someone other than she, and seemingly he had fallen under her spell for he seldom left her for more than a dance.

As Lauren watched him hold Coco, their hips swaying rhythmically to the beat of the drums, Lauren saw Lucienne in his arms the night of the ball. Except for the color of her hair, Coco was a younger replica of Lucienne. A green demon of jealousy ripped through Lauren's entrails with an intensity of feeling she thought had died. With an overwhelming sensation of impotence, Lauren drew her eyes away.

Edmond became the knight in shining armor who rescued her from despair. He insisted on teaching her the finer points of the provocative Haitian salon dance, the two giggling and laughing endlessly at her mistakes. More than once, she had noticed Roget's glare upbraiding her behavior as she cavorted with Murielle's brother.

The party in full swing, Gaston and Emile Rousse took rum and coffee and retreated upstairs to the library. Lauren watched Antoine grow sullen and recoil into his thoughts as he attempted to drown his fears in the rum.

After some time, the two men returned, and summoning Filene, Gaston ordered champagne. "Everything has been settled," Emile Rousse broke in, grinning from ear to ear. "The wedding is set for April. The exact date will be left to the bride and groom," he added, glancing toward his daughter. His grin made Lauren think of a Cheshire cat.

Champagne bottles popped open to spill their frothy liquid into sparkling glasses. Gaston grinned, smug and confident, as he offered a toast. Lauren's focus was caught by his devious smile, and she could not follow him as he lifted his glass.

"To the future Madame de Martier, a lady in every sense. We welcome your addition to our proud family." Glasses were raised to the future bride. Murielle giggled and clung to Antoine's arm as if she were a baby with a new toy, but the solemn groom exuded no emotion.

After many toasts and much merrymaking, the Rousses staggered pompously to their carriage and the de Martiers climbed the stairs to their bedchambers. Removing the pearl combs, Lauren brushed out her dark bushy hair. Raking the brush violently through the curly mass, her blood churned as she recalled the way Roget had held that vixen in his arms. The door between their rooms clicked open, and startled, Lauren whirled in a complete circle to stare at her husband as he entered. Divested of his elegant clothing, Roget wore nothing more than a silk robe. Lauren drew a deep breath and attempted to quell the butterflies that had gone awry in her stomach at the sight of him.

"Who were you expecting?" he said, hoisting an eyebrow in sarcasm.

"Certainly not you," she retorted.

"I must say, you did enjoy yourself cavorting with Edmond Rousse this evening," he scoffed in a grimly condescending tone. "Perhaps you expected him to walk through that door."

"Thanks to Edmond the day was rather pleasant," she replied acidly. Her fingers tightened about the brush handle as she raked it over her scalp.

"I didn't know you preferred them so young," he said, his finger absently tracing a line around the curved surface of a Chinese vase. "Most women like their men older, at least older than themselves."

Lauren swung around and faced him head on, her eyes glowing opalescent at his darker ones. "I did not see you turn Coco away!" She flared at him with a biting sarcasm that matched his own.

"She's a young girl having a harmless flirtation with an older man," Roget replied, quietly dismissing the issue.

"Harmless!" Lauren cried in disbelief. "I was beginning to think that she was your Siamese twin. That—that seventeen-year-old coquette!" Her voice faltered, searching for the right words. "At least Edmond is twenty-one."

"If you like them that young." Arching a raven black brow, his response was calm.

Disarmed by his seeming lack of emotion, Lauren struggled for words that would vent the pain of her rage, but her mind went blank. Finally she recognized the futility of their argument, and finding no other release, she let out her exasperation in a heavily audible sigh. With tears burning her eyelids, she questioned softly. "Roget, what does it matter to you what I do?"

"You *are* my wife," he replied sharply as though her inquiry had pricked a raw nerve.

"You would have a hard time proving that to anyone . . . except perhaps the priest who married us," she said grimly, her gaze dropping to the emerald ring on her finger.

"I don't know why it should matter," Roget murmured softly, "but it does." Jealousy was a new emotion for Roget, and its impact failed to cross his mind. His thoughts no longer caustic, his gaze fell to her mouth and lingered there as his eyes drank in the full, shapely contours of her lips. When she was laughing and frolicking with Edmond, he could have strangled her, but even then he ached to feel her in his arms. He had loved Lucienne for a good part of his life and had never experienced these ambivalent feelings.

Roget's abrupt change in mood took Lauren by surprise. Her lucid gaze sought to question him, but without warning, she was trapped in the smoldering depths of his gaze.

"Lauren . . .," his voice breathed in a sultry whisper. Trembling with desire, Roget felt the reins of control slip from his hands as he dragged her into his arms. His hungry mouth ravaged hers, forcing her lips apart as he plunged recklessly into the warm cavern he had denied himself for so long. Raggedly, he murmured her name against the sweetness of her breath. Burying his fingers deep in the softness of her hair, his right hand cradled her head while the left one slid over the curve of her derriere and drew her taut against him. Lauren's slender frame arched willingly over his arm, and her head swam in whirlpools of dizzying ecstasy as her body responded beyond reason to his touch. The brush dangled limp in her hand, threatening to plummet to the floor when she felt his male body harden and grow insistent against her. And then the stirrings of truth impaled her brain like an arrow. Lauren pulled her mouth away. Wrenching her body free of his caresses, she glared mutinously.

"How dare you!" she cried, hurling the silver brush at him. But with rapid-fire agility he avoided the blow. "Why don't you go back to your blue-blooded mistress?" Lauren felt the waves of pleasure that Roget's fondling had sent pulsing through her body and she hated him. His mere touch had turned her insides to putty. "So you can't crawl in bed with your precious Lucienne for one night. What a pity!" Bitterly she flung her hurt at him. "You spent the entire evening bantering with a seventeen-year-old version of Lucienne, and now you want to satisfy your lust with me."

Her rebuff struck him like a hammer. "Lauren, I . . ." Roget hesitated, knowing he had no valid recourse.

"I hate you!" she cried, her outburst not allowing him to finish. Covering her face with her hands, Lauren refused to let him see the tears brimming in her eyes.

Roget left quietly, not attempting to utter another word. A dismal ache seized Lauren's heart as she watched him leave. As much as she had wanted him, she shuddered with rage that he would use her to vent his lust for another woman.

The next evening, the two older brothers locked horns once more as Antoine convinced Roget to intervene again on his behalf.

"Gaston, Antoine is not ready to marry," Roget argued.

"No man is ready to marry. It's simply a duty he must perform. You eventually married, though your choice of a bride left much to be desired."

"There was one difference. I married of my own volition. No one held a loaded pistol to my head."

"We both know he may never marry of his own volition." Gaston's wide nostrils flared as he cocked an eyebrow in skepticism. "I intend to make damn sure that our brother is securely wed before his escapades bring us disgrace, and no woman will have him except some slut trying to better her station in life."

"In the process you will ruin two lives, not only his, but hers as well," Roget said sourly.

"The kind of husband he'll be does not interest me. I want the marriage consummated so that our family can reap the rewards. Once they are married, it is their problem."

"What gives you the right to manipulate lives?" Roget scoffed, his vexation slowly giving way to scorn. "Who the hell do you think you are: God?"

"In a sense, yes," he replied arrogantly. "I am lord of this household, and I decide what is best for the family name. Every de Martier has an obligation to his heritage, and he is expected to perform that duty for the good of the family. Antoine's marriage to Mademoiselle Rousse will bring a considerable dowry to this estate and, I might add, lucrative business advantages."

"At last you've told the truth," Roget expounded with vehemence. "I should have known that Antoine's naive behavior did not distress you nearly as much as the profits you may lose because of it."

"One can never have too much wealth," Gaston sneered. Striking a match to his thin Havana cigarette, he inhaled deeply and made a ritual of watching the exhaled smoke curl above his head. Gall rose in Roget's belly like a tide. "Besides, dear brother," he continued, his narrow lips twisting upward, "someone has to provide the family with a bride worthy of producing heirs since you have not."

"Then why don't you, Gaston, provide the family with that bride? That is, if you can find a woman who will have you." Roget's bitter scowl eased to a disarming grin. Turning sharply on his heel, he left.

On her way to the opposite corridor, Lauren witnessed her husband's explosive exit. Obviously, his pleas had fallen on deaf ears as well. As she fled past the open door, Gaston's huge hand shot out, imprisoning her arm, and with one swift motion, he forced her behind the ominous door. His massive body pinned her against the rosewood and ebony wall. His mouth forced its way brutally into hers, bruising her lips, and Lauren struggled with a vengeance.

"Why all the fuss? Your husband has gone for the evening, more than likely to see his mistress, and you, *madame,* are left alone. Alone except for me."

Lauren cringed. An icy wave of repulsion washed over her, causing her to shudder, but she said nothing. There was no one to hear.

"Don't think for one minute, my dear Sister-in-Law, that you have escaped my notice. I intend to get what I want. I always do." His voice harbored an oddly vindictive tone as though he meant to make her pay the price for Roget's audacity. The strong fingers crushed deeper in her arm, and she winced in pain, the grimace distorting her face. Yet she stood motionless.

"You owe me something," he said in a snide manner. "The next time I expect you to be more cooperative."

"I owe you nothing," Lauren retorted. "You will not use me again."

"Use you," he replied, mocking her. "You loved every minute of it. And the next time I want to hear your pleasure."

"There will not be a next time," Lauren asserted with a foolhardy lack of concern for the consequences.

"Come now. Let's not be foolish." His lewd manner taunted her. "You would not want your husband to hear of the last time, would you? It would give him perfect grounds for an annulment. And we both know how much you love him even though he's bedding another woman." Gaston's thin wide lips twisted with smug satisfaction, knowing that he had driven a spike into her heart.

In a fit of desperation, she twisted her arm free. His hand reached for the door and pulled it open, and through curling lips, he added, "There will be another time."

"Never!" Lauren flung her refusal at him.

"Madame, you will cooperate," he warned contemptuously, "or my brother will definitely learn of our secret."

"Then I suppose you'll have to tell him," she said, her voice dripping venom. Shaking with fear, Lauren fled into the hall. What was she going to do? Shivering at the thought of his hands mauling her, Lauren knew she would not endure his torture and humiliation again for any reason. She had to get away from him, but how?

Engrossed by the scope of her thoughts, Lauren bolted into Antoine as he emerged from his bedchamber. Dropping the hand from her throat, she managed a weak smile.

"Is everything all right?" His expression was openly concerned. "I heard you arguing with my bastard of a brother," he said, his dark eyes narrowing.

Shaking her head, Lauren shrugged, dismissing it as though it was nothing important.

"Antoine, I want to leave here," she said.

"And Roget?" His eyes widened in surprise.

"Roget," Lauren sighed as if thinking aloud. "There is nothing more to hope for there. Anything I say or do only makes him angry. I think he looks at me and hates me because I'm not Lucienne."

"I've made a decision as well," Antoine said, his voice hesitating. "I am not going through with the wedding."

Alarmed by his statement, Lauren studied him with empathy. "How will you avoid it? Gaston will make your life hell."

"I have a plan." Antoine's focus darted around as if he expected to find invisible ears implanted in the walls. "Meet me tomorrow when you go riding." Leaning forward, he whispered directions in her ear.

Chapter 21

Panic grabbed Lauren's throat as she approached the desolate plain on the outskirts of le Petit Cul-de-Sac. Timorously, Miel picked her way along the path at the foot of the mountain, her horse sense reacting to the skittishness of her rider. Silence hung from the sky like a giant rain cloud, while every living thing took cover to avoid the sun's deadly rays. Shivering despite the heat, Lauren removed her hat and fanned the white straw vigorously before her face. She was well aware that she should not be here, but this was the place where Antoine had instructed her to meet him. Spying a clump of trees that hid the entrance to an obscure path, Lauren reined Miel off the main road to mingle with the foliage that provided them shelter from the sun as well as from detection. Relaxing her grip on the reins, she waited.

Soon a horse pounded down the road, creating whirlwinds of sand as it was jerked to a halt in the center of the fork. Its rider surveyed the area around him in haste and then pulled in close to the cluster of trees where Lauren had taken cover.

"Antoine," she called softly. Drawing a labored breath, she guided Miel out of seclusion and onto the open road. "Thank heaven, you're here. I was horrified to be out here alone . . . since my accident." Her throat nearly choked on the word.

"This way," he said, urging the reluctant animal beneath him through the low-hanging foliage to the hidden road. Trees and vegetation were densely thick along the narrow path, making it difficult to see the earth underfoot, but Antoine plodded up the mountain with confidence, and Lauren followed in his tracks. "I used to come here when I was a boy," he continued, "to escape from my father. No one knows much about it except me. Everyone else avoids this mountain like the plague, but for me it was a welcome refuge." He smiled the way a little boy does when revealing his innermost secret to a treasured friend.

Halfway up the incline, Antoine pulled his horse from the path. "Right here," he said.

Off to the side, Lauren noticed a small, dilapidated cabin peering from behind a group of frangipani trees. Her companion slid from his mount, tethered the stallion to a post, and rushed inside, leaving her with no choice but to follow. The lopsided door hung limply off its rusty hinges, and jagged fragments of broken glass jutted from the windows. The door to the next room creaked with an eerie whine as he pushed it open, and vanishing inside, he beckoned her to follow. Remnants of fine furniture and intricate wall paneling, not unlike those at Villa de Martier, filled the two rooms inside. The pupils in Lauren's hazel eyes dilated to the size of *centimes*.

"Such fine things in a cabin?" Astonished, her voice echoed her surprise. "None of the other thatched-roof huts even have glass windows."

"This one is special," Antoine replied, smiling uneasily. "This is where my grandfather kept his *placée* wife."

Lauren had heard the word before but was still not sure of its implications. "What exactly is a *placée* wife?" she questioned, attempting to clarify, once and for all, what had to be a misunderstanding on her part. Having grown up Catholic, the idea of polygamy was so foreign to her that she could not imagine that it still existed.

Antoine reflected on her question a long while before he replied. He was not proud of the custom, but she had a right to know. *"Placage,"* he began hesitantly, "is a peculiar custom where a man can enter a marriage-type alliance with women other than his legal wife. A ceremony is performed, usually with the consent of the young woman's parents, and she is set up in her own household. She does not, however, have the sanction of the church or the law. A *placée* suffers no disgrace in society, but she lacks the honor a man bestows on the wife he marries in church."

"Hmmm . . ." Lauren sighed. The hum emitted from deep in her breast as she grappled with her thoughts. "Then it *is* a form of polygamy?" she asked finally, unable to accept the blatant inequality of a practice that pitted women against women.

"You could say that." He nodded in agreement.

Ironically, what riled her was not that it existed, but that it was, as always, the privilege only of their men.

"Why do you think Gaston detests you?" Antoine continued, his contempt dripping from each word. "Do you think he would care if you were Roget's *placée?* Huh!" The sound emerged indignantly from his throat. In a huff, Antoine folded two arms across his chest and hooked a long leg over the edge of the dining table. "He cares that Roget had the audacity to marry you before God and the state."

As she digested his words, Lauren's gaze wandered through the doorway to the next room, her eyes lingering on the termite-infested legs of a worn silk brocade sofa in what had pretended to be a salon. She could not help empathizing with the nameless woman who once occupied this isolated cabin.

"Why did he keep her here . . . in this godforsaken place?"

"She was a peasant. Here she was well hidden from society and my elite grandmother. I suppose she wanted some of the luxury that he enjoyed," Antoine said, "so he lavishly furnished the interior of this house, not daring to call attention to the outside."

"Did your father have a *placée?"*

"No, I don't believe so, but he did have a mistress. It seems to run in our family." Lauren caught the mournful glance that betrayed his feelings about the matter. "Roget hated him for it . . . and what it did to *Maman*. Roget was sixteen when he found out, and he was so upset that he disappeared for three days. *Maman* was frantic." Antoine stared into space as if the scene were being enacted again before his eyes.

"What was your father like?" Lauren queried with a nagging curiosity.

"Very much like Gaston." He laughed slightly, a low, ironic bitter kind of chuckle. "Roget is nothing like either of them, but sometimes I think he fears that he is. And at times he lets it spur his actions."

"Roget and your mother were very close . . . even when he was a child?"

"Roget was always *Maman*'s favorite, and she his. Perhaps because Roget can appreciate the beauty of a rose as easily as he fires a rifle," he mused.

Lauren envied her husband his precious treasure. He had known the warmth of his mother's love. Hers had been ripped from her before she was old enough to remember.

Antoine's brow wrinkled to a frown. "I will not go through with the wedding," he said, turning to face her. "I plan to leave here and go to France."

Her mouth open, Lauren stared dumbfounded. Recovering her senses, she reached out and grasped his arm. "I want to leave, too," she said. Unintentionally, her nails dug into his sinewy, muscled flesh.

"You would leave Roget?" he said, grimacing with the stab of pain.

Knowing it was the last thing in the world she wanted to do, Lauren had to bite back the sting of an overwhelming sadness that threatened to drown her in despair before she could answer. "Roget is gone most of the time. I'm terrified of being alone in the house with Gaston. He takes great pleasure in abusing me mentally . . . and physically."

"Have you told Roget?" he asked heatedly, his eyes narrowing with disgust.

"Would he believe me? I sometimes feel that he thinks I'm imagining these things, and Gaston would certainly twist it around so that the blame would be mine."

"Roget is more aware of our brother's tactics than you

think." His tone had grown adamant. "I think you should tell him."

"I doubt that he cares. Roget never loved me," she said, her tone pleading with him to understand. "He only used me to protect Lucienne."

For a brief moment both fell silent until Antoine's voice shattered her reverie.

"We could go together," he broke in excitedly. His brain examined the possibility. "I'm positive that I can manage the arrangements through a friend at the harbormaster's office." In one split second his expression faded from anticipation to utter despair and then rose again to anger. "Where would we get the money? I should have received my inheritance when I turned twenty-one, but if I know my brother, he will hold it up until after the wedding."

"I have some money," Lauren volunteered. "It's not much, only two thousand French francs, but perhaps it will be enough to pay our passage." Shrugging her shoulders, she spread her hands in a gesture of futility. "I have no idea what it amounts to in gourdes."

Antoine's poignant expression wondered at the existence of her newly discovered wealth.

"Roget knows nothing about it," she explained, answering his silent question. "It was left to me by my father." Slowly, her thoughts gave way to skepticism. "Will you be able to book passage for us without anyone learning of our plans?"

"I hope so," he replied. Lauren felt the agitated air of restlessness. This was a dangerous thing they were plotting. If Gaston learned of it, they could be thrown into depths worse than hell. Roget could be reasoned with, but Gaston . . .

"How soon will you need the money?" she inquired, talking merely to quell her rampant anxiety.

"I'll know when I make the arrangements."

All at once a dire thought struck her. "Antoine, what will you do for money when you get to France?"

"I haven't thought that far ahead." The handsome head dropped forlornly. "I will probably have to get a lawyer and fight Gaston for my money, but that could take months, even years. Roget will be on my side," he added, "that should help tremendously since he would be the next heir. If only the family fortune were in Roget's hands—" Lifting his gaze to meet hers, he bit off his words.

Lauren attempted to imagine the plight of someone born into wealth having to face life penniless.

"My aunt runs a small hotel in Paris. I'm sure she would put you up for a while."

"That's very kind, and I may have to accept the offer." Lifting her hand to his lips, he muttered apologetically, "I promise to pay you back one day. Your compassion and your money."

Lauren laughed, a nervous, uncertain kind of throaty chuckle.

"Why is that amusing?" he asked, dropping her hand as if it had become a heated poker.

"Not amusing, just ironic that I who have been penniless throughout my life can lend money to a de Martier."

"We had better go now." His tone was curt. "When I have more information, we will meet here again." Lauren sensed the shame he felt at being forced to accept what he thought was charity, not kindness. The de Martiers were too proud, she thought.

Nevertheless, his sullen mood disturbed her. At his suggestion, she left the dwelling and rode back over the Cul-de-Sac Plain alone. Antoine remained behind, giving her a good lead before he urged his stallion onto the same path, thus removing all chance of anyone seeing them together.

New Year's Day for the rest of the world was Independence Day in Haiti. January 1, 1804, was the day that Jean Jacques Dessalines had declared them free, and this celebration, needless to say, took precedence over welcoming in the new year. On the eve before Haitians toasted the dawn of 1892, they were not merely inaugurating the new year, but giving thanks for eighty-eight years of independence. Riding on the heel of the Môle Saint Nicolas fiasco, this year's jubilation was to be more heartfelt than usual. Giving thanks was the primary activity on the day's agenda, and the de Martiers, along with other élite families, attended mass at the cathedral. Following the solemn early-morning ceremonies, the parade of aristocratic carriages joined the flag-waving revelry in the streets, which would eventually give way to evening festivities celebrated at sumptuous dinners, gala receptions, and glittering balls and for the lower class many public dances.

The de Martiers had accepted an invitation to indulge in the evening's merriment at the home of their future in-laws, and upon returning home, Roget felt strangely as if he were living a recurrence of Christmas. Mutely, Lauren climbed the stairs beside him. The playful, carefree mood she had enjoyed with Edmond Rousse had turned decidedly somber. He made her laugh, and Roget found himself resenting the young man's ability to unlock her insouciant spirit.

"It was an interesting reception," he commented, knowing that his intent was merely to weaken her defiant composure, but lately she had become quite astute at eluding his bait.

"Yes, it was." Lauren smiled vaguely, her lips pressed tightly shut. As they parted like two strangers to enter separate doors to the same bedchamber, Roget felt his gaze slide off the curve of her throat and onto the rapidly heaving swell of her breasts where the gown ended.

"Lauren," he muttered inaudibly, reaching out to touch her. And then, just as abruptly, Roget let the outstretched arm drop back to his side. This insatiable lust was driving him to distraction. Why should she be more willing tonight than the last time he had lost his senses? Averting his gaze, he moved down the hall to his door. Remembering that he had felt an urge to strangle her but a few hours before when she was laughing so heartily with the Rousses' son, Roget shook from the intensely ambivalent scope of his desires. He pushed the heavy mahogany door ajar and stalked inside, leaving his clothes strewn in a neat path behind him.

When she was lying out there paralyzed and he thought he might never hold her again, bury his face in her hair, or hear her fingers enchant him as they danced over the piano, he had felt a terrible sense of loss. He could not recall when he had fought so desperately to hold back his tears. God knows, she had suffered enough, losing her mother at the age of three and growing up black in a white culture. Every Frenchman who sought to ease his lust for a dusky-skinned woman had probably approached her, thinking that because she was of mixed blood she would be easy. A flood of tender feelings melted his hard male torso to a column of liquid.

Crawling into the empty bed, Roget was unable to blot out his yearnings and fall asleep. He tossed from one side of the mattress to the other, reliving the days, the hours, and the minutes he had spent with her in Paris. All at once the scent of her wafted through the room, and the delicious body filled his arms. As he pulled her close, the warm curves of her flesh molded to him with a heat that singed through the fabric of her gown and set a fire raging in his soul. Roget felt his trembling hands span her waist, and his lips scorch the soft arch of her neck. But then as his hungry mouth sought hers, she bolted free of his grasp. "Why don't you go back to your magnificent lover!" she spat indignantly, her eyes glowing a fiery yellow.

Roget awakened in a cold sweat and knew that the only thing real about the dream was the excruciating ache in his groin.

Days dragged along one by one, and Lauren waited in anguished silence for some news of their plans, wondering if perhaps her accomplice had had second thoughts and abandoned the treacherous idea until one morning she was awakened by Antoine's knock at her door.

"I will meet you this afternoon," he whispered and was gone.

When she arrived, he was there sitting on the steps, his long legs propped against the railing.

"You're early," Lauren said, inhaling a few gusts of air to ease her breathlessness.

"We must talk fast. I can't stay long. Gaston is on me like a hawk these days." His tone was bitter as gall. "I spoke to Georges, and he can arrange it for March," he said, the bitter tone losing its edge. "Until then, I will pretend to go along with the wedding." He shrugged helplessly, burying his face in his hands. "I feel like the lowest kind of scoundrel, deceiving Murielle to save myself."

Lauren placed a consoling hand on his shoulder. Lifting his crisp dark head, he crossed the sleek leather boots in front of him. Would he truly be able to relinquish the luxury he was born to? Lauren wondered.

"The money will be enough at least for the tickets," he said. "But there's another problem . . ." Lauren's gaze questioned him. "Passports," he said looking at her. "We're going to need passports. Do you have yours?"

"Roget must have it. He always carried it with him."

"Do you know where it is? Could you get it without his knowing?"

What little her spirits had risen by the good news, they now sank to lower depths. "No," she said dejectedly. "I have no idea where he keeps it."

"I've never had one, and if I apply for it now, it will be a matter of days before the information reaches Gaston." Ruefully, he added, "It will cost five hundred gourdes to get one forged. That's more than a thousand francs."

Lauren sighed. Tapping her crop rhythmically against the railing post, she felt each vibration increase with the tide of rising frustration in her breast. "There must be another way," she said, "some other route we can take."

"How? I couldn't possibly get my hands on a gourde. Gaston guards the purse strings like Midas guarded his gold."

Lauren lashed out in vengeance with her crop, bringing the strap down hard against the wooden banister.

"We will find a way," she said, biting her lip to stave off the sting that burned in her head. "We have to!" Suddenly the silence was penetrating. Both were deep in thought.

"I have an idea," she cried, her excitement ringing through the quiet. "You could pass as my husband—use Roget's passport. You look enough like him." Her enthusiasm sunk to midstream. "But I still have to find them."

"It's a perfect idea," he agreed. A glimmer of hope returned to Antoine's eyes. "We must find those passports." His tone was adamant and then peculiarly pensive as if flirting with a flash of recollection. "Roget used to have a silver box, about the size of a jewelry case, where he kept personal things. It's very possible that he still uses it."

"I've never seen it," Lauren said anxiously. "Where does he keep it?"

"I don't know."

"You will have to find it."

During the next few days, Lauren searched the house, but there was no sign of anything that remotely resembled the documents they needed. She had looked in all the drawers, the closets, and the writing desk. In Roget's dressing room she had gone through drawers of his neatly arranged shirts; closets full of frock coats, trousers, and waistcoats; his huge armoire; and even the brass trunk. She had found nothing but a tiny silver key. Where would he put a passport? She could think of nowhere else except the silver box Antoine had mentioned, and there remained but one place to try.

Having waited until the maids had finished their duties in the west wing of the house, and Filene had gone on her way, Lauren swept along the hallway, her feet moving in rapid determination toward the library. Slipping into the room, she locked the door and pocketed the key. Better to be questioned about the locked door, she thought, then to be caught unaware.

Lauren gazed about the room at the volumes of books that went from floor to ceiling and wondered where to begin. Where would he hide a silver box? She began pulling out books at random to see what was behind them. Her scrutinizing eyes wandered restlessly about the room, skimming here, pausing there, until a thought flickered through her mind. Once she had come in the room unexpectedly, and Roget had hastily replaced a book. It was a folio-sized book, and even he had stretched to reach the shelf. Anxiously, her lucid gaze scanned that corner of the wall, and she located it. Lauren dragged a stool to the shelf and, climbing on it, pulled the navy and gold book from its space. Behind it was the silver case.

Clasping the treasure against her breast, Lauren jumped from the stool and fumbled with the tiny key until the lip popped open. As Antoine had said, it contained papers, documents, and personal items, among which was an adolescent love letter grown yellow with age. In it, Roget and Lucienne had sworn their love for each other, but below Roget had added a passage in a different ink: "I will love you forever, my love, but I will never marry you. I'll not condemn you to life in my family." Scalding tears swelled behind hazel eyes as Lauren folded the aging paper and replaced it in its envelope.

Rummaging further through his personal papers, she drew in a breath that anxiety did not allow her to exhale when her fingers fell on the flat red folder that contained their passports. She had found them! Now, she need only pray that their scheme would succeed.

"It's my game," the portly, brown-skinned Haitian chuckled. Slapping his thigh, he flipped his cards face up on the table. The inflated chest swelled with pride, because after years of trying, he had at last managed to beat his opponent. Reluctantly, Roget added the remaining stack of his chips to Louis Norville's hoard and considered how badly he had lost. He had not won a single game. Roget's gaze fled past the heads of his three partners and stopped short on the two men who had entered and gone to the bar. An irritated frown distorted his chiseled features.

"Deal me out of this one," he said as he saw the next hand flicking through Armand Benoit's fingers. Shoving his cards back to the dealer, Roget pushed the chair back and stood up, aiming his long strides toward the bar. He was in no mood for Gaston's antagonism, but how would it look if he ignored his brother?

Approaching them, he offered a hand to Henri Duval.

"Oho! Good to see you, Roget," the older man said, pumping his arm with jocular glee. "This should be quite an evening."

"Gaston," Roget nodded, acknowledging his brother.

"Mon cher frère, fancy meeting you here."

The sparks of antagonism that ignited the air between them completely escaped Henri Duval's notice. "Give my regards to your charming wife," he said. "We had no idea she possessed such talent."

"I will," Roget replied with wooden animation.

"If you gentlemen will excuse me, nature calls but I will return shortly," Duval said, his hands stroking his goatee in anticipation. Hurrying toward the privy, he called over his shoulder, "Don't deal the cards without me."

"What brings you here?" Roget inquired grimly. Resting a hip against the leather stool, he crossed his arms and feet simultaneously. "I thought you preferred more elite company."

"It was Duval's choice, not mine. You and he seem to enjoy the same class of people."

The ebony-skinned bartender, neatly attired in a crisp white jacket, made his way to where they sat. "The usual, Monsieur de Martier?"

"Oui," Roget nodded.

"And the gentleman?"

"He's my brother, Guillaume."

"It's a pleasure, *monsieur,"* he grinned, but Gaston ignored the amenity.

"Rum with water on the side," he said curtly, his rebuff hastening the man's departure. "I didn't come here to make the acquaintance of bartenders."

"Why did you come here?" Roget asked, his brow wrinkled with contempt.

"I should ask you the same question," Gaston replied in a mocking tone, "especially when you have so charming a wife waiting for you at home."

Roget shifted his weight uncomfortably against the leather stool. The bartender returned, quickly placed the drinks before them, and backed away. He would not risk another rebuff. This de Martier was nothing like his brother.

"Speaking of your talented wife," Gaston continued, a lascivious grin spread over his face, "why do you spend your time here? It seems you would be at home enjoying her talents while you can."

Roget felt the hair at the back of his neck stiffen like a porcupine. Lifting his glass, he swallowed a long, burning gulp of the amber liquid.

"She is a tasty morsel, my dear brother," Gaston taunted, raising the glass to Roget's face in a mock toast. "And so easy to arouse. Only a few pinches on those eager breasts, and her silken thighs spread royally."

Roget's eyes narrowed, his brain suddenly comprehending what his brother meant. All at once, the stiff wing-tipped collar was too tight, and his impeccably tailored jacket felt as if it would suffocate him. His head exploded into a thousand different pieces as he turned the glass up and emptied it.

"Having sampled her talents, at least now I know why you had the audacity to bring the wench into our family," Gaston scoffed leisurely, unaware of the violent war that waged in Roget's head. "However, you should have had the discretion to keep a wench like her as a *placée* or, better yet, a mistress. A church marriage should have been reserved for a lady such as Lucienne."

Roget's hand squeezed the empty glass. Struggling with the urge to clutch Gaston's wicked neck and strangle the life from him, he wondered if his boasting was true. But instead of exercising his murderous thoughts, Roget motioned to Guillaume to refill his glass. Blood bulged against his temples, and gulping down the second drink, he attempted to dull the pain. Alarmed, Guillaume filled his glass for the third round. Taking that down in two swallows, Roget proceeded to order another while Gaston looked on with amused scrutiny.

In all the years he had worked here, Guillaume thought, he had not seen Monsieur de Martier drink this heavily. He had rarely poured him more than two drinks during an evening. His uppity brother certainly had a powerful effect on him.

By the time he had dispensed the fourth, Henri Duval had returned, anxious to begin a game of bezique.

"I'll join you in a while," Roget begged off. The two men left him and settled at a card table.

After a weak attempt at trying to drown his rage in a fifth glass of rum and then a sixth, Roget felt the bile rise and overflow in his gut, leaving its sour taste in his mouth. He had wanted her all these months, and pride had not allowed him to claim her. And now, damn her, she had slept with Gaston. Like a serpent, Roget saw his brother slithering over her flesh, infecting her with his venom. The rum festered in Roget's belly. Hot blood pulsed through his temples as he imagined Gaston's hands mauling her body. But why should he care? He summoned Guillaume and ordered him to pour another drink.

The gilded Louis XV clock in the vestibule sounded midnight, and chimes echoed through the mansion like sirens, piercing Lauren's soul. Lauren awoke from a twilight sleep, her restless thrashings disallowing the deep slumber her body needed. Somewhere in the distance or perhaps in a dream, she heard the clattering of a carriage. Drowsiness overtook her, and she dozed once more in the land of dreams, this time to be awakened by the sound of footsteps in the hallway outside her door, footsteps with a rhythm and an intensity of purpose that she failed to recognize. Lauren drew a jagged breath that pricked her throat. Had Gaston returned so early? It was not yet midnight.

Turned from outside, the brass doorknob flashed against the darkness. Lauren felt the strength drain from her body. She lay there, paralyzed with fright as the inevitable was about to overtake her, feeling too weak to defend herself. The heavy mahogany door flew open with a force that shook the room as it connected sharply with the doorstop. Bracing herself against the wall, Lauren groped for the gas mantle beside the bed, but her hands trembled and she merely fumbled with the lamp, unable to light it. A man's figure stood silhouetted in the doorway, his ominous shadow cast by the rays of moonlight streaming through shimmering glass. Determinedly, the shadow moved into the room, pushing the door closed behind him. Still, her clumsy fingers could not ignite the lamp. Releasing it, she braced herself against the headboard and frantically clutched the sheets to cover her half-clothed body. She could hear Gaston's voice ringing in her head. That mocking laughter that had rung in her ears and stripped her of all pride.

The memory sprung loose from its prison in the back of her mind, intensely vivid, to haunt her once again. Towering over her, the dark figure loomed larger than life beside the bed. There was no chance to escape him. Drowsiness had rendered her immobile. Frantic, Lauren opened her mouth to scream, and even the sound froze in her throat. His hands reached for the lamp and ignited it, using more manual dexterity than she had been able to command. It flickered, and the room took on a soft, eerie glow. Vague shadows reflected against the pale ecru walls reminding Lauren of the grotesque drawings scrawled on the walls of the *houmfort*. The yellow furnishings of her bedchamber turned instantly gray, and suddenly she stared into a pair of fiery dark eyes, eyes that were etched on her memory. Lauren shuddered, realizing she was his captive again. But the eyes were not Gaston's.

"Roget!" Lauren gasped. The stench of liquor invaded her nostrils, and she sensed the perversity of her husband's mood. Instinctively, she pulled away.

"Whom did you expect?" he growled, his voice riddled with scorn.

"Roget, you're drunk!" she scolded, using the outburst of words as an effusive response to her fear.

"So I am, *ma chérie*. So I am."

The glibness of his words did not match the biting sarcasm in his voice. His ebony eyes glared cold and angry, and he was drunk, very drunk. Lauren had not seen him intoxicated before, and she reacted with the cold caution of apprehension. She was facing a stranger, a Roget she did not know, and without being fully aware of her action, she recoiled from him, binding the sheet against her bare shoulders.

"Oho!" Roget hoisted his raven black brows. "Now you cover yourself like an innocent virgin. I am your husband . . . or have you forgotten?"

His arrogance spurred her anger, and fear sunk into oblivion. "I haven't forgotten," she retorted, her voice suddenly biting, "but it seems that you have."

"Perhaps." His rejoinder employed the same glib tone. "But you're still my wife."

An icy chill raced through Lauren's body, causing a noticeable shudder. Roget reached for her, and she pulled away, but his grip was clad in steel, rendering her helpless to free herself. With one swift motion, he tore away the sheets that covered her and forced her back upon the pillows, anchoring her body with his own. She felt his weight as she had not felt it before. Unable to move, hardly able to breathe, she was welded to the bed by the dead weight of his lean, unyielding torso. Roget's mouth clamped down on hers hard as he claimed its softness, roughly, brutally, until her lips ached from the pressure. Hooking a finger in the bodice of her nightgown, he ripped the lace with fiendish glee and exposed the smooth rise of her honey-colored breasts. Lauren arched against him, fighting desperately to wrench free of his grasp, but struggling with him was like doing battle with Hercules.

Impetuously freeing an arm, Lauren shoved the palm of her hand into his face. Roget's head snapped back, and he balked, offering her a means of escape. In a split second, she drew trembling knees to her chest and thrust them into his groin. The blow stunned him. He sucked in a hissing breath and fell sideways across their canopied bed. Lauren scrambled to her feet and bolted for the door, but it was closed. Roget recovered with a vengeance for retaliation, and he lunged at her before she could turn the knob and open it. Blocking her path with his lean, well-honed frame, Roget crooked a finger in the elegant puff scarf knotted at his throat, and snatching it open, he tossed it aside. It landed on a chair and then toppled to the floor. He pulled off his linen jacket and flung it at the same yellow armchair. As he yanked the pleated shirt from his trousers, Lauren watched the studs scatter one by one over the carpet. His ebony gaze burrowing a hole through her middle, Roget unbuttoned his narrow trousers and let them fall to the floor, all the while blocking Lauren's access to freedom. Stunned and motionless, Lauren looked on as he reached behind him for the key and locked the door.

"Roget, this is insane," she pleaded. "You're drunk! You can't possibly know what you're doing."

His feet wavering, he moved forward in an uneven swagger. *"Ma chérie.* I may be drunk, but I know very well what I'm doing."

"You would not behave this way with Lucienne," Lauren rebuked sharply, the sarcasm in her voice ripping through his senses.

"That's quite true, I wouldn't . . . but then she is not a wench like you are."

Seething beneath the brunt of his contempt, Lauren lashed out, letting the flat of her hand connect hard with his face. The sound of flesh meeting flesh rang through the air, reverberating off the silence. Roget's head shook from the force of her blow, and his face grimaced at the sting. Glaring indignantly, Roget landed his open hand flat against her face, blunt and stinging, the force destroying her balance.

Lauren staggered to stay on her feet as the impact sent her reeling into the bedpost. The side of her jaw went numb, and acid tears welled like pools of despair in her eyes.

Roget's glare blazed with his fury, and Lauren felt the strength of his hostility now more than ever. Why did he hate her so? Grasping her by the arms, he flung her on the bed, and as her body bounced against the mattress, the entire room trembled amidst their disdain.

Leering down at her, his eyes drank in the naked breasts that heaved with alarm beneath his scrutiny, and then he saw Gaston's hands fondling her flesh. A green serpent crawled through his belly. With renewed vengeance, he fell on her, his weight pressing her into the mattress, his body controlling her as an anchor controls a ship. Like a ship, he allowed her sufficient movement to thrash about in rough seas but not enough to sever the rope and set herself free. Yet with everything in her she fought him—body, mind, and spirit—swearing that he would not force her into submission.

Like daggers, Lauren's nails slashed into the smooth sable muscles of his back. His face contorted with pain, and angered by her action, he pinned her arms beneath her. She felt Roget's hungry mouth descend on her breasts, and she tried to wrench herself free, but he shifted and pressed his hand against the soft hollow in her throat so that she could no longer move her head. His tongue invaded her mouth, and Lauren ground her teeth together on the foreign flesh. Pulling back sharply, Roget bellowed a loud cry. "You witch!"

Seizing the brief freedom, Lauren struggled with the insane effort to free her arms and break herself loose, but his furious determination manifested a Herculean strength and she was powerless against it. Fiendishly, he ripped the shreds of her nightgown from her, leaving her nude body exposed, and still she fought him. In the struggle, their naked bodies clashed like swords in the night.

"I'll not be your whore!" Lauren cried bitterly. "Vent your lust on your mistress!"

She gouged her nails into the flawless plane of his face and then drew them back when she felt the warm, sticky substance ooze between her fingers. Drawing them away, she saw his blood. Roget inhaled a deep, jagged breath that allowed his grip to falter. Lauren lurched forward and started for the door, and just barely, he caught her arm, hurling her once more onto the mattress. Her hand lashed against his face, but this time he did not flinch. Instead, one corner of his mouth twisted to a wry sneer.

"Did you fight Gaston so hard?"

Amid the deafening silence, her thoughts screamed, *He knows!* Shamefully, Lauren averted her eyes from the scrutinizing agony of his gaze. Roget's venomous tongue had accomplished what brute strength could never claim. Having lost the will to fight for anything, least of all her honor, Lauren relented and allowed him his way. Sagging hopelessly into the mattress, she realized that his words hurt more than Gaston's blows.

Nauseated by the overwhelming stench of alcohol that hung on his breath, the fumes potent enough to intoxicate her with a mere sniff, she recalled all those nights she had longed for his maleness to assuage the longing in her womb, but not like this—never like this.

Lauren felt Roget's lips roam ravenously over her cringing flesh, extracting the nectar that she was unwilling to give. Had he looked in her face, he would have seen the contrition, but he was oblivious to all but his own driving demons. His mouth claimed hers with the fury of pent-up lust, but as he penetrated her rigid body, she lay beneath him motionless, feeling nothing but the humiliation of the act. Roget convulsed and exploded in her, flooding her core with his essence, and having pleasured himself, he withdrew. Lauren turned her face away, not ever wanting to look into those eyes again. He had used her like a whore.

As Roget left her bed and stumbled blindly to his room, Lauren buried her face in the pillow and sobbed the bitter tears dredged up from her soul.

Morning came and Lauren dragged herself from the bed, her feet tangling in the clothes still strewn over the floor where Roget had left them. She rang for Cybele and ordered a hot bath drawn immediately, her only desire to wash him from her body. Shuffling to the balcony, she threw open the glass doors, letting the heat gush into her room. Already the sun was blistering hot. Perhaps it would burn away the taint on her soul and make her pure again.

Why had he been in such a drunken frenzy? Did liquor make him so vile and despicable? If she had not seen his face, she would have thought he was Gaston. There was no need to subject her to that kind of humiliating treatment. She would have taken him to her bed eagerly had he come like the man that she knew.

Immersed in the hot, foamy bubbles, Lauren let her body collapse against the porcelain tub as the soothing water flowed over her and soaked away her despair. Roget's face would be suffering more than a little today, she thought, but it could not begin to pay for the damage he had done to her pride.

Roget opened his eyes and then closed them instantly, squinting at the stream of sunlight that assaulted him from the window. A deafening hammer pounded in his head.

Rolling onto his side to evade the light, he tried to swallow, to pull the tongue from his throat, but his mouth felt as though it were stuffed with balls of cotton. Shooting pains ripped through his back as he attempted to move, and he remembered her nails cutting into his bare flesh. Vividly, the night came back to him, and Roget cringed with shame, realizing that he had taken her by force.

His soul scorching beneath the fires of disgrace, Roget entertained the unwelcome thought of getting up, but the slightest motion sent those flames licking through his limbs, and he eased back onto the mattress. Good Lord, he felt as if someone had used him as a trampoline. His hand reached up to sooth the burning sensation in his cheek and drew back in horror at the hardened gashes on his skin. Dragging himself from the mattress, he weaved, half walking, half stumbling, across the floor, grabbing the armoire and then a chair for support. Staggering to the mirror, Roget ran his fingers over the patches of dried blood that streaked his face.

"Blast her, the witch!" he snarled aloud. Angry bile rose in his gut, bringing back the encounter with Gaston. "So she has a penchant for my brother? Well, she can have him."

Roget felt his stomach retch with nausea from the stale liquor, and he doubled over, clutching it with his arm. She certainly wasted no time in letting the snake crawl into her bed, he thought as his gut churned once more. They deserved each other. She probably enjoyed his lecherous abuse. The bitter taste of gall rose to his throat, and clutching the hard muscles of his belly, Roget raced nature to the bathroom.

Lauren paced the carpet, her rage growing stronger with every step. She must see Antoine! It was almost six. Why had they not come in yet? Lauren bristled. It occurred to her that Roget would be coming in as well. Aware of the fact that she would have to confront him at dinner, irately she clenched her fists and wrestled with the notion of avoiding the ritual altogether. But pride would not allow her to surrender.

A tight constriction welled up in her chest, and hot tears scalded behind her eyes while she struggled to restrain them. She wanted nothing more than to gouge her nails into those handsome, arrogant features and make him feel the pain that she felt, but she would face him with the same audacity with which he would face her. Lauren's shapely lips curled to a smug grin as she wondered how he would explain the gashes on his cheek, especially to his mother. At least her wounds were not visible.

It was nearly seven when Lauren heard Roget moving about, and hopefully Antoine would be in his quarters. Slipping from her room, she went stealthily along the corridor to his, where her soft knock was issued an invitation to enter. Antoine looked up with alarm, realizing it was she. "Lauren, you should not be here," he whispered anxiously.

"No one saw me come. I'm sure."

"You can never be sure who sees what in this house. Invisible eyes peer around every corner."

"We must talk. Is everything all right?" she questioned.

"As far as I know." Lowering his voice to a whisper, he said, "We can't talk now. I will let you know the minute I have more information."

Antoine's behavior had been strange. With agitated motion, he had hurried her from the room, reminding Lauren of a dog with a buried bone.

Four weeks passed and Lauren heard not a word from Antoine about the progress of their plans. Lauren lay in bed staring at the yellow fringed canopy that swayed overhead. There was no need to get up, no need to do anything, she thought. Reluctantly, she climbed out of bed, placed her feet on the floor one by one, and stood up. All of a sudden she was dizzy. Her balance wavered, and unable to gain her equilibrium, she grasped the bedpost for support. Closing her eyes, she sat on the edge of the bed. The dizziness faded. Standing once more, she headed toward the bathroom, assuming that it was probably hunger. Washed and dressed, she went downstairs to breakfast.

Madame de Martier sat at the table sipping her small cup of black coffee. *"Bonjour, ma chérie,"* she said, her voice almost chiming.

"Bonjour, madame."

"Have you seen what a glorious day it is?"

"Oui, madame," Lauren replied, forcing a smile.

Lifting the china cup from its saucer, the older woman took another sip of black coffee as Lauren slipped into a chair. "It is such a beautiful day," she repeated. "You should go riding instead of moping around the house as you have been the last few days."

"I've been very tired." Lauren realized that if fatigue had not dominated her thoughts, she would have been taken aback by his mother's sudden concern for her welfare.

Lisa appeared and set plates of fresh pineapple, mango, and orange on the damask tablecloth. When she had left, Madame de Martier remarked idly. "Roget will have his hands full the next few days. No doubt he too will be exhausted." Lauren looked up with a question in her eyes. "Gaston left for Jacmel this morning," her mother-in-law added.

Lauren wavered. "But there's Antoine," she replied.

"He said something this morning about leaving also." Feeling faint, Lauren braced herself against the table.

"Are you feeling well?" the older woman inquired. "Perhaps you should eat something."

The sight of food made Lauren nauseated, but she reached for the fresh pineapple, the only thing tart enough to stop the cartwheels in her stomach.

Having devoured a reasonably healthy dinner that evening, Lauren used the feeble excuse of a headache and started for the stairs, preferring not to join Roget and his mother in the salon.

"Wait! I'll go with you," Antoine called after her as she hoisted the corner of her blue muslin skirt to place her foot on the step.

"Antoine!" She blurted out her anxiety. "We must talk. I'm going mad with—"

Roughly his hand covered her mouth. "Shhhhh," he whispered, removing his hand. "We will talk when I return. I promise." He gave a sly grin, like a signal between conspirators, and vanished into his private refuge.

Oddly, time had dulled the pain, and she was able to face Roget without rage. When she entered his mother's parlor the next evening and found him alone, glass in hand, leaning nonchalantly against the mantle, her eyes took in the white linen suit and the elegantly tied cravat, and it was hard to imagine that he was the same man she had fought so viciously that night.

The skirts of her jade green gown swished loudly as she swept over the floor and seated herself in the chair opposite the sofa. Roget's moody gaze followed her across the room.

"Sherry?" he said, moving to pour her drink.

"Sherry will be fine," she replied. Unwillingly, she gave him a sidelong glance. Her gaze lingered on the breadth of his shoulders, his crisp dark hair, and then fell to the sultry contours of his mouth. Her heart began to thump. Swallowing hard, Lauren smothered the sensation in her breast. The mere thought filled her with loathing. How could her traitorous heart still want him when he had violated her so abominably?

Roget handed her the tapered column of pale amber sherry, and each made doubly sure that their fingers did not touch. Her eyes traveled to the scratches that marred his face. He had not come near her since that night, but he behaved now as though nothing had happened.

The door flung open, and Madame de Martier swept between them, offering her glass to be refilled. Taking the stemmed goblet from her, Roget filled it with obvious distaste.

"*Maman,* this is the last," he said grimly. A deep anguish shrouded his handsome features as he remembered the last encounter with Lauren and how stinking drunk he had been.

"Dear, you look tired," the older woman commented, using the diversion to ignore her son's reprimand.

"Why was it so urgent that Gaston leave now? Could he not have waited a week or two?" The sharp tone drew Lauren's attention to his abrupt change in mood.

"I suppose, dear, that the matter could not wait," his mother replied.

Drawing his gaze from his mother, Roget focused his moody thoughts on his wife. "You're quiet this evening," he remarked.

"You appear to be in a foul enough mood already. Anything I said would only provoke you."

Roget laughed slightly, a low, uncertain chuckle. Lauren stared up at him and their gazes locked intimately for a fleeting second and then pulled away.

"You know me quite well," he said finally, bantering with her as though his mother were not present.

"Not very," she replied. A weak smile parted her lips. It was alarming the way his manner could make her forget, but she did not want to forget. She would never forget what he had done to her! Without warning, her fingers clenched into fists against the chair, while a surge of angry blood turned her face a ruddy burgundy.

"You're blushing," he remarked casually, his lips suppressing a smile. Strolling past her, he paused to study the Henry Tanner landscape on the adjoining wall.

The audacity of him—the way he was brazenly toying with her feelings. How she hated him! With foolhardy recklessness, she wanted to dig her nails into the other side of that arrogant face. Instead, she ground her nails silently into the palm of her own hand. She would be very glad when she was gone from here. Lucienne could have him. She never wanted to set eyes on that face again! Love and hate made a potent brew that simmered in her veins.

Filene came in to announce dinner, and Madame de Martier quickly claimed her son's right arm. Roget offered his wife the other.

Antoine returned with a newfound aura of confidence. As though gloating over some recent accomplishment, he appeared to have lost his crippling fear of Gaston. Lauren wondered if this would mean a change in their plans.

When he approached her and ushered her into the library, brusquely clamping a hand over her mouth, she heard the restless excitement that commanded his voice.

"Don't say anything," he said in a whisper. "Meet me tomorrow shortly after noon." With his hand covering her mouth, Lauren could only nod her head in reply. Slowly, he removed the hand and let it fall to his side. "I have something to tell you," he said.

Lauren arrived at the cabin feeling weak and nauseated from the hard ride and realized that she should not have abandoned the midday meal. Inside the hut, she planted herself in the nearest rickety chair to await her accomplice's arrival. Miel pawed anxiously at the dead foliage under her feet, creating a raucous disturbance, but Lauren was too weary to get up and scold the animal. Propping an elbow on the bare wooden table, she put her head against her hand and dozed off. Antoine's arrival shook her from the slumber.

"You must be tired," he grinned.

"What is wrong with me?" she smiled weakly, placing her hand over her forehead as if to erase the drowsiness. "I cannot seem to keep my eyes open."

"Perhaps you should see Dr. Mauriac," he said with concern.

"I suppose you're right. If it doesn't pass soon, I will." Suppressing the thought that had crept into her head, she inquired curiously, "Is there some new information?"

Shaking his head in disbelief, the tall, sepia young man pulled out another age-worn chair and sat opposite her, struggling inwardly with a way to begin. Propping his booted legs one by one on the edge of the table, he let the motion buy him time to think. "I think I can prove what Roget has suspected all along," he began, a reluctant tone guarding his voice, "that Gaston was responsible for Reinette's death."

Lauren gasped aloud. "Oh, no! Why?" she questioned, her mouth agape.

"I don't know why . . . not yet." A feral gleam danced in his eye. "I have a feeling that Roget knows more than he has ever told." Amid the silence, they were both aware that Roget's bitter distaste for le Petit Cul-de-Sac dominated their thoughts.

"Are you sure there couldn't be a mistake?" She wanted desperately for Roget not to be involved.

"I'm sure," he replied, nodding.

"What will you do?" She was compelled to ask the inevitable question.

He gazed at her with eyes so like Roget's that she was caught in them. "I don't know. I've not decided yet." He shrugged with indecision. "I only know what I want to do."

"Turn him in?"

"Oui. Roget has suspected it for a while. Though he has never said as much, I know he believes it. I'm sure that was the reason he went to France."

Nausea twisted like a snake in Lauren's stomach. "But if Roget knew, why would he not turn him in?" she questioned with a genuine feeling of alarm.

"He had no proof. And with Roget's strong sense of loyalty, it would have been difficult to condemn his own brother to death."

"He's your brother as well."

"By birth, yes, but he's as alien to me as that fly crawling on the wall." Devoid of expression, his dark eyes followed the tiny insect to the ceiling.

"Roget has no great love for Gaston either," Lauren added.

"I know that. But Roget dislikes him intensely . . . I *hate* him."

Lauren came in from her trip, opened the door, and flung her hat fiercely into the closet. Spending the afternoon shopping in Port-au-Prince had left her feeling refreshed until Georgette carelessly mentioned that Jacques had seen Roget and Lucienne picnicking on the mountainside one day. Lauren flopped face down across their canopied bed, determined not to care. All she wanted was to leave here and return to France. Burying her head in folded arms, she tried to shut out the throes of her imagination, but the only vision she saw before her closed eyes was Roget and Lucienne. Because closing her eyes was useless, she opened them and sat up, her dusty shoes leaving a smudge of dirt on the bedcover.

Lauren drew herself up and onto her feet and padded aimlessly to the balcony. Gazing out over de Martier lands, she realized that no matter where she focused she saw only one thing. Lucienne sharing a picnic lunch with Roget. She pictured Lucienne's beige marble skin and lustrous auburn hair as his lips plundered her full, enticing mouth. She imagined him making love to her beneath the rustling frangipani trees while their horses stood tethered nearby.

The scene quickly faded when the door to his dressing room slammed shut. Foolish as it was, a nagging doubt urged her to seek the truth she already knew. She had heard it from everyone else, but she had to hear it from him. Lauren's feet moved across the carpet, and she rapped lightly at his door.

"Entrez," he uttered, and she heeded the invitation.

Hot, dusty, and tired, he had just begun to undress. He glanced at her briefly and continued removing his sweat-drenched clothes.

"Roget," she began, the crack in her voice more than noticeable and then let loose her thoughts in one steady stream of words. "Why did you choose me to marry, since obviously it's no secret that you love Lucienne? Surely there were other women . . . who . . . Did you have any feelings for me at all?" Having said it, Lauren waited with dread for his reply.

Looping his belt over the brass hook, Roget pondered her question and wondered what he could possibly say that would not make matters worse. Deciding that truth was probably his best recourse, Roget replied. "There was an attraction," he said, his voice grounded in skepticism. "I would not have married someone who repelled me." He paused, trying to read the stolid expression that had frozen on her face. "You were different. I had not known a woman from your class. You had a naive charm and a talent that I found intriguing. I saw an opportunity to carry out a plan, and I seized it. I had made the unfortunate mistake of loving the woman I was destined to marry . . . My marriage to you enabled me to save Lucienne from a sordid alliance."

Lauren listened, her lips not uttering a sound as his words burned against her skull and tied painful knots in the wall of her stomach. Attempting to support wavering legs, she leaned her buttocks into the back of a chair. "I see," she replied after moments of weighted silence. Her downcast eyes never left the long, expressive fingers that spread limply on her lap. The gold and emerald band loomed at her like a mirror. "The times you made love to me . . . Was your passion, too . . . merely a wager?"

"No." His candor was more than she had expected. "I

would have to admit that what happened on our wedding night took me by surprise. I enjoyed tremendously the fruits of your love. That is until . . ." How could he imagine that she had forgotten that horrendous night? He had not been able to forget it. With sudden abruptness Roget shifted, masking his face in the shadows.

Lauren sprang to her feet. "Until what?" she queried.

"Nothing. Forget it." Roget shifted his thoughts. Could he expect her to forgive him when he could not forgive himself for what he had done?

Lauren's face went blank as he mumbled a vague excuse and strode into his bath.

It was true, even during their honeymoon he had never said that he loved her, but in her naïveté, she had just assumed that some men were uncomfortable saying the words. Seemingly, nothing was further from the truth. She was experienced enough now to know that his passion had been nothing more than lust.

Outside the day was warm and fragrant, and the chatter of birds assaulted her eardrums like the raucous cackle of magpies. Life went on around her; it was merely she who wanted it to cease. Roget was out there somewhere overseeing the plantation, and no doubt he would share the midday meal with Lucienne, the woman he loved. Lauren stared down at the emerald ring on her finger and realized the farce. As she lay beneath his brother, enduring his cruelty, it was because she loved Roget, but the marriage for him was a convenience.

How long could she sit here wallowing in despair before the walls closed in on her? This room had become her prison. The children at the orphanage were far happier in their unadorned dormitory enclaves than she had been in this one. Despite its grandeur, she doubted that another room could be as lonely as her own.

Exercising a strong will, Lauren pulled herself to her feet. The room whirled lucidly around her head, and she was forced to clutch the bedpost for support. With both hands clinging to the intricately carved column, she lowered herself with great care onto the bed. Brilliant colors darted before her eyes: reds, oranges, blues, all bright and all blinding. Her stomach retched, but there was nothing to come up. She had almost succeeded in blocking out the memory of that night and the way Roget had humiliated her, but if her dreaded suspicions of the past weeks were true, it would be etched in her memory for a long time to come.

Chapter
23

The Deffand carriage ground to a halt opposite the front entrance to Villa de Martier. Impressive as it was, the main portal yawned wide and uninviting against the tropical terrain, as Mulgrave leaped from his lofty perch and offered assistance to the young Madame de Martier. Around them the day was glorious, and the dry winter heat was deliciously permeated by sea breezes. Shrubs of camellia, poinsettia, and hibiscus that graced the veranda bloomed full and aromatic in the nurturing sunlight, but Lauren scarcely noticed when she stepped down from the carriage and met Mulgrave's extended hand.

"Lauren, I hate leaving you alone like this," Georgette said. "I can stay for a while if you'd like."

"No . . . I'm fine . . . just a little shaken." Lauren's farewell was an erratic flick of the wrist as she left Georgette and padded reluctantly into the house.

In the vestibule, she ran headlong into Filene who bid her a startled, *"Bonjour, madame."* Fortunately, she encountered no one else during the seemingly endless ascent to her private quarters, for if she had, her rigid composure would have dissolved into a flood of tears.

Feminine intuition had been foolproof. She was going to have a baby. Shoving the door closed behind her, Lauren's body shook from the jar. She could still feel the force with which Roget had flung open the door that night. The room had shuddered from the impact, and the sound deafened her ears. *Baby.* The word went round and round in her head, beating against her skull like a gong. What in heaven's name would she do with a baby! Especially now when Roget—Lauren buried her face between her hands to quell the bitter reality that pounded in her head. How would she bring up a child alone?

For want of a task to occupy her restless hands, Lauren reached for a brush, one of the silver monogrammed set Roget had given her during the delirious days of their honeymoon. Her gaze lingered on the engraved initials of her name placed artistically within the de Martier trademark. Then, she had foolishly believed that he loved her. Raking the bristles hard through her curly hair, she held it extended at the end until the strands appeared almost straight, but the moment she released them, the tight curls sprung back. She envisioned Lucienne's lustrous auburn hair and imagined Roget's hands buried deep in the silken mass. Ruthlessly, Lauren raked the brush until her scalp ached, and then, her eyes brimming with tears, she surrendered to exasperation. For a fleeting second, she stared at her reflection in the mirror, then dashed the silver brush against the wall. It nicked the molding with a loud crash and plummeted to the floor.

At that moment, she developed an insatiable desire to ride. Feeling an urgent need to lose herself, she wanted to saddle Miel and move at breakneck speed across the Cul-de-Sac Plain. Or was it that she dare not recognize her real intentions? Perhaps she wanted to dislodge his seed and abort the child Roget had planted there. Abruptly, she clamped the door shut on her wicked thoughts. She would ride—she had to—there was no other way to keep the walls of this house from closing in on her.

Lauren rode far into the Cul-de-Sac, driving Miel at an unmerciful speed. When finally they had drawn to a halt, she realized that she would suffer the after effects much more than her mount. The horse rested a few seconds and snorted anxiously to move on, but her mistress could not muster the strength. As much as she had needed that pounding ride, she knew now that it had been a mistake.

Lowering herself to the ground, Lauren abandoned her onerous weight to the sturdy arms of a tree trunk. Listlessly, her head fell back and she labored to draw in a breath of the tepid air.

It was very hot on the open plain, and oddly, she could feel nothing but gratitude for the solitary mapous tree that sheltered her from the scorching sun. Why had she been so impetuous? A pregnant woman should not ride like that. Drifting away with the thought, Lauren closed her eyes and dozed, allowing sleep to blot out her faculties.

The earth beneath her rumbled, but she was deep in slumber and the movement seemed very far away. Miel pawed the sandy earth with skittish hooves, agitated by an unseen force. Lauren opened her eyes, certain that she had felt motion beneath her, a subtle movement as though the earth were shifting position. No doubt she had dreamed it. Wearily, she picked herself up, dusted her breeches, and prepared to remount. Lifting her foot into the stirrup, she dangled against the animal's side, wondering if she had sufficient strength to pull into the saddle. How she hated feeling weak—and helpless. Through sheer determination, she managed to hoist her leg over Miel's back and let her mount carry her slowly back to the house. She was not going to enjoy being pregnant.

For the second time that day, she encountered Villa de Martier's officious housekeeper, this time in the upstairs hall.

"*Madame,* are you well? Did something frighten you? You look exhausted."

Was her anguish that visible that even the housekeeper was alarmed? "No, Filene. I'm tired, that's all . . . and hungry," Lauren added as an afterthought.

"You had better lie down, *madame.*" A subtle inquiry seeped into her statement. "You've missed the midday meal, but Emmeline has made a conch stew, her Jamaican recipe, the way you like it. Why don't I bring you some? A little soup would do you good."

"That sounds enticing." Lauren felt her mouth watering already in anticipation. "I would love some."

"I'll bring it up right away," she said as she turned to leave. "You should not ride so hard, *madame.* Not in your cond—" Stifling her tongue, she never finished the word, but Lauren knew she was aware of her secret. How did she know, Lauren wondered, when she herself had just learned of it this morning? She would have to meet with Antoine soon. She only prayed that they could get to France before her condition began to show.

A soft knock at her door produced Filene, balancing a tray on which sat a steaming bowl of Jamaican conch stew. Savoring the delicious aroma as it escaped into her nostrils, Lauren attacked the bowl with a ravenous hunger, but the first few spoonfuls dulled her appetite. It did not taste like Emmeline's usual conch stew. Disappointed and assuming that her condition had influenced her taste buds, she abandoned the idea of eating and gave in to her drowsy eyelids. By the time her head touched the cool linen pillow, Lauren was asleep. Soundly, she slept through the night and into the next morning.

Considerably refreshed and a lot less hampered by fatigue, Lauren sat up and opened her eyes to a head blurred with cobwebs. Another side effect of her condition, she thought as she vowed that today she would be more sensible. She would face things squarely and not try to run from her dilemma, and the first thing to be dealt with was getting passage to France. Lauren marveled at the calm that had overtaken her along with the ability to face her precarious plight without hysteria. Famished after her night of oblivion, Lauren bathed, dressed, and hurried down to breakfast.

Entering the dining room, she caught Filene's doe eyes watching her with scrutiny. *"Bonjour, madame.* I see you're feeling better this morning."

"Oui, Merci, Filene. I am." Inclining her head toward Roget's mother, she uttered an animated, *"Bonjour, madame."*

"At last you're up," she replied, settling the china cup in its saucer. "Roget could not wake you for dinner." Pausing, her light eyes searched Lauren's face for an answer. "You've missed an alarming number of meals."

"I know, *madame,"* Lauren responded absently. Averting her attention to the pale green folds of the drapery, she studied the way it hung in columns from the cornice. Had Roget really tried to awaken her? If he had touched her, she was sure she would have known.

"I took her a portion of stew yesterday before she fell asleep," Filene chimed in with ample self-praise as she filled Lauren's coffee with warm milk. "Surely that helped some."

"It helped tremendously. The conch stew was delicious," Lauren lied. She did not have the heart to tell her that she had not eaten more than three spoonfuls of the savory mixture.

"It's not like you to be tired," the older woman continued. "I think you should see Dr. Mauriac."

"I will," Lauren agreed, turning the silverware round in her fingers. Madame de Martier was unaware that she had seen a doctor and he had confirmed her suspicions. Purposely, she had gone to an unfamiliar town because she did not want them to know, and Georgette had nearly had to bribe Mulgrave to keep him from telling Jacques that they had not gone to the orphanage but to La Coupe.

"Poor Lisa had to be carried off to the hospital this morning," Madame de Martier said.

Filene's furtive glance darted from the elder woman to the younger one, and she scurried from the room.

"Oh?" Her interest pricked, Lauren looked up. "What happened to her?"

"She was deathly ill . . . pains and convulsions in her stomach. We have not heard the results. I presume Dr. Mauriac will contact us soon."

"What a shame," Lauren uttered. "I hope she will be all right."

After breakfast, she wandered out to the garden. The flowers and foliage were breathtakingly beautiful at this time of year. It was their last burst of life before being drowned out by the rains. Reaching down, Lauren cupped her hands about a snow white camellia and buried her nose in its center to savor the heady aroma. When it bloomed again, she would be gone. Having grown fond of this exotic tropical country, it would be sad to leave it, but what choice did she have? Roget would soon be rid of her.

"Roget." She muttered his name, and a lonely tear wound

its way down her cheek. She tarried a while longer and then walked on, up the triple flight of steps, across the veranda, and back into the cool shade of the house.

At the rear entrance, Old Jean shuffled to the door with a message for Madame de Martier, and Marie went scurrying to her parlor bearing the note. On her way from the parlor, the young maid intercepted Lauren's path. *"Madame,"* she said, her curtsey appearing skittish and agitated, "Madame de Martier want to see you right away."

"Merci, Marie." Gathering her soft pleated skirt, she went quickly to join her mother-in-law.

"This is from Dr. Mauriac." The older woman spoke with measured caution while Lauren waited anxiously for her to continue. "They have kept Lisa in the hospital; she's in critical condition."

Lauren released her bated breath. "What's the matter with her?"

"Dr. Mauriac says poison."

"Poison?" Astonished, Lauren repeated the word. "Who would poison Lisa?"

"He believes she may have tried to kill herself."

"Commit suicide?"

"The ironic thing is that she did not take enough to kill herself, merely enough to make herself very ill."

Lauren's honey-hued complexion drained to an ashen gray at the dire news. She left the parlor.

The entire household remained in an uproar of repressed excitement. Servants whispered among themselves in hushed voices, their expressions fearful of Lisa's poisoning. The family, meaning the men, dealt with it in private discourse behind closed doors, and the matter was only vaguely discussed with Lauren.

Approaching Roget about the attempted suicide was like gathering pumpkin seeds from a calabash.

"Have you learned anything more about Lisa?" she asked. Her inquiry was born of genuine concern.

"She ate something that she shouldn't have," Roget replied flatly. "Whether on purpose or by accident, only she knows," he added, shrugging the muscles in his shoulders. "She will recover. We can be thankful for that."

The hubbub of discussions and whisperings continued through the night. Seeing that there would be no chance to steal a moment alone with Antoine, Lauren retired to bed.

By morning the household had calmed to a normal buzz of activity. The servants went about their daily chores, assured that the young maid would recover. Adrift in her own thoughts as she reached the top of the stairwell, Lauren failed to hear the whispering and stealthy motions that emanated from Reinette's bedchamber. She was in her own room, half dressed, when she heard the voices suddenly bellow and then quiet again. Alarmed, she pulled a skirt on over her shirtwaist blouse, shoved her feet into the riding boots because they were the closest at hand, and rushed into the hall. Unmistakably, it was Gaston's baritone voice that blared from behind the closed door. A tremor shook the house, but no one seemed to notice. Lauren did notice, and the tremor sent a small chill of premonition snaking through her spine, but the ensuing argument diverted her attention.

"What you did was ridiculously careless! You could have destroyed me, my name, my family. I've warned you to be careful." It was not the mocking, derisive tone he employed with her, Lauren thought, but one of pure anger. The voice that answered him was Filene's.

"There is no time to be cautious! Nothing else has worked. Your brother's son will inherit everything that should rightfully belong to *my* son—*our* son."

"My brother's son," he repeated curiously. "Roget has no son."

"He may soon have one," she added. "She's pregnant." Her tone made Lauren aware of the desperation.

"Pregnant!" He laughed. "How in hell could she be pregnant? Roget has not slept with her in months."

"Then it was an immaculate conception." Filene's inflection reeked with sarcasm. "Believe me, she's pregnant. Women have a way of knowing these things. I would wager a bet that her husband doesn't yet know about the blessed event. And you are not aware of your brother's every move."

By the tone of her voice, Lauren could imagine the

haughty tilt of her head and the doe eyes that lifted toward the ceiling.

"No one wants to be rid of her more than I do." Calmer now, Gaston spoke in a tongue thick with malice. "But what you did was dangerous."

Lauren gasped as her heart sank to her stomach.

"My son is going to inherit what is rightfully his!" Filene screeched, her words piercing like a siren. "What other choice was there? How was I to know that the bitch would not eat the stew? She said she was hungry. I never thought when I sent Lisa to gather the tray that the girl would finish it. If I had thought—"

"*If* you had thought . . . Therein lies the problem. You never consider consequences. But then, you have nothing to lose. Your attempt at abortion could have cost me my family name."

Lauren recalled the bitter taste of the conch stew on her tongue and the cobwebs in her head when she awakened. She drew a deep, ragged breath and expelled it before allowing her brain to conclude the obvious. Filene had meant to kill her baby.

"I had to act quickly; time was growing short," Filene went on frantically. "I could not allow her to have that child. It would mean our son losing everything. He would be a pauper."

"Still, your recklessness was inexcusable."

"When Yves died, I was certain that my son would eventually be heir to his father's fortune. The two *were* half brothers. With Antoine odd as a duck and Roget reluctant to marry Lucienne de Luynes, there didn't seem much chance of another heir coming into the family, but then Roget arrived home with a bride. There was something about her—an earthy, sensuous nature lurked beneath those Paris gowns. The same lusty passion that burns in Roget. I knew it wouldn't be long before she produced heirs, and I couldn't allow that to happen." Her voice rose to an agitated contralto and then fell back to a hush. "Even the *ouanga* packet did not prevent her from housing his seed. It worked for a while, then she found it."

"So, that fiasco was your doing? I had thought you were above such things," he scoffed, his tone grounded in bitter derision. "After everything I've given you, you are no further advanced than the workers in the fields." With a thunder of sudden movement, he demanded vehemently, "How many more of these tricks did you try?"

In a hushed, frightened voice, she replied, "Only one."

"And what was that?"

"The vodun ceremony." Filene's tone remained agitated, and Lauren could imagine the woman's ebony skin cringing from the threat of his cruel hands.

"That was utterly foolish!" His powerful voice bellowed through the corridor. "It only drew attention to Reinette." Lauren shuddered at the strength of his wrath. "Heed what I say, woman, and heed it well," he growled. "I forbid any more *ouanga* packets, vodun spells, or the like in this house. Practice your primitive beliefs elsewhere. Madame Lauren will be dealt with in due time."

"In what way?" she demanded furiously.

"Leave that to me!" he snapped. "I forbid any more of your witchcraft in this house. I will not have my family name jeopardized under any circumstances."

"My concern is my son!" she cried. "You care more for your precious family name than you do for our son."

"Keep in mind that if you continue with these absurdities and our relationship becomes common knowledge, I will dismiss you from this household."

"How dare you threaten me when my child's life is at stake!"

"I'll do more than threaten you," he raged with mounting fury. "Don't force my hand, Filene!"

"What will you do?" she shrieked. "Have me suffer a mysterious accident far from the house like you did your wife, so that your precious name will remain unscathed?"

Paying little heed to the desperation that triggered her outburst, Gaston replied calmly, "At least I know better than to deal with such things personally."

"You would really do it, wouldn't you?" Her voice faltered, astonished, as if she had just realized his lack of compassion for her.

"Yes, I would," he said flatly, emitting no emotion. "Roget already suspects the relationship between us . . . He has for years. After I married Reinette, he scoured the orphanages searching for the child he was sure you abandoned. He knows about the boy; he knows about us. My brother has too much damn brain power for his own good, but there is one redeeming thing about Roget. His sense of honor will keep him from talking . . . at least until he has proof. If anyone else finds out . . ." A long pause hung in the air, and Gaston, collecting his thoughts, grinned contemptuously. "There are other ways to get rid of her. She's not worth risking murder."

"You risked murder with your wife," Filene retorted.

"I had no choice. She found out about us and threatened to expose me."

"You, who had your own wife murdered, have the audacity to look down your nose at my primitive beliefs. You bastard! You've never loved anyone," she ranted, her voice torn with hatred. "Not your wife, not me, nor our son."

"I loved Yves," he replied with an overwhelming sadness.

"Yvone is your son, too," Filene said bitterly.

"Yves was my rightful son, my heir."

"Your son from a wife that you detested! You loved him only because he was the child of your aristocratic wife, who brought prestige to the family. I want for my child what she would have had for hers."

"That's impossible!" His fury climbed to a deafening pitch. "Yvone is a bastard. He can never carry the de Martier name or inherit its property." There was a loud bang, like that of a heavy hand striking a table. "I will not allow it."

"You allowed him to be born. You allowed his mother to be your whore for twelve years, but you will not allow him to inherit your priceless name. Curse you! I hope the zombies dig up your grave!"

A sound of spitting and the sharp echo of a hand hitting naked flesh rang through the air. Filene let out a long shriek of pain. A flurry of violent movement burst from the room, and the servants who had heard the commotion converged on the hallway. Without being aware of her motion, Lauren had edged steadily closer and was now two doors away. The servants gasped in horror to hear the sounds and voices escaping from behind the mysterious locked door, their primitive imaginations conjuring up every sort of hideous explanation.

Madame de Martier emerged from her parlor, and grasping the folds of her peignoir in one hand, she rapidly ascended the stairs to the second floor. Rushing along the corridor, brusquely bypassing the scattering forms of her maids, she paused next to Lauren.

"What on earth is the matter? What is all the disturbance? Why are the servants standing around in the hall?" she inquired of her daughter-in-law. "First, it seemed that the house was shaking, and now I hear screaming."

"I don't know, *madame,*" Lauren whispered so that the servants could not hear her alarm. "Gaston and Filene seem to be arguing in there . . . in Reinette's room." Lauren inclined her head toward the locked door. In an instant, the brass knob was jerked round, and the door parted midway as Filene struggled to exit, but her red silk skirt was snatched from the door back into the room, not to emerge again. Angry voices trumpeted once more.

"Yvone is your heir!" she shouted.

"I have no heir! My son is dead!"

"But you have another son," she pleaded. "Why should the son of your mulatto wife have inherited everything? You didn't want her—only her son."

"He was my heir," he repeated with angry arrogance.

"Her son would have inherited everything, and our son would have had to scratch his way through life even though they were born of the same father." Her voice cracked, agitated by fury.

"I would have provided for him."

"How? A measly pittance thrown his way each year from the income of Yves's plantation?"

"There is no need to discuss it now," he said, his face wrenched with remorse. "My son is dead."

"Your son is dead because I willed him to die!" She flung the words at him viciously.

"What do you mean, you willed him to die?" Gaston's eyes glared venom.

Insatiable curiosity drew Lauren closer to the half-open door until she had full view of the irate pair.

"Just that." Filene lifted her head and laughed haughtily, taunting him as she flirted with danger, all the while her soul seething with the malice of revenge. "You sneer at my primitive beliefs, but they bring results. Your son died because I put a spell on him. Had he been strong willed and stubborn like your brother's wife, perhaps he would have survived, but he was young and vulnerable. The *goofer* dust worked easily." Her derisive laughter held a lust for revenge. "My son will get what is his."

"Over my dead body!" Gaston lunged at her with a vengeance bent on destruction. His huge hands closed around her throat and left her gasping for air. As Lauren shrank with fright at the scene, a tumultuous tremor rumbled the earth beneath them and Villa de Martier trembled violently atop its foundation. The stone walls vibrated as if the massive structure were merely a dollhouse being fluttered in the wind.

Servants screamed and clung to balustrades, their eyes bulging with fear of the encroaching unknown. Lauren and Madame de Martier clutched the doorjambs for support. Heavy potted plants overturned, glass bottles plummeted from dressing table tops, and furniture slid inch by inch across the floor. The mansion seemed to be breaking loose from the ground.

The tremor ceased, and Lauren's gaze sped to Reinette's bedchamber. The door gaped wide, exposing an opulent room that stood in shambles. Filene's limp body crumpled to the floor. He had strangled the breath from her. His hands still clutching her throat, he squeezed mercilessly until he had choked every ounce of life from her defiant body. Gaston rose to his feet. Staring down at her, his dark eyes bore the glassy, vacant look of a person who had lost his mind. He burst from the room half crazed, nearly sending Lauren to the floor as she stood stunned in the doorway.

Lucienne stretched her arms over the thick carpet of grass, her auburn head rustling the leaves that had become her pillow. Her gray eyes watched Roget as he lay propped on one elbow, toying with a blade of grass. A slow smile spread over her lips. Reaching up, she coiled a hand around his neck, and letting her fingers play in his crisp raven hair, she pulled his body on top of hers. Cringing at the thought that she was capable of seeking his pleasures with such brazenness, she plunged ahead, her senses driven by a desire that over the past months had festered to a fever. Her efforts to entice him had failed miserably, and disregarding that one aborted attempt, they had not made love at all since she had been home.

Her parted mouth offered him eager invitation. Tasting the sweetness that she put before him like a feast, Roget's lips plundered hers for a long, delicious moment that sent the blood racing through her veins and waves of desire lapping at her loins. But then, severing the contact, Roget rolled onto his back. "Not here," he said.

"Oh, Roget, *tonnerre!*" Lucienne grit her teeth and grunted in a paroxysm of bitter frustration as her beige skin flushed red with humiliation. "Not here! Not there! I wonder if you are even capable?" Her words spilled out in desperation.

"Our timing has been bad," he replied calmly, thinking that he might have questioned the truth himself if not for his abominable performance with Lauren.

Lucienne flung her head away, pursing her lips in an indignant pout. She should have stopped seeing him months ago, she knew that, but she could not bring herself to let him go. Not yet. Beside the fact that her aunt and uncle would be livid if they knew, she was beginning to see that she was making a colossal fool of herself.

Retrieving his panama, Roget propped the straw hat over his face to shut out the sun and closed his eyes to shut out the assault of his rampant thoughts.

Minutes passed in deafening silence, and then a thunderous rumble quaked the earth beneath them, vibrating through their bodies like an echo. Alarmed, Lucienne bolted up with a start, an array of leaves still clinging to her sleek, upswept hair.

"Did you feel that?" she asked. Getting no reply, her focus darted anxiously to Roget, only to meet with his hat. Lucienne tipped the brim up with her finger. How easily he fell asleep in her presence, she mused. There was a time . . . She sighed in resignation.

"Roget," she whispered. Letting her fingers caress the hard, muscled contour of his shoulder, she shook him. "Roget!"

His dark eyes flew open with the same intensity that had propelled her to an upright position. "Oh, it's you," he groaned. "I thought it was a dream."

"Roget, there was a . . . I felt a strange rumbling several minutes ago."

"Then I was not dreaming?" Raising himself to rest again on an elbow, he perused her intently from beneath the tightly knit frown of his brows, but the perusal was just that, a vacant stare from which his mind had fled. "I felt it, too," he said absently.

Another rumble rocked the ground, and they felt the earth undulate beneath them as if it were a swell of waves at sea. Lucienne saw an inscrutable haze of apprehension cloud Roget's face.

"Lauren . . . the house . . . ," he muttered, unaware that his unconscious thoughts had escaped his lips. But Lucienne *was* aware.

Roget leapt up, nearly dragging her from the bed of grass and set her on her feet. "I have to go back," he said, blurting his thoughts in a steady stream of effusion. "Get on your horse. Ride straight to Villa Condé as rapidly as you can." Lucienne pulled herself free of his grasp and headed toward her horse. "Will you be all right alone?" he called after her.

"I think so," she retorted. "I came here alone."

Roget noticed the haughty tilt of her head and the decidedly loose sway of her stride as she moved from him. No doubt his abrupt dismissal had upset her, but there was no time for amenities. Swinging his lithe frame into the saddle, Roget turned Bleu de Roi to the opposite road and raced toward home.

The raucous rumbling began again, accompanied by low booming noises that resembled distant thunder. Snapping bricks and tearing walls rang loud in Lauren's ears, and her eyes inadvertently followed the rippling sound of wood being torn apart. Gaston was midway on the staircase when the burnished mahogany severed from the second floor balustrade and hung suspended in space. The others were trapped on the floor above. Lauren drew a ragged breath as her heart sank with the weight of a lead ball to her stomach.

Marie, along with two upstairs maids who had been huddled in the corridor, scrambled for the staircase, attempting to salvage their last link with the ground, but the gaping space spread wider than their reach and sent two of them hurtling to the floor below. Their lifeless bodies crashed, broken and twisted, against the marble floor of the vestibule. "Oh, Lord," Marie cried, her eyes rolling back in her head. "It's the Judgment Day!" Managing to retain her foothold on the edge of the severed floor, she stumbled back against the wall where she fell into a heap of catatonia. She sat wide-eyed and motionless, the involuntary trembling the only sign of life in her young body.

Seeing the two bodies below, Madame de Martier let out a feeble scream and clutched Lauren's neck with the grip of hysteria.

"Roget . . . Where is Roget?" she sobbed, her voice sliding on the rim of senseless panic. In her fear, the older woman had developed an Amazonian strength, and her weight hung like a noose around Lauren's neck.

The echo of pounding hooves resounded through the earth, growing stronger and more intense amidst the rumble, until they were clearly audible from the other sounds of devastation and then came abruptly to a halt. In one desperate motion, Gaston jumped from the wreckage and landed on hands and knees in the vestibule below. Roget, arriving just seconds before Antoine, found the main door hopelessly wedged between a warped and twisted jamb, and aiming every ounce of his strength against the barrier, he forced it ajar. The heavy portal swung open, straining on its hinges. Face-to-face with Gaston, Roget's position in the doorway posed a major threat to his brother's flight for freedom.

Focusing a wild-eyed glare on Roget's searching expression, with the assumption that he would attempt to restrain him, Gaston's crazed mind aimed a powerful fist at his brother's jaw. With lightning-fast reflexes, Roget ducked and avoided the deadly blow. His quick action sent Gaston reeling forward, struggling to gain his balance, and Roget recalled what he had known since they were boys. Speed and agility had always been his best weapons against Gaston. What his size gained him in power, he lost in ease of movement.

Walking straight into the fight and using no means to protect himself, Antoine caught the full impact of the next blow. In a frenzy of motion, the massive man propelled both fists, aiming at nothing and striking anything in his path. Antoine foolishly walked headlong into that path.

"Antoine, get back!" Roget cried. "Can't you see he's mad? You would have to be a fool to go against a man in his condition . . . Those fists are worse than *cocomacque* clubs."

Antoine ignored the warning. It was if he were proving to himself that he was not afraid. "I've lived in fear of him for too long," he said. "It must end."

Again and again he moved toward the hated brother, unable to strike even one blow and seemingly oblivious to the pain of those that he took. Finally, the deadly clubs pummeled him to the ground. Blood trickled from the corners of his mouth, and one eye had swollen to a pulpy slit.

"The bastard will blind him," Roget thought aloud. "And Antoine doesn't have the sense to protect himself."

Stepping quickly into Gaston's range to shield Antoine from further attack, Roget smashed an irate fist square into the side of his brother's jaw and another flat up under his chin. His head snapping back against his collar, the elder brother stumbled backward. Regaining his equilibrium, his powerful fist shot at Roget, but moving with rapid-fire speed, Roget lunged away from the full force of it. Still, he felt it clip the side of his face.

With Gaston's attention once more on Antoine, Roget moved in behind him and manacled the deadly weapons by locking his own arms under his brother's armpits and bracing them against his thick neck. The maneuver restrained him momentarily as he struggled to throw Roget from his back, but as an aftershock rocked the wavering structure, their clashing bodies were flung across the floor. Gaston broke free, and the force sent Roget reeling against the door frame.

Lauren looked on, horrified as the shirt on Roget's back ripped to shreds beneath the strain and laid bare tense, angry flesh that gleamed with perspiration. Free from his grasp, Gaston fled through the gaping door.

At last feeling his pain, Antoine dragged his battered body to his feet. Just as Roget had recovered his foothold with the ground, another giant tremor rocked the house, uprooting it from the base. Jacquard-upholstered chairs slid over the floor and smashed to bits as they met with walls and pieces of heavier furniture. The mansion shook, its quoins bursting at the seams. Antoine was hurled against a pillar, while Roget, thrown by the impact of an armchair that slammed into his leg, employed total strength just to remain upright. In the ensuing struggle, they had been oblivious to the surrounding disaster, but no longer menaced by Gaston, Roget's mind had begun to assess the hopelessness of their situation. His mother clung to Lauren with a strangling grip, and she rallied bravely under the weight of her burden. As Roget looked up, Lauren gazed down, and his eyes met hers for the barest whisper of a moment.

The tremor ceased, but the aftershocks ripped through the house, section by section, crashing giant blocks of it into piles of rubble. Primitive chants mingled with screams as superstitious servants fled from every corner of the crumbling structure. In their eerie way of calculating things, the earthquake was evidence of God's displeasure.

Lauren read Roget's expression like a reflection in a mirror and knew that time was running out. The crystal chandelier that dominated the vestibule swayed dangerously to and fro. Ornate cornices and chunks of plaster ceiling showered them like hailstones in a storm, filling the air with suffocating clouds of dust. Furiously waving a hand before her face, Lauren fought to clear the air in front of her. Suddenly, there was a skin-crawling tear, and a wooden beam broke loose and crashed down upon the two women, striking the elder in the back of the head. Her grip on Lauren's neck faltered and grew slack as Lauren struggled to hold her. With one loud moan, she slumped to the floor at Lauren's feet. The falling timber had gouged a deep gash in the back of her skull, from which her blue blood oozed profusely. Lauren stared at the limp body, her limbs immobile, her hands still clutching her mother-in-law's peignoir. Disaster, it seemed, played no favorites.

Her sons witnessed the near fatal blow, both faces contorted in agony. "How badly is she hurt?" Roget's voice rose through the dust, but Lauren could not hear. Her senses were paralyzed along with her body.

"Lauren!" he shouted in desperation. Shielding his eyes with his hand, Roget attempted to look up. Still, she did not move.

"Lauren!" His tone grew louder and more harsh. "Can you hear me?"

His voice melted her frozen senses and she was jolted from the stupor. Her gaze traveled to the floor below, and she saw her husband there pleading with her, his shirt in shreds, his breeches and boots buried beneath a layer of dust. The carefully sculptured hair had caught the fine mist in the air, leaving him white haired like Old Jean.

"Lauren!" His voice rang in her ears. "How badly is my mother hurt?"

At last she gained comprehension. "I—I don't know . . ."

She hesitated, glancing down at the body sprawled across her feet.

"Is . . . is she breathing?" He had difficulty phrasing the words. Slowly, Lauren crouched beside the lifeless form. Probing the head gently with her fingers, she pulled back a handful of blood. Blood spilled in a trickling stream from the base of her skull, while her mother-in-law's chestnut hair lay in a pool of red liquid that threatened to drown her. Lauren's eyes searched the area for something to cover the gaping cut, but she found nothing.

"How is she?" Roget demanded again, this time the sound of desperation distorting his voice.

"She's badly hurt . . . There's a gash in her head . . . She's losing a lot of blood."

"Is she breathing?" His tone was anxious—restless in a way she had never heard him.

"I think so," she said, glancing downward again to be sure of her diagnosis. "She appears to be unconscious."

"You'll have to revive her. We can't possibly get her down in that condition."

"Revive her?" Lauren cried out in frustration. "I can't even stop the bleeding!" Her empty hand spread in a gesture of defeat.

"Lauren, you will have to try," Roget pleaded. For the first time, Roget needed her for something, and the circumstances were too futile to bring satisfaction. "Lauren, listen to me!" he bellowed through the thunderous commotion, his voice commanding her full attention. "Can you get to *Maman*'s room?" Lauren nodded vaguely, not certain if she had the strength to accomplish what he was asking. "Somewhere in there she kept smelling salts. Try to find them."

"She keeps them in the little drawer beneath the dressing table," Antoine said, joining in.

Lauren rose from the floor and gently retrieved her feet from the weight of her mother-in-law's inert body. The riding boots she had pulled on so hastily were soaked through with the precious liquid, and the hem of her skirt was no longer ice blue but blood red. Using her arms to shield herself, Lauren made her way to Madame de Martier's bedchamber in the east wing of the house. While her hands were kept occupied, clearing the air in front of her face, bits of gray plaster landed in her hair and buried themselves in the dark curly mass. Dodging from one side of the hall to the other, she narrowly escaped the impact of a falling timber.

Through grotesquely battered lips, Antoine turned to Roget and asked, "Do you have any idea how we are going to get them down . . . before we're all buried alive?"

"No. None whatsoever. But we have to find a way." There was a pause and a devastating silence as Roget stared fixedly at the wreckage. Finally, he said, "Get some rope from the stables, and bring Old Jean . . . and Paul if they're around. We will need help."

Lauren entered the bedchamber, still weaving from side to side. A hole yawned wide in the ceiling where the plaster had fallen onto the bed, reducing the elegant canopy to broken posts and torn fabric. The room's furniture had been thrown to one side, barricading the dressing table six layers deep against the wall. Drawers lay strewn across the floor, the expensive contents spilling out like coffee from an overflowing cup. Linen handkerchiefs, fine lace nightgowns, and French underwear lay draped about the furniture as if it had been discarded on a junk heap.

Lauren had not the vaguest notion how she would reach the smelling salts. She would have to move six pieces of furniture. Her task was impossible! But if she failed, Roget's mother would die.

On hands and knees she climbed over the broken bed. Chunks of concrete tore through her skirt and cut sharply into her knee, causing her to wince in pain. With fabric burns searing her bruised knuckles, she hauled the draperies from her path and gave one good push to the chaise lounge, moving it enough for her slender body to squeeze around. She heaved loose beams and fallen bricks until a spell of dizziness made her unsteady, and giving in to human frailty, Lauren was compelled to rest.

Determined to go on, she faced the last and most difficult obstacle. The heavy armoire lay wedged next to the dressing table, making it impossible for her to reach the drawer. She pushed the ponderous piece of furniture, but it did not budge. How could she possibly move it? She doubted that even Gaston would have been able to move it. Giving up to defeat, she had just leaned her body dejectedly against the armoir when another tremor rocked the house. The furniture shifted position and slid across the floor as though it had no more weight than fixtures in a dollhouse. Lauren clung to the heavy chest for support, but that, too, moved. The vibrating ceased, but it was moments before Lauren realized that the elusive drawer was no longer imprisoned, but set free and sprung open. As she reached into the boxlike enclosure, her fingers met with broken perfume bottles and pools of aromatic liquid that dripped silently on the remnants of the carpet. Then her anxious eye spied the violet blue bottle clinging to the corner. That must be it!

Nimble fingers plucked the small bottle from the drawer and deposited it safely in her pocket. On the way out she stooped to grab a handful of the linen handkerchiefs, and her mission accomplished, Lauren scrambled from the room.

The crystal pellets on the chandelier jangled noisily as Lauren picked her way along what remained of the corridor. Approaching the west wing, she felt the tear as the glittering mass broke loose from its perch and crashed to the floor below. Her hands flew to her face and covered it in horror as she watched Roget leap away from the thundering crash and shield his gray head behind folded arms. Splinters of glass flew everywhere. Millions of diamond-cut pellets whirled through the air, piercing every obscure corner, and then settled to form a sea of shimmering, shattered crystal.

A sharp cracking sound echoed off the walls, and when Lauren could again focus her eyes, the floor connecting the east wing to the west had split in two, leaving her and Madame de Martier separated by a gaping space. Roget looked up at his mother sprawled prostrate over the edge of the floor. The anguish in his look stung like the thrust of a blade. For a moment, his gaze remained fixed, and then he dragged it away, despair shrouding his features.

The villa was disintegrating piece by piece. Except for that small section where Lauren and Madame de Martier were trapped, the third story had already collapsed into the second, and Roget's brain comprehended what his heart was not yet ready to acknowledge. The wide gap separating the two women made it impossible for him to reach them both in a single maneuver, and there was not time for a second attempt. No sooner had he formulated the thought than another tremor erupted, sending the remainder of the west wing crashing into a pile of opulent rubble. While parts of the floor beneath her feet crumbled away, Lauren clung in desperation to the last remaining beam and watched motionless as Reinette's Marie Antoinette bed landed, smashed and battered, atop the pile.

Antoine rushed through the open door, his arms weighted down with ropes and a large iron hook. "Roget, the stables are a mountain of rubble. The horses are loose, running wild. Old Jean is nowhere to be found."

Roget's glance shot from Antoine to his mother and then to Lauren. Lauren felt the icy fingers that grabbed her spine, and she knew that Miel had been one of those caught in the havoc. Without warning, Bleu de Roi reared against the archway and galloped through the open door.

"Bleu de Roi is loose!" Antoine shouted. Dropping the hook, he lunged for the reins. The black stallion reared back, lashing out with his front feet. Large, limpid eyes were pools of reflecting terror as he snorted through flaring nostrils.

"Down boy, down!" Roget soothed him, talking the animal into submission. Responding to the gentle strokes against his side, the horse allowed his master to catch the reins and lead him outside. Tethering the frantic animal to a part of the balustrade that had not yet fallen to disaster, Roget came face-to-face with the crucial moments that remained.

As he made his way back to the vestibule, Roget studied the precariously weakened condition of that portion of the second floor that still stood. His mother's arm dangled listlessly over the ledge, hanging like a rag doll in the vast gaping space. Now and then, there was a twitch of movement, but for the most part she was unconscious. Blood still oozed from the wound in her head.

"We must get them down from there," Roget said, thinking aloud.

"How?" Antoine replied. As his brother's eyes clouded in thought, he felt the stab of his futile response.

Brusquely grabbing the rope Antoine had circled over his

shoulder, Roget knotted it around the double-pronged hook. Flinging the heavy iron claw upward, he was able to propel the weighted rope to the second floor. Trusting that the hooks had clawed their way into the wooden cross-beams, he yanked it to test its strength, and when he did, the rope came crashing back to the floor. In desperation, he flung it up again, only to have the metal come crashing back, bringing with it chunks of weakened concrete.

"Tonnerre!" he cried, his fists tightening at his sides. While his voice cursed the bitterness of frustration, he realized the hopelessness of the task.

Antoine heaved aside fallen bricks and broken furniture, attempting to clear a path for them through the debris, but without a second's warning, an ear-splitting rumble reverberated through the lull, and their home caved in on top of them. Draperies fell into gas lamps, igniting fires that choked the air with smoke. Paintings plunged from walls, and windows shattered as doorjambs and window frames collapsed.

Sputtering and coughing through lungs that were filled with smoke and shielding their faces with bleeding arms, the two de Martier men stumbled blindly through the holocaust. Forced to abandon the futile attempts to rescue his mother, Roget ducked beneath the archway to avoid being buried alive himself. There was little time left. He could not save them both. A force greater than his own was in control. Lifting his focus to the floor above him, Roget's face bore the expression of a man about to make a heart-rending decision.

For Lauren it seemed like the end. She thought of her unborn child and the love for Roget that had brought her to this gruesome death. If she had not wanted him so desperately, she would still be in France with Claude, Pierre, and Bertrand and not here, facing her death. Lauren felt her throat swell. A tear escaped and trickled over her cheek as she realized she would not see them again.

Baring a strength she had not known she possessed, her arms clung, paralyzed, to a lone wooden beam. She imagined that she would die calmly. There was nothing to live for anyway. Her baby—what should it live for? To be a poor orphan and black in France was a fate worse than death. But as she lingered there, tasting death, Lauren knew she was not ready to die. She wanted very much to live, but her life was in God's hands.

"Lauren, you'll have to jump." She heard Roget's voice penetrate her stupor. "In a few seconds the house will be leveled to the ground—there is no other way. I can't get to you!" Through the crashing pillars and the cacophony of confusion, she wondered if it were another of his deceptions. "Lauren, jump," he pleaded, but she clung futilely to the wavering beam. She imagined throwing herself into space and then watching him step back, deliberately allowing her body to fall, crumpled amidst the wreckage. He could say it was an accident. In the midst of the devastation, who would doubt his word?

"Jump, Lauren! For God's sake, jump! It's your only chance," he pleaded. "I will catch you!" Lifting his outstretched arms, he gestured for her to save herself, but Lauren stubbornly refused to move.

Shock after shock wrenched the walls. Bricks and timbers thundered down through the ceiling like hail on Judgment Day. And judging from the screams of hysteria, the servants believed this to be it. Unable to withstand the constant, trembling agitation, what was left of the east wing swung in space as if supported from above by a single wisp of invisible thread. As their mother lay on the edge, wounded and unconscious, the thread suddenly snapped: Villa de Martier buckled to the ground.

From its grand, high, lofty perch, it went down layer upon layer, as though the knees had given way beneath it. Madame de Martier's sons looked on in helpless frustration as it took their mother with it. Roget's breath locked in his chest. Rigidly clenching his jaw, he felt as if his heart had been ripped from his bosom. Turning away from the scene, he lowered his eyes, and bridging an open hand over his forehead, he stifled the tears that swelled behind them. Antoine merely let the tears trickle over his swollen face.

As Lauren had learned, Haitians were a proud people. Roget would face what he had to, and if she had learned anything about him at all, he would do it without flinching. Even Antoine had acquired a strength of character that astounded her.

The air exploded with the hum of moans and chants pouring forth from invisible mouths. Servants ran, stumbling, from the house only to find the same devastation in the fields. A piercing scream rang through the havoc and drowned out all other sounds. Lauren shuddered. Once again, Roget's eyes were on her, pleading. Looking down, she met her husband's gaze.

"Lauren, you must jump. It's your only chance." His glance moved swiftly over the obstacles, assessing the alternatives. His sable skin covered with thick gray dust, she barely recognized him, but nothing could change his eyes.

"Lauren!" he bellowed aloud, clearly exasperated by her obstinance. Racked with a feeling of frustration that was getting the better of him, Roget had never felt so helpless. "Damn it, Lauren, come down from there! A few seconds more . . . there will be nothing left. Lauren!" he ranted in desperation. "Do you hear me?"

She had heard him, but fear forbade her to move. If she jumped, could she trust him to break her fall? *He loves Lucienne. He will be glad to be rid of me,* she thought. All of a sudden, she was dizzy, weak—everything seemed foggy.

"Lauren come to the edge of the floor. Antoine and I are both here beneath you. We'll catch you. Lauren, please . . ." His pleas trailed into dust as Lauren clung with foolhardy recklessness to the timber that supported her.

"Lauren, you have to jump." Antoine joined him. "If you don't, Roget will try to come up, and that beam will not hold his weight."

Lauren did not stir. Her arms frozen round the beam, she prayed, while the floor beneath her feet disintegrated piece by piece.

Raw fear spread over Roget's face. "I'm going up," he said as he started toward the remaining buttress. Frantically, Antoine clamped a hand on his arm to force him back.

"Roget, that won't support you," the younger brother pleaded, afraid of losing the one thing that he loved. "You'll be killed."

"I have to try," he replied. With a force born of determination, Roget yanked his arm free of his brother's grasp. Antoine struggled to hold him, and Lauren witnessed the harsh confrontation that ensued. Words shot between them like arrows as the two argued, but Lauren could hear only slurred snatches of their disagreement, and it was impossible for her to know what was being said. All at once, the voices fell to a whisper.

"Roget, you'll be killed," Antoine said with somber resignation. Roget's tone softened, and he purposely met his brother's gaze.

Roget's thoughts struck him like a hammer as he heard the words that escaped his own lips. "If she dies . . . I die, too."

Reluctantly, Antoine drew his hand away.

Heaving boulders and broken timbers, Roget trod over shattered glass and sumptuous ruin until he approached the base of the buttress.

"Roget, don't!" Antoine called after him. "It will never hold you." Ignoring the pleas, Roget propelled himself onto the winged buttress and attempted to scale its heights. If anyone could have scaled that structure, he could, but it would not have supported a mere babe much less a six-foot man. Midway, the feeble column, racked by a series of endless shocks and vibrations, crumbled pitifully under his weight, and Roget was thrown savagely back to the ground. Bruised and bleeding, he lay stunned amidst the wreckage as blood stained his white shirt. Lauren and Antoine, separated by a floor, felt their hearts stop simultaneously, both thinking that he was dead.

Recovering from the shock, Roget dragged his battered body from the waste. Antoine swelled with gratitude to a higher being as he helped him to his feet. With the final buttress gone, the floor beneath Lauren's feet fractured and fell away. Seeing the nature of her death, her heart thumped frantically.

"Lauren . . . please." Roget's voice choked back the tears. But his pleas were lost to her as she stood trembling with uncertainty, her body frozen to the beam. Her final chance was to jump. This would be the end for her . . . and her baby. Roget would never know about his child. She had loved him so, and now it would end like this. But she had run out of choices.

His nerves raw with desperation, Roget watched the base

beneath her feet crumble piece by piece by piece. "Dear God . . . please don't take her from me now." As the tears streamed over his face, Roget found himself praying, and he had not prayed in a very long time.

Lauren moved to the ledge and looked down. Fear churned in her stomach, tying it in a mass of tangled knots. Beads of cold sweat broke out on her forehead, causing her to shiver. Her clothes, soaked with blood, dust, and perspiration, stuck to her body as if they were glued. Hovering on the edge of the rapidly disintegrating floor, Lauren labored to conjure up the courage that would propel her body into space. In that split second, as she stood perched on the ledge, ready to fling herself into the air, her eye caught sight of an article of clothing that seemed very familiar. Familiar, because lying atop the heap of broken furniture that had once housed Reinette's belongings, Lauren recognized her peach nightgown.

Roget and Antoine stood beneath her with as strong a foothold as providence would allow. Questions whirled round in her crowded brain, but there was little chance to decipher any of them. Lauren closed her eyes and lunged, feet first, from the crumbling partition, expecting not to open them again. Instead, she met with two pairs of outstretched arms, the impact of her fall flattening their well-muscled bodies to the ground. Opening her eyes to what she assumed must be death, Lauren looked up and stared into Roget's face and realized that she was most definitely alive. He had not let her die.

Roget struggled to his feet, her limp, pliant form filling his arms. As his own body took the weight of her plunge, he was oblivious to the leg being crushed beneath him. But instantly, the jabbing needles of numbness pierced his senses, making him aware of the injured limb. Limping, as he heeded the searing pain in his right leg, Roget cast one long glance toward the mountain of rubble where his mother lay buried, and then drawing away, he carried Lauren through the destruction to his horse.

Old Jean hobbled to the door, accompanied by several field hands in various stages of hysteria. "Monsieur Roget, they say the mountain has slid into the plains." The old man gasped, taking short, jagged breaths. "Their houses is covered with mud. They has nowhere to go."

"Tell them to go to the main warehouse. I will meet them there as soon as I can."

"There's one more thing." The old man hesitated, thinking that what he had to say could only add to his burden. "Some workers is trapped underneath the rocks. We need your help to break them loose. With my crippled leg, I can't be of no use," he said, his weather-beaten hand rubbing the injured knee.

"Where are they?" Roget questioned with concern.

"Show us where they are," Antoine volunteered, following close behind the withered old liveryman.

Vaguely, Lauren was aware of lying on the rumbling ground while Roget helped to rescue his field hands. Wails and moans stung in her ears, but it was difficult for her to know whether they wailed in pain or in terror. And then, strong arms lifted her and hoisted her onto Bleu de Roi's back. Awkwardly, guided by the stiffness in his right leg, Roget swung himself into the saddle. Lauren felt his arms close around her as his hands took the reins. A wave of blackness swept over her, and she was drowned in oblivion.

Chapter

25

Filmy columns of lawn billowed and fluttered, tangled and then unwound again, gently propelled by the afternoon breeze. Lauren stirred in the strange bed, rolled over, and parted her eyelids. Where was she? There was no noise, no dust. It was quiet and peaceful. Perhaps she had died. But as her blurred vision grew clearer and her senses more astute, she realized that the white spirals she saw were not clouds, but curtains. About to sit up, she heard the door click open.

"Bonjour, madame. We meet again," Dr. Mauriac said, bowing his head slightly. "It seems I've arrived none too soon. I don't want you out of bed just yet, not before morning." Lauren leaned back into the pillows. At least his was a familiar face.

After taking her pulse and examining the dilation in her eyes, he said, "There are some anxious visitors waiting to see you. Do you feel up to company?"

"I suppose so," Lauren replied, her words tinged with uncertainty.

Moving toward the door, he pushed it ajar. "Madame Deffand, you may go in now." Georgette rushed through the open door, barely able to contain her grief, but determined not to upset her guest with her own anxiety, she feigned a jovial smile.

"I was beginning to think you might sleep forever," she

teased. Seeing the opalescent eyes wide open and the honey brown shoulders propped against the pillows, Georgette breathed an obvious sigh of relief. She swept her lavender skirt aside and sat on the bed.

Lauren looked up at the concerned face, questioning its compassion. "How long have I been here?"

"Three days."

"Georgette," Lauren uttered, her fingers impaling the other woman's arm. "Roget? Antoine? Where are they?" But in that instant, she had remembered everything—the whole gruesome catastrophe. "Roget . . . is he . . .?"

"He's fine," Georgette replied. Taking Lauren's trembling hand between her own two, she added, "He and Jacques and Jacques's father rode over to Villa de Martier . . . or what's left of it . . ." Her voice caught in her throat. Grief made her pause before finishing the sentence. "They should return shortly. I expect them any minute."

"Antoine . . . isn't he with them?"

Georgette glanced at the doctor, who stood lounging in the doorway and searched his face for the proper reply. "Has something happened to Antoine?" Lauren demanded, her focus darting from one feigned expression to the other.

"No," the doctor replied, straightening his posture. "He's merely away for a few days."

"Away where?"

"We have no idea," Georgette added. "I believe he's taking care of some business for Roget."

"Madame de Martier, I shall return in the morning," the doctor broke in, flashing a handsome smile. "Until then, I want you to remain in bed. Madame Deffand, I will trust you to see that our patient eats." He pulled the door closed and left.

"Your baby?" Georgette questioned anxiously once he had gone.

"I suppose it's all right. Dr. Mauriac did not mention it."

"Perhaps he doesn't know."

Lauren shrugged indifferently and gazed down at the emerald band circling her finger.

"Lauren, isn't it time Roget knew that he's going to be a father?"

"Not yet," she said, alarmed. "I need time to think." And then, seeing the sad look in her friend's eyes, she was overwhelmed by remorse. How could she have been so unthinking? Georgette had wanted her baby so badly, and here she was, selfishly treating hers with indifference. Empathy for the other woman's loss altered her tone. "If only yours had clung to life as tenaciously as mine," she said. Clasping the consoling hand, she clung to it.

"There will be another time," Georgette smiled bravely. "I'll come back later. I must see about your dinner." She kissed each of Lauren's burning cheeks and left.

Turning her face to the wall, Lauren stubbornly dug her teeth into her lower lip, refusing to cry. In spite of everything that had happened, she was still pregnant. Another woman would have miscarried, but Roget had planted his seed deep in her womb, and nothing seemed able to destroy it. His child was determined to have life.

The stream of visitors was like a parade, and included were Jacques Deffand, his father, and even Old Jean. Everyone except Roget. He was probably shedding his grief with Lucienne. Everything was in ruin, and all he could think about was venting his lust. But why should she care? She would be gone soon. Through suppressed drops of water, she noticed the brilliant reflection of emeralds that imprisoned her finger, and her eyes burned as she attempted to sever the ring from her hand. She would not need it anymore; she should have removed it months ago. A dry sob choking her throat, she struggled to pull the jeweled band free, but it would not slide over the joint in her finger. Forced to relent, she swore that tomorrow she would find a way to remove it.

Mutton broth, boiled plantain, and poached red snapper arrived on the dinner tray that accompanied the serving maid sent to assist Lauren with her meal. Mechanically, she swallowed a meager portion of the food, barely chewing or tasting it.

"Madame, doctor say you must eat something," the girl said. On the verge of scolding when a soft rap at the door scattered her plea, the young maid ambled to the entrance and bashfully ushered Roget into the room. Then gathering the tray, she scurried like a rabbit through the open door.

Lauren sat forward, startled. She had buried any expectations of seeing him this evening. Walking toward her, his easy stride was hampered by the limp in his right leg, and he was putting considerable weight on a walking stick. His dark gaze ricocheted off her face to the slender, sinuous curves of her body.

"How do you feel?" he asked softly.

Unknowingly, Lauren drew the sheet up to her neck. "Pretty well . . . a little weak, I think."

"You ate very little. You'll not get out of bed that way."

Would it matter if she spent the rest of her life lying here? she said to herself wordlessly. But to him she replied, "I don't much feel like getting out of bed right now."

"That's not surprising," he said. "You have been through hell." Shifting his weight, he tried to ease the pain in his leg.

My love, you're hurt. Lauren heard a small voice inside of her cry out as Roget laid the silver-handled walking stick aside, flipped the tail of his frock coat back, and sat on the bed.

The clothes were definitely not his, she mused. They were the subdued classic style of an older man, and the fit was nowhere near the perfection that Roget demanded.

"You disapprove of my clothes," he said, perceiving her thoughts. He had meant it in jest, but Lauren heard the desolation that crept into his voice.

"No," she said, her bottom lip quivering with anxiety. "They're just not you."

"Thanks to Paul Deffand, I'm not naked," he replied absently, letting his thoughts rest on more imminent matters that needed his attention. He had not had a moment to consider anything so trivial as clothing, and yet he knew it had to be done.

"Was everything lost?" she questioned.

"*Oui.* Everything."

She felt the sadness that crept over him, and for a moment, he looked as if it would devour him. All of a sudden, her heart swelled and reached out to him, and her arms ached to hold him, offer him comfort, but she smothered the impulse, thinking it would be a foolish display of her longing. Swallowing hard, she asked, "Could nothing be saved?"

Roget moved his head in resignation. "If it were possible, I would have recovered my mother's body to give her a proper burial, but even that was beyond the realm of possibility. It was by the grace of God that we were able to save you."

Lauren fidgeted uneasily, her fingers playing with the quilted coverlet. She could not shake the fear that Antoine, too, was dead.

"Where is Antoine? Georgette told me he had gone to take care of business for you."

"I sent him nowhere. He left of his own accord shortly after I brought you here."

"And you're not worried about him?" she insisted, still unable to release the breath that hung in her throat. "Aren't you going to look for him?"

"Antoine is a grown man. He will do what he has to do."

Lauren leaned back, surrendering her weight to the pillows. "Gaston?" she said quizzically.

"No doubt."

Recalling the scene she had witnessed before the tremors, Lauren shuddered at the thought but felt oddly compelled to confess. "Roget, Gaston killed Filene . . . I watched him strangle her . . ."

"I know," Roget said with unexpected calm. "You were heavily sedated for two days, and you had some nightmares. You also talked in your sleep. I heard the whole sordid story."

Their eyes locked for a fleeting moment, and then the same young maid appeared at the door. "Monsieur de Martier, *madame* say that dinner is served."

Retrieving the walking stick, he rose to his feet, unable to conceal the grimace of pain that contorted his face.

"How did you injure your leg?"

"I caught my foot in a crevice," he said as his labored strides carried him from the room.

Daybreak found Lauren stronger, clearheaded, and ready to get up. Telling Roget about Filene seemed to have lifted the burden from her mind as well as her body, and she was bursting with a renewed energy. Georgette had insisted on joining her for breakfast in the room, but she had since gone, and Lauren was up, ambling about the confines of her prison. Not having noticed it before, she ran her fingers along the molding that decorated the door to an adjoining room. Roget's room, she thought. How else would he have heard her nightmares? She padded back across the carpet. Pausing to look down on the garden below, she remembered the magnificent grounds at Villa de Martier that were now in ruin. Here, the green walls, flanked with ivory Directoire furniture, seemed an indoor extension of the tropical flora outside. Sculptured roses spilled over the pale carpet, tickling like kittens beneath her bare feet.

Lauren wandered to the long bay windows that climbed from floor to ceiling, and pushed back the curtains. It must be about noon, she mused, her eyes squinting at the sun that blazed overhead. In the distance, she heard a horse gallop into the stable followed minutes later by another. Her eyes skimmed the titles of some books Georgette had left, but she could not concentrate on serious novels anymore than she could flip through fashion magazines.

Suddenly, familiar voices drew her back to the window. Glancing down again, for the nineteenth time, her sight plummeted to Roget and Lucienne. Apparently, they had been riding together. Engaged in a serious discussion, they talked for a period of time that to Lauren seemed endless. She moved from the windowpane and tried to occupy herself with the books, but it was no use. Seeing Roget and the woman he loved together was no comforting vision.

Roget turned from the grape arbor to face the irate woman who stood before him waiting for an answer. He had to say it, get it over with. "Lucienne, I *am* sorry. I never meant . . ." The words came harder than he had imagined.

Her eyes studied his ebony ones, and she knew what he would say, yet her anger melted into resignation.

"You don't have to say it," she uttered with a sigh, covering his lips with her hand. "My darling, I think I knew it before you did. I just could not bear to let you go. I watched you fall in love, and I watched you deny it."

"I do love you . . . I always will," he said. If there had

been any way to make the blow easier, any way to ease the hurt she hid behind a gracious demeanor, he would have welcomed it.

"Oui, as you would have loved a sister. I've watched you these past months; you were miserable without her. That aborted attempt at making love to me . . . you were merely going through the motions. Do you think a woman doesn't know?"

Roget bristled, feeling his sense of honor wounded. "A dilapidated cabin was hardly the place to make love to you."

She sighed and buried her face against the hardness of his chest. "Roget, you would make love to Lauren in a barn."

Once more, Lauren forced herself to read the opening paragraph. It seemed she had read it a hundred times and still she had no idea what the words said. The book might as well have been written in Japanese instead of her native French. She closed the cover and, minutes later, found herself reluctantly drawn back to the window. Approaching her illicit view of the garden, she saw the two as Adam and Eve wrapped in each other's arms. Lucienne's soft, voluptuous arms enclosed him, offering the comfort he so desperately needed, and as her head lay nuzzled against his chest, Roget pressed his face to her hair. Both appeared to be weeping.

Lauren remembered the impulse to comfort him that she had smothered, and feeling it push its way to the surface, her heart ached. She pulled away sharply. Like a green-bellied serpent, envy slithered through her soul. Fleeing to the refuge of her bed, she crawled beneath the sheets and attempted to sleep.

A soft rap disturbed the troubled sleep, and Lauren awoke in a cold sweat. "Who is it?" she inquired numbly.

"Lucienne de Luynes," said the voice behind the door.

There was a long pause. *What on earth does she want?* Lauren thought. *I can't see her now. I must be a sight!*

"I would like to speak with you a moment if I may." Her soft aristocratic voice echoed through the door.

Refusing to see her would be ill-mannered, not to mention cowardly. *"Un instant, s'il vous plaît,"* Lauren called out as she scrambled from under the sheets. Grabbing a brush, she pulled her bushy hair into an unruly pouf, pinning it in place with two combs. Reaching for the peignoir that Georgette had left on the chair, she shoved her arms in the leg-of-mutton sleeves and said, *"Entrez."*

The door opened, and Lucienne strode with grace into the room. Lauren had forgotten, perhaps purposely, how breathtaking Lucienne really was. She would never have believed such perfection, had she not stood face to face with it.

"Please sit down," Lauren said, motioning to a chair.

"How are you feeling?" she asked. She lowered herself to the seat as if there were a basket balanced on her head.

"Quite well," Lauren lied, trying to sound calm and unperturbed when it was all she could do not to scream. If she had followed her impulses, she would have torn the hair from the lady's elegantly coiffured head.

"Roget said that you had been through a frightening ordeal."

Lauren balked at how easily his name rolled off her tongue. "We both have," she replied, feeling a need to share the sympathy. "But I'm trying to put it behind me."

"Lauren . . ." Lucienne began and then dropped her gaze to the gloves in her lap.

Lauren sensed that she had something to say and was not sure how to proceed. The great lady had lost her tongue. Lauren hated herself for gloating but was unable to stop it.

"Roget has lost a great deal," she began again.

The vision of Roget in this woman's arms flashed through Lauren's memory, causing her to twist sideways in the chair.

"Please do not turn away . . . You must listen to me." Her tone was almost pleading.

"Forgive me," Lauren apologized, her hazel eyes squarely meeting the cool gray ones opposite her. "I didn't mean to be rude."

"The de Martier fortune is in his hands, and it will rest on his shoulders to carry the estate through this disaster. He's more than capable, but . . . he is going to need you."

Lauren heard the slight quiver in her voice, but ignorance

made her oblivious to the point that she was making. Uncrossing her ankles, Lucienne shifted her position and stood up. Wisps of auburn hair fell in tendrils from under her straw hat. Lauren took in the feline gray eyes that languished behind silky lashes, nearly obscured by the hat. Was it any wonder that he loved her? Could she blame Roget for wanting to possess a rare jewel?

"Why should he need me now?" she answered finally. "He never has before."

"Lauren, he needs you more than you know." Again, her tone was pleading. "All my life, I've lived in extreme luxury. I've been spoiled, I realize that, but I doubt that I could exist without it. I'm used to a grand home and many servants. I would not know how to . . ." Her voice faltered and caught in her throat. She mouthed the words, knowing full well that she would have lived with Roget in a wattle hut if he had asked her. "He needs a wife who can work beside him and help him rebuild his family's plantation, not one who would be put on a pedestal."

Lauren sprang from the chair and stalked across the room, her opalescent eyes glowing fire yellow. The nerve of her! Smothering her impulses, she drew in a slow breath and exhaled it even more slowly. "Mademoiselle de Luynes, are you attempting to tell me that you are a lady and I am not and what Roget needs at this moment is a wife who is not so much a lady?" Lauren's tone reeked acid. "Is that what you and Roget spent so many hours in the garden deciding?" Lauren moved from her abruptly, refusing to let Lucienne see the wound that dagger had carved in her heart.

Realizing she had committed a gross faux pas, Lucienne pleaded, "I didn't mean it that way."

"Roget has never, ever needed my help," Lauren flung back at her. "Why should he now? Roget has never loved anyone but you." Looking away, Lauren stared blindly through the window. Lucienne walked quietly to the door and let herself out.

Hearing the barrier between them click shut, Lauren released the hold on her temper, and her eyes sparkled with tears. Distress festered to fury. "The nerve of him!" she raved. Grinding her teeth together, she paced the floor.

What a tidy scheme they had concocted. And he had the audacity to send his mistress to convince her to comply. So he planned to use her again. Well, she would not be his workhorse!

Remembering that she had seen a bottle of oil there, Lauren tramped to the bathroom. Plunging her finger in the bottle, she pulled it out, covered with the hibiscus-scented lubricant. One pull, and the emerald band slipped from her finger. Sorely tempted to toss it out the bay window, a better idea rankled in her head, and she placed it back on her finger for safekeeping.

Roget appeared that evening, still nursing the limp in his right leg, but Lauren's rage had calmed little. It lay like a wounded jungle cat in her breast.

"Apparently, you've recovered," he said, his focus drawn to the rigidly determined contours of her mouth. Without warning, an errant thought possessed him and all he could think was that it seemed a lifetime since he had felt her lips surrender to his.

"*Oui.* I'm afraid so," she replied.

Ignoring her sardonic tone, he asked, "What did you do today?"

How she loathed polite, meaningless chatter. The words spilled from her mouth mechanically, lacking thought or emotion. "I was up for a while, but there was nothing to do, so I went back to bed. Georgette brought some books, but I did not feel much like reading."

A smile curled his lips. "Reading has always been too sedentary for you. Dr. Mauriac says that you can go downstairs tomorrow. That should please you."

His smile melted a part of her that she was determined to keep frozen. Tearing her gaze from his, Lauren poured her bound-up energy into her hands, shoving her fingers together and then apart again while the silent rage gnawed a hole through her belly. Finally she looked up at her husband. "Your mistress was here today," she said, her glare shooting sparks of fire yellow. "How dare you send her to carry your message!"

Roget cringed at her spiteful emphasis on *mistress*. He resented the fact that the anger he incited was being directed at Lucienne. He deserved it. Lucienne did not. "I was not in favor of the idea," he replied flatly, "but she insisted. What did she say?"

"She informed me that she was a lady and I was not, and what you need now is not a lady, but a mule and a brood mare, and she was not raised to be either."

Roget slapped the heel of his hand against his forehead, not knowing whether to laugh or cry. Surely Lucienne had not made so grotesque a statement, but obviously, Lauren had comprehended it that way.

"Lauren, I don't think——"

"You need not try to cover the bitter truth with rushes of sugarcane!"

Never would she accept their scheme. Grasping her wedding ring, she yanked it from her finger.

Roget felt his heart stop as the jeweled band severed easily from her hand. She walked toward him, a definite purpose in her stride and extended her arm. The emeralds sparkled between her brown fingers.

"I won't need this any longer."

"And what do you suggest I do with it?"

"You could give it to the next Madame de Martier, but I'm sure a great lady such as she is entitled to a much grander one."

"Lauren . . ." He began to apologize, but giving in to exasperation, his voice faded. What could he say to her? He was mistaken to think that their differences could be resolved. It seemed all they did was lock horns.

A deadly, penetrating silence stood between them, and both felt its discomfort. Roget moved from her and strode awkwardly to the window, even though the pain in his leg was less acute than it had been. He stood with his arm outstretched against the casement, staring into the blackness that shrouded the garden.

Lauren jerked her head from him, her breast filled with a potent brew of love and hate. He and Lucienne deserved each other. She was welcome to him!

Roget retrieved the silver-handled walking stick and left.

Lauren waited idly for Georgette to join her. After inspecting the flower beds, she let her feet wander to the grape arbor where she had seen Roget and Lucienne. Occupied with household chores for most of the morning, Georgette had just found her when the sound of horses pounded in their ears.

"There you are," Georgette grinned puckishly. "You've hidden yourself among the jasmine."

"It's so beautiful here," Lauren said with a sigh, her nostrils drinking in the fragrant perfume emitted by the flowers.

"I think I hear our men returning." Lauren shot her friend an inquisitive glance. "Jacques and Roget rode to le Petit Cul-de-Sac this morning. Roget wanted to estimate the damage before seeing his banker. A Monsieur Muller from Banque Nationale d'Haiti is coming to dinner Friday." Appalled at her own ignorance, Lauren realized that Georgette Deffand knew more about Roget's business affairs than she did.

"Darling, we are in the garden," Georgette called as the two Haitians sauntered around the house and crossed the driveway. Beaming, Madame Deffand intercepted her husband halfway, her lips brushing his in a tender greeting.

With a faintly visible limp still restricting his leg, Roget moved to the bench where Lauren sat. At least he was walking without a cane, she thought as he approached.

Joining Roget, Jacques inquired in a teasing manner, "How is our patient today?"

"I feel fine, almost as good as new." Lauren smiled, enjoying his playful banter.

"She would say anything not to stay in that room," Roget broke in, his forced smile baring a glimmer of white teeth.

Madame Deffand glanced from one to the other. "We will see you at dinner," she said. Taking her husband's arm, she strolled with him along the path and into the house.

Roget remained, and for a long drawn-out moment, they could hear only the buzz of a bee. His dark gaze swept over her. She met his eyes briefly, and then disturbed by his scrutiny, she dropped her head. With her hand, Lauren held together the neckline of Georgette's gown where it gaped over her bosom.

Roget stared at the ill-fitting garment, realizing that she as well as he needed clothes. She was almost comical in

Georgette's gown, but he dared not laugh. The ground between them was already strewn with eggshells.

Lauren rose from the bench and, with trembling fingers, bent to cradle a flower. Before he could form a word, she dreaded hearing what he was about to say.

"I know that you and Antoine were planning to leave," he said. His voice held a huskiness that was unfamiliar to her. "I married you for my own selfish reasons. I have no right to hold you. If you want to go, I'll book your passage. I can have our marriage annulled from here."

Annulled. There it was—the reality she had fought against for months. When she had given him the ring back, she had not realized that it would cut so deeply into her heart. Her back still to him, Lauren felt the despair swelling in her head. No doubt, he would be glad to be rid of her, but as Georgette had said, he had a right to know about his child.

"To erase it as though it never happened . . . might be difficult," she said. Her voice faltered as she turned to face him. "I'm going to have a child."

"Mine?" The expression on his face questioned her.

"Of course yours." Humiliation made her stiffen at his assumption. "Do you think I've been carrying on a wild affair with your dastardly brother these past months? What happened with Gaston," she said, her voice trembling, "was because he forced me. What I endured at his hands was because I wanted our marriage so much, I couldn't bear to be sent back to France . . . cast off like an obsolete toy. It happened only once!" Bitterly, she flung the words at him and stalked in blind circles around the flower bed.

Damn Gaston! Roget thought. *If I ever get my hands on him again . . .* If he had been rational that night, he would have realized that Lauren would never give herself to Gaston willingly—she hated him. But he had not been rational, he had allowed Gaston to get the better of him.

Catching her, Roget closed a strong hand on her arm. "Woman, will you stand still for a moment," he growled irritably. Her pacing was driving him mad. Wrenching her arm free, Lauren planted her feet in their tracks. "You should have come to me," he said, his tone softening.

"How could I?" she replied warily. "It was our marriage he was using against me."

Roget's sable features contorted to question what she had said.

"He told me that he had received information from France concerning my birth, information that would provide grounds for an annulment."

"What information?" Roget demanded harshly.

"About my being born illegitimate . . ." As her voice faltered, she found it impossible to look at his face.

"The bastard!" Roget uttered the words in a compressed whisper. Drawing a slow breath, he attempted to quell the blood that pulsed through his temples.

Taking in the slightly flaring nostrils, Lauren recoiled as she remembered the other time she had seen him so furious. Noticing how she drew away from him, Roget softened for the moment, letting his rage dissipate.

"Lauren, didn't it occur to you that I would have had that verified? I could not afford to leave Gaston any loopholes. What my brother neglected to tell you was that your parents were married some weeks after your birth, and according to French law, that legitimized your birth." He paused and studied her reaction. "I may have been rash but not that foolish."

The color drained from her face, and she grabbed the rosebush to keep from falling, never feeling the thorns as they pricked her fingers. Enduring Gaston's abuse had been for nothing.

"Are you all right?" Roget questioned. Alarmed by her stupor, he slipped his arm around her back and propelled her body onto the marble bench.

"I'm fine." Lauren bristled irately, preferring not to feel his touch.

Roget drew his arm from her resistant body as though he had been burned. After all he had put her through, how could he expect her to forgive him? Yet he could not let her go. Perhaps with time . . . "Lauren." He uttered her name softly, a noticeable apprehension controlling his voice. "Despite all claims to the contrary and devious efforts to undo it, you are my wife. I would like you to stay."

Lauren gazed up at him, her stoic expression giving way to no emotion. Had he made the same request six months ago, she would have been delirious with joy, but now the idea lay like lead in her breast. *Roget wanted his child.* She would not delude herself into believing that the request was anything more than his sense of duty.

Lauren plodded through the remainder of the day in a daze. By the time night fell, she had sidled between the sheets, extinguished the mantle, and prayed that sleep might provide an answer. But sleep never came, and tired of lying in bed, she got up. Tramping across the carpet, her path illuminated by the white rays from the moon, she could not resist feeling that the entire matter seemed like a business arrangement. "If only he had not asked me to stay," she thought aloud, her feet padding mechanically into the water closet, "the decision would be out of my hands. But he did . . . and I have to choose."

Lauren padded back to the room, stared at the huge empty bed and chose a chair in its place. She could not shed the feeling of despair that came over her. Her mind had been dead set on leaving, but how could she go when her belly was filled with his child? She would end up being a burden to Claude, and where else could she go? Her aunt had graciously raised her; she could not expect her to take on her child as well. And then, like a star shooting across the sky, the image of Lucienne in Roget's arms flashed before her, and she realized that if she remained, she would have to live with this picture for the rest of her life. How would she endure the years ahead, living with him, being so close and knowing that he wanted someone else? It would be easier to go, she decided.

With nature prodding her, once more she padded across the floor to the water closet, vaguely aware that she was heeding nature's call more often than usual. Was this another symptom of being pregnant? She exhaled a loud sigh, and as if carrying a yoke on her shoulders, she dragged herself through the darkened room. Unable to spend another night in the empty bed, Lauren curled up in the cushioned armchair, uncomfortable as it was, and eventually fell asleep.

Her cramped limbs tingling from lack of circulation,

Lauren opened her eyes to bright streams of morning sun. An annoying thought tugged at her brain as needles stung the soles of her feet and the piercing sensation went right up to her knees. Straightening her legs, one by one she shook them, her involvement in the physical action allowing her to postpone the activity of thought.

Hastily dressing herself in clothes that fit like coffee sacks, Lauren fled down the stairs, praying she would not meet anyone who might try to detain her. She felt a desperate need to be free from that room. Perhaps, out of doors she could think more clearly. Before going to sleep, she had foolishly thought her decision was made, but in the light of day she could find no peace with it. How could she turn her child loose in France—black, penniless, and nearly nameless, where it had not the slightest chance. Life had been a struggle enough for her; she did not want her child to suffer the same fate, especially if it was a girl.

Everything that she could not give her child, Roget could. Here with its father, it would share his name, wealth, and position and not have to suffer the pangs of poverty or the humiliation of being out of place. It would never have to face the fears of uncertainty that had plagued her life. Her daughter would be a lady.

Blindly unaware of the path that she had taken, Lauren's stride carried her to the stables, but along the way, she missed the morning dew that glistened on the foliage. She could perhaps leave later, but she would be leaving her child without a mother, and she knew too well what it was like to grow up motherless. No! She had to put her feelings aside. All along she had thought of it as being Roget's child—not hers. Suddenly she was ashamed for having had such ambivalent feelings about her own baby, thinking solely of herself. But this decision had to be made for her child's welfare—not hers. She was already grown, but her baby would need many years of nurturing and care, care that she could not provide alone. She was the one who had made the mistake, and no matter how painful life might be for her, the tiny life she was carrying should not have to bear the brunt of it. It would take courage to return to France, she thought, but even more to remain here and live with him everyday, yet she knew she could not do otherwise.

Lauren found herself standing outside the stables, totally unaware of how she got there. She heard the morning snorts and yawns that came from the horses but refrained from entering their shelter. She could not bear to see them prancing around when Miel was lying dead somewhere. She would have given anything to be able to ride, but she had no riding clothes, and requesting them from Georgette would only get her a lecture about her condition. What on earth would she do to occupy herself for the next seven months?

Hunger growled in her stomach, and reluctantly Lauren turned and walked back to Villa Deffand. Well aware of Roget's sense of duty, Lauren shuddered at the idea of being just another of his obligations, another task he performed perfunctorily. And oh, how she hated the fact that she would be forced to comply with their scheme. Scalding tears formed in her eyes while she searched through blurred vision for her handkerchief.

Chapter 26

Two days flew by, and by dinnertime Friday, Lauren had had scarcely little time to reconcile her convictions when she found herself seated opposite an incredibly handsome Roget, still attired in borrowed clothes. Feeling her pulse quicken, she tried to imagine him fat, ugly, and unappealing.

The stocky German seated next to her wiped either side of his face and replaced the napkin across his lap. As he parted his lips to speak, the bushy mustache and beard almost obscuring the fact that he had a mouth, Lauren felt his eyes glide timidly over her bare, gaping neckline. Why, she wondered, did every male assume that she would be party to his lust, including her own husband. Lucienne had his love, and she knew that as his wife, she could expect nothing more than an occasional venting of his lust.

"Have you been able to calculate the total damage?" the German inquired, drawing Roget's attention from Paul Deffand.

"Pretty nearly, I think," Roget replied. "Our losses are bad." Lauren saw the sorrow that clouded his features, and the reins on her heart would not restrain it from going out to him. "There is major damage to le Petit Cul-de-Sac . . . The workers' village is completely destroyed. Villa de Martier is a mountain of ruin, as you saw," he said, glancing

419

at Jacques. Jacques nodded with glum resignation. "The workers have to be housed immediately, and of course, so do we."

Pétion appeared, and the aroma from the steaming tray of roast lamb that was set before them invaded Lauren's nostrils, reminding her that for the first time in two days she was hungry.

"Fortunately, the coffee groves are intact . . . and one warehouse," Roget said, resuming his assessment after the interruption. "The other is destroyed. And most of our horses were buried in a mud slide."

"We were lucky," Jacques said, helping himself to the succulent slices of meat. "Our sole damage was the strip of flamboyant trees bordering your property, but the Dupins and the Brunets were hit pretty badly as well."

Monsieur Muller cleared his palate and tasted a mouthful of the red wine. "This claret is superb," he said, lifting the glass to Jacques, and then his focus returned to Roget. "According to our figures," he injected, "your financial condition is good. You had an exceptional crop in '91. Certainly, your assets outweigh your liabilities. Of course, losing the villa was like losing a treasure chest."

"You need not remind me," Roget replied in a tone that was sadly lacking in animation.

"You're still a rich man," the banker added.

Roget looked at the stocky German as if that fact held no importance and replied, "The first thing is to allocate money for the workers' cabins. I would like them built sturdier, brick perhaps, at least concrete floors. I'm appalled at the conditions under which these people have been forced to live." His stoic expression masked the fact that he was attempting to atone for years of injustice.

"How much do you want to assign?" the banker questioned.

"I've drawn up some figures. We can look at them after dinner."

Unwillingly, Lauren was lured to Georgette who was privately engaged in playful banter with her husband. "You mean you were eavesdropping again," Jacques chided, his eyes dancing with laughter.

"I was not eavesdropping, darling. I merely overheard it."

Lauren swallowed hard. How she envied Georgette her love, but there was no time for self-pity. She had made the decision for the welfare of her child, and she would see it through. Forcing her attention back to the somber discourse between her husband and his banker, she caught Roget's fleeting glance as he pulled it from her. Had he noticed how the Deffands' love affected her?

Idly, her thoughts traveled to the future. There must be a point at which love and longing died, a place in time where indifference prevailed. Lauren prayed she would reach that place soon, so the future that lay ahead might be less unbearable.

At the sound of Georgette's voice, Lauren started from her reverie. "Pétion, the gentlemen will have their rum and coffee in the billiard room. On that note, *messieurs,*" she quipped flippantly, "we will leave you to discuss your manly affairs. Are you coming, Lauren?" Madame Deffand stood, and the men stood as well.

"Oui . . . bien sûr." Flustered, Lauren hurriedly wiped her mouth, placed the napkin on the table, and followed her hostess to the foyer.

Excusing himself, Paul Deffand joined the women. "I will leave this discussion to you younger men," he said. "I'm afraid I was too willing to abandon those responsibilities when I gave the place over to Jacques."

At the foot of their impressive white staircase, the Deffands let their lips meet, and Georgette whispered a breathless, *"Bonsoir, mon amour,"* before sweeping up the stairs.

Lauren bit down on her lip, unaware that it was blood she tasted. "Oh, God, give me strength," she prayed, her voice less than a whisper.

Jacques took Monsieur Muller by the arm and showed him the way to the game room, leaving Lauren and Roget alone. In a vain attempt to stifle the loneliness that overwhelmed her, and not knowing what else to say to him, she volunteered her services. "Roget, I would like to help . . . There must be something I can do."

She watched her husband's back stiffen at the idea as though it were the recurring sting of an old wound, and then having a second thought, his broad shoulders relaxed.

"Probably . . . I will need your help. I need all the help I can get."

The words were not easy for him to say, and Lauren noticed that he struggled to meet her eyes as he said them. No doubt he was gloating at how easily she had agreed to their scheme.

"Are you going to bed now?" he asked quietly.

"No, I think I may read for a few hours."

"Lauren." He murmured her name as if wanting to say something and then pulled back and extinguished the thought. "I'll be up in a while," he said and strode toward the billiard room.

Roget took the steps slowly. Today had been the first day since the earthquake that he had been able to manage without the walking stick, and it had taken its toll on his leg. How could he approach her after the way he had used her? *I'm sorry* seemed a pitiful apology, he thought. Feeling the ache in his groin, Roget balked at the intensity of his desire.

Comprehending nothing of what she had read, Lauren's fingers continued to turn the pages of the book. And then, hearing Roget's muffled footsteps next door, she lifted her head from the novel and stared at the shadows created by the flicker of the gas mantle on his door. Taking her by surprise, the formidable barrier between their rooms clicked open, causing her to feel a fluster of self-consciousness that she foolishly thought she had outgrown. But even pregnant, she could not fill out Georgette's gown.

Roget walked in, his easy stride still hampered as he favored the injured leg. The brocade dressing gown was far more lavish then he preferred, and she almost smiled at the calculated habit he had of shoving his hands in his pockets and leaving the thumbs extended. His dark eyes took in the palpitating swell of her breasts, and feeling dissected beneath his scrutiny, Lauren tried to pull the gown up to her neck.

"Do you want to talk about something?" she asked with apprehension.

"That depends. What do you have in mind?"

Lauren hated him for being so self-assured when she felt as if she would burst apart at the seams. Pushing the sheets aside, he left barely inches between them as he sat on the mattress. Lauren felt the close proximity of his body to hers, and she felt every heartbeat as his chest rose and fell.

Harboring an amused grin, he said, "I think tomorrow you should see about ordering new clothes. Madame Deffand's do nothing for you. I'm afraid she's far more amply endowed than you are." The barest smile still curled the corners of Roget's lips as he lifted her hand to his mouth.

And so is Lucienne! Lauren thought acidly as she yanked her hand from him.

"Roget, I know my shortcomings. You don't have to point them out to me." Bitter defiance escalated in her tone.

Standing abruptly, he moved away from her. Why the devil had he said that? The thought pummeled his brain as he stalked to the window. Placing one hand above his head on the casement, he stared blindly into the darkness. He had never felt so incompetent in his life. He felt like a bumbling schoolboy suffering his first crush. And like a schoolboy, he had said the wrong thing, masking his feelings behind a teasing remark. His memory fled back to Paris and the way he had teased her by calling her a wanton hussy, because he himself was overwhelmed by the magnitude of their pleasure. He could still see her face flushing a deep burgundy the morning after their wedding night. And at this moment, his mother was dead, Gaston would be tried for murder, his home lay in ruin, and all he could think about was whether she would love him that way again. Of course, from his wife, he could claim marital rights, but duty was the last thing he wanted from her.

Lauren's trembling fingers lifted and laid down the pages, though her eyes had seen nothing that was written on them. *Why does he not go and leave me alone,* she thought. Her eyes followed the well-defined contours of his body beneath the robe, and realizing her thoughts, she quickly averted them back to the book.

Drawing his arm from the window, Roget approached her once more, his reservation slowing his stride.

"When I asked you to stay, it was because I—"

"I know perfectly well why you asked me to stay," she broke in, not allowing him to finish the statement. "Your mistress made it quite clear. You need not try to whitewash it. I've agreed to stay . . . What more do you want?"

"Lauren, you are going to listen to me," he said, glaring down at her, "if I have to put you over my knee." Seizing her arms, he dragged her to the edge of the bed, his hands nearly bruising her thinly clad shoulders.

"Why not?" she spat at him. "That seems to be your way of dealing with a woman who was not born a lady."

Roget felt his insides coil, and relaxing his grip, he let his hands fall to his sides. Her remark had cut more deeply than she knew.

Seething with rage at his audacity, Lauren yanked the quilt over her shoulders and turned her back to him. *Blast him anyhow! Why does he insist on tormenting me?*

Her lips clamped shut, making Roget very much aware of her anger but even more aware of how badly he wanted to coax them apart.

"Since I'm not a lady, there is no need for a man of your class to treat me as one," she said caustically.

"That's nonsense," Roget replied, the back of his neck bristling with pent-up frustration.

"Is it? Lucienne made it very clear what you needed me for: a workhorse."

"She did not mean it that way; she just didn't know what else to say!" Throwing up his hands in exasperation, slowly he let them fall back to his sides. He would have liked nothing better at the moment than to put her over his knee and whack the stubbornness out of her.

How blindly he defends Lucienne, Lauren thought, *when from the beginning he has done nothing but oppose me.* As resignation burned fire yellow from her eyes, Lauren faced him. "I've already agreed to your scheme, so everything will be perfect for you and your lover."

"Will it?" he said, arching two raven black brows. Awed by the strength of her determination, he knew that she would stand beside him with the same wholehearted tenacity. In that instant his heart was laid bare. His hand went to her breast and pried loose the fingers that clutched the quilt.

"You've gotten what you wanted. Why don't you go and leave me alone?" she said acridly. Her bottom lip quivering, she retrieved her hand. His easy charm would not fool her again.

But Roget did not go. Instead, he drew her hand back into his, tentatively examining the long, graceful fingers and the carefully manicured nails. "You do have beautiful hands," he murmured in a low, husky tone, "the hands of a pianist." His lips brushed over the quivering tips, his teeth gently nibbling each fleshy mound.

Lauren felt a fierce, tingling desire race through her arm, down her spine, and find its way to the inner recesses of her soul. Irately, she snatched her hand from him.

"Damn it, woman!" he said, pulling back. "I don't want to fight with you . . . I want to love you."

Dragging her to her knees, his lips sought hers with all the awkwardness of two adolescents sharing their first kiss. A kiss full of uncertainty, it was racked by the pain of frustration that spurred it. Disconcerted, Roget was shaken by his sudden loss of self-assurance. Severing his lips from hers, he muttered almost inaudibly, "It's not like us to be so awkward."

Ebony eyes locked with her hazel ones, and two mesmerizing pools lured her into their depths, making it impossible for her to separate herself from the magic of his touch.

"It's been a long time," she uttered softly.

"Too long," he replied with a huskiness in his voice that made her tremble. Again she felt his lips on hers, and this time, the awkwardness was gone. *Blast him,* she thought, her breath coming in short, ragged gasps. *Why are his lips so convincing?* Lauren felt her blood surge, and much against her will, she felt her lips part and her mouth surrender to the urgent demands of his until they were lost in their own sweet paradise.

The hardened muscles of his chest and belly pressed against her, smothering her senses, while his touch ignited scorching flames of passion in her traitorous soul. Lauren struggled against his persuasive plundering, but her eyelids fluttered closed and the core of her melted to molten liquid. Although her brain said no, every nerve in her body screamed *yes, yes.* As much as she longed to hate him, she still loved him.

Skillfully, Roget's body maneuvered her down to the pillows, and the oversized nightgown fell from her shoulders. Lauren wanted to resist, say no, push him from her, but his lips made her weak as his mouth claimed the warm, eager passion of hers. Trembling with desire, Lauren pushed her conviction aside and let her arms caress the hard sinuous muscles of his back. *Just this once,* she thought as she abandoned her pride, her honor, and her resolve.

Roget's mouth moved over the column of her neck to her throat to the firm swell of her breasts. With an excruciatingly deliberate slowness, he savored every inch of her velvet skin until she would literally have begged for the fulfillment she knew only he could give. Chills of feverish anticipation shivered through her body as she felt his lips burn a trail of kisses along her stomach to her navel and then circle the small concave with his tongue.

Roget devoured the sweetness of her as though he were a man approaching food after months of starvation. He wanted to taste every precious moment, have it etched in his memory, the flavor of her skin, the scent of her hair, the heaving rise and fall of her breasts, and the cries of pleasure that escaped her throat as he loved her.

Moving one hand down over the delicate swell of her chest, Roget unbuttoned the remaining closures on the loose-fitting garment. His dark eyes devoured her. Wanting to bury himself in her, he pressed his face into the softness of her belly. His own body threatened to gorge and explode in his gut he wanted her so badly, but he denied himself, knowing that the pleasure would be so much greater if he prolonged the release until she was ready.

Lauren ran her fingers along his back and his narrow waist, clawing at the robe, anxious to rid him of the obstacle that stood between her and the delicious sensation she had been anticipating. Resting his weight on one elbow, Roget untied the sash and let her remove the hampering garment. Her eyes drank in his maleness and then pulled away. Amused by her obvious discomfort, Roget slid one hand along the curve of her waist.

"Would you rather not?" he questioned, bating his breath for her reply.

"Yes . . . no . . . I mean . . . ," Lauren stammered, unable to think with his hand searing her flesh.

Roget felt her body throbbing beneath his touch, and at the same time he saw her mind's struggle to resist. The decision would have to be his. He reached for her arm in an attempt to bring her closer, but his awkward position threw him off balance and he plummeted sideways from the edge of the mattress to the floor. Landing with a thud, his right leg took much of the weight of the fall. His face contorted with pain as he rubbed the injured limb.

Before Lauren could realize what she had done, she had scrambled from the bed and knelt beside him, alarmed by the contortions of pain in his face. "Are you hurt?" she asked, compassion filling her eyes.

The pain in his leg was very real, but he could not resist the temptation to use the mishap to his advantage. "I think I'll live," he said, straining to control the grin that threatened his masquerade.

Lauren saw the laughter dancing in his eyes. She was not amused. "Oh, you!" she cried. Sucking her teeth, she felt disgusted that she had allowed herself to be taken in by him again. As she moved to get up, Roget seized her wasplike waist between his hands and pulled her down to him.

"No, Roget!" Lauren protested with burning indignation as she struggled against his grasp. And then, in one lightning quick motion, Roget had hooked his uninjured leg around hers, hopelessly intertwining them as he rolled her onto the carpet. Rigidly, her back sank into the rose-patterned pile as he covered her body with his own.

"Woman, you will drive me to drink," he growled. Locking her gaze into his, Roget lowered his head.

"No, Roget, no," she murmured, knowing that she would rather die than not let him finish what he had started.

Cradling her head in the palm of his hand, Roget tangled his fingers in the soft, bushy mass of her hair, and his lips met hers with a raw hunger that set two heads spinning. He held her to him, his mouth fusing with hers in a long, plundering kiss that sought to assuage the gnawing hunger created by months of abstinence.

Clutching his back, Lauren's fingers kneaded, grasped,

and nearly impaled his smooth, taut torso as her mouth tangled with his and her lips met the urgency of his kiss. Caressing his sable skin, she marveled at the trim hips and the firm, muscular buttocks that commanded so much power during their union. A hot flush raced from her cheeks, through her spine, to her toes as she felt compelled to draw him closer.

Roget's heart soared with the essence that rose and swelled within him, and his aching body clamored for the sweet agony of release but only when she was ready. He remembered too well their last encounter when he had pleasured himself, meager as it was, with no thought for her feelings.

Moving his hand over the delectable sinew of curves that shaped her back, Roget let his fingertips explore her softness. The heat of his touch laid his brand on her soul, and the vulnerable position gave him easy access to the heart of her womanhood. As she clung to him, her body molding into his, no longer could she deny her longing for him. In her desire to bring him even closer, Lauren arched wildly against him, and as she did, he claimed her, surrendering to her everything he had to give. Lauren gulped, and the rush of air colored her face burgundy red. "Roget," she gasped in a whisper. "It's been so long."

Roget felt her silken honey-hued limbs enclose him and draw him further into the depths of her soul. Sharp, ragged gasps of breath strained to fill his lungs as he sunk deeper and deeper into a whirlpool of excruciating ecstasy. "Lauren . . . Lauren . . . Lauren," he whispered, his lips muttering her name like a prayer. Roget moved skillfully, keeping a tight rein on his craving, and as he wallowed in the sweetness that flowed from her, he allowed her the lead on the journey to ecstasy.

Lauren's body filled to overflowing as the heat of his passion flowed through her, and inside, she exploded with fireworks of brilliantly scorching color. Sparks of fuschia, orange, and yellow shot through her and then faded, only to give way to another spray that came bursting forth, more intricate and more brilliant than the last. Lauren's brain traveled beyond all sense of reason. Her teeth clenched against his shoulder, and her fingers raked his skin like a purring jungle cat.

Roget savored each spasm of pleasure that burst forth from his body as she tightened around him. They made love like two people facing the gallows, as though it were their last meal. For hours it seemed they were soldered together by the heat of an insatiable hunger, their hearts beating as one, their souls clinging to each other for their lifes' blood, while their bodies climbed every mountain and descended every plain in a glorious, magnificent union of love consummated in smoldering passion.

An early dawn mist had seeped through the window before Roget lifted Lauren from the rose-patterned carpet and they reclined, exhausted, on the bed. Their bodies finally, reluctantly pulled away. Roget looked down at her, his ebony eyes drugged and intoxicated, and mused at the sheen of perspiration that covered her skin and dampened her hair. He had loved every inch of her, and her cries of joy had been like music to his ears.

Ashamed to meet his gaze, ashamed that her traitorous body had betrayed her so wantonly, Lauren averted her eyes from his scrutiny. She had sworn not to be swayed by his charm, sworn to accept this devil's arrangement for exactly what it was, and what had she done? Was she so weak? Would she never be able to resist his touch, even knowing that she was merely a vessel for his lust?

Langorously, Roget moved his hand and pushed the wild, tangled mass of hair from her face. "I didn't think you would ever love me like that again."

"I didn't know you wanted me to," she said, the reply almost catching in her throat.

"I've not been able to concentrate on much else these past months," he said, his tone sounding vaguely like a confession.

A slight, nervous smile quivered Lauren's bottom lip. "But you had Lucienne."

His raven brows lifted slightly. "I doubt that she would agree. There was one disastrous attempt after which she accused me of being distant."

"Attempt!" Lauren's eyes dilated in surprise.

"Oui," he replied, resting his head against a loosely formed fist, "and I was unable to consummate it."

"Roget, surely you don't think I'm that naive?"

Smiling sheepishly, he added, "It seems my flesh was willing, but my soul was not. And for some strange reason, my heart kept remembering you."

His smile could disarm an army, Lauren thought, but she was determined not to let it deceive her again. "But all those nights . . . You didn't come home until almost morning . . ."

"Did you think I was wallowing in wanton pleasure?" His eyes narrowed with amusement, and she went weak, realizing he was teasing her. Then without warning, his expression went from playful to somber as if he really meant to confess.

"Lauren, I won't promise you that I'll be a perfect husband. I will probably never be the kind of husband Jacques is; I don't know if it's in me. I come from a long line of notoriously bad husbands." He paused and waited as if expecting a reply. "But I love you . . . Dear Lord, I do love you."

Lauren felt the heart in her leap against her chest, beating so wildly she feared it would break loose and flutter from her body. Afraid to move, afraid to even breathe, she lay there beneath his gaze, petrified, waiting for his next word to shatter the illusion. But his teeth merely nibbled her neck. *Oh, my love,* her heart cried out in silence. *You could not have said what I think you did. I must be imagining things.* Holding her breath, Lauren muttered, "Did you say . . . what I . . .?"

But as though reading her thoughts, Roget gave her no time to finish. "Mm-mmm," he grunted, his teeth wickedly nibbling her earlobe.

Exasperated, because he seemed not to be taking her distress seriously, Lauren heard the tone of her voice escalating. "Roget. You are not listening to me," she insisted.

"But, I am," he replied, moving his head so that his mouth hovered inches above hers. "I said, I love you."

Lauren felt her bottom lip quiver, and as his lips brushed hers, she froze, not knowing how or when her arms had encircled his neck. "And I've loved you," she murmured, "from the moment I first saw you." Her hands held his crisp dark head, allowing him to bury his mouth in the sensitive hollow where her neck met her shoulder. "But I'll never be a docile Haitian wife," she added.

"Did I ask you to be?" he mumbled.

The sound of his breath tickled her neck, and Lauren chuckled. "Have you given up trying to make a Haitienne of me?"

"Not given up, just engaging different tactics. If we de Martiers have anything, it's perseverance. I've finally learned that there's but one way to tame a woman as stubborn as you."

"And how is that? Beat me?"

"No . . . love you. Then I have you purring in my hand." Riled by his smug grin, Lauren opened her mouth to protest, but the softness in his eyes rendered her speechless. "And, yes, I do need your help," he said with an expression on his face that melted her resistance. "We both need clothes desperately. Your first responsibility is to go shopping."

"Roget," she uttered softly, still attempting a protest, but her lips were soon occupied satisfying the demands of his. Drifting off to sleep in his arms was like a gift from heaven, and Lauren recalled the nights she had lain awake aching to feel him beside her and thinking that he was with Lucienne.

Chapter

27

Lauren could hardly contain her elation as she stepped into the black taffeta skirt and poufed sleeve jacket even though it was a solemn occasion. It mattered little that it was a mourning dress. It fit. The skirt hugged her slightly expanded waist, and the bodice clung to her bosom.

"Madame, I hear that you was almost died," her young maid said. As Cybele hooked her into the gown, Lauren thought of Madame de Martier lying dead beneath the tons of wreckage. Whatever her differences with Roget's mother had been, she would never have wished so horrendous a death on her. Remembering that she herself might well have been buried there with her, Lauren shuddered and clasped her shoulders to ward off the chill.

"Thank God, Cybele, that you had gone home to see your family."

"Oh, *madame,* when I come back and they tell me what happen, I am so upset!"

Lauren had forgotten the sound of Cybele's Jamaican-accented French, and hearing it again, she chuckled at the way she always managed to use the wrong tense of the verb.

Hearing a barely audible knock, the maid pulled the door open and stood aside. Georgette's maid lounged in the doorway. "Madame de Martier, they are waiting for you," she said.

Lauren placed the veiled black hat on her upswept hair, securing it with pins, and working her hands into the kid gloves, she tread down the stairs to join her husband.

Roget and Antoine had opted for a simple requiem mass. Since their mother's body could not be recovered and given a proper burial, they chose to forego the elaborate pomp and pageantry that normally accompanied Haitian funerals. There would be no march through the streets with gilded carriages and high-stepping horses bedecked with purple plumes. And there would be no martial band blurting military music as the spirited musicians led the procession to the cemetery. But because of the de Martier position in society, the bishop would preside over her final mass.

The chapel bells pealed a sad lament of farewell as their party was ushered into the cathedral. Hundreds of mourners, along with the Duvals, the Clerveaux, and the Rousses, were already seated. Familiar faces that Lauren recognized from the balls and receptions they had attended nodded discreetly to Justine de Martier's surviving sons. Adorned with opulent purple robes and a gold-encrusted crown, the bishop entered, accompanied by his cross-bearing acolytes, and as he climbed to his dias, a hush fell over the room.

Seated between Roget and Antoine, Lauren stood, kneeled, and prayed at the various intervals commanded by the mass, her compassion radiating from one brother to the other. Antoine's eyes grew moist, and more than once she had seen him brush the tears from his face, whereas the expression coloring Roget's features remained decidedly stoic. But then in the midst of the eulogy, when Madame de Martier was commended for her vivacious spirit as a young wife and mother, Lauren saw her husband struggling with the swell of emotion that invaded his soul. *"Maman beauté,"* he uttered softly, the words spilling from his lips as from a cup that had filled to overflowing. The barriers at last crumbled, and Roget sobbed.

Lauren trembled at the quake of emotion that shook his body, and as she slipped her hand into his, she felt him grasp it and cling to it, drawing from her the strength that she offered.

The elegant mourners poured from the cathedral and

climbed into waiting carriages, many of whom would make the journey to Villa Deffand, where they would formally offer their condolences at the reception.

"At last he is walking without a limp," Lauren commented as Antoine lifted her into the stifling black vehicle. Her eyes followed Roget as he was drawn aside to accept expressions of sympathy from a group of his card-playing friends.

"His leg was crushed pretty badly," Antoine replied.

"Crushed? He said he caught his foot in a crevice."

Antoine's look told her it was an inane idea. "Not that I know. His leg was injured when he took the weight of your fall."

Lauren's heart swelled with emotion until she thought it would burst.

"Dr. Mauriac wanted him off of it for a while, but there were too many things needing his attention, including his wife." Antoine's lips curled slightly as he focused on the opalescent glow that came from her eyes. "And he was terribly concerned about the workers needing shelter."

Georgette climbed into the adjacent vehicle. Closing her parasol, she waved a gloved hand at them to get Lauren's attention. "We will see you at the house," she said.

"Antoine, are you coming?" Paul Deffand inquired anxiously, clamping a hand on the younger man's arm. Contrary to custom, Antoine accepted the older man's invitation to make the return trip with the Deffands, because the old man was curious to hear every detail of Gaston's arrest. Lauren was left alone to comfort her husband.

Its closed hood allowing the entrance of little light, the carriage rumbled noisily over the dirt roads that led from Port-au-Prince, and Lauren was instantly aware of the small, nagging ache in her back.

Breaking the silence, Roget spoke as if he were confessing a sin for which he had no feeling of penitence. "In spite of everything, I am not sorry about my mother's death, just the manner in which it happened."

"You saved me. Why not—?"

"Why do you think?" His expression told her he could have done nothing else. "I had no choice . . . I could only save one of you," he muttered sadly. "My mother died years ago. She was only drinking her way through the motions."

"Maman beauté." Curiously, Lauren repeated the words he had uttered. "I heard you say that during the eulogy."

Hearing her repeat those words, Roget's lips twisted into an ironic smile. "That was my name for her when I was a boy. Once I grew up . . ." His voice drifted langourously, and then reining in his thoughts, he added, "I hadn't used it in years until recently."

Through the silence, Roget was intensely aware of Lauren's presence, and abruptly he dragged his reflections back to the present. "Will you ever forgive the abominable thing I did to you?" The dark handsome features grimaced with self-reproach.

"My love, I already have," Lauren replied softly. "It's you who must forgive yourself."

"Well, I certainly will not be able to ignore it."

"There was never any need for you to force yourself on me."

"It had nothing to do with you," Roget said with a sigh of resignation. "It was me. Gaston made a point of telling me that he had slept with you and made it sound as though you had done it willingly. The thought of my brother's hands on you drove me beyond reason to a jealous rage. If I had been rational . . ." Lauren watched the cords in his neck tighten, and as he pressed his fingers against throbbing temples, he added, "But a man in love is hardly rational."

Arriving at Villa Deffand, once again they had to face the scores of friends and acquaintances that came to offer their condolences.

"A tragic accident . . . tragic," Henri Duval murmured to Roget, his fingers pinching the point of his goatee.

"I know this is not the time to ask," Madame Duval said, hesitantly addressing Lauren, "but would you be willing to play for our concert this year?"

"If it is possible, I would be happy to," Lauren replied graciously.

The Duvals left, and Lauren could not help noticing the light that flashed in Roget's eyes when Lucienne glided toward them. Observing him as he took her two hands in his and passionately kissed them, Lauren recoiled inside, but outwardly she maintained her most dignified manner. "Lucienne, it was good of you to come," she said, offering a reluctant hand. Lucienne replied by taking her hand in the same restrained manner.

Among the guests were Lucienne's friends, the Clerveaux and the Louis, and throughout the reception, Roget had looked up and seen Lauren graciously greeting people who had been anything but kind to her. *Whether she knows it or not, she is a lady,* he thought.

With the last carriage gone from the gravel driveway, Roget and Jacques Deffand strolled the length of the veranda.

"Thank you . . . for everything," Roget said, the gratitude swelling in his breast.

"It's the least we could have done. It could just as well have been us." Jacques paused reflectively. After some minutes, he said, "We will see you in the morning," and disappeared into the house.

Roget strode to the balustrade, and clasping both hands on the railing, he stared up at what his mind imagined to be diamonds glittering on a black velvet dress. "Lord, you sent me a magnificent love, more than I ever could have chosen for myself. Help me to be worthy of her." He drew a deep breath of the still night air and entered the house.

Coming up from the veranda, he found Lauren dozing in an armchair, one tempting bare foot dangling over its arm. Provoked by a delectable notion, Roget closed his hand around the slender ankle as the fingers of his other hand wreaked havoc along the sole of her foot. Squirming from the ambiguous sensation of delight and discomfort, Lauren's eyes flew open and she struggled to free her captive foot from the excruciatingly unbearable tickle.

His face harboring a puckish grin, Roget teased the sensitive extremity until his delicate stroke drove her to a frenzy. Lauren pounded her fist against the chair, twisting and wrenching her body into every conceivable position, but she was unable to rescue her imprisoned foot.

"Roget, please—let go!" she pleaded, gasping for breath. He merely chuckled. "I don't think you should be thrashing about like a *Banda* dancer," he said, his gaze dancing with mischievous amusement. "Have you forgotten, *madame*, that you're carrying my child?"

Again, without warning, he trailed his fingers along the sole of her foot. The pain became pleasure, and squealing with delight, Lauren felt the titillating sparks of desire race through her limbs and invade her womb.

"*Ma chérie,* you'll wake the entire house," Roget chided, releasing her foot. "You must learn to behave like a lady."

Lauren yanked the pillow from under her and hurled it at him, but he was too quick, and her ammunition barely clipped his side. Bristling with irritation, Lauren drew her legs under her and sat Buddha fashion, her lips provocatively clamped shut. But she could not remain angry for long. Within seconds, Roget was hovering above her, his lips so close she could taste his kiss.

"Does it give you pleasure to torment me?" Feigning anger, she turned her mouth from his reach. But then his lips found the curve of her neck, and her nose inhaled the musky scent of his cologne.

"No," he replied, the vibrations of his voice tickling her neck, "but I do discover things that you have kept hidden."

"And what might that be?"

"That your feet are as beautiful and sensitive as your hands," he whispered huskily.

Coiling her arms about his neck, Lauren's mouth sought his with the hunger of an unrelenting passion.

Roget approached the high pink-hued concrete walls with trepidation. Forced to enter sideways, he lowered his head and passed through the narrow door to the inner room, where he met with the first sign of resistance. The general of the prison sat with his dirty boots propped on a desk, attentively cleaning his nails, and as he looked up to question Roget's purpose, he grinned, showing two broken teeth.

"I am here to see Gaston de Martier," Roget said. "I'm his brother."

"You must mean the high and mighty one," he quipped, not bothering to alter his position. "The one who thinks the bullets won't cut through his chest."

Roget could not resist thinking that the general's description definitely sounded like Gaston, but he would not give the man reason for further insolence.

"Don't matter how rich he is," the man continued. Eyeing Roget from silk cravat to kidskin gaiter boots, he lingered on the silver handle of his walking stick. "Those bullets going to rip through his guts just like everybody else's."

"You can spare me the graphic details," Roget growled impatiently. "If you don't mind, I would like to see my brother."

"Oui, monsieur." His attitude changed abruptly. Dragging his feet from the desk, he stood upright and at attention, as if he was intrigued by the idea of playing soldier. "Follow me, *monsieur,"* he said in a harshly clipped tone. Clicking his heels together, he wound his way through another narrow passageway that forced a grown man to turn sideways.

As they emerged into the courtyard, common criminals, their legs in iron anklets with short chains between, stumbled to the bars begging for food. *"S'il vous plaît, monsieur . . . J'ai faim,"* they pleaded, clamoring after him. Roget felt his stomach retch when prisoners too weak to speak merely pointed to parched mouths in desperation. It dawned on him that the only thing separating him from these wretched souls was a row of iron bars.

"Your brother's there," the general informed him. And pointing with his finger, he led Roget to the next courtyard.

Scores of gentlemen, still wearing ragged remnants of the black frock coats and white shirts they had worn when they were arrested, huddled near wooden sheds, their legs chained to a bar. Rickety sheds, the floors strewn with straw, were their only shelter from the sun. Roget cringed with disgust. The de Martiers had kept their horses in better conditions than these, he thought, as the squallor penetrated his senses.

It was then that he noticed Gaston, his leg chained to a bar with four other men, all gentlemen, but prisoners as well. The general opened the gate and let Roget de Martier into the court. He heard the heavy metal clank shut behind him, and the sound of iron grating against iron shot right through his gut. With hesitating steps, he walked toward Gaston. As much as he had detested his brother, he had not expected to see him like this. Gaunt and emaciated, his face covered with a nappy, matted growth of beard, Gaston looked up.

"Well, if it isn't my scholarly brother." Lifting an arm to his face, he mopped up streams of sweat with the remaining shreds of his sleeve.

"It is not a pleasant place, is it?" Roget commented flatly. The stench assaulted his nostrils.

"They have no consideration of class. Gentlemen are allowed no more privileges than common criminals."

"You could have come to your mother's funeral," Roget replied caustically. "The law would have allowed you at least that privilege."

"I had no intention of showing up there in chains, escorted by armed guards as though I were a common thief."

Averting his eyes in disgust, Roget's focus rested on the other inmates who hobbled toward him to beg for food.

"Besides," Gaston continued, waving the haggard souls away, "I see no sense in crying over the dead."

"She was your mother."

"Nevertheless, she is dead."

"Of course, you cared little for her when she was alive, and you haven't changed." Roget's glare held no pity. "You are still an insensitive bastard."

"I leave things like sensitivity to you, dear brother." His thin lips spread into a satisfied smirk that Roget knew well. That smirk once before had provoked his anger beyond reason. But reacting calmly to his brother's mockery, his rejoinder was sharp and to the point.

"I think you had better concern yourself with more crucial things—like your trial."

"My trial is of little consequence," he replied with indifference. "I will be free in a matter of weeks."

"You have the blood of two murders on your hands," Roget said, his voice choking with alarm. "But I should not be appalled that you can treat it so lightly."

"I was nowhere near Reinette when she died. It was done by others."

439

"But you planned it and you paid for its execution." The younger brother ground the tip of his walking stick into the dirt.

"That cannot be proved."

Roget met his mockery with a look of disgust. "Perhaps, perhaps not, but Antoine believes otherwise."

"Antoine is a sniveling fool bent on revenge," Gaston replied sharply. Turning his back, he dismissed the interrogation.

"There were witnesses that saw you strangle Filene."

"She was a peasant."

"She was also your *placée* . . . and long before you married Reinette."

"So she was," he said, lifting an eyebrow. "That changes nothing. She was a peasant and the witnesses nothing more than servants. It will be their word against mine. No court will accept the word of a servant against that of an elite peer." He grinned, confident with satisfaction.

"You forget that Lauren was there as well."

"Like I said, no court will take the word of a peasant over mine." Roget bristled as Gaston's mockery burned through his gut. "Besides, dear brother, your wife is easy enough to silence. A few minutes with me between her thighs, and I assure you she will do as I say."

Roget swallowed the bitter venom, his dark eyes glaring with suppressed hatred. "Like you did once before, you bastard!" he growled. "You forced yourself on her with a lie, and I was gullible enough to believe you."

"Forced?" Gaston repeated the word. Throwing his head back in laughter, he mopped the stream of perspiration from his face. "Believe me, *mon cher frère,* she put up no fight."

"Of course not, you were blackmailing her." Roget felt the sun burning through his cravat, and he reached up to loosen the knot.

"The lusty wench loved every minute of it."

Roget's forehead wrinkled to a scowl, and he wondered why he had allowed himself to engage in this inane battle. "I will make you a promise. If you touch her again," Roget snarled in a controlled whisper, "you will not need a trial;

I'll kill you myself." He turned his back on his brother and strode with impetuous strides across the courtyard, his body grappling with an uncontrollable rage.

Facing the iron gate, he rapped on it with his cane and let the dankness fill his nostrils while he waited for the general to release him. The gateway clanked ajar, and as Roget ducked his head beneath the bars, Gaston's voice called after him. "If you have any notion of being brotherly, you could supply me with fresh clothes and some decent food. We are still de Martiers."

Gaston de Martier hobbled back to the wooden shed, dragging with him the other four men attached to the bar who were too weak to resist. Inside, he sank onto the filthy straw. So, that African wench would be mistress of the new Villa de Martier instead of a lady such as Lucienne. The de Martier men would roll in their graves at the way he had lost control of things. He had known when they brought him here that he was doomed, but he would take these thoughts with him to the grave before he would let Roget know that he was the victor. The huge shoulders collapsed, racked with sobs, as he cupped his face in the palms of his hands and whimpered like a baby at the prospect of his death.

The following afternoon, the prison general decided to occupy himself by sorting through the slew of crates that had just arrived. Dragging them one by one back to the second courtyard, he opened the gate and shoved them through onto the dirt. "De Martier, these are for you," he yelled.

The inmates swarmed like ants around the crates, their eyes glued on Gaston as he feverishly ripped them open. Inside, he found trousers and shirts, blankets, and enough cooked rice, corn, and pancakes stuffed with smoked fish to feed the prisoners in the courtyard for several days.

The remaining crates were designated for the common criminals in the first court, and upon eyeing the means of survival, they too swarmed over them like locusts when their hungry noses inhaled the smell of food. Violently, the nailed coverings were ripped to shreds, and filthy hands plunged in and out with handfuls of plantain and yams to shove into empty bellies. "You can thank someone named de Martier," the general said as the gate clanked shut behind him, but he was sure that no one heard.

The ship blew its whistle for the third time, the *twang* of the siren cutting sharply through the thick, hot Port-au-Prince air. The gangplank was ready to go up.

"I will always welcome you back," Roget said. "This place is yours as much as mine."

Antoine looked squarely into his brother's eyes and acknowledged the pride he saw there. "You know I must go," he said wistfully. "But who knows, I may be back one day. I may even marry. But I need the chance to become my own man, the same chance that you and Gaston had."

Roget nodded in silent resignation. "I *am* proud of you."

"I merely did what had to be done."

"Agreed, but I'm not sure I could have done it."

"You do not hate Gaston the way I do." His voice still quaking with vengeance, he glanced at his sister-in-law. "I doubt that Lauren would nurture the same sentiments."

Lauren drew a prolonged breath, not realizing she had sidled into the curve of her husband's arm. Like sour ale, the bile churned in her belly.

"A poignant perception," Roget replied, his expression growing somber. "Still, it's not a pleasant sight seeing your brother behind bars."

"I know . . ." Antoine clearly shared Roget's remorse. "I shudder at the sight myself, but he deserves to be hanged for what he did to Reinette. It was a clever plot they mastermined. Gaston came out smelling like a rose."

Roget's lips twisted at the acrid taste of irony. "A mock vodun ceremony was clever indeed. It placed the finger of suspicion on the cults. Somehow it always smelled like foul play, but there was no proof."

"I'm not surprised that Filene dared to try it again with Lauren. The first time had been foolproof."

"And Gaston was not involved?" Lauren questioned. Her suspicions had not been completely abated.

Antoine nodded. "He intended to get rid of you," he replied, "but legally. You were not important enough for him to risk involvement in another murder."

"And Reinette was?"

"Reinette forced his hand. When she discovered that Filene was his *placée* wife, she threatened to take her son and return to her family. Our brother did not want to lose his son, and more than that, his greed did not want to part with her dowry. Her family wielded a lot of power in the government, and the last thing he wanted was to face the wrath of their revenge. Her legitimate death was his only alternative."

"You look puzzled," Roget commented, curiously observing the expression that slid over her face.

"It seems feasible . . . except how did they get a dumb animal to comply?"

"Easier than we would imagine," Antoine replied. "It just took time and patience. When Reinette saw a young filly in Santo Domingo and fell in love with her, Gaston bought the animal for her and then had it trained to serve his purpose. In both cases, the horse was probably drugged into its frenzied state by Filene."

"That would account for neither of us being able to control her," Lauren said, "but was Reinette forced to experience the same horrendous ritual?"

"We believe so. But most likely she died of the poison." Roget choked on the words, unaware that his hand had tightened around Lauren's arm. "When I knelt over her body, I thanked God that she was dead. She would have been deformed for life."

"I don't know what possessed me to do it," Lauren said, "but I am thankful that I was delirious enough to swallow the oil."

"So am I," Roget replied, his voice not more than a whisper.

Seeing that the two were momentarily engrossed in each other, Antoine used the moment as his cue to leave. "Unless I want this ship to sail without me," he cut in jocularly, "I had better get on board. Roget, you can forward the remainder of my inheritance when the de Martiers are again prosperous. I won't need it for a while."

"It should be no problem in a year or two," Roget replied, forcing a weak smile. "We will recover with a few good crops."

As Antoine pressed his lips against each of Lauren's

cheeks, she pulled a letter from her pocketbook and shoved it gently into his hand. "See that my aunt Claude receives this. She's expecting you, and she will be anxious to hear from me."

Roget and his younger brother embraced with more genuine affection than she had seen displayed by any member of the de Martier family. Both pairs of dark eyes grew moist, and the two men wrenched apart before emotion overtook their discretion. Antoine turned toward the gangplank, and seconds later he was gone.

Climbing into the carriage, Lauren glanced over her shoulder for one final look at the ocean liner as it steamed away from Haiti's harbor and into the horizon. Mulgrave swung the horses around and headed the vehicle back to Villa Deffand. The wheels created a lulling rhythm as they rolled over pavement, gravel, and finally red dirt roads. Idly contemplating the colorful bouquet of blooms on the spring foliage, Lauren suddenly felt Roget's gaze penetrating her thoughts.

"What will happen to Gaston?" she questioned curiously.

"If he is found guilty, he'll face a firing squad."

Shuddering at the idea, she pondered the fate of the child. "And Filene's son?"

"I will see that the de Martier estate provides for him, but he can never inherit even a small parcel of the property. Filene's scheming was for nothing." Stretching his legs before him, Roget shifted uneasily in the leather seat, and Lauren's ear was drawn to the muffled sound of his toe drumming against the base.

"You're still thinking about Gaston," she said, perceptively reading his thoughts.

"When I think of what his greed would have done . . . how he would have destroyed Lucienne."

"And me," she added quietly.

"But you're stronger."

"My peasant blood," she retorted. Lauren stiffened at the familiar prick of jealousy.

"I didn't mean it facetiously. It's just that she was born to be a lady."

"So I was informed by the lady herself."

"She merely tried to make matters as comfortable for me as she could."

"And you still love her," Lauren murmured, her irritation calming considerably. It seemed Lucienne would forever be a sore spot between them.

"I will always love her, her beauty . . . She's the sister I never had. Perhaps if there had been women in our family, the men would have been more benevolent, but for ninety years there have been only sons."

"There were women—your mother, your grandmother, Reinette . . ."

"I mean women born in the family. A daughter brings out the tender feelings in her father, and sisters teach men to understand other women. You need women in a family to keep it humane."

"You do pretty well," she said, smiling mischievously, "not having had a sister." A faint, fluttering motion vibrated through her womb, and Lauren focused her hazel eyes on him with a satisfied grin. "I have a feeling that the de Martiers may have their first daughter."

The wrinkled brow that showed his disbelief caught her by surprise, but his face smoothed gradually as he entertained the possibility. "I would like to have a daughter," Roget said, sounding pleased with the idea. "And under the circumstances we had better consider our living arrangements unless you want our daughter to come into the world homeless." His lips curved delectably, baring his teeth. "I doubt that the Deffands want us as permanent houseguests."

"What choices do we have?" Lauren questioned, somewhat curiously.

"We have a summer house in La Coupe. It's about twelve rooms. It hasn't been used in years, and I have no idea what condition it might be in. We could possibly make it livable, at least until we build another house."

"Are we building another house?" Lauren blurted out the question, interrogating him as though he had just disclosed a secret plot in which she had no part.

"I think we will have to," Roget replied. His sly grin jolted her senses.

Admonishing herself, she thought, *How foolish of me.* Of

course they would have to build another house. Villa de Martier was gone. In all the confusion, it had just not occurred to her.

Roget could not resist the urge to chuckle at Lauren's bashful retreat when she realized that she had put her foot squarely in her mouth. "I had been mulling over the idea of building another house, one that was more to my liking or my wife's . . . if I decided to marry." He saw the fire yellow glow that flashed from her eyes, but he was not yet ready to ease her embarrassment. Continuing, he added, "I did not intend to spend my life under the same roof with Gaston.

"How long will it take?" she asked, sheepishly turning back to look at him.

"Two years, perhaps more."

"Some of the houses I've seen here are so charming," she said as her rigid pose melted. "Could we build a house and not a mausoleum?"

"Whatever you wish, *ma chérie.*" Meeting her gaze, his eyes danced with suppressed amusement. "Meanwhile, we have to live somewhere. If you can make it livable, the house in La Coupe would do." His voice held a note of skepticism. "You would have to run your own household, and it would only house two or three servants."

"I helped Claude run a hotel, surely I can manage a twelve-room house," Lauren retorted. Her wounded pride bristled at his questioning her capabilities. *"I was not born to be a lady."*

"You would have to train new maids, hire kitchen help, a gardener—"

"Is it far?" she broke in, staunchly dismissing his skepticism.

"About nine kilometers from Port-au-Prince. Tomorrow we can ride there and look at it if you like."

"Your mother mentioned that house to me once in a sober moment," Lauren said sadly as memories of Madame de Martier trailed through her mind.

"Maman loved that house. My father closed it up, and we never went there again."

"Why?" she questioned softly.

"Who knows?" Roget shrugged his broad shoulders with

an air of indifference. "No doubt because my mother was happy there."

As her husband's voice faded into his thoughts, Lauren watched his right hand pass absently over his cheek. The marks had faded, but his smooth skin would never be free of faint scars. She winced to think that out of desperation she had marred his incredible face.

"*Madame,* you left quite a lasting impression," he said soberly.

Placing a hand on her rounded belly, Lauren replied sheepishly, "So did you, *monsieur* . . . so did you."

Chapter
28

Roget had not known that one woman could be so all consuming. He was like a schoolboy in love for the first time and could not drink his fill of her. Reveling in the pleasures that he had foolishly denied himself, he adored her. Mornings, he hated tearing himself from the warmth of her body, from the taste of her lips and the scent of her honey-hued skin, and if not for the fact that there were urgent duties pressing on him, he probably would have wallowed in indolent pleasures for life.

In the weeks that followed, Lauren was more occupied than she could have imagined. A new crop of "black gold" bloomed and was harvested and while Roget nurtured coffee beans and rebuilt warehouses, Lauren ordered repairs on the plumbing, hired painters, had the gardens weeded and pruned, bought furniture, trained maids, and decorated a nursery. In her spare time she assisted her husband with his bookkeeping. The months passed so rapidly that Lauren hardly knew they had gone. But as her baby's birth drew nearer and her belly grew heavy and cumbersome, Lauren was forced to curtail her rigorous activities.

Slowly, Roget surrendered his skepticism and in its place was awe. Awe of what one slender, sinuous, hourglass figure of a woman could accomplish in a span of five months. She had turned a neglected, weatherbeaten, twelve-room wooden frame into a home.

A rectangular structure, its carved latticework balustrades surrounded a veranda that fanned into a half-circular staircase, which descended from the main door to the driveway. Admiring the two-story villa as it lay nestled among the pomegranate trees and coconut palms, Roget's comment became an apology. "I am amazed."

"I wanted to help before," Lauren replied smugly, "but you were so stubborn. You seem to forget that I was not born to be a lady." Thrusting her chin in the air, her intent was to stalk proudly around the fountain and up the circular staircase, but the size of her belly made her resemble a waddling duck.

"A foolish mistake on my part," Roget said, conceding gracefully as he doggedly tried to suppress the chuckle that was triggered by her awkwardness.

Six months to the day after they had seen Antoine off to France, a new de Martier entered the world to fill the place Gaston had vacated. As Lauren went into labor, Roget, like most other men, paced the floor, feeling useless.

Strolling into the mahogany-paneled library that she had had decorated for him, he poured himself a shot of rum and gulped it down. Through the French doors, he stared at the rose garden. For someone who had always been so capable, he felt utterly helpless. Sitting at the ebony-inlaid desk, Roget attempted to wade through the pile of receipts that needed his attention, but hearing her cries distracted him. There was nothing he could do. It was in her hands . . . and God's, he thought with futile resignation. *Oh God, I love her so—and I've not often told her.*

Unable to decipher the figures that blurred before his eyes, Roget got up and ambled outside to the rose garden, where he prodded and poked at a colorful array of white, pink, and red blossoms. Her waist had been so narrow, that could hardly be an advantage in childbearing. Georgette, who was quite well endowed with feminine attributes, was having difficulty carrying a child to term. Moving a stem here and freeing a petal there, he poked at the roses and remembered the touch of her hands exploring his body—

the delicious trembling in his belly that spread like wildfire through his limbs. Stalking back into the library, Roget seized the crystal decanter, poured the liquid into a glass, and gulped down another shot of rum.

Lauren was in labor a mere seven hours when her impatient daughter burst into the world. Justine Ndate Yala de Martier slid from her mother's womb, a squalling, healthy baby who had her father's sable skin and dark eyes and her mother's magnificent mouth.

"Roget, you have a fine, wailing baby girl," Dr. Mauriac said as he inclined his head toward their bedchamber. "I'm sure you heard her."

"A daughter?" Roget murmured, almost speechless. "And Lauren?"

"She's fine . . . just very tired."

"Her waist was so small, I was afraid . . ." Roget released the breath that had been imprisoned in his throat, it seemed, for hours.

"It will probably be an inch or two wider after this, but she'll be fine. She has quite a healthy pelvic area. As a matter of fact, for a first birth it was relatively easy. I would venture a guess that you can expect several more," he said, flashing Roget a sly grin.

"How soon can I see her?" Roget inquired anxiously.

"She's waiting for you now. But just a few minutes. She needs to rest."

Once the doctor had gone, he walked slowly toward the ebony sideboard. More pleased than he realized, Roget threw back his head and howled, "I have a daughter!" His spontaneous outburst brought León scurrying to the room.

"Is something wrong, *monsieur?*"

"Nothing at all, León, nothing at all."

Roget stood by their bed and gazed at the tiny wrinkled creature nestled in her mother's arms, and the sting of tears swelled behind his eyes. As he turned away, Lauren clasped his hand and brought it to her breast.

"Are you pleased?" she asked.

"Very," he replied softly. "What irony that *Maman* did not live to see her. She had always wanted a daughter. When Antoine was born, she wanted very badly for it to be a girl.

Ma chérie," he said, his dark eyes enveloping her, "I have a feeling she would have been pleased with your contribution."

"Would you do something for me?" Lauren asked drowsily.

"Anything you wish."

"Send a telegram to Claude."

"I would have anyway," he whispered. As the nurses took the baby from Lauren's arms, she drifted off to sleep.

From the moment Justine curled her tiny sable hand around Roget's finger and refused to let go, she was her father's child. But as far as Lauren was concerned, she had been Roget's child from the moment of conception.

Roget had chosen not to attend the execution. Though his sentiments for Gaston did not much surpass contempt, he had no desire to see his brother's body riddled with bullets. Claiming the body for burial in the family crypt had been painful enough. But now, as he was about to meet with the family lawyers, the grisly details drifted back to haunt him.

"Roget," the older man greeted him, offering his hand as he strode into the provincial office. "Of course, you know my son and partner, Pierre Brunet."

"Comment allez-vous, Monsieur de Martier?" the young lawyer volunteered, zealously pumping Roget's hand.

"Bien, merci," Roget replied.

"I was sorry to hear about Gaston . . . Unfortunate to say the least," the elder Brunet commented. Masking his obvious discomfort, he stroked his graying goatee. "I was your father's lawyer as well as your brother's. Due to Gaston's death, you are heir to the de Martier holdings, and I trust we can represent you as successfully as I did them." Moving behind the desk, he offered his client a seat and sat down. "Of course, you know that the stipulations of your patriarch, Valery de Martier, still stand." Roget merely nodded. "As for that other matter you discussed with me, as soon as Madame de Martier is well, she can come in and sign the papers."

Roget left the office, satisfied that Lauren would be an independent woman.

* * *

With her strength returning, there were days when Lauren grew anxious for her convalescing period to end. The infant suckling at her breast made her long for the moment when Roget's sultry lips could once again give her pleasure. And then there were times when she wondered if he would still desire her in that way now that she was a mother. During the last months of her pregnancy, he had shown little interest except for the sympathetic pats he had placed on her protruding belly. And since Justine's birth, it was obvious that he was overjoyed with his child.

Anxious to see the little miracle they had created, Roget took the steps two by two and strode into their sitting room, not bothering to remove his dusty boots. Tossing his gloves haphazardly on the cushioned armchair, he stopped in his tracks as his eye caught Lauren, breasts exposed, nursing Justine on the chaise longue. The tightening in his groin almost made him immobile.

"Haitiennes would let a wet nurse take care of that job," he commented lightly.

Lauren cast him a wicked opalescent glance that said he should know better than to compare her with a Haitienne. "No one else will nurse my baby," she replied firmly.

"As you wish, *madame,*" he grinned.

Approaching them, Roget nuzzled his nose in Justine's belly, and she gurgled, awkwardly kicking her tiny brown legs as father and daughter giggled and frolicked in their own private revelry. And then noticing the other plump, chocolate crest that stood erect and neglected just inches from his face, he could not resist nuzzling its softness with his nose.

Waves of pleasure ripped through Lauren's body. "Roget don't," she pleaded. "You're torturing me." Cradling his crisp, dark head in her hand, she trembled. "You know I can't . . . not yet."

"I know," he said reluctantly, and then flashing a puckish grin, he added, "But how I wish you could."

Roget watched the child cuddled in her arms and the love Lauren showered on her and wondered if there would still be love enough for him. He had heard many cases where a woman, after giving birth, poured all of her love on the child and had little or none to give her mate. He hated the twinge of jealousy that he felt and pondered the fact that so tiny a bundle of human flesh could make him entertain the idea of being obsolete.

"Madame, Carmelite say the baby is dressed. She was bring in." Clasping both hands together, Cybele purred with delight. "She look like a little angel."

The nurse brought the infant into Lauren and Roget's bedchamber and placed her in her mother's arms. "Your godmother is responsible for making you a fashion plate," Lauren said, playfully nuzzling her daughter's nose. Tying the silk bonnet under Justine's chin, Lauren adjusted the long white dress, smoothed the yellow ribbons on the coverlet, and wrapped her in it. "No one but Georgette would send to Paris for a baptismal gown," she said. Smiling up at her husband, her voice held a note of inconceivable wonder.

"I hope that we can soon do the same for their child," Roget replied.

"Perhaps sooner than you know. Georgette thinks she may be pregnant again."

Once inside the church, Lauren and Roget de Martier stood aside while the Deffands approached the altar, Georgette holding their daughter in her arms. As the priest annointed her forehead and made the sign of the cross on her body, Justine gurgled and cooed. Raising his hand above her, the priest proclaimed, "In the name of the Father, the Son, and the Holy Ghost, I christen this child Justine Ndate Yala de Martier," but before the last word left his mouth, Justine had grabbed a fistful of his glimmering gold vestment and refused to let go. Smiling with embarrassment, Georgette was forced to pry the tiny hand loose.

With uncommonly rapid haste, Jacques paid the priest's fee while Roget paid the civil officer to register his daughter's birth. Together the four emerged from the cathedral, discreetly smothering their snickers, to face the blazing midday sun.

By the time evening fell, Lauren breathed a sigh of relief that the hectic, but joyful day was at an end. Justine had been put to bed and her proud godparents had reluctantly departed for home. Alone with Roget, Lauren wondered if he would ever touch her again. In the past week she had done everything to entice him, but he remained coolly aloof, often pulling away when she came close. Stepping out of her gown, she grinned wryly. "Your daughter made quite a spectacle of herself this morning."

"I'm not surprised. She takes after her mother." Roget removed his white linen jacket, untied the silk cravat, and tossed them both on the nearest chair. His eye took in the honey-hued swell of her breasts and then slid down over the curve of her waist. "It seems I have not one stubborn woman to tame, but two." The corners of his eyes crinkled with amusement, but Lauren was preoccupied with her own thoughts and failed to see that he was teasing.

"Why should you have to tame either of us?" she retorted coldly. "Taming is for horses."

"Haitian women, like horses, are supposed to obey their fathers and husbands."

"You will not break my daughter's spirit and turn her into a spineless, subservient female."

"Your daughter?" he said, hoisting an eyebrow. "A moment ago she was my daughter."

Lauren flung her face away from him in a fury. Here she was standing before him, half naked, and all he could talk about was Justine. She stalked past him in a huff, but her irritation lost its fire when her eyes paused to drink in the easy, rhythmic strides that carried him to the other room. Clamping her mouth shut, she turned to the wall and dug her teeth into her lower lip. *Blast him!* If she stood here naked, he probably would not care. She had been right from the beginning: all he had ever wanted was his child.

As Roget returned, Lauren heard his footsteps and quickly busied herself brushing out her hair. But suddenly he was behind her, and she heard him whisper, "Close your eyes." His breath so hot on her neck that it made her shiver. Not knowing why, she obeyed his command without question. Something cool, like stones, circled her neck and then the burning touch of his fingers before he drew them away. Opening her eyes to the mirror, she gasped, the breath smothering in her lungs. Brilliant green gems fell in teardrops from her throat, cascading into one superb emerald that nestled in her cleavage. And in a case lay two perfect emerald drops to hang from her ears.

"Roget, they are magnificent . . . ," she murmured. "They must be worth a fortune."

"Only a small one," he said, his lips curling into a satisfied grin.

"But why?" Her opalescent eyes dilated wide with wonder.

"For starting the de Martier family over again." Pausing for an endless moment, he continued. "If anything should happen to me, these will keep you in comfort for the rest of your life. Once you sign the papers, they are yours, not even I can take them from you. Of course, I hope you will pass them on to our daughter, but should you ever need them, these are your security."

Lauren's mouth twisted into a curious smile as she asked, "Are you trying to get rid of me?" And Roget had the strange feeling that she had not meant it entirely in jest.

"I know how fiercely independent you are," he said. "According to the stipulations of Valery de Martier's will, the estate can only pass through de Martier offspring. Wives cannot inherit the property. If I should die, you would be living on your daughter's land. My mother spent the last thirteen years of her life as a guest on her children's property. I would not see that happen to you."

Speechless, Lauren swallowed hard when it dawned on her that for giving him a child, he had given her a precious gift of independence.

"Roget . . . I . . ." Her voice was silenced by his lips against her neck.

Roget felt the curve of that delectably ample derriere press into him, and his pulse quickened. His arms aching to hold her, he wondered how much longer he could possibly keep his hands off her. The throbbing wrenched in his groin, and he pulled away.

With painstaking care, Lauren removed the jewels from her neck and placed them in the velvet case. "Dr. Mauriac said I could resume riding again . . . among other things." The faintest blush of burgundy colored her cheeks as she mused at her wantonness.

"Oh?" Roget looked up hungrily.

His dark eyes locked with her lighter ones in the mirror, and desire stirred in her womb in a way she had not experienced in months. As she turned in his arms, she felt his hands once again span her waist. Lauren's lips parted, the bottom one quivering with anticipation. Roget lowered his head, and their lips met with a fiery, ravenous hunger that rekindled the desire that had waned during her pregnancy. Throughout the night, Roget reveled in her cries and gasps of pleasure, his own breath catching in his throat each time she fondled him. If he thought that motherhood had quelled her passion for him, he was mistaken.

"Christophe, I'll be at home," Roget called out to his foreman. Circumstances had compelled him to give Christophe the responsibility for which he had trained him. As the tall, ebony-skinned man crossed the road to approach the benefactor of his good fortune, Roget gathered Bleu de Roi's reins and swung into his saddle.

"My woman, she is very, very pleased over the new house," he said in a melodic Creole.

"It goes with the job," Roget replied.

His eyes curiously studying his employer's wife as she sat astride her mount, the foreman's attention shifted to the new mistress of Villa de Martier. "Madame Lauren, soon Ernée goes to thank you for the good good things you bought for us for the house . . . and for stopping me from hitting her. She say I am to stop beating her. She say, 'Monsieur Roget don't hit his wife. You always talking to me about Monsieur Roget . . . wanting to be like him. Well, he don't beat his wife.' So I stopped beating on her."

"I'm pleased to hear that," Roget replied hastily, anxious to dismiss the subject.

Smugly pursing her lips, Lauren covered the delight in her victory with the brim of her hat. For nothing in the world would she have missed the expression on her husband's face.

"We had better go," Roget said curtly, yanking the gold watch from his pocket. "Alexis is arriving today, and it is already past noon. If we are going to beat the rain, we had better fly." Urging his horse into a gallop, Roget sped down the road toward the fork, and reluctantly, Lauren attempted to keep pace behind him.

Unaccustomed to the mare she was riding, she had no idea what the animal's capacity was. Had it been Miel, she thought sadly, she would have had no qualms about keeping his pace. But Miel was gone, and she would soon have to choose another horse.

When he noticed her lagging behind, Roget reined Bleu de Roi in and slowed to a trot. "You miss your horse," he said, empathizing with her loss. "Sometimes, I think we foolishly put too much trust in them. They become almost human."

Lauren swallowed hard, remembering the solace she had sought in her rides with Miel. "For months, she was the only companion I had."

Leaning sideways, Roget stroked his hand along the animal's gleaming brown side. "She's a fine mare. Give her her head."

Trusting his judgment, Lauren did as he suggested. Copper red dust whirled in a tornado from the pounding hooves as they raced over the dirt to La Coupe, but they had covered barely half the distance when the blue sky grew ominously dark. Swaying coconut palms bent and twisted in the sudden wind, their leaves rustling like silk about the riders' heads.

Roget sniffed the air, smelling the dampness and the rain. "There's an old cabin near here," he said. "We had best try to reach it."

Lauren felt one drop, then two, and then they were falling all around her, beating on her straw panama and dripping off the brim into her face. Clutching her legs about the horse's middle as they plowed through the red mud, she followed her husband to shelter. By the time they had drawn their mounts to a halt, Blue de Roi and his female companion were dripping wet. So wet that Lauren and Roget nearly slid from their backs without dismounting. Securing the animals under the roof of the porch, the two fell, stumbling and laughing, into the cabin.

Must invaded Lauren's nostrils, and as she cleared the cobwebs from in front of her face, a rush of warm air caressed her skin. Roget searched the room for a chair strong enough to sit on, but the two he found had barely three legs and were shrouded in spider webs. "We'll have to make the best of it," he said, spreading his hands in defeat. Pensively, he propped one booted leg on the windowsill. "What did you think of the warehouses? I haven't yet heard your opinion, and I know you have one." He grinned slightly.

"They certainly get built faster than houses," she said, her lips matching his grin.

"Warehouses don't have inlaid satinwood floors, hand-carved staircases, and chandeliers powered by electricity."

Musing, Lauren mulled over the fact that their new Villa de Martier would be lit with electricity. "Have you realized," she said, "that our daughter may not know what gas lights are."

The drenched clothes began to chill her skin, and Lauren wrapped her arms about her shoulders to ward off an involuntary shaking.

"There are ways we can keep warm," he said.

"We could build a—" Lauren's thought was rapidly extinguished when she looked up at him and noticed the mischievous gleam that flickered in his eye.

"Roget, not here," she protested, scanning the dilapidated cabin's meager furnishings.

"Can you think of a better idea?"

Suddenly she felt his lips burning against her neck. Roget pulled Lauren's wet body to his and enclosed her in his arms. His hands eased over her with a deliberate slowness.

Shivering beneath the sopping wet clothes, she felt the heat of his touch burn through the clothes and, like a raging fire, set flame to every inch of her. "Roget," she sighed, the breath smothering in her throat. Her teeth bit into his earlobe, because it was the one part of him near her mouth on which she could vent the excruciating sensation of ecstasy that escalated in her loins. At this point she would have made love in the dirt.

Roget lifted his head to seek her mouth and paused abruptly. A second thought had taken precedence over the first. "This is not a good idea," he said, wrenching his body from hers. "The place is full of cobwebs and termites and heaven knows what else."

Lauren looked up at him, perplexed by his change in mood, but refusing to be cheated, she took matters into her own hands. "You instigated this, my love, and if you think for one minute you're going to back out now . . ." Her cheeks flushed to a ruddy burgundy, and her eyes glowed with sparks of yellow when she became aware of what she was thinking. As Lauren moved in close to him, Roget saw the gleam in her determined eye.

Untying the laces on his wet breeches, she stroked him with the soft cushions of her fingertips, and as she dragged her nails lightly over his strong male body, he trembled with the force of an earthquake.

Moments later, arms entwined and breeches tangled, they were on the floor wallowing in the dust, not realizing how they got there. Rain murmured against the roof, the wind rustled the trees, and Roget shuddered in ecstasy beneath the shapely body that claimed him.

At last, the rain stopped. Roget rolled onto his back and stretched langourously. Lauren watched a slow ironic smile spread over his face. "Whatever you're thinking must be a deep, dark, delicious secret," she whispered, trailing the fullness of her mouth along his ear.

"I was thinking of something that Lucienne said to me once." He replied in a tone that suggested he was musing aloud.

"Lucienne!" Lauren bolted upright. "You have the nerve to think of her when you have just made love with me?"

"The irony is, what she said was true. She told me that I would make love to you anywhere, even in a barn."

"Why would she think that?"

"Probably because she could not entice me to make love to her in this same cabin."

Lauren's expression melted to a limpid glow as she realized what he was saying.

Standing, Roget offered her his hand. "We had better start for home." Lauren put her hand in his and used his strength to propel her upright. Once she was on her feet, her face contorted with pain as she felt the stab in the small of her back.

"Is something wrong with your back?" His voice bordered on alarm.

"Yes, you," she replied, rubbing the bruised area of her anatomy. "You seem to have a passion for making love on floors."

He met her smile with a sensuous grin. "The next time, my love, we'll keep you on top."

Rapidly, they buttoned, tied, and rearranged their not merely damp, but dirty and noticeably wrinkled clothing. They emerged from their refuge with Lauren feeling embarrassed that she had to arrive home in this condition.

"Perhaps we can still get home before our guest arrives," Roget said, settling himself in the saddle. "I would rather Alexis not see us like this."

Alarmed, Lauren bit down on her lip, thinking that they were committing some gross faux pas.

"Your backside in those breeches is a little too tempting."

"Oh, you!" she said, sucking her teeth. Smiling secretly to herself, she had to admit that every minute had been worth it.

However, it seemed their moment of reckless passion was not to be kept from their guest. They had no sooner ridden into the stable than Old Jean informed them that they had guests. "I met Monsieur Vauxvelle at the dock as you say. He waits for you at the house with a lady."

"A lady?" Roget's tone questioned the old man.

"*Oui*, Monsieur Roget." Curiously stroking the white hair on his chin, he added, "A lady with hair red like fire."

Lauren and Roget stared at each other as each saw their thoughts in the other's face. "Marie?" Lauren questioned.

"We will soon find out," Roget replied as they tread rapidly along the path to the house.

Entering through the rear door, they were met in the vestibule by León. "*Madame, monsieur,* there are guests waiting in the salon," he said, his eyes discreetly ignoring their clothing.

"*Merci,* León." Removing his hat and gloves, Roget placed them along with his wife's riding crop in the older man's outstretched hand.

The first thing that caught Lauren's eye as they entered the room was Marie, her red hair swirled into an enormous pouf beneath a pink-feathered hat. Seated with her back to the door, she failed to see the de Martiers when they came in.

"Marie. It *is* you!" Roget bellowed. Rushing toward her, he planted a kiss on each of the porcelain white cheeks.

"Roget!" She squealed with delight, wrapping her arms around the only part of him she could reach, his waist. "It's so good to see a familiar face. You really do live in this part of the world after all. I was beginning to think it was a cockeyed story that Alexis concocted in order to drag me halfway around the world to a godforsaken island where I will know no one."

Clearing his throat rather ostentatiously, Alexis broke in. "You two look as though you've been rolling in the mud." He stood with an arm extended from his body, a Victorian birdcage dangling from his fingers. "Madame de Martier, I believe these are for you."

"My birds!" Lauren cried. Her eyes danced with joy as she glanced from the Frenchman to her husband and then back to Alexis. Opening the door to the cage, she put her finger inside, encouraging one of the frightened birds to hop on it. "It's all right," she purred. "You're safe now." Gently, she stroked her finger along the tiny flaxen head.

Alexis's blue eyes crinkled at the corners, and he turned his attention to the noticeably pleased Haitian. "Do you have any idea what I've gone through to get these birds from France to Haiti?" he quipped. "Roget, old man, I would not have done it for anyone but you."

Lauren rushed across the room and flung herself at her husband, winding her arms about his neck. "My love, how can I ever thank you?" she whispered.

"I'll think of something," he answered softly.

Feeling eyes on her back, Lauren pulled away. "Do forgive us for not being here when you arrived," she apologized. "We were caught by the rain, as you can see."

"I know you were not expecting two of us," Alexis said, his glance fleeting to Roget, "but circumstances have changed. And since you're too damn much of a gentleman to ask," he chided, "may I present Madame Alexis Vauxvelle."

Roget's face broke into an expression of utter surprise,

but gathering his senses, he grasped the Frenchman's hand. "You have our best wishes. Welcome to the stormy sea of matrimony."

Proudly displaying the diamond on her finger, Marie entwined herself around Alexis's arm as though she were a vine.

"Roget, old man, I could use a shot of that rum that you Haitians thrive on," he said. Surreptitiously, he freed his arm from his wife's grasp.

"Let me show you to your room," Lauren volunteered amiably, "since the men are about to lock themselves in the library." Flashing Roget a perceptive glance, she beckoned to the other woman to follow her.

"I would like to rest before dinner," Marie confessed.

"And I desperately need to bathe," Lauren chuckled, looking down at her clothes, "as well as feed my daughter. She has probably howled her lungs out."

Madame Vauxvelle lifted a small white hand to her forehead. "How on earth do you bear this heat?"

"I've grown used to it," Lauren replied, her gaze taking in the fragile texture of the other woman's skin. "My skin is not as delicate as yours."

"In this part of the world, it's definitely an advantage," Marie added. "You know, when we met on your wedding day, I never dreamed that I'd be a guest in your home halfway round the world. Or that I would even marry Alexis," she added wistfully.

"God does have a way of turning our lives around and putting us in places we dared not hope to be." Lauren replied.

Meanwhile, the Frenchman flopped in the cane armchair, crossing his legs before him. Roget hung one leg over the corner of his polished ebony desk and took a swallow of the liquid in his glass. "I must smell like a goat," he said, his lips breaking into a grin.

"I never noticed," the Frenchman retorted puckishly, his hand reaching up to swipe a lock of yellow hair from his face.

Hoisting two raven brows, the Haitian peered at him from the tops of his eyelids, and Alexis read the silent question.

"You should have seen the woman my family wanted me to marry . . . The ugliest, pale white creature with a hook nose I have ever seen."

"And Marie was the lesser of the two evils?" With skepticism rampant in his tone, Roget emptied his glass and set it aside.

"I would have preferred Eurydice." Alexis turned up his glass and emptied it as well. "But," he said, releasing a loud sigh, *"c'est la vie."*

Later in the evening, bathed and dressed, the de Martiers sat down with their guests to dinner. After sating their palates with roast turkey, yams, plantain relish, and claret wine, they moved from the dining room to the salon. Rising to leave the room, Alexis made a strong gesture of offering Lauren his arm, and then pulling an envelope from his breast pocket, he handed it to her. *"Madame,* this is for you from your aunt Claude."

"Merci beaucoup," she replied, smiling radiantly.

"And I must say, motherhood has only made you more lovely."

Lauren blushed openly. *"Merci encore une fois, monsieur."*

"Perhaps the lady of the house will play for us," he said.

Marie placed a frigid hand in the bend of Roget's arm. Her gaze lingered on the creamy white walls and yellow damask draperies, and suddenly she felt the love and the warmth that emanated from the room fill her soul with a ray of sunshine. "Alexis has told me what a superb pianist you are," she said. "I would love to hear you play."

Graciously, Lauren obliged her guests, and for each night of their stay they requested that she entertain them. By the third night, their evening soirees had become boisterous sing-alongs with her playing all the bawdy songs they had sung at the Saint Germain. At the end of the week, Alexis and his bride reluctantly tore them themselves away and set sail for Martinique.

Lauren coaxed Justine's greedy little mouth from her breast and placed her in Carmelite's outstretched arms. "She should sleep now," she said, looking up at the nurse. As the woman's footsteps disappeared into the nursery,

Lauren heard Roget's long, rhythmic strides crossing the carpet in their bedchamber.

Stopping at the low chiffonier, he poured a glass of water and then stretched the full length of his body sideways across the brass bed.

"Roget, your boots are dusty," she chided smugly.

"So they are." Idly, his gaze wandered along his crossed legs to the boots.

"Did their ship sail before noon?"

Roget nodded. "They should have docked in Martinique by now." Lounging on one elbow, he turned the glass round in his hand. "I don't envy Marie. She's going to have the devil to pay for Alexis. He will probably go through every dusky-skinned woman on the place."

"Perhaps he will fall in love with her," Lauren said, her voice tinted with optimism.

"It's unlikely . . . given his penchant for mulatto women."

"Mmm . . . I don't know," she mused aloud. "You had a penchant for beautiful women."

"I did, didn't I," Roget replied. His dark eyes gazed up at her.

"Do you still?"

His arm circled her waist and pulled her down beside him. "I might," he said, nibbling her fingertips. And then following a long pause, he added, "But after you, how could I be content with a marble goddess? You make love like a demimondaine, fall on your face like a schoolgirl, and still manage to behave like a lady in the salon. My ancestors will probably rise from their graves, but, *ma chéri,* I would not trade you for all the black gold in Haiti. I want to live with you, make love with you, fight with you, and die with you . . . if our Father in heaven so desires."

Lauren's graceful fingers closed around his, and as their hands clung to each other in an embrace, she knew heaven had granted him that wish.

464

Author's Note

I am still in awe of the fact that I, who was bored by history and uninterested in reading, was destined to become a historical writer. But once out of school, I began to travel and, much to my surprise, discovered that I loved history. What I had hated was the way it was taught. History is not memorizing names and dates. History is people. When the human foibles of their lives unfold and we can relate to them as human beings, then the events and places that surround them become not only real, but fascinating.

Having always been drawn to love stories, twenty years ago when I stumbled upon and read my first Gothic novel, I was intrigued, because at last I had found a genre that could hold my attention and keep me turning pages until the end of the book. I realized that what I enjoyed reading most was the love story set in the gloomy, sinister surroundings of an ancient time period, or at least a period different from my own. So, several years later when I discovered my first historical romance, I was hooked! Here at last were books that fired my imagination, and I became an avid reader. There is nothing more captivating to my imagination than the covenant relationship that God ordained between man and woman, and here it was, played out against the backdrop of intrigue, adventure, and the lifestyle of another time period. Yet, after reading a number of romances, I felt a growing desire to see novels of this type with heroes and heroines from my own ethnic group.

Marrying the two became inevitable for me as a writer when it was revealed to me that this was an exciting way to present the many obscure facets of black history that lay buried in boring history books that no one, black or otherwise, would ever read. So what began as a gothic novel evolved over the years into a multifaceted historical novel, as Roget and Lauren de Martier propelled me through the adventure of their lives. The story and the characters are from my imagination, but the historical facts are real.

For those of you who share my love of history and are interested in reading about Haiti's illustrious past and the glory of her bygone days, I am including a brief list of the books that were invaluable to me during my research for *Murmur of Rain*.

Heinl, Robert, and Nancy Heinl. *Written in Blood.* New York: Houghton Mifflin, 1978.

Korngold, Ralph. *Citizen Toussaint.* Boston: Little, Brown & Company, 1944.

Leyburn, James G. *The Haitian People.* New Haven/London: Yale University Press, 1941.

Niles, Blair. *Black Haiti: A Biography of Africa's Eldest Daughter.* New York: G.P. Putnam & Sons, 1926.

Rodman, Selden. *Haiti: The Black Republic.* New York: Devin-Adair, 1961.

Simpson, J. Montaque. *Six Months in Port-au-Prince.* Philadelphia: G.S. Ferguson & Company, 1905.

Vandercook, John W. *Black Majesty.* New York: Literary Guild, 1928.

JUDE DEVERAUX

America's favorite historical romance author!

"Jude Deveraux always spins a gripping tale...
Plenty of passion —and the plot never slackens."
— ALA *Booklist*

"Deveraux's tales are tender, funny, warm,
and endearing...." —*Baton Rouge Advocate*

⚜ *The James River Trilogy* ⚜

❑ COUNTERFEIT LADY...............73976-X/$6.99
❑ LOST LADY.................................73977-8/$6.99
❑ RIVER LADY...............................73978-6/$6.99

⚜ *The Chandler Twins* ⚜

❑ TWIN OF ICE.............................73971-9/$5.99
❑ TWIN OF FIRE...........................73979-4/$6.99

⚜ *The Montgomery Annals* ⚜

❑ HIGHLAND VELVET.................73972-7/$6.99
❑ VELVET ANGEL..,.....................73973-5/$6.99
❑ THE VELVET PROMISE...........73974-3/$6.99
❑ VELVET SONG...........................73975-1/$6.99